These Hands

A love story

DARCY DANIEL

DEDICATION

To my mum. Thank you for always being there.

- 1 -

LUCAS

I OPEN MY BUREAU drawer and pluck out a pair of tan leather gloves. On rare occasions, the sight of all these neatly arranged little prisons takes me back to my childhood. Apparently, today is one of those days. As the memories well up in me, I look in the mirror above the bureau to assure myself that the image of the man reflected there is not that scared little boy.

No. There's no trace of the skinny, pale kid I'd once been. That boy died a long time ago. The man staring at me now has made it to the grand old age of thirty. I've managed to live longer than any known relative with the same disorder. My father, also afflicted, only made it to twenty, not even long enough to see me, his only child, enter the world.

Scratching at my five-day growth, I lean closer to the reflection and study my face. Still tanned from a long summer and autumn in the sun, the small wrinkles around my eyes are, for me, something I should be happy about; proof that I've outlived my predecessors. But the price of living this long is high.

I may be alive, but I only live half a life. I suppose half a life is better than no life at all, though sometimes, when the loneliness weighs down on me, I wonder. It's always there in the background. Occasionally I can smother it for weeks before it makes an appearance, sometimes only a day or so, but it always comes back to remind me. I'm alone, and probably always will be.

I run a hand through my thick, short-cropped hair, which had gradually grown darker when I hit my teenage years. I prefer it this way, believing it makes me appear stronger than the scrawny blond boy I'd been. And the transformation helped me embrace the new identity my mother created for me when she changed my name to protect me from a threat she perceived as life or death.

Though I would forever think of myself as Lucas Daniel, the rest of my world, small as it is, only knows me as Daniel Clark.

After my near-death experience, my mother's paranoia that Kelsey's father would either hunt me down, or reveal my secret to the world, overtook our lives. She moved us around constantly, never settling anywhere for more than a few months. Finally, she found someone shady enough to forge new birth certificates for both of us. Although she kept her given name, Emily, she insisted I change mine. I never had the chance to meet my father, but I wanted to keep a part of him close, and his name was the only way I knew how to do that. So, I stood up to my mother and demanded I keep the name Daniel. She relented, but she only ever calls me Dan.

I sigh and step away from the mirror. Although I need a shave, I know women find me attractive. My time at university taught me that women tended to look my way, their gazes lingering that fraction too long. But soon enough, my rudeness and gloves made them see past the face they once found attractive. Soon enough, they agreed with everyone else.

I'm a freak. A freak to be avoided, to be left alone.

Something else I can't hide, even beneath the warm layers of clothing, is my tall, muscular frame. If anyone knew I ate whatever I liked, that I never went through the drudgery of working out to stay in shape, they'd probably want to kill me for that alone.

Fortunately, no one but my mother really knows me.

Unfortunately, I have to keep it that way.

I look at the soft gloves in my hand and take comfort in them. They're a necessity I'd once hated, but eventually learned to embrace. Slipping them into the back pocket of my jeans, I head out of the bedroom, down the short hallway and into the open-plan living area.

The two-bedroom cottage is cosy enough for me and the only other occupant, my border collie, Sam. Who's sitting at the front door waiting to begin our daily routine.

Rubbing my hands against the crisp winter chill, I stride over the polished floorboards in my thick socks and stoop to pat her. That bushy tail wags at an astounding rate as I run a hand over her back. She's one of only two living things I allow myself to feel with my bare hands. With the sensation of touch such a rare experience, her soft fur is a luxury I never take for granted.

As I make my way around the kitchen bench, a faint plume appears before my lips. Halfway into winter and it's still getting colder.

While I wait for the kettle to boil, I prepare the open fireplace for my return in the evening. Then I make my morning coffee in a travel mug, shrug into a warm parka and slip into the work boots waiting for me beside the front door.

Sam follows me onto the verandah and sits at my side when I stop at the top of the steps. I take a sip of the hot coffee and stare into the white wall of fog before me.

I love these mornings. The utter silence, the way the fog engulfs everything. It gives me the sense of being in my own silent world of solitude. When there's nothing but this white void, I can imagine the world beyond no longer exists. And I don't mind that idea one bit. If it were only true, I'd never have to wear these gloves again.

Walking over the gravel driveway towards the invisible stables, the classic red barn with white trim soon looms before me. I place a hand on the large metal door, enjoying the wet, sharp coldness beneath my bare fingers. It rumbles and vibrates as I slide it open enough to step inside, out of the damp air, and into the familiar smell of horse manure and leather.

Sam charges ahead, sniffs at the ground and follows a scent only she can detect. While she's busy, I dry my hands on my jeans and slip on my gloves.

The large barn houses four stables—two on each side of the wide walkway—an area for lucerne, hay, oats, chaff and molasses. Opposite the feed is a tack room where I keep riding gear, rugs and brushes. Nothing special, just practical and well maintained, but it happens to be one of my favourite places.

I enter the first stable to my left, scratch the chestnut mare behind her ears, then unbuckle the front of her rug and pull it halfway along her back. She watches me with curious eyes as I slide a gloved hand over her swollen belly, checking for any abnormalities. She has a month or so before she's ready to foal, and everything seems to be going smoothly.

After I tip a bucket of prepared food into her feed bin, I cross to the other side of the walkway, open the stable door and stand back.

Beau, a sixteen-hand bay stallion, emerges, walks right up to me and nuzzles one of my leather gloves. My pride and joy, this horse is the only other living thing I allow myself to touch, because just like Sam, I know it's completely safe to do so.

I bought Beau at the stockyard auctions when I first moved to Cascade almost six years ago, paying next to nothing for him. In fact, I'd been the only bidder, and I almost hadn't raised my hand at all. When the handler led the young colt into the arena, I watched the feisty beast rear up and almost strike the poor sap trying to hold on to him. Then, with all four legs firmly planted on the ground, he'd strained against his halter, dragging the handler across the dirt floor like a water skier. As the colt's rump connected with the arena's railing, he'd spun around. Only then did I see he was not only missing his left eye, but crude scars covered the left side of his face and neck. And in that instant, I knew he was meant to be mine.

Once the handler finally managed to get a semblance of control over the colt, I saw his beauty and potential. Though I knew the horse would be forever physically scarred, I also knew I could do something about his behaviour, knew I had to save him from what was bound to be his destiny.

Since then, Beau has sired over thirty horses, two of which I still own. My miniscule horse stud costs more than it makes, but it's a hobby I take great pleasure in, and something I can do with a minimum of human interaction.

Removing a glove, I run my fingers over the criss-crossing scars on Beau's face and neck, feeling the uneven, crudely healed wounds. I give the stallion an affectionate slap, then slip my glove on.

Beau follows my every move as I break off a biscuit of lucerne and tuck it under my arm. At the rear of the barn, I slide open the large door and head into a small yard.

Behind me, Beau snatches a bite from the biscuit.

I spin around. 'Hey, we've spoken about that.'

Beau's ears twitch as he chews the stolen morsel.

'Come on.' I grin as I walk over to an open gate, grip the biscuit and spin it like a frisbee into the fog. Beau gallops after it, disappearing into the thick shroud of mist.

I close and secure the gate, then check my watch. Time to get to work.

After I lock up and climb into my beaten-up Landcruiser with Sam, I travel down the long gravel driveway. Through the fog, the gnarled winter trees appear in pairs on both sides, at first like ghosts, then solid and black, leaning towards me, as if reaching for me with deformed, arthritic fingers. At times like this, they remind me of my mother's warnings when I was a kid. Warnings that if anyone found out about my disorder, that people, both good and bad, would all want a piece of me. And they'd take every piece they could lay their greedy fingers on until there was nothing left.

The thought makes me shiver. I reach out and turn up the heater to full blast.

<><><>

As I pass the 'Welcome to Cascade' placard, the fog thins just enough to let the sun's white orb shine through, but the town beyond the white barrier remains hidden. The first sign of civilisation stands on the corner of Tucker Road and Main Street; the only petrol station in town, which charges outrageous prices due to a lack of competition.

As I take a left, I soon pass the two-hundred-year-old church, which has been used in several Australian TV series over the years. Then I slow for the school zone. Even though school started half an hour ago, a few groups of mothers huddle together, chatting. Some glance my way, but when they recognise the Landcruiser, they quickly avert their eyes.

Good.

Further along the road, the street opens up to allow for parking in front of the quaint collection of shops. Majestic old oak trees flank the street, their limbs bare now, but in summer their canopy reaches high overhead, providing abundant shade from a magnificent archway all the way to the end of town.

She'd been right.

I quickly push down the surge of thoughts that want to race through my brain every time I think of her.

Slowing for the raised pedestrian crossing at the town's centre, I continue on to the very last building on the right. I pull into my parking space, climb out and hold the door open for Sam.

Eager to get inside before anyone comes along, I push on the glass door's handle. Locked. I shake my head.

Emily's late. Again.

Finding the key, I let myself and Sam inside, pull on the blind over the door and let it fly up with a rattle. Behind the glass stencilled with 'Cascade Vet Clinic', I turn the 'closed' sign around.

Sam trots behind the reception desk and snuggles into her bed in the corner. I turn on the ducted air, shrug off my parka and flick on the lights as I walk towards the rear of the clinic. When I reach the examination room, I hear the bell over the front door tinkle.

Ready to reprimand my mother for her tardiness— which is becoming quite a habit lately—I hurry up the hallway and stop short.

Mrs Winston, the well-to-do sixty-something busybody, and wife of Cascade's mayor, stands at the reception desk with a confused expression. In her arms, she holds Poppet, her white Chihuahua.

She spots me. 'Dr Clark. Am I too early?'

'No.' The familiar tension created by having to deal with someone like Mrs Winston enters my body. Most of the locals have long ago received the message that I prefer to be left alone, but Mrs Winston seems oblivious.

She stares at me, shifting Poppet from her left arm to her right. I know she's waiting for me to say more. I suppose I could be polite and explain why no one's here to greet clients, but I refuse to indulge her with small talk.

'Well,' she says, 'Poppet's here for her yearly shots.'

By way of invitation, I simply tilt my head towards the hallway and head to the examination room.

As I remove my leather gloves and replace them with the latex variety, Mrs Winston appears in the doorway. Without a word, I indicate for her to place Poppet on the exam table. She obliges, but refuses to let go of the trembling dog.

I sigh on the inside. Becoming a vet had been my dream since I was ten years old. I love animals, and they seem to love me. It's that simple.

Unfortunately, there's one problem. Animals come with owners. And owners are a pain in the arse I can do without. I have no problem giving them a diagnosis or explaining the treatment or what an operation might involve. That's easy, part of my job. It's the chitchat that I loathe.

'Let her go,' I say.

Mrs Winston hesitates a fraction of a second before she releases the little dog and clutches her purse, instead.

As soon as I place my hands on Poppet, she stops shaking and licks at my latex gloves. Her bulging eyes lock with mine as her tail begins a rapid sweep against the stainless-steel table.

'You know,' Mrs Winston says, 'I saw Nora Dawson yesterday.'

I ignore her and concentrate on easing Poppet's lips back so I can get a good look at her teeth. Next, I check her ears, then listen to her heartbeat.

'She's just broken up with Ray McKnight.'

Mrs Winston seems determined to ruin my examination. Without giving her even a grunt of encouragement, I open the small bar fridge, which contains an array of vaccinations, antibiotics and anti-inflammatory vials. I hear her release a small scoff, an obvious sign that I've offended her, but my deliberate rudeness does nothing to discourage her.

'She'd be perfect for you, Dr Clark.'

Why was it she felt she had to play matchmaker for me? I hate being reminded of just how lonely I am, have always been and always will be. Yes, I'd love to share my life with someone special, but I can't, and that's that.

After preparing the two injections, I return to the exam table, avoiding Mrs Winston's curious stare. I can feel her eyes on me as I give Poppet her shots. Why Mrs Winston thinks any woman would be interested in me is so ridiculous I actually struggle to keep a straight face.

'Well, maybe that new woman who's moving into the old Edwards' farm might be more to your liking. Unless you're one of those …'

Avoiding any eye contact, I move Poppet closer to Mrs Winston, turn away from her once again and pretend to tidy the bench.

'All done,' I say.

She releases a huff before her footsteps retreat down the hallway. I grin to myself. Let her think I'm gay. It doesn't bother me. In fact, it' give the town gossips something new to add to the list of things they already believe. Plus, Mrs Winston might finally give up on her matchmaking crusade.

When I hear her voice in reception, I let out a breath of relief. Emily's finally arrived. Curious about what Mrs Winston has to say, I inch towards the doorway.

'Well, it was a good morning until I had to deal with that son of yours. If you ask me, he's in desperate need of psychological help.'

I grin.

'For his germaphobia?' my mother asks.

'Among other things. Manners being one of them.'

'I've talked to him,' Emily says. 'I really have. But you know how men are about shrinks. And since we don't have one in town, there's not much I can do about him, I'm afraid. Anyway, how's Poppet?'

'As always, for some strange reason, she just seems to adore Dr Clark.'

'He's never had any complaints from his patients, that's for sure.'

I wait for Mrs Winston to leave before wandering out to reception. My mother watches me enter, an amused glint in her eyes.

'What did you say to her this time?'

'Not much. Hopefully, she finally got the message to leave me the hell alone. Seems she's the only one around here who forgets.' I lean on the desk's high counter as my mother files away a copy of Poppet's vaccination record. 'You were late again.'

She gives me an innocent look. 'I was?'

'You know damn well you were. I really should fire you.'

She laughs. 'Then who'd deal with people like Mrs Winston for you?'

I like to see her happy. Growing up, she'd been so tense, always on edge, always because of me.

When I'd first discovered the clinic, it'd been run by a husband-and-wife team who were ready to retire to the coast. The timing couldn't have been better, the set-up perfect for me to step right in. When I'd told Emily, she'd quickly jumped in with an offer to help me run the place. At first I'd objected, but her arguments eventually persuaded me. With her help, my dealings with people had been limited. Usually, she'd greet the patient's owner and find out exactly what they thought was wrong. Before showing the patient in, she'd bring me up to speed, saving me a lot of unnecessary talk. She also handled all the administration and purchasing duties.

But most importantly of all, it meant I didn't have to hire a stranger who would expect conversation from me.

It had also been an opportunity to forgive her without having to say the words. For a long time there, I'd resented her for keeping me so isolated I was almost socially inept. When I'd gone to university on a full scholarship at the age of seventeen, I'd realised she'd been right on so many levels. My disorder handicapped me when it came to social interactions, but thankfully it hadn't prevented me from following my chosen path in life. By the time I'd realised how right my mother had been, I'd believed I'd damaged our relationship so profoundly that I just couldn't admit I'd been wrong to resent her. Not when all she'd been trying to do was be a good mother. The circumstances she found herself in when she discovered my disorder were anything but normal. Giving her this job was my apology for the coldness I'd shown her during that turbulent time in our lives.

The phone rings and Emily snatches it up. 'Cascade Vet Clinic … Oh, Jess, glad you called … Of course I can talk.'

I stare at her as she scribbles something on a post-it note and passes it to me, never missing a beat in her personal conversation. The note simply says, *Coffee!* Which means she expects me to go and get it. I try to make eye contact with her, to show my annoyance, but she knows better and keeps her head down.

I remove my latex gloves and flick them at her, but her only response is to swivel around in her chair and turn her back on me.

Shrugging into my parka, I grab my leather gloves and shove my hands inside them. Outside, the sun's almost broken through the thinning fog, but the air still has plenty of bite. I hurry past the small hardware store next to my clinic, past the goodwill shop and the newsagency. As I walk past the only supermarket in town, I see Ned Jamison heading my way. It's almost imperceptible, but I notice Ned arc around me, even though we're in no danger of wandering into each other's paths.

It doesn't surprise me. After all, the town sees me as an oddity to gossip about. The reason everyone believes I constantly wear gloves may be an outright lie, but what isn't a lie is my self-imposed solitude. And the locals love to speculate on that one.

When I reach the Little Drop of Heaven café, I push through the door and stride inside.

Behind the counter, Josephine Little places sweet pastries in the display case. At only seventeen, she's dropped out of high school to help her parents run the café after her father suffered a heart attack. I know all this through Emily, and I also know Jo wants to sell the place and move to Sydney once her parents pass away. I respect her for that. It shows how much she cares for them. She could, after all, already be gone.

As she turns towards me, I see her eyes flick to my gloves. She does nothing to hide her distaste. Nor does she bother smiling. Fine with me. Smiles are just something else I've learned to do without.

- 2 -

BRYCE

BRYCE HARGRAVES WALKS ALONG the street towards the Little Drop of Heaven café, eager to get that hot liquid coursing through his body. Shoving his hands in his pockets, he can't deny the chill in the air this morning is doing a number on his arthritic knee. But he refuses to give into it. Refuses to limp. He's a tough old bastard and he plans to keep it that way.

Squinting against the emerging sun, the wrinkles on his face from sixty-five years of work on his own cattle farm, deepen even further.

From the road, a car horn toots. Bryce glances up to see John Greentree, another born-and-bred local, wave from his beaten-up ute. Bryce raises his hand in return.

'Hey, Bryce!' Tom Packer calls from the other side of the street, then hurries across the road.

Bryce stops on the footpath and waits. Tom's only been a Cascade resident for ten years, but he'd fit in almost immediately and had become a close friend.

'Comin' to the pub tonight?' Tom asks, panting a little.

'You betcha. My shout, right?'

'Thought ya shouted last time?'

Bryce gives him a sociable pat on the shoulder. 'What's it matter? All works out in the end, right?'

'Good man. I'll see ya there.'

In an upbeat mood, Bryce watches Tom hurry off in the opposite direction. His good mood doesn't last long. Guilt courses through him, putting an end to any thoughts of the carefree life he'd led until a few days ago. But he also knows he can return to that life again.

Just a matter of time. That's all there is to it.

Until then, he knows what to do to prevent the spread of the highly contagious disease. A disease his cattle developed just a week after his daughter, Georgia, returned from a Year Twelve trip to Japan.

Once the symptoms began to take hold, he'd figured out what was wrong with his cattle. Since then, his full-time job has consisted of hiding the disease from the rest of the community, and Georgia. It'd been easy to begin with. Still recovering from jet lag and feeling homesick, she hadn't wanted to go anywhere. And even now, she hasn't been too interested in the cattle since her return, so she hasn't noticed the signs of the disease. Not that she'd know what they were. But over the last couple of days, she's started making noises about coming into town to visit her friends.

Bryce doesn't like to lie to her, but if it means protecting her and the farm, he has no choice. A week ago, he'd disabled her car. Pretending he had no idea what was wrong with it, he'd told her he'd get someone to look at it as soon as he could. She'd been upset, but that was a far better alternative than having her know what she'd unintentionally done.

Every time he's come into town, Bryce has left home before Georgia wakes. Not too difficult since she's seventeen and prone to sleeping until midday.

Though the decontamination process is a pain in the goddamn arse, she would have been suspicious had he completely ceased coming into town. So, when he does, he fills a couple of buckets with industrial-strength disinfectant and steaming hot water, places them in the ute's tray with a hard, bristled scrubbing brush and drives to the end of the kilometre-long driveway.

Once there, he scrubs and rinses the ute's tyres until every pebble and clump of dirt falls away, and does the same with his shoes. Only then does he drive onto the public road. With all the precautions he takes, there's no chance the disease will spread. And in another week or so, the symptoms will disappear, and the threat of an outbreak will be gone. And no one, including Georgia, will be any wiser.

Stepping inside the warm café, Bryce freezes. There, sitting at a table in the corner, is his rotten neighbour, Dan Clark. The bastard who broke Georgia's heart when he killed her prized bull.

'Hi, Mr Hargraves,' Jo sings out from behind the counter.

He glares at Clark, waiting for any sign of acknowledgement, but as always, the rude son of a bitch doesn't even lift his head.

Plastering on a smile, her strides over to the counter. 'Hiya, Jo. Whatcha got for me today?'

Jo gives him a wide grin. 'Those cinnamon buns you love. You want me to warm up a couple?'

'That'd be great.'

He watches her place them in the toaster oven, then busy herself with a couple of takeaway coffees. She fits the lids and pushes them across the counter, rolling her eyes at him as if they share a secret.

'Ah, Dr Clark?' she calls, clearly uncomfortable.

Bryce steps back as Clark approaches the counter and finally glances at him. For a split second. Long enough to acknowledge the animosity between them, before his eyes skitter away.

The freak slides a twenty-dollar note onto the counter with a gloved hand. Jo waits unit he releases it before she dare touch it. She places the change on the counter and slides it over to Clark. Smiling inwardly, Bryce knows she'll do anything to avoid contact with the freak.

When the bell over the door sounds, Bryce turns to see eighteen-year-old Mike Turnbull enter. He briefly wonders why the twit hasn't left town to pursue a career as a drug addict in the city. From the looks of his long, greasy hair and threadbare clothes, that's all he seems qualified for.

They give each other a nod, and Bryce moves to allow Mike enough room to step up to the counter. As Clark clumsily tries to stuff his change in his pocket with his gloves on, a coin drops to the floor.

Mike bends, retrieves the coin and offers it to Clark. Without a word, Clark ignores him, grabs his coffees and leaves.

'What a freak,' Mike says as he leans on the counter and grins at Jo.

At least that's one opinion Bryce has in common with the kid.

Jo checks on the cinnamon buns, returns to the counter and looks at Mike. 'You know, I've been thinking. Maybe he's not a germaphobe at all. Maybe he's really a serial killer afraid of leaving fingerprints. Ever thought of that?'

Bryce likes the way the girl thinks.

'Nah,' Mike says. 'I like your Freddy Krueger–hands theory better. Pus and sinew and burnt flesh—' He suddenly grabs Jo's shoulders. She squeals and pulls away in disgust.

'Gross! You buying something?'

'Nah. Just here to look at you.'

'Then get outta here,' she says.

Bryce watches with amusement as Mike gives her a small bow.

'Your wish is my command,' he says in a pathetic attempt at an English accent.

Bryce waits until Mike leaves before he says, 'I see that boy hasn't given up.'

Jo shrugs, removing the cinnamon buns from the toaster. When she returns to the counter, she takes his payment.

'Guys are idiots. 'Cept for you, Mr Hargraves. I wish my dad'd let me go to Japan … or anywhere besides here. Georgia's lucky to have an awesome dad like you.'

'Well, that's kinda you to say, Jo.'

When he leaves, he feels a slight spring in his step as he replays Jo's words in his head. Yep, Georgia is lucky to have him. If it wasn't for his insatiable need to protect his only child and farm, if it wasn't for the actions he's taken to keep the outbreak on his property a secret, they'd both be thought of as traitors by the entire town.

- 3 -

GEORGIA

WEARING EARMUFFS, GEORGIA WATCHES her father aim his rifle at the target they'd set up against a stack of hay bales in the distance. This is one thing she actually loves about living here.

Bryce squeezes the trigger, the shot ringing out across the rolling hills.

The smell of gun smoke wafts into Georgia's nostrils, bringing up memories of her father teaching her to shoot when she was just five. She loves that smell. Probably because it'd been the first time she'd found a genuine connection with her father, the man who'd raised her on his own since then.

Not wanting to think about her mother's death right now, Georgia grabs the binoculars hanging around her neck and raises them to her eyes. Damn him. A bullseye. When she looks his way, he's already grinning at her. Annoyed, she shoves the binoculars at him, raises her own rifle and cradles it against her shoulder. The trigger's cold metal seeps into her index finger as she lines up the sights, then slowly, slowly squeezes. The muffled shot cracks in her ear at the same instant the kickback punches her shoulder. Without even looking, she knows she's missed the bullseye.

Bryce doesn't raise the binoculars and gloat. He simply passes them to her and lets her take the first look. When she does, she sees that she hit the target's outer ring. Not as bad as she thought, but not great, either.

She takes off her earmuffs and waits for Bryce to do the same.

'I suck,' she says, handing him the binoculars.

He doesn't bother looking. Instead, he puts a comforting arm around her shoulders and squeezes. 'That's what you get for tripping off overseas. Outta practice. But you'll be kicking my arse again before you know it.'

Pretending to be annoyed by his affection, she shrugs off his arm, though she really doesn't want to. 'When're you gonna cut that out? I've been home for two weeks.'

'Doesn't mean I've forgotten how much I missed you.'

She can't keep the smile from curling her lips. 'I know. I missed you, too, but I'm home now.' The words on her tongue feel thick with the lie. She had missed him, but she no longer feels like she's home. Not anymore.

'Here,' he says, handing her his rifle. 'I'm going in for my nap. You remember how to clean those, right?'

'Unfortunately, yeah.'

He smiles, clamps a hand on her shoulder with affection and walks towards the house. As she watches him, she notices the faintest hint of a limp. A hollow pit opens up in her stomach. He's trying to hide it, but the pain must be especially bad today for him to show any sign at all that he's hurting.

Then again, she's hurting too. Just not physically, though it feels that way sometimes.

When she'd started her Higher School Certificate last year, it'd been the first time the tiny high school offered textiles as an elective. Just as she'd known she would, she'd instantly fallen in love with every aspect of it.

She'd raved about it to her father, but he'd only given her obligatory grunts, his eyes miles away. So, she'd stopped talking about it.

Then came the opportunity to go to Japan and experience their fashion. She'd known Bryce would never let her go, would never spend money on something so frivolous. So, she'd deceived him by making her own permission slip on the school computer, changing every textiles and design reference to agricultural studies.

He'd claimed she already knew everything there was to know. But she'd explained that part of the syllabus was to gather information on another country's agricultural techniques, and that the best way to experience such a thing was to be there in person. Convincing him that her attendance on the trip would help with her overall marks in her final year at high school, he'd finally coughed up a cheque.

She'd forged his signature on the real permission slip, knowing she wouldn't get caught. What did the school care as long as they had the money? And it wasn't like her father would bother talking to her teachers.

Yes, she'd lied to him. But she *had* visited a farm in Japan. Once. She'd sent Bryce a bunch of photos to make it look like that's where she'd been the whole time. After that single day on the farm, she'd wrapped her muddy boots in a plastic bag, stuffed them in the bottom of her suitcase and forgotten all about farms and cows and mud and manure. Until she'd unpacked those boots two weeks ago.

For the rest of her trip, the teacher had taken the textiles class to fashion shows and design schools. And she'd had a revelation. A passion had welled up inside her, one she'd never been able to summon for farming. And now it simmered within her. Every time she stepped into the textiles class, every time her fingers touched the different textures of the fabric she worked with. Every time she heard the rhythmic rise and fall of the sewing-machine needle punching thread through fabric, joining it together in a unique way that seemed to flow from her hands as she guided the material.

Her throat constricts. This life, the one her father wants for her, isn't the one she wants for herself anymore. She has to tell him. She knows that. But she loves him and doesn't want to hurt him.

Taking a deep breath, she turns away from the house and looks at the rolling hills that are all theirs. Her father's, anyway. As beautiful as it is, it's not where she wants to be. She has no idea how she's going to break that news.

Bending down, she grabs her Akubra, shoves it on her head and glances at her gumboots. They're not warm and comfortable like her favourite boots, but she hasn't been able to find them since she'd unpacked them and worn them on a walk around the property her first day home.

Not eager to get on with her task of cleaning the guns, she lets her gaze travel over the familiar contours of the land until they come to rest on one large, brown paddock. A paddock that also happens to contain every single head of cattle they own. Frowning, she places the rifles on the ground and takes the long walk over to the fence.

Once there, she finds that all the grass has been eaten. Worse still, the cattle seem so hungry, they're salivating. For the life of her, she can't figure out why her father would subject the cows to this hunger when the adjoining paddock is twice the size and lush with pasture. He's only sixty-five, old by other teenagers' parents, she knows, but is he that old he's forgotten to move the herd?

Well, the least she can do is save him the trouble.

- 4 -

LUCAS

SAM SITS ON THE passenger seat, gazing through the windscreen. As I take the left-hand turn onto my property, she adjusts her weight to keep her balance.

Halfway down the long driveway, I jerk the Landcruiser to a sudden stop and stare at the cattle in the Hargraves' adjoining paddock. On the other side of the boundary fence, it seems Hargraves' entire herd is occupying this single paddock. That in itself is unusual. But that's not why I stopped.

The cattle simply stand in the paddock. Not a single one eats the lush pasture. Instead, they drool. A calf limps over to its mother and presses against her.

Facing forward, I stare straight ahead as the last remnants of sunshine slips behind a hill. I want nothing more than to ignore what I've seen, to just drive home and pretend I haven't witnessed anything out of the ordinary.

But I can't do that.

It's my job, my responsibility.

'Fuck,' I say under my breath.

Sam looks at me, her head cocked slightly to the side. I give her a pat, tell her to stay put and climb out into the already frigid air.

Opening the rear door, I find some latex gloves in the medical bag I keep in the back and head towards the boundary separating Bryce's property from my own. After I duck through the post-and-rail fence, I remove my leather gloves and replace them with latex.

Stopping beside the calf I'd observed limping, I run a comforting hand over its face. Like all animals, it senses that I'm no threat and allows me to ease up its saliva-covered lips. And I discover exactly what I'd feared. Fluid-filled blisters.

This can't be happening.

With reluctance, I run a hand over the calf's shoulder, down its leg and lift its hoof off the ground. A raw, painful ulcer protrudes from the heel. I gently release the calf and take a step back.

'Jesus.'

Dismayed, I stare at the miserable herd. Then my gaze shifts to the Hargraves' homestead in the distance. I don't want another confrontation with Bryce, but the choice isn't mine.

Knowing the last thing I should do is drive onto the infected property, I leave Sam in the car, where she'll be safe and warm until I return. At least the walk across the expansive field delays the unavoidable for a few more minutes.

By the time I stomp up the paved steps to Bryce's front door, I've replaced the latex with my warm leather gloves. I press a hesitant finger to the doorbell. Inside, it chimes a pleasant tune, as if the Hargraves expect whoever visits to be a welcome guest.

They're in for a rude surprise.

As footsteps approach, I steel myself.

The door swings open, and at the sight of me, Georgia's face instantly hardens. Usually a pretty girl, when she's not glaring at me that is, she crosses her arms over her chest, offering no greeting.

'Just get your father,' I say.

She gives me a death stare before turning on her heel and stomping around a corner.

'Dad!' she shouts. 'The germaphobe freak's here!'

Uncomfortable, but taking the open door as an invitation, I step into the warm, slate-tiled foyer. On the right, blue rosettes, ribbons and sashes cover the wall like wallpaper. To my left, photographs in various-sized frames litter the wall.

Curious, I move closer to the photos. Old black-and-whites show proud men and their sons with bulls draped in champion sashes. As I move along the wall, the photos change to colour shots, right up to a recent picture of Georgia and Bryce smiling proudly as they flank a bull with a supreme-champion sash draped around its neck.

The bull I had to put down. The bull that'd caused all this animosity between us.

'What the hell do *you* want?' Bryce demands, striding into the foyer, Georgia right behind him.

'There's a problem with your cattle.'

Bryce squints with suspicion. 'You been snooping around my land?'

'Pretty hard to miss them. They're right on our boundary.'

'Bullshit. They're nowhere near your property.'

I catch the guilty look on Georgia's face as she bites her lip.

'I might've moved them,' she admits.

Bryce shoots her a glare, his mouth clamping into a thin line of disapproval. 'Go make dinner,' he barks at her, then turns to me. 'Outside.'

I oblige, but flinch when Bryce slams the door with a loud crack. I turn and face the older man, dreading what's coming.

'Reported it yet?' I ask, knowing full well Bryce has done no such thing.

'You're trespassing.'

'Then I'll have to.' I pull my phone from my pocket, but of course, I can't unlock the damn thing without taking off a glove. And from the way Bryce is acting, I don't want to risk any chance my bare hand might come into contact with him. He's old and sure as hell isn't in great shape. When it comes to me, he's the very definition of danger. I knew all this before I even reached for the phone, but I'd hoped he'd come to his senses. Maybe I can fool him by pretending to scroll through my contacts and—

He snatches the phone from my hand, flings it to the pavers and crushes it under his boot.

'What the fuck?'

Bryce advances on me, and I back up, not wanting him to touch me.

'It's not enough that you killed Georgia's prized bull?' he accuses.

'That bull was riddled with cancer and you know it. There was nothing to do but put it out of its misery.'

With real menace, Bryce steps right into my personal space and grabs my parka before I have a chance to escape.

'How about I put *you* out of your misery, you goddamned freak?'

I jerk out of his grasp, just managing to keep my balance as my foot catches the edge of the step behind me. 'Is that a threat?'

'You bet your fucking life it is,' he says, his face red with rage.

Calm on the outside, my heart's thundering like a goddamn jackhammer. I've never seen him like this, not even when I'd injected Georgia's bull with the lethal dose of Phenobarbital. He'd been angry, yes, but he didn't have this wild, desperate look his eyes.

'You know I'm legally obligated to report this, Bryce. So are you.'

'Get the fuck off my property.'

I back down the steps, the unease in my chest building. Still, I can't let Bryce know he's rattled me. 'You've got until I get home to do the right thing.'

I turn, and even though my whole body coils with tension, even though every instinct tells me to run, I slowly amble towards my property in the distance.

- 5 -

BRYCE

SHAKING WITH RAGE, BRYCE watches the freak walk across his freshly mown lawn, slip between the fence railing and set off through the paddocks. Confused, he glances at the driveway.

No car.

So, Clark walked over.

Bryce knows from Clark's slow, unhurried gait that it'll take him at least five minutes, if not more, to reach the boundary fence. He also knows that if Clark makes it home, makes that phone call, he'll lose everything. His life is farming and farming is his life. It's as simple as that. If that's taken away from him, he has no idea who he'll be.

And he'll most certainly lose his daughter. He already has the uneasy feeling she's slipping away from him since her return from Japan, but if he loses the farm, there'll be nothing keeping her here.

There's only one solution.

Clark has to be stopped.

Permanently.

He stares at freak's retreating figure. Twilight's taken hold and the clear, open sky sports pinpricks of light here and there. Complete darkness isn't far off. He needs to decide.

Is he capable of murder?

The answer comes in a rush.

Yes.

To save who he is, to keep his daughter … *yes.*

Darting inside, heart pounding, he hurries into the study, unlocks the rifle cabinet and takes out a Remington 7600, his most powerful and accurate weapon.

'Dad?' Georgia calls from the kitchen.

'I'll be back in a couple of minutes,' he yells as he slips through the front door and closes it softly behind him.

Then he breaks into a run. His arthritic knee screams in protest, but fear and determination override everything now. He has to catch up to Clark before he gets to his own property.

By the time he reaches the paddock Georgia moved the herd into, his breath wheezes on the cold, thin air and his knee wants to buckle. But he keeps going. He can see Clark weaving through the cattle, making a tough target of himself.

In that instant, he realises he won't catch up to Clark before he makes it to the boundary fence.

When Bryce reaches the first cow, he stops beside it, raises the rifle to his shoulder and points it over the top of the animal's back. He pumps a round into the chamber and looks through the scope. Burning up from the exertion, warm sweat trickles down the side of his face. He needs to get Clark to stop moving.

Taking a deep gulp of air, he yells, 'Hey!'

Clark hesitates and turns, his face confused as he searches for the source of the voice.

It gives Bryce enough time to steady his aim. He squeezes the trigger.

Then the kickback comes, the crack in his ear, the herd startling. He knows Georgia will hear the shot from the house. Nothing he can do about that.

Clark stands motionless for a long moment.

Fear grips Bryce. Did he miss? He's sure he hasn't, but if he has, he's just given Clark a reason to get the fuck out of here.

Then Clark's legs buckle and he drops to his knees. A second later, he falls forward and disappears into the long grass.

As Bryce circles around the cow, his own leg almost gives way as he limps towards the collapsed body. By the time he reaches Clark, the freak's turned onto his back and unzipped his jacket. A neat bullet hole to the right side of his chest pumps blood into his flannelette shirt.

Disappointed, Bryce glares down at him. He'd been aiming for the centre of the freak's chest. But the disappointment's short-lived. When Clark lets out a body-racking cough, blood mists on his lips. Then he starts gasping for air.

He's hit Clark's lung. Which means his prick of a neighbour is done for. Maybe not as quickly and efficiently as a bullet to the heart, but Bryce knows a collapsed lung when he sees it. Clark will soon pass out from lack of oxygen, and either suffocate or bleed to death. Either way, without immediate help, he's dead.

Relieved, Bryce leans over him and watches as the freak gasps for breath like a fish out of water, watches blood trickle from the corner of his mouth, watches his pasty face grow pale.

Clark makes eye contact, blinking with what Bryce can only interpret as confusion.

'You think for one second I'd let you destroy my life? My daughter's?'

Clark coughs again, spewing up more blood.

Good.

'Dad! Dinner!'

Bryce jerks away. Georgia's voice is distant, but the sound of it shocks him. He knows she heard the gunshot. That's not what worries him. Putting down cattle and shooting rabbits is nothing new, easy to explain. But if she sees what he's done, he'll be in the same mess Clark wanted to put him in.

He can just make her out in the distance. She's turned the outside light on and stands on the front verandah. Then she starts down the steps. His heart thunders as he raises his hand above his head and waves at her in acknowledgement. When she waves and turns towards the house, he lets out a groan of relief.

Limping close to Clark again, Bryce takes a good look at him. In the fast-fading light, the blood on the freak's mouth looks black against his white face. Already, his eyes seem sunken, resigned to the fact that life is seeping from him.

Satisfied, Bryce says, 'I'll be back to bury you later.'

He turns away and begins the painful journey towards his now safe existence.

- 6 -

LUCAS

I BLINK UP AT the darkening sky, the wheezing loud in my ears. I can't catch my breath, yet with each rapid exhale, the air forms a white cloud for a second, then vanishes. I wonder if my soul will do the same when it leaves my body; the frigid air exposing what's usually invisible to the naked eye.

When the bullet first entered my chest, I think the shock kept me standing. The shock that Bryce Hargraves shot me. A man who's lived his whole life in Cascade, who's farmed the land just as his ancestors had, a man the whole town respects.

A man who shot me for doing my job.

I found it hard to believe. Until my body collapsed.

I don't have long. The pain's excruciating. The lack of air suffocating. Every muscle in my body trembles, and even though the ground beneath me chills my bones and the air above presses a thin blanket of condensation over me, I know that tremble has nothing to do with the cold and everything to do with the bullet in my chest.

Life pumps from my body with each heartbeat, with each breath I can't take.

I have two choices, and I'm not sure which decision to make. I never thought I'd be in this position. It certainly isn't the situation my mother warned me about, but the consequences are the same.

Live or die. The choice is in my hands.

Literally.

I almost laugh at that, but can't. I'm sure any harsh movement might intensify the pain and reel me into unconsciousness.

Every beat of my heart feels like a ticking time bomb. I need to hurry, need to decide. Just let go and drift away, or is there something worth living for? What sort of life do I have anyway? A never-ending stretch of lonely isolation interspersed with work. Is that living?

Then there's the hollow ache I constantly feel in my chest, one that's been with me from the moment I lost my only friend.

Kelsey.

Not only had I lost her, but the pain of having failed her has never left me.

I have an existence, but I'm not living life. Which makes it so easy to die right here and now.

But one tiny spark of hope does exist. A hope that both lifts my spirit every time I think about it, but also shoots fear through my heart.

Kelsey.

There's just the slimmest chance that she'll one day arrive in Cascade. And I can't bear the thought of not being here if she does.

With every ounce of strength I have left, I raise my head, tear open my shirt and expose my bare skin to the icy air. To my horror, I can actually see the blood pulse from the wound in my chest. Worse still, the pain's fading. Numbness is setting in and I know what that means.

Gasping and wheezing, I try to pull off a glove, but my fingers are numb, useless, leaving me incapable of wrenching it free.

I panic. I've left it too late. If I can't remove the glove …

The corners of my vision grow dark. I can't be sure if it's the encroaching night taking hold, or if I'm about to pass out.

Suddenly, it comes to me.

I bring my right hand up to my mouth, bite down on the glove's fingertips and pull it free. Just as the entire world begins to spin and fade away, I find the bullet hole with my bare fingers and press over the wound. And as I do, I fall into the memory of her.

THEN

- 7 -

LUCAS

'LUKE?'

My sleepy eyes blink open, then close again. The dream I'd been having wants to pull me back under. And I want it to.

'Luke? Come on, honey. I have to get to work.'

I groan. The dream had been so good because I'd been normal and surrounded by friends.

'Lucas!'

'I'm awake,' I mumble without opening my eyes.

'Look at me.'

I grumble at her. This has been our routine ever since Mum started working at a nursing home six months ago. Which meant she had to leave me alone for the first time in my life.

She's been homeschooling me since I can remember, constantly telling me that I'm smart, years ahead of other ten-year-olds. She's also told me most ten-year-olds aren't allowed to stay home on their own, so I'm lucky. But I'm not sure I believe that. I'm not sure I believe a lot of what she tells me lately. The problem is, I have no one else to ask, so the truth remains elusive.

What matters most is being alone, being away from her constant, stifling supervision. There are rules, of course. I can never leave the apartment—nothing new there. The door has to stay locked at all times. I'm only to use the microwave to prepare food, not the stove or the oven. Never answer the phone if it rings. Though who'll call, I have no idea. As far as I know, Mum has no friends, either. No one's ever been to our apartment.

'Come on, you know what you have to do or I'm not leaving.' Her voice has taken on a stern note. I know better than to push her further. Opening my eyes, I look at her.

She stands in my doorway, wearing her uniform and sensible shoes. I love her, but I also love this new sliver of freedom.

'That's better.' She smiles, relief in her eyes.

That's another thing I've started to understand now that I'm ten. Just as I enjoy the tiny freedom of being on my own, I'm sure Mum enjoys not being stuck with me every day in our small apartment. I wish she understood that, like her, I want to go out into the world and experience new things, new people.

But she doesn't understand. I don't think she ever will.

Pushing myself up, I swing my feet out of bed, raise my naked arms above my head and give an exaggerated stretch that brings bright pinpricks of light to my vision. When I take a step towards her, she backs right out of the room, like I'm a magnet, and the closer I get, the more I repel her.

It's not because I repulse her, it's just her way of keeping me safe.

I follow her through the small open-plan living room and past the round dining table behind the battered couch. When she reaches the front door and opens it, I stop, leaving a few metres between us.

She turns towards me and smiles. 'Your schoolwork's on the table.'

I nod, and after she steps into the corridor and closes the door, I turn the deadbolt with a loud clack.

'I'll see you tonight,' she calls through the door.

'Okay,' I mumble, resenting that she doesn't trust me to lock the door after all this time. Besides, I think it's stupid of her to wait for me to lock it. If I want to, I can simply unlock it again after she leaves.

Before she started working, she'd leave me alone briefly to get groceries and run errands. Back then, she'd locked me in the apartment from the outside, literally imprisoning me. She'd also done the same thing when she first started working. But one night, when we'd been watching TV, we'd seen a devastating apartment fire on the news. I remembered turning to her in fear, and before I could even say the words, she'd told me that from then on, I'd have to lock the door from the inside so I could get out if there was an emergency.

Sighing, I brush my long hair from my eyes and hurry to my bedroom.

At the dresser, I open the top drawer, grab a long-sleeved shirt and shoved it over my head. From the next drawer, I find a pair of ragged khaki shorts and slip them on.

Shuffling to the window, I part the worn curtains. Since we live on the fifth floor, there's no lock, so I simply slide it open. As I stretch my sleeves over my hands, hot air blows inside, stirring the shaggy fringe out of my eyes. Across the alleyway stands the fantastic view of the building a mere four metres from where I stand. The red bricks contain no windows. I only know from Mum that the lower level houses a small supermarket, a café and hairdresser, and the levels above are offices.

Between the gaps in the dumpsters below, I catch movement. About a month ago, a stray cat carried her kittens, one by one, into the alley and placed them in between the dumpsters, making a new home for her new family. I itch to go down there and pet them, touch their soft fur, listen to their purrs.

But I don't dare. If Mum catches me, there'll be hell to pay. She might quit her job. Then I'll be stuck in the apartment with her again, day after day, week after week.

No, thank you.

I give the alley below a quick glance, then lean out further to get a good look at the busy street beyond. For the millionth time, I wish we had a corner apartment, not one on the side, a good ten metres back from the street. I wonder if Mum deliberately chose this apartment so I wouldn't be able to see what I was missing out on.

I hope not, but the older I grow, the less sure I become.

On the street, the rumble of traffic mixes with the occasional blare of a horn. But in that four-metre gap between both buildings, I see the usual kids waiting at the bus stop. Kids who are allowed to go to school, kids who wear uniforms. Boys with neatly cut short hair and girls with long ponytails. Kids Mum tells me hate school, hate wearing uniforms and hate catching the bus. Kids that'd be jealous of me being homeschooled.

If that's true, why am *I* the one who's jealous? Why do *I* want to be the boy at the bus stop whose friend puts him in a headlock? Or the boy who pulls on the girl's ponytail, then gets shoved or punched in the arm? Or any of them who get to talk, argue and laugh with one another?

I watch with longing as the school bus pulls up, the doors hiss open, and the kids shove at each other as they clamber on.

Frustrated, the heat already making me sweat, I'm about to shut the window when a removalist truck parks at the bus stop. I know from years of studying the traffic that no vehicle except the bus is allowed to stop there. Then the passenger door opens.

And the prettiest girl I've ever seen jumps out.

I hold my breath as she slams the truck door. When she turns around again, she places her hands on her hips, her eyes scanning the apartment building with disgust. I watch in fascination as what seems like a million emotions pass over her face.

Then her eyes find mine.

I stumble back, smack my head on the window frame above and trip over my tangled feet. As I drop to the threadbare carpet, I let out a huff of air.

What an idiot! A girl notices you, and you hide?

Hauling myself up, I shove up my sleeve and place my hand on the back of my head. Heat radiates into my scalp, the dull pain vanishing in an instant. Quickly pulling my sleeve down again, I step to the window and lean out.

The truck's still there, but the girl has gone.

Annoyed with myself for being such a wimp, I lower the window and close the curtains against the heat.

But I can't help wondering if I'll ever see the girl again.

- 8 -

KELSEY

I STAND ON THE busy city street, my arms crossed over breasts that haven't begun to form yet. I think about that sometimes, but my ten years on this earth has been filled with so much drama, it leaves little room for imagining what the future holds. Except for one thing. Living with my dad.

'Kelsey?' my mother calls.

I remain rooted to the spot, my eyes fixed on the dark cavity at the back of the open truck, wishing it'd swallow my mother into a magical black hole.

'Kelsey!' Lisa Wells materialises from the darkness like an angry ghost, her face pale and drawn from years of too many cigarettes and too many intimate kisses with a million different bottles of scotch. In desperate need of a cut, her dirty-blonde hair hangs in frizzy strands around her shoulders. I've only ever seen her as a pretty, hopeful woman in old photos Dad's shown me. They'd been teenagers in high school when they'd met. Back then, my mother seemed happy and carefree, the whole world an endless possibility.

I know something bad happened to her a long time ago, but neither of my parents will tell me anything. It's always the same excuse; I'm too young.

But I won't be too young forever. Then I'll find out, then I'll know why she's a miserable bitch. The one thing I don't know is whether the reason for my mother's shitty personality will change the way I feel about her. I doubt it. Too much damage has been done. But in the deepest parts of myself, in the parts I barely ever let see the light, I hope it'll change everything.

I hope, but still can't wrap my head around the sort of trauma that could cause someone to hate their only child.

'What the hell's wrong with you?' Lisa shouts from the edge of the truck's tailgate.

I snap out of my thoughts and peer up at her towering above me, a box in her arms.

'Jesus Christ, girl. Stop bloody daydreaming and help.'

I glare at her as a removalist takes the box from her arms and heads towards the apartment block.

'No!' she yells at him.

He flinches as he turns back.

'Ma'am?' he asks innocently.

'Give the box to her,' she demands. 'It's as light as all get-out. She can carry it. I'm not paying you guys to move stuff we can do ourselves.'

The man gives me a sheepish shrug as he hands over the box, then hops into the truck again.

I stomp towards the apartment block's door, which the removalists have propped open with a wooden chock.

'And don't dawdle!' Lisa yells.

If my hands weren't full, I'd give he the finger. I've done it before, and I'll do it again. It doesn't worry me if it results in a slap across the face. It's always worth it. If there's anything that gets under my mother's skin, the finger is it.

I enter the building. The place is so cheap and nasty it doesn't even have a foyer, just a concrete corridor leading to the ground-floor apartments and a set of concrete steps leading to the rest.

I climb and climb before stopping to lean over the inside railing, which wraps around and around until a dark patch at the top of the ten-storey structure signifies their end. With no elevator, I'm glad we only live halfway up.

When I get to the fifth-floor exit, I fumble with the box as I pull the door open and step into the corridor. My footsteps echo slightly on the cheap lino as I walk towards my new home.

At number 516, I turn the handle and slip inside, into the open-plan lounge room with a kitchen to the left.

Lisa's bedroom stands off to the right of the living room, the bathroom straight ahead, and my room to the left. That's the only thing I like about the apartment; the fact that I'm separated from my mother.

I traipse into the bathroom and put everything in the box away, knowing Lisa won't thank me for helping; she probably won't even notice.

If only I could live with Dad. That's been my wish for over a year now.

Seeing him every second weekend sucks big time. It's not fair, and it's not right. He looks after me and treats me properly, while my mother couldn't care less. Yet the court gave her custody.

Shane, my dad, said it's just the way courts are. One of the reasons, he'd told me, was because Lisa doesn't work, and he does. My mother would be there for me every day before and after school, something he couldn't do.

I'd told him that Lisa doesn't even bother getting up in the morning. And when I come home from school, she's nearly always drunk. I've pleaded with him, tried to convince him I'm old enough to get myself ready for school and come home to an empty house and be safe. He's gone back to his solicitor to see what they can do.

Now we're just waiting for a new court date, but Dad keeps warning me that the law's a horse's arse, and although I don't know what that means, I wholeheartedly agree. The law seems to be an invisible enemy standing in the way of our happiness. But still, every night before I go to sleep, that's what I wish for.

It isn't fair, it isn't fair, it isn't fair.

Even I'm getting sick of hearing those words in my head.

Swallowing over the lump forming in my throat, I leave the apartment to get more boxes.

It's not until the removalists take the very last item out of the truck that I realise I haven't packed my guitar. Absolutely gutted, I drag my feet up the last of the steps to my new apartment. Stopping in the corridor, I lean against the wall, in no hurry to get there.

Up ahead, the removalists disappear inside the doorway. Lisa stops on the threshold, takes a long suck on her cigarette and glares.

'Kelsey! Move your arse!'

As she slips inside the apartment, I notice the door to apartment 514 crack open.

A single eye, barely visible behind a shaggy blond fringe, stares at me. I stare back, realising the eye belongs to a kid, but I can't tell if it's a boy or a girl.

I push away from the wall, and when I move closer, the door slams shut.

Hello to you, too.

'Kel,' a deep male voice says from behind me.

I spin around to find Dad standing there with my battered acoustic guitar in his hand.

'Daddy!'

The sight of my instrument lifts my mood, but the sight of Dad lifts my whole heart a millionfold. I run at him hard, thump into him and wrap my arms around his waist, holding on for dear life.

I'm too old to call him Daddy, but I don't care. This man is the only person on the entire planet who loves me, cares for me, encourages me and makes me laugh.

'Hey, pumpkin,' he wheezes jokingly.

I reluctantly release my hold and take a step away so I can look up at him. My heart feels like it might burst with hope. But when he smiles at me, I see the force behind the curve of his lips, see the lack of lines around his eyes, and my hope deflates.

He likely sees it in my face, too, because he pulls me in close and kisses the top of my head. 'Not yet, pumpkin, not yet. But I'm working on it. Real hard. Here, look at me.' He places his fingers under my chin so I'll meet his gaze. 'I promise. Okay?'

I nod as he hugs me, the lump in my throat as big as a shooter marble. Tears well in my eyes and I hate myself for being so weak.

'Look what you forgot,' he says, holding up the guitar.

I know he's trying to distract me so I won't cry.

'I thought I'd left it at the old apartment,' I mumble, trying to push down the disappointment and just be happy he's here now. He won't be able to stay long. My mother will make sure of that.

I take the guitar and sling the worn strap over my shoulder.

'What's the new place like?' he asks.

'It sucks.'

'Come on. How about you show me?' He puts an arm around my shoulders and turns me towards the apartment.

As we move, I spot the kid next door watching me again, the strangest expression on his face. It gives me the creeps, so I stick out my tongue. In a flash, the door slams shut.

As we walk past, my own apartment door flies open.

Lisa steps out and glares at us. My heart sinks.

'What the hell're you doing here? It's not your day,' she barks.

'I know, Lisa. I just wanted to see where my daughter's going to be living,' Dad explains.

'So now you have. See ya.' My mother grabs hold of my arm and pulls me inside, the guitar crashing into the doorframe.

'Mum!'

Before I have a chance to look at Dad, the door slams shut, and Lisa snaps the lock in place.

'What's wrong with you? I was talking to him!' This time, I can't stop the tears from sliding down my cheeks.

She studies me, and for just a second, I think she's about to relent. Instead, she sweeps past me and stomps into the kitchen. Opening the cupboard above the microwave, she pulls out a cheap bottle of scotch.

'Mum!'

'You can see him when it's his day, so stop whining.'

'I should be able to talk to him anytime I want.'

'Tough.'

I watch with growing anger as she pours a small amount of scotch into a tumbler. I can never understand why she doesn't just fill the glass all the way to the top, why she makes herself come back over and over for refills. It makes no sense.

'It's not fair!'

She shrugs, then downs the scotch in one hit.

'You suck,' I say under my breath.

'Yeah, I know, so you can stop telling me.' She pours another nip of scotch, avoids my glare and gazes at the remaining moving boxes. 'Finish unpacking this lot, and I'll let you call him tonight.'

My nails dig into my palms as I tighten my fists. I know the more I scream and yell, the more infuriating she becomes. Stomping over to the nearest box, I open it and remove a newspaper-wrapped object. I unwrap it and stare at the pretty pink music box Dad gave me for my seventh birthday.

Unable to help myself, I glance at the front door and wish with all my might that he'd break it down and take me away. But I know that won't happen. Dad always does the right thing. It's one of the things I love most about him. He's a good man, the type I want to marry when I grow up.

I stare at the music box, wanting to lift the lid, but don't dare. The tune will set Lisa off, and she'll probably snatch it from my hands and smash it to pieces.

Instead, I place it carefully in the cardboard box and lift it as I rise to my feet. When I turn, I notice my mother watching over the rim of the glass as she downs the golden liquid.

She smacks her lips together.

I can't help but glare at her.

She glares back. 'Don't forget the other boxes. All of them. That's the deal.'

Hating her more with every step I take, I stomp into my bedroom, drop the box on the bed, turn around and slam the door as hard as I can.

- 9 -

LUCAS

I JERK AWAY FROM my bedroom wall, the slam of the door on the other side still ringing in my ear.

'I hate you!' Kelsey screams so loudly it seems like she's in the room with me.

I shouldn't be listening, but who can blame me? No one's lived in the apartment next door for close to a year. Before then, old Mrs Riley was our neighbour. Nothing worth listening to when she'd lived there alone. Her bedroom hadn't been the one on the other side of mine. I hadn't even known there *was* a bedroom on the other side of my wall. Not until a few seconds ago.

So, I figure, the apartment next door's a mirror image of ours.

Interesting.

In fact, today's been the most interesting day I've had since ... well, I can't remember.

I'd stood with the front door slightly ajar, watching and listening to Kelsey's excitement over her father arriving. Something I'd never experience myself. My own father died before I was born. At least I can't miss him. But I miss the *idea* of him, of having another male to talk to. Someone who might have a different opinion to my mother, since, according to her, my father had been like me.

Not only have I missed out on a father, I've missed out on a man who knew how I felt, who could have guided me through life, who could have kept me safe without hiding me away from the rest of the world. It's obvious he hadn't lived the way I was living. If he had, he never would have met Mum, never would have had a son who desperately needed him.

Sometimes I hate him for leaving me here alone with only a mother. But it never lasts long. It's hard to hate someone you never knew in the first place.

Now, at last, I might have a chance to get to know someone else, even if it's a girl called Kelsey.

Kelsey. I like that name, a lot.

When I'd first heard the commotion in the corridor, I'd cracked the door open and watched. First the removalists went past, then a woman with frizzy blonde hair that looked like it needed a good wash and brush. My mother would never leave the apartment without looking presentable to the outside world. Something I don't have to worry about.

And then the girl appeared, emerging from the stairwell into the corridor like it might be slithering with snakes. I could tell she didn't want to be there. She stopped and leaned against the wall almost across from my apartment in an attempt, I guessed, to delay going into her new home. Only a few minutes later, I understood why.

But in that moment, with her so close, I studied her features with pure fascination. Sure, I've seen people hurry along the corridor, but none have stopped to give me a chance to really look at them.

Kelsey had. And I drank her in the way I imagined you'd drink water after being rescued from the desert. Her thick, shiny dark hair fell to her waist, her bright blue eyes sad and intelligent. Her smooth skin featured a few freckles spattered over her nose and cheeks, her full lips a deep pink.

In just a few seconds, I knew I wanted to know her, knew there had to be a reason for her moving in right next door. Deep inside, I felt a desperate need to be her friend.

Then she'd met my eyes, and that feeling had intensified. She'd stared at me with curiosity. Her lips curved upwards slightly, and she took a step towards me. I slammed the door like a coward and stumbled backwards.

Of course, I instantly regretted it. Too late, I realised how rude I'd been. But a lifetime of warnings had kicked in, and that strange feeling in my stomach made my heart thunder, and my body took over before my brain could control it.

When I'd cracked open the door again, Kelsey's father called her name.

I'd seen the look of joy on her face, and I'd experienced that happiness right along with her. Until her mother ruined it all by dragging Kelsey away. That seemed pretty mean. I'd watched her father as he'd disappeared into the stairwell, his whole body filled with sadness and something else. Hopelessness, I thought. I know that feeling all too well.

Another new sound comes from the other side of the wall. An angry, jarring attack on what has to be the old guitar. There seems to be no rhythm or melody, just a loud, riotous noise that expresses her anger, I guess. And why shouldn't she be angry?

I get angry at Mum a lot, but I'd never speak to her like that.

After a moment, the guitar grows quiet.

'What?' I hear Kelsey ask.

'I said, quit that racket and finish unpacking,' her mother says.

Muffled movements follow, and I guess Kelsey's doing what her mother asked.

I leave the bedroom, flop into my chair at the kitchen table and stare at the textbooks. They no longer hold any appeal, but if I don't finish the section Mum assigned, I'll be in trouble. Usually, that isn't even a problem. I'd learned a long time ago to pretend that the work takes me all day. But it's so easy, I always breeze through it well before lunchtime, then watch TV for the rest of the day.

And study it like it's another assignment. I study the people, how they stand and express themselves physically. But more than that, I study how they interacted with each other, what upsets them, what makes them happy. I know that one day, no matter what Mum says, I'll have to talk to people, know how to behave like everyone else. So, just as much as my schoolwork, TV is my teacher.

As I pick up a pen, I catch the quick movement of a mouse as it scurries across the kitchen floor, stops and sniffs at the cheap lino.

I slide off my chair and stealthily walk towards it. When it doesn't seem to notice me, I kneel on the floor before the furry creature. Slowly, I lower the side of my face to the warm lino. Once I have a better view, I suck in a breath.

The mouse's nose twitches as it sniffs the air and raises its one dark eye to look at me. I stare back, taking in the old scar covering the mouse's left eye, welding it shut.

I grin, excitement flooding my bloodstream at the opportunity before me. Of course, I'm forbidden to act on such an opportunity, but how will Mum know? I rarely break her rules, but I *have* broken them. Months ago, a small bird—a swallow, I think—flew in through my bedroom window and crashed into my mirror. Mum had been in the shower, so when it flopped to the floor and flapped around weakly, I couldn't help myself. The only other experience I'd had up until then was with an insect here and there. But the bird was different. That was the first time I remember feeling *the pull*. A pull I couldn't resist. And when I'd shoved up my sleeves and moved closer, my hands had tingled and heated with something that came up through me from deep inside.

When I kneeled before the bird, it grew still, and at first I thought it might have died. But as it lay on its back, its eye moved, watching me. My hands throbbed and I seemed to have no control over my body. I scooped it into my bare hands. Whatever was inside me flowed through my fingers and palms and into the bird, and a feeling of warmth and pleasure and love overcame me. I felt connected to the bird, like we were welded together in that moment. Too soon the feeling stopped, but when it did, the bird struggled to its feet.

It made no attempt to fly away, and I'll never forget the soft feathers brushing against my palm as it sat there, looking at me.

Worried Mum would find me with it, I'd taken it to the window. For a moment, it seemed like it never wanted to leave me, and although I wished it wouldn't, it turned and flew into the alley and disappeared into the city.

Less than a minute later, my knees grew weak and the room began to spin. I stumbled to my bed and lay down, overcome with exhaustion. I fell asleep and didn't wake up until Mum came in to tell me dinner was ready. I'd been so hungry I couldn't get the food down fast enough.

I never told her what I'd done. Because I understood then, that doing what I did to the bird took something from me, something I gave to it. Mum had been right about that. What she didn't know was that after I'd rested and eaten, I felt just as good as new again. But I'd wondered what would happen if I touched something much bigger. How much would it take from me then? Mum told me it'd kill me. But she only knew that from my father. She might be wrong, but it seemed like she was probably right.

Now, here in front of me is another opportunity. If it makes me feel weak, I'm pretty sure the feeling will be gone by the time Mum comes home from work. Even if I'm not better, I can just make up a story that I have a stomach ache.

Slipping my sleeve over my right hand so it's completely covered, I place it palm down on the floor and hold my breath. I slide my hand closer and closer to the mouse, millimetre by millimetre, expecting it to scamper away. But it doesn't. Instead, when my hand is a mere centimetre from it, the mouse stretches its neck and sniffs my sleeve.

I freeze. And wait.

After a few seconds, the mouse steps forward. Then takes another step, placing its tiny paw on my sleeve. The pressure's only light, but I feel every gram. It stops, sniffs at the fabric covering my hand again, before taking four more steps and placing itself completely on top of my hand.

Very, very carefully and very, very slowly, I raise my head from the floor. As I lift the mouse on my hand, I sit up and cross my legs. Still, the mouse sits calmly on my sleeve without a hint of fear.

I draw it closer to my face so I can inspect the scar covering its eye. It looks old, showing no sign of blood or pus. I wonder what happened to the little guy. Had a cat been close to a nice juicy meal and scratched the mouse but somehow lost it?

With great care, I bring my bare left palm up next to my other hand and watch the mouse switch hands. And for the first time, I feel the tickle of its tiny claws against my skin.

Once it rests safely in my palm, I ease my right index finger free of my sleeve. Slowly, not wanting to scare it, I inch my bare finger closer to the small creature.

To my surprise, the mouse stands up on its hind legs, using its tail to balance, as if reaching towards me, too.

With my breaths fanning the mouse's fur, I gently touch my bare finger to its old scar. I let it rest there for a few moments, watching the mouse watch me, still showing nothing but total trust.

But something's missing. I don't feel *the pull*. That irresistible feeling that makes my whole body tingle, my skin prickle. I feel nothing. And now, with my finger touching the mouse, I don't feel glued to it, like I had with the bird.

I draw my finger back. The mouse continues to stare at me with its one good eye.

'Huh?'

I frown, shake my hand, and again touch the mouse's scar. And again, nothing changes.

As I gently stroke the soft fur, I don't feel weak or hungry.

Because I've failed. Failed to do what I'm supposed to do.

I just can't figure out why.

<><><>

After Mum returns home, I itch to ask her a question I know I shouldn't. Her answer will be *no*. I know it with every fibre of my body, but what I want, what I've always longed for, now lives so close, that I find myself willing to risk her inevitable anger and disappointment.

Still, it's not easy. All through dinner I've fidgeted, the tight knot in my stomach churning. I've hardly eaten a thing or spoken a word while Mum talks about her day. Her chatter about the people she's interacted with has given me hope. False hope, I'm sure, but still, I cling to it with all my might.

While we stand at the kitchen sink together, I watch her, trying to gauge her mood.

'Oh, I forgot to tell you,' she says. 'I'll be doing quite a few more shifts at the nursing home over the next month or so. You don't mind, do you? It'll give us a bit more money.'

'Okay.' I twist the tea towel in my hands, knowing I have to get it over with.

As I carefully adjust my sleeves so they cover my hands, I pick up the wet plate she's just placed in the rack. My heart speeds up as I open my mouth.

'Any reason you keep staring?' she asks.

I feel the plate in my sleeve-covered hand slip. I fumble, just managing to clutch it before it shatters on the floor.

Mum stares at me. My heart thunders.

'New people moved in next door today,' I manage, my voice quavering a little.

She places another plate in the rack. 'And?'

As I reach for a plate, my arm trembles. I swallow hard. 'There's a lady … and a girl. I thought, maybe … I could have a friend?'

The moment the words leave my mouth, I know I'm right. Mum's whole body tenses and her face hardens. In the water, her hands scrub vigorously at the cutlery. Never a good sign.

'How many times do we have to go over this, Lucas? A million? A trillion?'

She keeps her focus firmly on the soapy water as she scrubs. Not looking at me is one of her many ways of showing her disappointment. Usually, I'd leave it alone, not rile her up more. But this time, something new swells in my gut.

'But I'm older now. I thought—'

'I said no!' The moment the words burst from her, she flinches in pain. 'Damn it!'

At first, I think her reaction seems over the top. Then, with fascination, I watch the soap suds turn pink. She tosses our sharpest knife onto the drying rack and eases her other hand clear of the water.

Captivated, I watch her blood seep from a shallow slash across her fingers. In that moment, everything stands still. Every thought in my head vanishes as the need to touch those wounds consumes me. Hands tingling, I shove up my sleeve and reach towards her cuts.

She recoils as if I'm a deadly snake about to strike.

'What're you doing?' She takes three steps back, her face contorted with fear and anger. 'Have you forgotten everything I've ever taught you?'

Ashamed, I drop my head and stare at the floor. 'No.'

She reaches towards me and snatches the tea towel from my hand, wrapping it around her fingers.

'I hate being a freak,' I mumble, sneaking a look at her through my long fringe.

Her face softens, and she releases a long sigh. 'You're not a freak, honey. You're special. There's a difference.'

'But I don't want to be special. I just want to be normal and have a friend like everyone else. Just one. I know the rules. I can be super careful.'

She holds up her injured hand, her eyes sad. 'This— what just happened—proves otherwise. You almost touched it, Luke.'

'I know, but—'

'No buts. If you get close to someone, you won't be able to help yourself. And being who you are …'

We stare at each other. I sigh, knowing what she wants to hear.

'Can kill me,' I finish. 'I know, okay.'

'Luke, the only way to prevent that is to stay away from people. Your father, his father—they all had short lives because of this … thing. How many times do I have to tell you?'

'It's not fair!' I choke, trying to swallow the lump in my throat.

She gives me that sympathetic look I hate, then draws me into her arms.

'Don't you think I know that? But it's my job to protect you. And this is the only way I know how, okay?'

As she gives my back a comforting rub, I nod, knowing in my heart she's telling the truth.

'Go on,' she coaxes. 'Go and put your gloves on. You'd better start wearing them again.'

I jerk away from her, anger suddenly blooming into a fury stronger than I've ever experienced. I shake my head, taking another step away as I pull at my sleeves, even though they're already covering my hands.

'Lucas. Until you prove that you can remember the rules, you're to wear your gloves again. Now go and get them on. No arguments.'

'No! Not ever!' I yell, shocking myself as much as her. Running past, I barrel into my bedroom and slam the door.

Swallowing, I turn to the bureau, my gaze riveted on the bottom drawer. I've only been free of its contents since my tenth birthday, the best birthday present I've ever had. A present she wants to snatch away. I hate what that drawer contains. Just the thought of it makes me feel like I'm being put in a straitjacket so all the world can see the freak that I am.

Of course, that's not true. No one will see me except Mum.

I reluctantly edge closer and wrench it open. The drawer contains nothing but gloves. Gloves of all sizes and types. Woollen, cotton, leather. It doesn't matter which. They all make my hands sweat. They all say the same thing about me. They all make me want to scream.

- 10 -

KELSEY

SOMETHING TICKLES THE SIDE of my face as I stare at the perfectly straight-edged shadow cast on the ceiling by the building next to mine. I swipe at the tickle, the back of my hand coming away damp. Nine am and sweating already.

I roll onto my side and stare at the bricks outside my window. I hadn't bothered closing the flimsy curtains the night before. What's the point when only bricks can look in on me?

At least at my old apartment, I'd been on the second floor. Low enough so a large liquidambar kept my room cool in summer by casting a shadow on my window, and warm in winter when it lost its red leaves and let the sun inside.

Much better than a brick wall.

Bored to death already, I roll out of bed and rub my tired eyes.

Stretching, I let Dad's large T-shirt unravel from where it'd twisted around my waist. Thinking of him reminds me of something he always told me. First thing in the morning and last thing at night, I should try to think of at least one thing to be grateful for. Well, already I can think of two. One: it's the second day of school holidays. Two: having a drunk for a mother means no one bugs me to get out of bed early. Will there be a third by tonight?

Feeling the press of a full bladder, I hurry across the cheap carpet, the nylon fibres already warm under my bare feet. I grab the old doorhandle and turn. Instead of the door unlatching, the handle turns freely, spinning around loosely. Bladder aching for release, I rattle the handle, spin it some more, then yank on it.

And it comes right off in my hand.

I stare at the round, rusty knob with dread before letting it fall from my grasp. As a flutter of fear travels through my empty belly, I poke a finger in the hole where the doorknob used to live and try to pull the door open.

Nope. That isn't working.

'Muuuuum!' I yell. 'Muuuuum!'

Now I'm not so grateful for having a drunk for a mother. If she's out cold, she might not wake up until midday.

I cross my legs and squeeze. I won't make it another five minutes.

Clenching my hands into fists, I pound on the door as hard as I can. 'Muuuuum! Muuuuum! Wake up!'

Desperate, I continue to bang relentlessly on the cheap hollow wood, the noise deafening.

The door suddenly swings inwards hard and fast. 'What the hell's wrong with you? I'm tryin' to sleep!'

I shove past her. Even in my desperation to get to the toilet, I don't miss her troll-like appearance; the hair sticking out at all angles, the haggard face etched with deep lines and broken capillaries.

I bolt into the bathroom, not even bothering to shut the door, pull down my undies and sit on the toilet. At first, nothing happens. I've held on too long.

'I asked you a question,' she says from the open door.

Finally, my bladder lets go. I groan with relief.

'The stupid knob came off and I was busting. I couldn't get out.'

'Hmm,' Lisa barely mumbles.

'Thanks for waking up and letting me out,' I say, relief still coursing through my body.

'Whatever. I'm goin' back to bed. Will you please just let me sleep?'

'Uh-huh.'

I listen to her footsteps stagger away. And flinch when the bedroom door slams. This time, I don't let her response upset me. Because I've found a third thing to be grateful for already. I hadn't left a pool of urine on my bedroom floor. Urine that'd stain and leave a stench for weeks. I'll never forget the time Lisa, passed out drunk, had peed herself on the living-room floor of the apartment we'd rented a year ago. That'd been gross.

Finished, I clean up then turn on the TV and watch cartoons with the volume barely more than a whisper until midday.

Afterwards, I slink into my bedroom, grab a worn sneaker and place it against the doorjamb. If the door accidentally swings shut, it'll just bounce off the shoe. One problem solved. But now I can't close my door and have privacy.

Pouting, the room getting hotter, I decide to explore outside.

As I pull a clean shirt over my head, I wonder when I'll start to get boobs. It isn't something I look forward to. Some of the sixth graders at my last school already had them, but to me, they seemed like nothing but trouble. The boys were always staring and giggling, especially at sports carnivals, when those girls had to run in races. Their boobs bounced around everywhere, even though everyone could see the outline of their bras.

Nothing about the stupid things appeal to me at all, especially since I like to play touch footy with the boys at lunchtime. The last thing I need are boobs flopping around and boys laughing at me instead of chasing me and trying to get the ball. It isn't fair.

Nothing about life seems fair lately.

As I swing the wardrobe doors shut, I spot the guitar leaning against my bed.

Well, maybe one thing's fair. Music. Music won't care if I grow boobs.

I grab the guitar and take it over to my bed. Scooting up to my pillow, I cross my legs and cradle the guitar in my lap. Plucking at the strings, I make a few minor adjustments before launching into Dad's favourite tune.

When my parents first separated, I'd had a lot of trouble adjusting to Dad not being around. I'd soon discovered that if I played his favourite songs, I could close my eyes and imagine him standing there with that goofy grin on his face.

Lately though, it hadn't been enough to simply play the tune. I needed the words, as well. Without even thinking about it, I'd begun to sing. That first time, Lisa had banged on my door and told me to turn down the radio. At first, I'd just smirked and thought about how stupid that was. She knew I didn't have a radio in my bedroom.

After a few moments, something had dawned on me. If my mother thought the music had come from the radio, then I must have sounded like someone *on* the radio. And the only people allowed on the radio were singers who were pretty good. Well, more than pretty good.

Though I knew my mother's judgement wasn't the best, I'd clung to the belief that, for once, she might be onto something.

From then on, I sang every chance I could, and the feeling that it was easy, something that came naturally to me, grew. I'd practised for a month to get Dad's favourite song just right. Then I'd had to work up the guts to sing for him.

I'll never forget that day. The moment he'd picked me up for the weekend, I realised I'd be devastated if he didn't like my voice. I'd instantly broken into a sweat, soon accompanied by the shakes. Dad thought I was coming down with the flu and I'd been too nervous to tell him the truth. So I'd kept my mouth shut and let him dote on me all weekend while I lay on the couch under a warm blanket watching TV.

But by Sunday afternoon, as the hours drew closer to going back to my mother's, I'd realised it would be another fortnight before I could try again.

Listening to him washing up dishes, I'd finally convinced myself to just do it. Heart racing, I'd grabbed my guitar. My fingers trembled as I'd placed them on the strings. As I'd played, the kitchen noises continued. Dad had heard me play the tune a million times.

Then I began to sing. Softly at first, afraid and insecure. But when I'd closed my eyes, I'd disappeared into the music and let go of the outside world.

As the last note left my mouth, I'd opened my eyes. Dad stood in front of me, tears on his cheeks. I'd never seen him cry before. He wasn't sobbing like a baby. Tears were just leaking from his eyes.

And then he'd given me a smile I'd loved instantly. When I'd asked him what he thought, he'd seemed incapable of speech. Instead, he'd held out his arms, and I'd rushed into them. He hadn't needed to say anything at all.

Later, when the shock wore off, he'd told me I had a gift, that he'd do everything he could to help me get better ... if that was even possible. My confidence had soared, and I've been singing ever since.

But now, as I sing that song again, I still haven't attended a single singing lesson. The whole custody thing, along with the child support Dad has to pay, is a huge drain on his money. But he promised me, as soon as he has custody, I'll be going to singing lessons that very day.

With every ounce of my soul, I pray he'll keep that promise.

- 11 -

LUCAS

WHEN I BOLTED UPRIGHT in bed, I could hear my new neighbour thumping and yelling at the top of her lungs. I pressed my ear to the wall, discovering her doorknob had broken and she couldn't get out of her room. Her mother didn't sound too happy about being woken up.

When Kelsey's footsteps faded away, I flopped onto my pillow and grinned.

Right next to me. She's sleeping right next to me.

We're so close to each other, but she doesn't even know I exist. Well, that's not true. She'd poked her tongue out at me yesterday. Still, I'd bet my life that she's forgotten all about me, that she has no idea I'm on the other side of her bedroom wall.

A surge of hope rushes through me. I just *have* to make her my friend. It'll be perfect. We can see each other whenever Mum isn't home. I don't even care that she's a girl. That makes no difference. She's a person. She's my age. No matter what Mum says, I have a right to a friend.

Sitting at the kitchen table, I'm determined to get through the lessons set for me in record time.

As I put my head down, I hear something that surprises me. I thought she'd be at school.

I rush into my bedroom, scramble onto my bed, press my ear up against the wall we share, and feel the guitar's vibrations in my skull.

And then something amazing happens.

She begins to sing.

At first, she sings softly, like she's trying to be quiet. I've only heard people sing on the radio or TV, never in real life, but something in me shifts as I listen. I'm not sure what it is or why. I just know I don't want it to stop.

The tune she plays picks up momentum, and as she sings the chorus, her voice rises, and I understand that she's caught up in the moment. Just like I am.

I shove up my sleeves and press my bare hands to the wall, wanting to feel her voice as much as hear it.

'Hey! Hey!' a woman shouts.

The music cuts off abruptly.

'Thanks so bloody much for wakin' me up.' Obviously, Kelsey's mum.

'You're welcome,' Kelsey says.

I smile. I already like her.

'Put that piece of junk down and go get me some milk. I need coffee.'

'Can't you get it?'

'You're already dressed. Now move it.'

'Fine.'

Kelsey isn't happy, but I don't understand why. If Mum asked me to actually leave the apartment and run an errand, I'd be thrilled.

As I hear muffled movements, it suddenly hits me. This is my chance.

My stomach churns. I'll be breaking one of Mum's rules. It's not her number-one rule, but it's near the top of the list. If I obey most of the others, I'll be okay. It's not like she'll find out, anyway.

I race out of the bedroom and straight to the front door. With my hand on the lock, I freeze. I don't want to look like I'm following her. I need something, an excuse to go to the shops, too, but Mum never leaves any money in the apartment. Better that I'm not tempted.

Turning around, I scan the living room, the kitchen. My eyes skitter to a stop when they spot the garbage bin. I can't go into the general store, but I can go into the alley, to the dumpsters.

Grabbing the garbage bag, I disengage the deadbolt, swing open the door and step into the corridor. Down the far end, Kelsey disappears into the stairwell.

I take a big breath and break into a run. The garbage bag bangs and bounces off my leg all the way to the stairwell door. I burst through, leap down the stairs two and three at a time, not caring if I fall and hurt myself.

I'm so intent on catching up to Kelsey, I haven't realised I've closed so much distance between us until I round one of the bends on the stairs and come face to face with her. She stands motionless on the second-floor landing and stares up at me.

The first expression I see on her face is alarm. I hope it's because of the racket I've been making, and not my appearance. But when she gets a good look at me, she rolls her eyes, turns away and disappears around the next bend.

Once I remember to breathe, I take the steps one at a time, to make sure I'm not too close. When I hear the echo of a door slam shut, I break into a run again, until I reach the door that leads outside. Stepping out onto the hot, crowded street, the footpath warm under my bare feet, I feel small and alone as people push past me in a hurry.

Pulling my stretched sleeves over my hands, I scan the people but can't see Kelsey. She's probably already at the grocery store. I walk away from my building, past the alleyway, and stop in front of the store's huge window.

I let the garbage bag drop to the ground, press my sleeve-covered hands to the glass and cup them around my face. I can't see her, so I wait and wait. Finally, carrying a carton of milk, she joins the long queue at the checkout, not looking too pleased with the wait.

If I went in right now, I could line up behind her. And then what? What would I say to her? No. I need to know every step before I speak to her for the first time.

Without warning, she turns slightly and looks right at me.

I step back, grab the garbage bag and, heart racing, take off into the alley. Lifting a dumpster lid, I throw in the garbage bag and let the lid close with a clang. Then I kick it with all my might until my toes throb and I can't stand the pain anymore. Shoving up a sleeve, I balance on one leg and grab my injured foot.

Heat pulses from my hand into my toes, and in seconds the pain vanishes.

Now she knows, without a doubt, that I followed her. I'm so stupid. Do I even deserve a friend? Who wants an idiot like me hanging around? Maybe my total lack of social skills will prevent me from ever knowing how to talk to anyone. Except Mum, of course.

A tremor of desperation passes through me. Surely, that isn't what my life will amount to. No, I won't let that happen. I don't want to be alone my whole life.

Steeling myself, I know I have to go out there and face her or I'll regret it.

When I try to push away from the wall, I can't.

Stop being a baby!

That's when I feel something press against my ankle. I jerk away and stare down. A ginger-and-white kitten presses up against me again.

Surprised by the cute little bundle of fur, I forget all about the tight knot of cowardice in my stomach. After watching the litter and their mother from my window, I've longed to come down here and take a closer look. But of course, I'm not allowed. Now that I'm here, though, I wonder why I haven't just snuck down before. Here I am, and the world hasn't collapsed in on me.

The kitten circles my ankle, pressing all its weight against me, before it changes course and does a lap of my other leg. It feels so soft against my bare skin. Smiling, I crouch and gently stroke it with my sleeve. Although I can't hear the kitten purring over the street noise, I feel the vibrations beneath my hand.

Further along the alley, the kitten's mother calls, but the kitten seems oblivious as it licks my sleeve.

Having the affection of something other than my mother feels like heaven. I've wanted a pet for as long as I can remember, but Mum refuses, claiming it'll be far too dangerous. Well, I can't see how. All I can see and feel is a sense of being wanted and appreciated by another living thing.

I sit on my butt, not caring about the dirt my shorts will collect or how I'll explain it to Mum. The kitten instantly leaps onto my lap. I hold it close, pressing my cheek to the top of its head. Now I can hear it purr.

'It's so cute. Is it yours?'

Startled, I look up to find Kelsey standing before me, the milk in a plastic bag at her side.

Struck dumb, I shake my head. How long has she been standing there watching me? I realise it doesn't matter. All that matters is saying something before she leaves.

'You want to hold it?' I ask.

She nods eagerly, puts aside the plastic bag and kneels on the ground in front of me.

I place the kitten between us and release it. Before Kelsey can even reach for it, the kitten leaps back onto my lap and presses up against my belly.

'Boy, does it like you or what?' she says.

I can tell by her tone she's not impressed. Giving her a tentative smile, I pick up the kitten in my sleeves again, and going against all my mother's training, I hand it to Kelsey.

Her hands brush against my sleeves as she takes the kitten from me. She cradles it against her chest and runs her fingers through its fur. A streak of jealousy surges through me. I want to feel its softness, its silkiness with my bare hands.

The kitten wriggles in her arms, presses its little paws against her chest and pushes away. Kelsey tries to hold on, but the kitten's too agile. It wriggles free and leaps straight onto my lap.

'Jeez,' she says. 'You got cat food in your pocket or something?'

I shake my head and pet the kitten with my sleeve. That's when her eyes latch onto them. She stares for what seems like an eternity before her gaze drifts to my dirty bare feet, then my face. I blink through my fringe and hand her the kitten again, hoping to distract her.

'How come you're not at school?' I ask.

Once again, the kitten wriggles from her grip and returns to my lap.

She lets out a frustrated huff. 'It's school holidays, stupid.' She glances at the kitten, then at me. 'How come you were following me?'

'I wasn't.'

'What a liar.'

My hands freeze on the kitten. She's right. I am a liar. Great way to impress someone.

'You want to try holding it again?' I ask.

Kelsey stands up. 'Stuff it. If the dumb thing wants a freakazoid who wears long sleeves when it's a million degrees and has girlie hair, then let it.' She picks up her bag and walks away.

'Wait!' The shout's out of my mouth before I know it.

She turns but walks backwards, putting distance between us. 'Don't follow me, you weirdo.' And she disappears around the corner.

My stomach bunches. I rise with the kitten in my arms, hurry deeper into the alley and hide behind the last dumpster. There, I slump to the ground with my back against the brick wall, and let cool tears flow over my burning cheeks.

When I open my eyes, I find three more kittens in my lap, their mother in front of me, keeping a watch over them. All but the kitten I hold in my arms are black and white. I reach towards their mother and she comes forward, rubbing her head into my sleeve.

I still, in awe at the trust they all have in me. This is what I want, what I've been missing from my life, what I believe every other person has.

Comfort and companionship.

Maybe I don't need people. Maybe animals will be enough.

- 12 -

KELSEY

FROM MY BEDROOM, I stare down at the weirdest boy I've ever met. And I've known some weird ones from school.

He sits in the dirty alley like the Pied Piper. The mother cat and her kittens can't seem to get enough of him. And they don't care that he has those stupid long sleeves stretched over his hands. I wonder if maybe something's wrong with them. Maybe he hides them because they're deformed?

Whatever the reason, he's weird, and what I'm looking at is weird.

But there's something about him. Something I can't name. Something that draws me to him.

Maybe, I try to rationalise, I'm just lonely. None of my friends from my old neighbourhood live close anymore, and because of Lisa, no one will visit.

I want friends. *Need* them. How else will I survive the boredom of six weeks of summer holidays?

But what's with the long sleeves? If it'd been the middle of winter, I might not have noticed, but in thirty-five-degree heat? It's insane. There has to be something he's hiding under there.

And that hair. No wonder I hadn't been able to figure out if he was a boy or girl when I'd first noticed him spying from his apartment.

Then something hits me in the chest. Can it be that his mother's as neglectful as mine? So uncaring, she won't take him to the hairdresser or even bother cutting his hair herself? Not to mention he doesn't even know it's school holidays. How's that even possible?

I wonder if he has a father, then wonder why I'm wondering about him at all.

Before he can look up and catch me staring, I step back and plonk myself on my bed.

Maybe, if I see him again, I'll try to find out more about him. Anything's better than the weeks of boredom that stretch before me.

<><><>

I don't see the boy again until I return home from a weekend with Dad. The best weekend ever.

He'd taken me on a long drive to the small country town of Cascade. We'd stayed overnight and gone horse riding the next day. Apart from music, I now know my second favourite thing in the whole world is riding a horse.

Not only do I now have two favourite things to *do*, I also have a new favourite *place*. The rolling green hills, wide-open spaces, cows and sheep and horses and alpacas, all captivated me. Maybe it was being away from my mother, but when I'd been in Cascade, I could *breathe*.

The town itself felt like coming home. It bustled with activity, and while I'd sat with Dad outside a café, I'd watched people stop and talk as if they all knew each other. That spread a warmth through my heart, a comfort the cold city filled with strangers could never match. I wanted what those country people had, wanted to feel part of something, cared about by an entire community.

But now, as I climb the depressing concrete steps with Dad, my heart sinks. Back to the hot hovel with my pathetic mother.

Pulling on the fifth-floor door, we walk into the corridor and I look up at Dad. He instantly draws me close to his side and rubs my shoulder.

'I know, pumpkin, I know. I'm working on it real hard, I promise,' he says.

That's how well he knows me. I don't even have to say what I'm thinking.

From the corner of my eye, I notice the neighbour's apartment door creep open. The boy's watching.

Then I have another thought. 'Can we go to Cascade next weekend? I really want to ride the pony again.'

'I don't know, Kel. It's a long drive. We can't do it every weekend.'

'But I think it's my favourite place in the whole world. Pleeeease,' I beg.

He gives my shoulders a squeeze, guiding me towards my apartment. 'We'll see.'

I know what that means. Not likely.

When we reach my front door, Dad raises his hand to knocks, but I pull on his arm.

'What?' he asks.

'You'll only get in a fight.' I throw my arms around his waist, hugging him hard.

He returns the hug. 'I should make sure she's home before I leave.'

I look up into his eyes. 'What difference does it make whether she's home or not?'

He tries to hide it behind a smile, but I don't miss the anger in his eyes. 'Humour me, pumpkin.'

I sigh, release him, unlock the door and swing it open. Taking a few steps inside, I hear running water.

'She's in the shower.'

'Okay.' He steps forward and plants a kiss on top of my head.

After he leaves, I stand in the living room for a while, letting the heat envelop me. I can't help the snide thought that my mother's under the cool water, downing a bottle of scotch.

Moving closer to the closed bathroom door, I yell, 'Mum? I'm home.'

'Great,' comes the sarcastic reply.

Why can't she just be nice for once?

Already fed up, I grab my guitar, unlock the front door and step into the corridor, not bothering to tell her I'm leaving. What would she care?

As I walk past the weird boy's door, a pang of disappointment hits me. His door's closed. He isn't there, spying on me. I might've talked to him this time. Or maybe not. Now I don't have a choice.

Pushing into the stairwell, feet smacking on the concrete steps, I climb higher and higher, faster and faster, thighs burning. And trip.

Sprawling, my hands slap the landing and skid forward, the concrete rough and unforgiving. I cry out, palms on fire as I come to a stop. Twisting onto my butt, my guitar still safe on my back, I turn my palms upwards and stare at their grazed surfaces, watching as the blood starts beading through the scrapes.

The tears come. Sobs of self-pity rip from my throat and tumble down the steps below before echoing back to me. I cry and cry, leaning against the cool wall, letting it all out, not even caring if anyone hears.

No one does.

After what seems like an eternity, I manage to gain control of myself. Wiping my blood-smeared palms on my T-shirt, I pull the front of it up to my face and rub away the tears and snot. Lisa will kill me for ruining the shirt, but I don't care. She won't even ask if I've been hurt.

Nose stuffy and eyes puffy, I drag the guitar onto my lap. My scraped palms hurt when I strum, but I ignore the pain and concentrate on the music, tuning out the world.

After a few minutes, a distant noise from outside catches my attention. Surprised I can hear anything this high up, I rest the guitar against the landing wall and rise.

At the dusty landing window, I look way down into the alley. Something's going on. A fight? Curious, I rub at the window with my forearm until I can see through the grime.

These Hands

Even though the angle's awkward, I see a group of teenage boys. They're shouting and jeering and pushing another boy out in front of them.

- 13 -

LUCAS

WHEN I HEAR THE shouting outside, I jerk away from my schoolwork.

Hearing the shouts again, I hurry into my bedroom and poke my head through the open window.

In the alley below, a group of teenage boys mill around the dumpsters. One of the boys crouches in front of a gap between two bins. Even from five storeys up, I see the knife in his hand.

'Do it! Do it! Do it!' the older boys chant.

When the boy holding the knife turns to look at his friends, I see fear on his face.

'Do it, or you're out!' the boy who seems in charge shouts.

The boy with the knife faces the gap between the dumpsters again, his knuckles white from his fierce grip on the handle. Then he lunges into the gap, slashing at something I can't see.

A screech echoes off the brick walls.

'Yeah! Get it again!' another boy yells.

Another screech, and I suddenly realises what they're doing.

Without thinking, I lean further out the window, cupping my hands around my mouth. 'Hey!'

The boys look up in surprise.

'I'm calling the cops!' I shout at them.

The boys laugh as the leader gives me the finger. Then he grabs the boy with the knife and pushes him towards the street. A moment later, the group take off.

I bolt into the living room, fling open the front door and sprint to the stairwell. My bare feet slap hard on the concrete steps as I leap down them three and four at a time, not caring about the pain. I'll deal with that later. All that matters is getting to the alley.

I fling myself at the exit door and run onto the street. Arms pumping, I turn into the alley and sprint to the gap between the dumpsters.

Peering into the narrow, dark space, I see it. The ginger kitten lying on its side.

Pulling my long sleeves over my hands, I reach in and carefully pick it up. Its little body trembles. Clear liquid runs from its sliced eye and sticky blood oozes from a deep cut to its side.

Already my whole body tingles, my skin prickling as the hairs stand on end in anticipation. Deep in the pit of my belly, a vibration radiates outwards, consuming me.

I look towards the alley's entrance, at all the people rushing past, all the people completely unaware of the precious life I hold in my hands, a life I know is slipping away second by second.

Needing privacy, I cradle the kitten against my chest with my sleeves, and run into the apartment building. By the time I reach the third landing, my body's vibrating with energy.

Making sure I'm alone, I shove up my blood-stained sleeves. My breath quickens, my chest rising and falling hard and fast as the tingling ripples through my body like a wave until it reaches my hands. The vibrations in my fingertips are what I imagine electricity might feel like if I plugged myself into a power socket.

The kitten's tummy rises and falls with shallow breaths as more blood leaks from the wound. Every cell in my body screams, *the pull* intense. My hands vibrate and throb painfully, the energy contained within them desperate for release. Taking a deep breath, I do the very thing Mum forbids me to ever do.

I place one bare hand over the kitten's eye and one over the slash in its side. And then the energy flows. It comes from my toes, up through my body and out through my hands, the rush so exhilarating I can't breathe. It's the best feeling in the entire universe.

But the kitten's huge compared to an insect and much bigger than the bird. I can feel the extra power it's taking from me, the energy it drains from my cells.

Suddenly, my elation becomes fear, and I try to remove my hands. But the energy welds us together, making us one so my body can do what it's been built to do.

Then, as suddenly as it began, I feel the release. I jerk my hands away and stare at the kitten.

First, I notice that the rise and fall of its tummy seems deeper, steadier. Then I look at its face. It blinks at me, its injured eye just as perfect as it'd been the other day. But its side remains matted with so much blood, I can't see if the cut has gone.

Then it purrs.

I grin from ear to ear.

I've done it.

Reaching out, I sink my hand into its bloody fur. Nothing. No wound, no reaction except more purrs. I stare in amazement at its perfect eye and briefly wonder why it hadn't worked when I'd touched the eye of the mouse. But I shake off the thought. All that matters is that it *had* worked this time.

I saved its life.

It feels like nothing I can describe.

And I'm not dead.

My heart swells and tears roll over my cheeks, my body overflowing with such happiness and amazement I just can't contain it.

Then the kitten rises and presses its face into my hands, its little body vibrating with purrs.

A gasp echoes down the stairwell.

I jerk my head up in surprise. There she is, about three flights up, her face peering at me over the railing. Our eyes lock, and I know without a doubt she's seen everything.

She knows!

I've broken every rule my mother has ever laid down, every promise I've made. Terrified, I scoop the kitten into my arms, turn and run down the steps.

'Wait!' Kelsey yells.

As I round the first landing, my legs begin to shake. I take one more step and stop, feeling as if I'm going to pitch headfirst down the steps. Then my legs buckle. I sit on the landing with a thump. Holding the kitten to my chest, I fall backwards. The last thing I feel before the world goes black, is my head cracking on concrete.

- 14 -

KELSEY

I THUNDER DOWN THE stairs, heart galloping, mind so confused by what I've seen I'm actually scared. And I'm never scared.

As I round what seems like the millionth landing, I stop dead. My breath catches in my throat, my eyes wide with fear.

The boy lies on his back, eyes closed, unmoving.

But not the kitten. It curls into a ball on his chest. I can hear it purring from where I stand.

Cautious, I inch forward until I'm standing over the boy. The kitten looks at me with interest, but makes no sign that it has any intention of moving.

With the toe of my tattered sneaker, I nudge the boy's out-splayed arm.

'Hey?' I whisper.

Getting no response, I crouch beside him. The kitten stares at me as I touch the boy's shoulder and give it a light shake.

'Hey? You okay?'

He groans. I leap up, take a step back and wait. As my gaze flicks from the kitten to the boy's face, his eyes flutter open and he lets out a puff of air. Then they drift closed again.

What if he's dying? And I just stand here like an idiot watching?

Moving forward again, I kneel on the cool concrete and lean closer, watching the kitten rise and fall as the boy takes steady breaths. He probably isn't dying, but what do I know? What if he'd hit his head and had brain damage?

I don't want to touch him. He's covered in blood, especially his hands, but I grab his shoulder and shake it.

He groans.

'I'm gonna get your mum,' I tell him.

As I release his shoulder, he grabs my hand and shouts, 'No!'

The panic in his voice makes my blood run cold. Then I stare at my hand in his, knowing the kitten's blood is all over me now, too. And my palm is grazed, littered with breaks in my skin, breaks the kitten's blood can get through.

Disgusted, I try to wrench free, but his grip is super strong.

Before I can gather my strength and free myself from his grasp, the strangest warmth enters my hand. Suddenly, I'm no longer afraid. Instead, a wave of love, of comfort and safety, consume me all at once.

It's the most amazing feeling I've ever experienced. I never want it to end. But the moment the boy releases me, it stops.

He sits up slowly, cradles the kitten to his chest and uses the wall to rise on wobbly legs.

'H-hang on,' I say, still trying to bring myself back to reality, to process everything I've seen and felt in the last few minutes.

He ignores me, grips the railing and steps unsteadily down the stairs.

'Wait,' I plead. 'What … what did you do?'

He continues down the steps, his footfalls growing faster, steadier. I hurry after him.

'Hey!' What'd you do to the kitty?'

'Nothing!' he shouts as he keeps moving downwards.

'Liar! I saw!' I catch up to him and grab his shoulder. This time he stops, seeming shocked by the contact. He quickly shrugs free of my grasp.

'I didn't do anything!' With wide, panicked eyes, he bolts down the rest of the steps.

'I saw you!' I yell after him.

The stairwell door slams shut in response.

Confused, heart still hammering, I sink onto the closest step. I want that warm, comforting feeling again, but now that it's gone, I'm not even sure if it'd been real. In fact, it won't surprise me if I wake up in a moment. None of what just happened could be real.

Then I look at my hands resting on my bare knees, and see the boy's bloody fingerprints where they'd wrapped around my right hand.

Grossed out, I use my T-shirt like a towel and frantically rub my palm on the material before checking to see if I've wiped away all the blood.

My eyes widen in disbelief.

It can't be true. I have to be seeing things. I *have* to be. Because it's just not possible.

But it is, isn't it? After what I'd thought I'd seen him do to the kitty, it has to be true.

Heart almost bursting from my chest, I wipe my right palm on my bare thigh, over and over, until I'm sure I've removed every trace of blood.

Then I turn them both up and study them. My left palm is still grazed and bruised from my fall, but my right palm is ... completely flawless.

- 15 -

LUCAS

I SIT IN THE alley for what seems like hours, holding the kitten, indulging in the incredible feel of its soft fur beneath my bare fingers. An instinct deep inside me tells me that now I've touched it, healed it, I don't have to worry there might be something else wrong with it.

Mum had been right. And wrong. Healing the kitten's injuries *had* taken strength from me. I'd felt it flowing from my body into the kitten. But it hadn't killed me. She'd told me that if I touched someone who was dying, then I'd save their life but lose my own.

Well, now I hold the proof in my arms. She's wrong. Or is she?

I have no way of knowing if the kitten would have died from its wounds. It'd been badly injured and losing a lot of blood, but maybe it might have survived. I guess I'll never know.

What I do know is that I'd taken the risk. I'd been scared of dying, but *the pull*, the need, had been all that mattered.

And just after, I thought Mum was an outright liar. Because I'd felt fantastic ... for about half a minute. Then came the effect of the drain, and I thought I *was* dying. But I was just weak from what I'd done, that was all. The other times, when I'd healed the insects, the only thing I'd really felt afterwards was hungry. With the bird, I'd felt the weakness, the drain and the hunger.

But there was a gigantic difference with the kitten. Mum had never explained that. She'd barely explained anything. Was it because she didn't want to, or because she didn't know? Had my father explained everything to her, or only some things? Had he kept secrets from her? The same secrets I'm going to keep from her?

The elation I'd experienced was overwhelming, but the fear at being discovered by Kelsey dampened everything. What if she told someone? Would Mum's other warnings come true? If everyone finds out what I can do, they'll all want me to fix them.

After what I'd just done with the kitten, I understand that sort of attention will kill me. The size of the creature matters.

Hoping against hope that Kelsey has given up waiting for me in the stairwell, I return the kitten to its litter, give it one last stroke on the head and walk away.

After silently opening the stairwell door, I creep up the steps, peeking around each turn on each landing. When I get to the fifth floor, disappointment seeps in.

While I don't want to be confronted by her, at the same time, I do.

I hurry towards my apartment door and stop. Someone's closed it.

Is she inside, waiting for me?

I hope so.

And hope not.

Taking a deep breath, I turn the handle and step inside. The room is empty, nothing out of place.

Had Kelsey closed the door for me when she'd gone home?

I smile. That was nice of her.

In the kitchen, I check the time on the microwave. Only four-thirty. Sighing with relief, I desperately want a shower, but more than that, I need food. I've never felt so hungry in my entire life.

After washing my hands, I pull a frozen loaf of bread from the freezer and make myself slice after slice of toast, lathering on thick layers of butter, peanut butter and topping it off with thick honey.

Six pieces later, I finally feel satisfied. Mum will notice that extra food has disappeared, like she had before, but like before, she doesn't know why. Last time, with the bird, she'd just thought I was going through a growth spurt.

I'm allowed to keep my own secrets, to know more about my hands than my mother. They're my hands, not hers. And now I'm glad she doesn't know why I suddenly get so hungry I think I'm going to die.

Finally, I feel strong enough to take a shower. I run the water and step in with all my clothes on. Once I'm soaking wet, I take everything off and try with all my might to get the blood out. The shorts are okay. It just looks like I've dropped some food or sauce on them. But the shirt has to go.

In the kitchen, I grab a garbage bag, put my shirt inside and hide it under my bed. Tomorrow I'll go down to the alley and toss it in a dumpster. Mum will never know.

I pick up a pen and try to concentrate on the geometry I've been working on, but I can't focus. I've just had the scariest, most exciting day of my life. Nothing comes close. And everything's changed.

Rapid knocks come from the front door.

I freeze.

No one ever knocks on my door.

The rapping comes again, more insistent this time.

'I know you're in there.'

Kelsey.

My heart skips a beat. Can I ignore her? I don't think so. She doesn't seem like the type to give up, not after what she saw me do.

I walk over to the door and crack it open.

Kelsey stares at me through the thin slit, arms crossed, foot tapping with impatience.

'Well?' she says, 'aren't you gonna let me in?'

In?

That hadn't occurred to me. No one's ever been in this apartment except me and Mum.

I frown and glance at the clock. Five-thirty. A little over half an hour before Mum comes home. Under no circumstances can she find Kelsey in this apartment.

But I can't resist. Opening the door wider, I step aside. Kelsey barges past.

Subconsciously pulling at my long sleeves, I cover my hands then close the door.

Turning, I find Kelsey right in my personal space. Surprised, I press up against the unyielding wood at my back.

'What'd you do to that kitty?' she asks, her face a mask of seriousness.

'Nothing,' I lie. Pulling at my sleeves again, I sidestep around her, hurry to the dining table and plonk in my seat. I pick up a pen and stare at the textbook in front of me while watching Kelsey from the corner of my eye.

She wanders over and takes in the messy table. Picking up my history textbook, she flicks through the pages. 'What's this?'

'My homework,' I say. When she doesn't reply, I finally look up at her.

'What sort of moron does school stuff in the holidays?'

'I don't go to school.'

Her mouth drops open, eyes wide with awe. 'Wow. That's pretty cool.'

'Not really.'

She plonks herself on the chair opposite. 'So,' she says. 'I'm Kelsey. What's your name?'

'Luke. You'd better go.'

She frowns, her eyes flicking over me. I drop my head, realising my damp hair won't allow me to hide this time.

'Jeez, Luke, what's the hurry?'

Hearing her say my name startles me so much I look at her again. I've only ever heard it come from my mother's mouth.

'My mum,' I say. 'She'll be home soon. You can't be here.'

She sits back and folds her arms. 'Why not?'

'I'm not allowed to have friends.' I say matter-of-factly, like it's normal. Because to me, it is.

She stares at me with disbelief, the frown on her forehead growing deeper. 'That's crazy. Everyone has friends.'

'Not me.'

She studies my face, her gaze boring into me as I nervously pull at my sleeves.

She gasps, understanding filling her wide eyes. My gut lurches.

'Because of what you can do, right?' she asks.

'Yeah,' I say without thinking. The weight of that one short word hits me with terror. 'No! I-I mean, I can't do anything. I don't know what you're talking about.'

'What a liar,' she says, but her face remains friendly, her eyes sparkling with mischief.

To my horror, she stands up and leans across the table, not caring when textbooks topple over the edge and crash to the floor. I watch her with wide eyes, utterly confused about her creeping approach. Then she slaps her arm on the table and turns her palm upwards.

'You see that?' she asks.

Perplexed, I study her smooth palm, the zigzagging lines everyone has the only imperfections. 'What?'

'Exactly!' she says with an explosion of happiness.

I frown, glancing at her face then at her palm.

She places her other arm on the table and turns her hand over as if she's performing a magic trick. This palm shows grazes and raw patches of skin, and what looks like the beginning of a bruise.

I feel the stirrings of that familiar vibration and try to push it down, try to concentrate on what she's showing me.

'I don't understand,' I say.

'They both looked like this,' she holds up her injured palm. 'Until you grabbed my other hand. In the stairwell.'

I stare at her uninjured hand. Had I really done that? It comes back to me then. When she'd said something about getting my mother, I'd grabbed her hand without thinking. But that doesn't mean she's telling the truth. It might be a trick to get me to admit what I can do.

Rattled, not sure what to believe, I glance at the microwave clock.

'You've gotta go,' I tell her in the sternest voice I can manage.

'No way. I wanna know how you fixed my hand, how you fixed the kitty.'

'Just go away,' I insist.

Her eyes narrow and I can tell that she won't give up.

'So … if your mum won't let you have any friends, then I guess she'd be pretty mad if she found out you've got one … and that I know what you can do.'

I bolt to my feet. 'You can't tell her!' I yell, fear blooming through my entire body.

'Ha!' Kelsey says, beaming as she comes around the table towards me, a finger pointed at my chest. 'So it's true!'

'No!'

We stare at each other. She seems so strong, so used to standing up for herself. I know that she has no problem telling her mother what she thinks. Doubt creeps into the pit of my stomach. How can I convince her when I have no experience in convincing anyone of anything?

'Bullshit,' she says, suddenly calm. 'You'd better meet me on the roof at midnight, or I'll tell.'

Without waiting for a reply, she stomps over to the door, wrenches it open and marches out.

I run to the door and lock it. Leaning against it, my knees buckle and I slide down the smooth surface until my butt touches the floor.

Once I gain control of myself, I realises something. This is my chance to make a friend, to know what everyone else knows. I don't have to convince her it isn't true. All I have to do is convince her not to tell.

As I collect the fallen textbooks from the floor, I grin.

<><><>

Biting my lip, I pad through the living room to Mum's bedroom. I stare into the blackness of her room, my ears straining to hear her breath. When I hear the steady rhythm, I reach in and close her door.

At the front door, I twist the deadbolt as slowly as I can, but that doesn't stop the loud clack. I freeze. Hold my breath.

Silence.

Satisfied, I open the door and swing it closed very, very slowly.

Hurrying away, my footsteps grow faster and faster until I break into a run, and finally push through the stairwell door. Then I climb, flight after flight, going where I've never ventured. I'm not sure if my beating heart comes from exertion or fear and excitement. Both, I guess.

When I finally round the last landing, I stop and stared at the EXIT sign flickering above the roof-access door. The sign buzzes with electricity, just like my body. As I take one step at a time towards it, I wonder if pushing through that door will mean exiting the only life I've known.

- 16 -

KELSEY

KNOWING HE'LL BE HERE any minute, I lean against the wall next to the rooftop door. I try to calm my racing heart by taking deep breaths, but the warm, humid air makes slowing my pulse difficult. Sweat trickles down my spine, dampening my T-shirt and shorts. Even my feet slip and slide around in my thongs.

If he turns up—which, after my threat to tell his mum, I believed he will—what I plan to do is both insane and brilliant. It'll either backfire spectacularly, or completely prove my theory right.

The door rattles. I stare as it creaks open, my heart jackhammering when Luke steps onto the roof. I meet his wide eyes and realise he's truly scared. Fear hasn't been something I've experienced much of, but I fear one thing. Losing Dad. So, I kind of understand where he's coming from.

'Hey.' I smile at him.

He pulls at those long, stretched sleeves, glancing around nervously. 'Hi.'

I watch him look up at the immense sky and do a slight double-take. Taking a sharp breath, he stares in wonder at the full moon and bright stars.

'Haven't you been up here before?' I ask.

He shakes his head. 'I'm not allowed,' he says, as if that explains everything.

'Is there anything you *are* allowed to do?'

He shoves his hands in his pockets and looks at his feet. 'Stay inside and keep to myself. That's pretty much it.'

Only half believing him, I let out a ragged laugh. 'Yeah, right.'

He turns towards me slightly, and really looks at me this time. 'It's true.'

I stare into his eyes and see something else there behind the fear. Pain.

'Jeez,' I sigh. 'You're like a … I don't know, a prisoner or something.'

He shrugs. 'Maybe.'

Breaking my gaze, he pulls nervously at his sleeves again.

An uneasiness sweeps over me. If he's telling the truth, I feel guilty about what I have planned. But, I try to convince myself, what I'd seen him do is something that I just can't let go of.

'Come on,' I blurt, before I change my mind. 'Come see the view. It's pretty amazing.'

Without waiting for him to respond, I casually stroll towards the edge of the roof, deliberately walking towards a wood paling on the ground. I'd found it earlier when I'd scoured the area looking for something that might work.

Lining myself up, grateful for the full moon, I brace myself. And step on the paling, on the protruding rusty nail. The spongy rubber of my thong resists, then suddenly gives way. The nail spikes right through my foot.

And then I scream.

- 17 -

LUCAS

KELSEY'S PIERCING SCREAM FREEZES me to the spot. My already thudding heart lurches as she doubles over.

I race the few steps to her side. Her hands flutter over her foot, then they move out of the way enough for me to see the spike of a rusty nail poking right through the top, blood spilling between her toes.

The sight of it sends my body spiralling into an urge to heal.

She looks up at me, tears streaking her face, her eyes pleading. 'Get it out,' she sobs. 'Please.'

I do my best to clamp down on what I really have no control over and try to concentrate on helping free her foot. As I take everything in, I notice the plank of wood beneath her thong and realise that's what the nail is attached to. If I lift her foot, the plank will come with it.

'You'll have to stand up,' I tell her.

With sobs shuddering her whole body, she grips onto my arm and I help her rise. For a moment, I wonder why she can't just lift her foot off on her own. But when I look into her eyes, the moonlight sparkling on her tears, I know she's scared, know she's hurting. There's something else there, too, but I can't quite figure it out, I move in front of her and stand on the plank.

Instinctively, I know getting it over fast is the best thing for her. Pulling my sleeves over my hands, making sure they're completely covered, I grip her ankle and, hard and fast, yank upwards.

She screams again and I can only imagine the pain.

I release her leg, step back and watch her drop to the ground in a fit of sobs. She rips off her thong and tosses it aside. Gripping her ankle, she pulls her injured foot onto her other knee and leans forward to study the blood as it drips onto the ground.

I squat in front of her to get a closer look, my hands on fire now, the urge to touch her injury pulling at me so hard and deep I can barely resist. But I have to.

She sniffs loudly, wiping at the tears sliding over her cheeks. 'It hurts,' she chokes. 'It hurts so bad!'

Blood drips from her sole, but only trickles from the hole on top of her foot. So fascinating … pulling me in.

'Please,' she begs. 'Can't you … can't you fix it?'

My breath catches. I meet her eyes.

Now I know what I'd seen there before, amongst the pain and the fear.

Guilt.

'You did this on purpose?' I ask.

Her sobs stop abruptly. She stares at me, biting her trembling lip. Slowly, ashamed, she nods.

All the air leaves my lungs. How could she do that? What sort of crazy person deliberately hurts themselves so they can … what? Test me?

'I'm sorry,' she mumbles as more tears river down her cheeks.

It's a dirty trick, and I don't like it one bit.

Resisting *the pull*, I stand and move away from her. And I feel like I've lost something. Something that could have been special. Something that might have changed my life.

Appalled, afraid if I don't leave now, she'll see my own tears, I turn away and hurry towards the rooftop door.

'Wait!' she calls.

I don't slow down.

'Luke, wait! Please!'

I slow a little. It's just so hard to leave when there's something I can do about her injury, when my hands throb with anticipation. With *need*.

'I'll be your friend! If you fix it, I'll be your friend. Forever.'

I stop completely then, take a deep breath and ball my hands into fists.

A friend. What I've wanted all along. Isn't that why I'm standing on the rooftop I've never dared visit?

'I promise,' she says.

I sigh. How does she know what I want most in the world? Then to use it to blackmail me? How's that fair?

But I guess I'm used to nothing being fair, so what does one more thing matter?

Defeated, I walk back and sit across from her. She stills, watching my every move as I shove my sleeves up past my elbows. I hold out my hands, which now throb in time with my pounding heart. Carefully, she eases the heel of her foot onto my palm.

My hands feel electrified and *the pull* takes over. There's no going back. I cover the entry wound with one hand and the exit wound with the other. Energy rushes through me, from the soles of my own feet all the way through my being until it pours through my hands and into Kelsey.

Our eyes lock, and in the pit of my stomach, I feel an intense connection with another human being. From the look in her eyes, she feels it, too.

'Oh my God,' she whispers, her breaths coming a little faster. 'It feels so ... I don't ... so ... good.'

She closes her eyes and lets out a long sigh, almost a groan. And it's it written all over her face. My touch, what I'm doing to her ... is giving her pleasure.

This is something new. Something I haven't seen before. I guess because insects and birds and kittens can't talk.

Then it's done, and slick with her blood, my hands slip from her foot. She draws it back, stares at it, then touches the top where the wound no longer exists.

New tears slip from her eyes as she looks at me.

'Luke ...' she whispers in amazement, her face changing before me with a million different emotions.

Then she beams. 'This is so awesome!' she squeals.

I try not to grin, but her excitement and happiness are contagious. Pulling my sleeves over my hands, aware that I've ruined another shirt, a wave of dizziness suddenly takes hold. As the corners of my vision blur, I sway slightly.

Lying down before I pass out and hit my head, I stare up at the expanse of sky. The stars spin and dip, leaving thin streaks across the darkness. I wait for everything to go completely black, but it doesn't happen.

'You okay?' she asks, her face blocking my view.

'Will be … in a second.'

Her eyes crinkle with genuine concern. She moves her face a little closer to mine. Never in my life have I been this close to another person. Well, besides Mum, but she doesn't count.

'Is this what happened after you fixed the kitty?' she asks.

I've discovered something new again. Healing Kelsey's foot hadn't taken as much out of me as the kitten, even though she's so much bigger. So it seems like I'd been wrong about that. It isn't the size of the creature, but the size of the injury. The kitten's had been worse; it might have died.

'I think … I'm just dizzy this time. The kitten was … harder,' I explain.

She frowns in confusion. After a moment, she grins, her eyes lighting up. 'This's so cool.'

I take a deep breath, let it out and do it again. Soon I notice that the stars surrounding her face are sharp and clear, not swirling anymore.

'No, it's not,' I say, cautiously sitting up. 'I'm a freak.'

'Are you crazy? You're like a … a superhero. If people knew what you could do—'

Terrified by her words, I grab her arm, my bare hand against her warm skin.

'You can't tell anyone!' I shout. 'They'll kill me!'

She looks at me like I'm crazy. 'Why would anyone wanna kill you?'

'Because they'd want me to fix them. It'd be too much.'

'Too much what?' she asks, her forehead furrowing. I kind of like that.

'It's like …' I pause, trying to figure out how to explain it to someone when I can barely explain it to myself. 'It's like I have to give away something to do it. Does that make any sense?'

She shakes her head. 'Not really.'

'Okay, so … maybe I'm like a battery. If I fix something small, then it hardly takes any power out of the battery. And I can recharge it pretty quick. But the bigger it is, the more power it takes and the longer it takes to recharge.' I watch her face, see the understanding, and realise that's the first time I've put into words what *I've* learned, not what my mother has told me.

My mind races over everything Mum explained. 'If I touch someone who's dying of cancer or something like that, then it'd totally drain the battery … and I wouldn't be able to recharge, because there'd be nothing left … I'd die.'

The crinkles on Kelsey's forehead furrow deeper. 'But … can't you just turn it on and off?'

I shake my head. 'It's on. All the time. That's why I'm not allowed to touch anyone. Mum says you just never know what might be wrong inside them, what you can't see. And I don't have X-ray vision, so there's no way for me to know.'

'Well, that's not fair.'

'No kidding.' I look at my sleeves with distaste. 'That's why I have to keep it secret, stay away from people. Mum says if anyone found out, even if there was nothing wrong with them, they might have a kid or someone they love who needs help. They could take me and force me to heal the one they love … and then I'd die instead.'

Her eyes widen, and I can see she understands. And if she understands how dangerous it is if anyone finds out, then she'll keep my secret.

'Okay,' she says, 'so what happens if *you* get hurt?'

'Nothing. I can fix myself, and it doesn't take anything from me. Sort of like … I'm keeping it inside instead of giving it away … instead of it draining out of me.'

She gazes at me with utter fascination. 'So, you can't die if you get hurt?'

Surprised, I stare at her. I've never really thought about that.

'I don't know,' I say honestly.

'But you can fix yourself, so …'

'I think, as long as I can touch the injury, I'll be okay.' I blink, trying to figure it out. 'But maybe, if someone shot me in the head, I'd die straightaway, just like anyone else.'

I watch her face, trying to read her thoughts.

'What if you got sick?'

I shake my head quickly, already knowing the answer to that. 'I've never been sick. I don't think I *can* get sick.'

'Holy crap,' she breaths, then bites her lip. 'But how do you know for sure you'll die if you fix something big?'

'My mum told me that's what happened to my dad.'

Her eyes widen. 'He's like you?'

I nod. 'And his granddad. Mum said even he didn't know how far back it went.'

I glance at my sleeves, then at her. On a shaking breath, I say, 'Please don't tell.'

She gives me the warmest smile I've ever seen. 'I won't. I promise.'

She holds out her hand as if to shake on it.

I hesitate. I've touched her a few times now. If she has any sort of disease, I would have already paid the price.

I pull up my right sleeve, and reaching out, I grip her hand and give it a gentle shake. In awe, I stare at our connected hands. The touch of her flesh against mine seems magical. And I know that even if she was the sickest girl in the world, I'd still touch her.

- 18 -

LUCAS

A FEW WEEKS LATER, I'm leaning against the warm roof-access wall, sitting across from Kelsey, lost in her voice as she sings and plays the guitar.

She's the most amazing person I've ever known. I guess that isn't saying much, since I don't know anyone except Mum, but still, I can't imagine there are many people like Kelsey in the world.

I let her voice transport me to a place I never knew existed. I've heard her before, but there's something different, special, about watching her sing.

Her eyes are closed, head tilted slightly to the side. Her fingers pluck and strum over the old guitar strings as if they have a mind of their own. If I practised for a year, I'm sure I'd never be able to play like she can.

Her voice—even in the blazing heat on the roof—gives me goosepimples. And I know without a doubt that my body's reaction has everything to do with how amazingly talented she is.

After a moment, the crescendo of her voice softens and drops before falling away altogether, giving the guitar the last few notes. Only when her fingers leave the strings does she open her eyes and look at me.

I see the anticipation there, but also see doubt. That takes me by surprise.

Hesitant, she asks, 'Well?'

I stare at her in amazement. 'No way anyone'll beat you.'

She hugs the guitar a little tighter and beams at me. After a moment, doubt clouds her face again. 'It's my first competition.'

Earlier, Kelsey had told me about the contest her father signed her up for as a surprise. She'd been so excited, she'd wanted to show me what she could do, but now, that confidence she always brings to everything falters.

'I think … I'll be too nervous,' she admits.

'You weren't nervous just now.'

'I know. But that's different.'

'How?'

She looks away quickly, her face flushing. 'Can't you come with me?' she mumbles.

My shoulders sag. After what she's done for me, opening up my tiny world, I want more than anything to be there for her.

'My mum's not working this weekend … she'll be watching me like a hawk.'

I used to like the weekends. Now I hate them. Now they're another prison, a kind of torture. I have to revert to my old life and pretend nothing's changed. Which is easy to do during the weeknights after a full day with Kelsey. But on the weekends, Kelsey goes to her father's, leaving me under Mum's ever-watchful eye. I still desperately want to go up to the roof, but I can't. It drives me crazy, and Mum isn't stupid. She picks up on my bad moods. Of course, I refuse to tell her anything. Instead, I keep myself locked in my room most of the time.

Worse still, there's only a few more weeks of summer holidays left. Kelsey will have to go back to school. I'll barely see her. After school will be the only opportunity, and then we'll only have around an hour together. I have no idea how I'll cope during the long days without her.

Disappointed, she squints at the harsh sunlight glaring down on the roof.

I hate seeing her like this.

'Hey,' I say. 'You know what you should do?'

She looks at me, her eyes hopeful.

'Just pretend you're here. Just you and me. Then you won't be nervous.'

Even as the words come out of my mouth, they sound lame. Now I'm the one who wants to look away, but I can't. Not when she's smiling at me like that.

She drags the guitar strap over her head and sets it aside. Then she rises to her bare knees on the hard concrete, leans forward, places her hands on my shoulders and kisses my cheek.

When she pulls away and sits down again, I realise her flushed face has nothing to do with the temperature, because now my own face is overheating. Even though strange emotions whirl around in my gut,

I don't look away. Instead, I put a hand to my cheek where she kissed me, and grin.

And she grins back.

- 19 -

LUCAS

MONDAY MORNING, EXACTLY FIVE minutes after Mum leaves for work, a frantic pounding on the door startles me so much I drop my spoon into my cereal bowl and splatter milk all over myself.

I race to the door and swing it wide.

On the floor before me stands a tall trophy with a white marble base and a long wooden stem topped with a golden girl singing into a microphone.

'You won!' I shout.

Kelsey leaps from her hiding place beside the door, her face flushed with happiness.

'Yes!' she squeals, jumping up and down on the spot. 'I won! I won! I won!'

'Ha! I knew you would.'

'I didn't,' she says, calming down.

I laugh as I touch the golden girl atop the trophy with a sleeve-covered finger. 'It's almost as tall as you.'

'Can we do something to celebrate?' she asks.

I nod. 'On the roof?'

She shakes her head. 'Let's go to the park.'

I swallow. She's wanted to take me to the park for weeks. There's one problem. There'll be other kids there, and parents, too. But how can I say no when she's so happy?

'Okay,' I whisper.

She squeals and claps her hands, then grabs the trophy. 'We'll have to go now, before it gets too hot. I'll just put this away.'

She races to her apartment and disappears inside.

Gently closing the door, I lean against it. Hearing raised voices from Kelsey's apartment, I hurry over to the connecting wall.

'I'll find it when I come back!' Kelsey yells.

'You've been sayin' that all summer! Why do you always have ta fight me? Why can't ya just do somethin' for me without kickin' up a stink?'

'Are you kidding?' Kelsey shoots back. 'Like the dishes I wash up every night because you're passed out? Like the vacuuming and cleaning I have to do because you're too busy getting drunk? I'm supposed to be a kid, not your slave!'

The loud slam of the door jerks me away from the wall. After a moment, a couple of taps come from the door.

When I open it, Kelsey stands there with a pair of runners in one hand and socks in the other. She shoves them at me and tells me to hurry up. I pull them on then stare at the laces.

'Here,' she says as she kneels before me and ties them with the same fluid movements she uses when she plays the guitar.

'Let's go,' she says and holds out her hand.

I take it with my bare hand, noting again that nothing bad ever happens when I touch her.

As we walk away, I notice how strange the shoes feel on my feet. They're a little too small, but I like how they make the ground seem soft and spongy.

'So, what was going on with your mum?' I ask.

'She's sooooo stupid. She's been bugging me to paint her nails since we moved in, but I've hidden all that stuff at the back of the bathroom vanity.'

'Won't she be mad if she finds it?' I ask.

'Stuff her. If she was a normal mum, I'd like painting her nails. And besides, that doesn't even matter. She doesn't *go* anywhere, so why the hell does she need her stupid nails painted?'

'Yeah, that's pretty dumb,' I agreed, not fully understanding what she's talking about.

She pushes through the stairwell door, and I follow.

'Anyway, forget about her. Let's go have some fun!'

And just like that, she bounds down the stairs like the gazelles I've seen on TV.

Five minutes later, we reach the park. Kelsey challenges me to race her to the play equipment. I accept, and she takes off. Following close behind, I realise I've never in my life been able to run so far and so fast, and that I could easily overtake her. But I don't know the way, so I let her win.

When we stop in front of the slide, she places her hands on her knees and tries to catch her breath. I watch her, fascinated. Because although my heart beats faster than usual, I'm not breathing the way she is. I know she wants to celebrate her win, but she can't get the words out.

After a moment, still panting, she straightens up and stares at me. Her eyes widen.

'No way!' she manages to get out.

'What? You won.'

She moves closer, right into my space, and studies me. 'You're not … even puffed!'

I shrug. 'I can't help it.'

She shakes her head in disbelief. 'Sometimes I really hate you.' Seeing the look on my face, she gives my arm a light punch. 'Not really, stupid. I'm just jealous.'

'So, not being puffed is good?'

'Are you kidding?' She gives her eyes an exaggerated roll. 'You could've beaten me, right?'

'I guess.' I won't lie to her.

Letting out a huff, she spins away and runs over to the swings. I follow and watch as she sits on a swing and begins to sway.

To my amazement, every time the swing comes forward, she rises higher and higher into the air. Her long, dark hair streams out behind her, then flattens against her back. When she reaches the top of the arc, her hair takes flight again.

'Come on!' she yells at me.

I take a seat on the swing beside her and try to copy her actions. I swoop forward and my stomach drops away, but I like it. Too soon, the swing's momentum stops. After a few more attempts, I give up.

'What's wrong? You don't like it?' she asks.

'I do. I just can't … I can't do it like you can,' I admit.

She stares at me a moment, frowning. 'You've never been on a swing before?'

Ashamed, I look at the ground and shake my head.

'That's insane!' she gasps. 'I'm really not liking your mum right now.'

That surprises me. 'Why?'

'For not letting you do things like other kids. It's mean.'

'She just wants to keep me safe.' I'm not sure why I'm defending my mother, but I feel in my gut that I'm supposed to, even if Kelsey's right.

She shrugs. 'I know. But it still sucks. Hey, let me teach you.'

I feel stupid that she has to teach me something little kids can do, but she doesn't seem to care.

'Okay, watch.' As she swings and shouts instructions at me, I copy her.

I start to feel the rhythm as I gain momentum. Before I know it, everything clicks and I'm flying high.

Laughing, a deep sense of happiness sweeps through me. I can do things like other kids. I'm not that different, am I?

Dragging my feet on the ground, I come to a stop and Kelsey does the same.

'That was … like flying!' I say.

'There's something way more like flying than that. Wanna try?'

I nod vigorously.

She gets the swing moving high in no time, and as she reaches the top of the forward arc, she lets go.

My heart seems to stop when she flies from the seat, floats upwards for just a second, then drops back to earth. When her feet hit the thick grass, she tucks and rolls until she uncurls onto her back.

My eyes bulge as I bolt towards her and drop to my knees at her side. Her eyes are closed. She isn't moving. Is she doing it again? Trying to test me?

'*Kelsey? Kel?*' I whisper, hovering over her.

One eyelid slowly squints at me. Then both eyes spring open, and she laughs. 'Your face! You're way too easy.'

'That's not funny!' I tell her off. 'That was crazy!'

She shakes her head and rolls onto her side, propping herself up. 'That was flying.'

'Really?' It seems pretty dangerous to me.

'Really. For just a second, it's like you don't weigh anything. It's amazing.' She sits up. 'C'mon. Both of us this time.'

'I ... I don't know ...'

'Don't be a chicken.'

'We could get hurt,' I try to reason.

'No, we won't. This grass is super soft. I'm not an idiot.'

I hesitate.

Kelsey stands, puts her hands on her hips and looks at me. 'What're you worried about? No one's around. Even if we do get hurt, so what? You should be the bravest kid in the whole world, right?'

Still on my knees, I gaze up at her, allowing myself to acknowledge that she's beautiful. Not just the way she looks, but her spirit. I want to feel like that. I also don't want her thinking I'm a wimp. She'd never be best friends with a wimp.

'Right,' I agree and get to my feet.

She beams and grabs my hand. The contact seems to mean nothing to her, but it means everything to me.

She can hold my hand anytime she wants.

We reach the swings and too soon she releases me.

'You ready?' she asks.

I nod, my heart pounding.

'We need to swing at the same time, so we can jump together, okay?'

'Okay,' I agree.

I follow her lead, matching her rhythm and we swing in unison, higher and higher.

'Ready?' she yells.

'Ready!'

'On three ... one ...' she counts as we swing forward. 'Two ...'

My heart thunders as we swing backwards one last time.

'... three!'

Together, we leap off the swings. And I'm weightless. Until gravity yanks at me, but I'm still flying, still totally out of control.

For a few seconds, I'm completely and utterly free.

When the earth rushes up to meet me, my feet slam down. My knees buckle, and I roll just like I'd seen Kelsey do.

Before I know it, my body comes to a grinding halt, Kelsey right beside me.

I look at her, and she looks at me. And we both burst into fits of giggles.

Gasping for breath, my stomach muscles aching, I realise that the laughter—the emotion—takes my breath, while the physical exertion doesn't.

'Told you it was fun,' she says between gulps of air. 'See how stupid your mum's rules are?'

Of course, she's right. Unlike the last time she criticised my mother, I feel a surge of anger at Emily.

'Yeah,' I agree. 'Bet she's made me miss out on heaps of fun things.'

'Yep,' Kelsey says. 'But I'm here now. I can show you.'

I grin, believing her, trying to stop the thought that she'll be at school in a week and I'll be all alone again.

'I wish I could've seen you win,' I say.

'Yeah, I was pretty great.'

I laugh and move just a little closer to her.

Then a horrible thought spikes into my brain. My smile vanishes.

'Remember when you called me a freakazoid?' I ask.

She hesitates, glancing away. 'Uh-huh.'

'Did you only change your mind about me ... because of what I can do?' I don't want to know the answer, but I desperately need to know the truth.

She bites her lip, shame filling her eyes as she meets mine and nods.

My heart drops into my gut. Even though I've never had a friend before, I'm certain what I have with Kelsey is true friendship. Does she really only like me because of what I can do?

'But,' she says slowly, 'if I hadn't found out, I wouldn't have got to know you. That's how friends work. They start talking for whatever reason, then they get to know each other and they get to be friends ... or not. Nobody's friends right away.'

I think about that for a moment and know she's telling the truth. Although I'd wanted to be her friend from the moment I saw her, I hadn't known her. Now that I do, I understand that wanting to be friends and actually *being* friends are very different things.

'Besides,' she says, 'you really are a freak.'

My heart drops again.

'Just in a totally awesome way,' she adds. 'Is that okay?'

I grin, wondering if a roller-coaster would make me feel as up and down and twisted all around the way she does. 'Yeah, that's okay.'

She smiles, then looks up at the sky.

I stare at her for a moment, watching her eyes flick back and forth as she concentrates.

Raising a hand, she points to the sky. 'Look. A pony.'

I wrench my gaze from her face and squint up at the clouds. Following her finger, I see the slightly deformed shape of a four-legged creature that could be any animal.

'I'm gonna be a famous singer and make heaps of money,' she blurts. 'Then I'm gonna move to Cascade and get lots of horses.'

'That's your favourite place in the whole world, right?'

She turns to me in surprise. 'How'd you know that?'

I shrug, not wanting her to know I'd been listening in all those weeks ago. Instead, I ask, 'Where is it?'

'In the country. Dad takes me on his weekends sometimes. We go horse riding and everything. It's awesome.' She stops for a moment, and I know she's thinking about being there. When her eyes meet mine again, she says, 'So, that's where I'm gonna live. What're you gonna do?'

'Go with you?' I say before my stupid brain catches up to my mouth.

She laughs. 'I mean, what're you gonna *be* when you grow up?'

A wave of sadness seeps into me. When my own mother doesn't even want me to go to school, what hope do I have of being anything worthwhile? Or worse still, of being anything at all?

'I don't think I can be anything,' I tell her honestly.

'You could be an athlete … but I guess people might want to know why you don't get puffed, so that wouldn't be good.'

She must see the sadness on my face, because she reaches out and covers my bare hand with hers. 'Oh! I think I know!'

'No, you don't,' I say. How can she know if I don't?

Her eyes sparkle like they do whenever she's excited. 'Remember when you tried to give me the kitty? In the alley that time?'

I nod, unsure of what that has to do with anything.

'Remember how it just wanted you? How you kept giving it to me, but it just went straight back to you?'

'Yeah, but—'

'I think it sorta … *knew*,' she says.

'Knew what?' I ask, totally confused.

'You know, how animals know stuff people don't? I bet animals can tell about you.'

My heart gives a little kick in my chest, the idea blossoming through my whole body. Not just the kitten. The bird and the mouse, too.

'You really think so?' I ask.

'Yep. And you know the best part?'

I shake my head, all too aware of the tears forming in my eyes. I'd had no idea tears could come when I feel happy.

'If you fix animals,' she says, 'they can't tell anyone.'

The idea's so shocking yet so logical, it leaves me speechless for a moment. She's right. If I'm careful, if I can somehow tell before I touch an animal that it's safe, that it doesn't have something terribly wrong with it, something that would kill it, I'd be able to heal it and no one would ever know. Animals would always keep my secret.

For the first time in my life, I see a future that doesn't involve being stuck in a house on my own, that will allow me to take advantage of this thing I have, that will allow me to use it the way I'm sure it's meant to be used.

To help.

I blink hard, and the tears roll down my face.

Kelsey frowns at me with concern. 'What's wrong?'

I turn my hand in hers so our palms touch, and I squeeze. 'I really have a friend,' I say, my throat tight.

She gives me a goofy look. ''Course you do, stupid. I'm the best friend you'll ever have.'

- 20 -

KELSEY

EYES CLOSED, FOOT TAPPING on my bed, I relax, letting the loud music transport me away. After winning the singing contest, Dad bought me a mini-stereo. Knowing Lisa would complain about the noise, he also bought a pair of headphones. Besides my guitar, the stereo and headphones are the best things I own.

As I mouth the words to one of my favourite songs, something lands on my stomach. I jerk upright. Clutching my tummy, I discover the makeup bag in my lap.

'Look what I found,' Lisa slurs from the doorway.

I take in the bottle of scotch swinging back and forth at her side. Sliding off the headphones and placing them carefully on the bedside table, I give her an innocent look.

'Wow. Where was it?'

She frowns with suspicion, but her eyes are red and far away. 'Under the bathroom sink. Don't remember puttin' it there.'

'Me either,' I say as I unzip the makeup bag and upend it, spilling bottles of nail polish, cotton balls and polish remover onto my tattered bedspread.

Lisa takes a sip from the bottle of scotch, wobbles into the room and plonks herself on the bed. If she's already given up on a glass, she's really drunk.

'What colour do you want?'

'Don't matter,' she says. 'You choose.'

As I line up the colours to get a better look, she lights a cigarette, takes a long drag, then an even longer swig of scotch.

Disgusted, I say, 'You promised not to smoke in here. Remember?'

Ignoring me, she swaps the cigarette to the hand holding the bottle of scotch and shows me the fingernails on her free hand.

'Old stuff's gotta come off first,' she instructs.

I sigh. This is going to take longer than I want.

I sit up straighter and struggle for a moment with the kid-proof lid on the nail polish remover. Opening it, I slosh some onto a cotton ball. Carefully resting the bottle against my thigh, I grab her hand and begin rubbing at the chipped polish.

After a minute of silence, Lisa nods towards the new stereo. 'Where'd ya get that?'

'Dad,' I reluctantly admit. She hates it when Dad gives me presents.

'Spoils you rotten,' she say predictably. 'I never saw you bring it home.'

I rub harder at the stubborn nail polish.

'That's 'cause you were passed out.'

'Do you ever stop?' she asks as she takes another swig of scotch.

I glare at her, fury rising. 'Do you?'

She gives me a long, sideways glance and takes yet another drink. After a moment, she snatches her hand from mine and stands on unsteady legs.

'Think we'd better drown out your whinin',' she drawls.

Shuffling over to the stereo, she pulls out the headphone jack and cranks up the volume. Then she begins to dance and gyrate, the music vibrating all around us.

Unable to help myself, I grin at the crazy sight of my mother actually enjoying herself for once. To my surprise, she has some pretty good moves.

As the beat increases, Lisa closes her eyes and moves faster and faster. Lost in the music, she raises the cigarette and scotch bottle above her head and performs a spin. Thrown off balance, she lurches to the side and crashes into the open door.

It slams shut so hard I hear it above the thumping music.

'No!' I scream as she dances on, oblivious.

Leaping off the bed, I totally forget about the open nail polish remover until it tips over. Before I can grab it, the liquid sloshes onto the bedspread, down the side and empties itself in a small pool on the threadbare carpet.

I rush to the dresser, grab the doorknob and run to the door. That's when I realise I've forgotten to replace the runners I'd given to Luke with something else to stop the door closing.

Even though I already know it's useless, I shove the stem of the handle into its hole. Jiggling and wiggling it, the knob spins freely in my hand.

I turn around, furious. Still dancing, eyes closed, Lisa places the cigarette between her lips and sucks. I jab at the stereo's power button. The room descends into instant silence.

'Hey!' she yells, her eyes flying open.

'You idiot!' I scream, my face inches from hers as I pointed to the door. 'We can't get out!'

'Jesus! Overreact, why don't you!' She pushes past me and turns the stereo back on.

Hoping to make her realise we're both trapped, I shove her. Hard.

She loses her balance and falls onto the bed, landing in the wet patch of spilt nail polish remover. Unconcerned, she clamps the cigarette between her lips and stretches towards the stereo, turning the volume up to a deafening level.

Unable to contain my rage, I snatch the scotch from her grasp and hurl it towards the closed door.

The glass hits the door frame and shatters. Alcohol splashes up the wall, over the door and onto the carpet. I stand rooted to the spot, stunned by what I've done, the booming music forgotten. I hadn't meant to do anything so violent.

When I turn to my mother, she stares at me in shock, her mouth gaping open. The cigarette hangs from her bottom lip for just a moment before falling, tumbling over itself as it skims down the side of the bedspread and lands in the puddle of nail polish remover on the carpet.

Flames instantly burst to life.

'Mum!' I yell, unable to believe what I'm seeing.

The flames leap up the side of the bedspread, following the path of the spilt chemicals, up higher and higher until they engulf Lisa's leg.

I scream.

Her reactions slow, Lisa scrambles backwards, trying to escape the flames eating at her jeans. As she bends her knees to push herself backwards, the flames whoosh over the back of her thighs where she'd sat in the flammable liquid.

It's all happening way, way too fast. So fast, I can barely grasp the reality of it.

Screaming herself now, Lisa furiously scrabbles backwards until she topples off the other side of the bed and lands with a thump.

Paralysed, I watch the flames race over the cheap carpet straight towards me. Startled out of my shock, I leap aside and bolt around to the other side of the bed.

On the floor, crammed into the narrow space between the window and the bed, my mother screams as she slaps the flames still licking at her jeans.

Unable to help her in the cramped space, I grab her beneath the armpits and pull her backwards with every ounce of strength I have. She slides along the carpet, scrabbling at the floor with her feet as I pull again and again, trying to get her past the end of the bed where I'll have enough space.

That's when the curtains draping each side of the window catch alight.

This isn't happening.

Except it is.

Putting everything I have into it, I wrench my mother free from the gap between the bed and wall and roll her over and over. Miraculously, the flames on her jeans go out. But I can't miss the large holes in the denim, the blistering skin straining against the charred fabric.

The terror on her face spikes into my gut. I've never once seen my mother afraid.

She scrambles up, eyes riveted on the centre of the room as she backs away and hits the dresser.

I follow her stare. Fire eats at the alcohol-splashed wallpaper on the other side of the room, spreading impossibly fast.

My eyes jerk to the bed. Engulfed in flames, a thick cloud of black, toxic smoke billows upwards. And the heat. It feels like it's searing my skin right off my bones.

'Mum!' I scream, realising that there's a very real possibility we aren't getting out. I grab onto her. She seems mesmerised and petrified by the fire all at once. 'Mum!'

'Can't ...' she chokes as she shakes her head. 'Can't burn alive ... can't bur—'

'Mum! Get us outta here!'

Eyes glazed over, staring straight through me, she shrugs me off and begins to blubber. To my horror, she stumbles towards the burning door and grabs the handle.

Instantly crying out in pain, she jerks her hand away, the doorknob falling to the floor. In a blind panic, she pounds on the burning door.

'Help! Help!' she screams, her voice already hoarse from the acrid smoke.

Feeling the effects of the smoke myself, I drop to the floor and crawl to the far side of the dresser, pressing into the corner as tightly as I can. For a moment, the radiant heat eases, the dresser blocking its path to me.

'Mum!' I cry, and wretch on my first cough.

You're not going to make it out of here alive.

I wipe at the hot tears on my face as a flood of thoughts rocket through me. Self-pity consumes me first. I've only just been told by a bunch of total strangers that I'm actually good at what I want to do, that I just might have a chance to turn my dream into reality.

And then there's Luke.

Besides Dad, he's the best person I know in the whole world. The most special person ever. But even with everything he can do, he can't save us from a fire. He can't help me now.

Giving up on the door, the fire ferocious, Lisa staggers backwards. Choking, she limps across the room and rounds the burning bed. Then she reaches for the window lock.

'No!' I scream as she turns the latch. 'You're not supposed to—'

She yanks up on the window, sending it crashing into the frame above.

Fuelled by the new source of oxygen, the fire flares brighter. All around me, the room burns faster and faster, the far side completely engulfed in flames. I can barely breathe, the air scorching, the fumes poisonous.

'Mum!' I scream, the thick smoke cutting off my next cry.

Terrified, I watch her put one burnt leg through the open window and straddle the windowsill. The smoke grows thicker as it races over her and through the opening.

Tears streak down her face. As our lock eyes, she reaches a hand out to me.

'Come on!' she cries.

Though I can't actually hear the words over the music, I can see them on her lips.

Eyes almost bugging out of their sockets, I shake my head, pull my knees up to my chest and hug them tight. 'It's too high!' I yell, spluttering and coughing.

Lisa screams something, but the black smoke swallows her whole, and that's even more terrifying than being able to see my usually fearless mother.

Suddenly, the stereo cuts off, the music replaced by the roar and crackle of the fire, a sound I haven't been aware existed until that moment.

'Kelsey!'

The shrill shriek sounds like nothing I've ever heard from my mother's mouth. It's wild, guttural, petrified.

I stare at the place where she straddled the windowsill, and as the smoke swirls through the gap, it clears for just a second.

And what I see terrified me to the bone.

The open window gapes wide and empty.

- 21 -

LUCAS

AS LIGHTS FLICKER OVERHEAD, I freeze, my fork halfway to my mouth. Mum looks at me, and I'm sure her expression mirrors mine. The scream we'd both just heard was nothing like the thudding music we'd listened to during our meal.

When Mum first served dinner, loud, thumping music started blaring from Kelsey's apartment. I knew it was coming from Kelsey's bedroom even before Mum insisted I close my door.

I couldn't figure out why Kelsey was playing her music so loud, or why she wasn't using her headphones. Unless she was in another fight with her mother.

Clearly agitated, Mum muttered something about putting a complaint in tomorrow morning, that she couldn't believe she had to put up with such low-life, inconsiderate neighbours.

I'd wanted so badly to defend Kelsey, but knew better, knew to keep our friendship secret or Mum would make sure it no longer existed. And if that happens, I don't think I'll be able to exist, either.

Then sudden silence descends, both a relief and eerie.

Mum sighs. 'Thank goodne—'

'Kelsey!' The scream that pierces the silence hurts my ears more than the music.

Without a thought, I bolt up.

'Leave it,' Mum commands.

'Muuuuum!' The terror in Kelsey's scream shoots me into action, and I run towards the sound, towards my room.

When I fling open the door, a wave of intense heat hits me so hard I almost back out again.

'Lucas! Come here this instant!' Mum shouts from the living room.

That's when I see my bedroom wall. Wallpaper peels off as it steams, the corners drooping low like dog-eared pages in a book.

It's turning black. And so is the bare wall it reveals beneath.

'Muuuum!' Kelsey screams.

Broken out of my trance, I rush to the window and stick my head through. What I see shocks me to my core.

Lisa hangs from Kelsey's bedroom window, her body fully outside the building, legs kicking, fingers white as they strain to grip the windowsill. Kelsey clutches her mother's wrists, but already, I see her fingers slipping.

'No!' she screams. 'Mum! No!'

I stare in horror as Lisa's wrists slide through Kelsey's hands.

I let out a cry at the same time Kelsey screams.

Lisa falls fast through the air, her terrified eyes staring up at us … until she catches the corner of a dumpster and flips, landing facedown in the alley.

'*Mum!*' Kelsey screams, staring down as thick, toxic smoke billows around her.

I have to get her out of there.

'Kelsey!'

She tears her gaze away from her mother and looks at me, seeing me for the first time.

'Luke!' she yells, tears leaving clean streaks down her grimy face.

I lean out of the window as far as I can and reach towards her. She leans further out, reaching for me, but the distance is too great.

She shakes her head, the sobs coming fast now. And then a cloud of black smoke engulfs her. As she disappears, I hear her coughing, choking.

'Hold on, Kelsey. I'm—'

Arms suddenly wrap around my waist and haul me backwards. My hands catch the windowsill for just long enough to hear Kelsey squeal in pain. Letting go, I fly back into the bedroom with such force, Mum loses her balance and falls, taking me with her to the floor. But she doesn't release her hold around my waist.

'Kelsey!' I scream, struggling against my mother.

'Stop it!' she yells in my ear. 'Lucas, you have to stop!'

If I don't get free of her grip, I'll lose Kelsey forever. Going against every fibre in my body, I force my muscles to relax.

'Mum! We have to get out of here. The fire … it's coming right through the wall!'

'We get up, grab some clothes and go. Don't even think about trying anything. Okay?'

'Okay,' I lie.

Slowly, her arms loosen, but if I try anything, she'll still easily restrain me.

As we sit up together, she grips my upper arm.

'Okay, up,' she instructs.

We rise together. She steers me towards the tallboy, keeping herself between me and the bedroom door. She pulls open the top drawer. 'Grab some short, T-shirts, quick.'

I do as I'm told, bunching anything I can grab in my fists.

Mum slams the drawer shut and opens the next one.

I fumble with the clothes, my hands already full. 'We need a bag,' I whine, the searing heat at our backs almost unbearable.

'Here,' she releases my arm and grabs at the clothes in the drawer.

In an instant, I take off.

'No!' she yells, her fingers brushing the back of my shirt.

I fly through the living room, fumble hard and fast with the lock, too scared to look behind me, too scared to see her right there, her hands reaching for me.

And then I'm in the hallway, sprinting as fast as I can towards Kelsey's door.

What if it's locked?

With my heart in my throat, I twist the doorknob and almost fall into the apartment when the door springs open.

A thin haze of smoke fills the living area, but it's nothing compared to what I'd seen coming from Kelsey's window.

'Lucas!' Mum yells.

Taking in the reverse layout of the apartment, I dash towards Kelsey's bedroom door and grip the metal handle.

And scream.

I recoil, shocked by the burning pain searing through my palm. But I don't even look at it. I pull down my sleeve, cover my burnt hand and turn the knob.

Barrelling inside, the toxic smoke instantly consumes me. Even through the thick black cloud, I can see the walls ablaze with hungry fire.

'Kelsey!' I choke out as I drop to my hands and knees.

Crawling forward, the fire flares in front of me from what I can only guess was the bed.

I know I have to get to the window, to where I'd last seen her, but the heat's so intense, the smoke so poisonous, I fear I might not get out of here alive, either.

Putting that thought out of my mind, I crawl around the flaming bed until I touch the wall. Then I crawl towards the window.

And see her bare foot.

I shoot forward until I can see all of her. She lies on her back, a wooden curtain rod ablaze against the left side of her face, her hair singed away to small stubs on her scalp.

I try to scream her name, but my constricted throat cuts me off.

Through the crackle and roar of the fire, I hear sirens.

'Lucas!' Mum's scream drifts to me from somewhere far away.

Everything seems to happen in slow motion, yet all at once. Pulling my sleeves over my hands, knowing now isn't the time to lose consciousness, I grab Kelsey's ankles and wrench her towards me with everything I have. As she slides across the carpet, the curtain rod falls from her face.

When she's far enough past the end of the bed, I drop her legs and grab her under her armpits. Shoving her limp body into a sitting position, I wrap both of my arms around her chest and grip my sleeve-covered hands in front of her. Still down low, I take the biggest breath my seared throat allows, then rise. Holding Kelsey against my chest, I back towards the burning doorway, bursting through as fast as I can so neither of us catch fire.

'Lucas!' Mum shouts in my ear as I stumble into the living room.

Mum suddenly pulls Kelsey from my arms and lifts her, hugging her tight.

'Quick,' she coughs. 'Go!'

With my eyes watering and my lungs screaming for fresh air, I obey her and run towards the front door. When we burst from the apartment, I slam the door shut and drop to my knees, overcome with racking coughs I can't control.

Beside me, Mum lowers herself to the floor and lays Kelsey down. I can't miss the horror on my mother's face.

I follow her gaze and let out a sharp, involuntary cry that starts another coughing fit. Although I'd seen

Kelsey in the bedroom, the smoke had obscured so much. Now, I can clearly see her missing hair and the ugly burn on the side of her face from the curtain rod. Only one thing makes me thankful, and that's the fact that she's unconscious.

I shove up my sleeves and reach towards her face.

'No!' Mum yells, knocking me sideways with her body, pinning me under her weight.

Desperate to get to Kelsey, I struggle furiously beneath her, pummelling her with my fists and trying to kick her away.

'Get off me!' I scream on a choked breath.

'I won't let you. You know I can't—'

'I have to!'

Mum struggles with me until she traps my wrists in each of her hands. She holds them against the floor and looks at me. To my surprise, she's not angry. The look in her eyes is pure sympathy.

Quieter now, she says, 'You can't, Luke. You can't.'

'But,' I say, swallowing over my ruined throat, 'she's my ... best friend. Please ...'

The utter surprise in her eyes tells me she's never once suspected I've formed a friendship with the girl next door, that I've blatantly broken the rules.

A sudden bang catches her attention, and from my distorted position on the floor, I watch as four firefighters burst from the stairwell and jog towards us.

For just a moment, I think Mum's going to release me, giving me an opportunity to help Kelsey, but she holds on firmly as another coughing fit burns my lungs and throat.

'Anyone else in there!' the first firefighter shouts as he draws closer.

'No one else,' Mum tells him.

Three firefighters charge past us and into Kelsey's apartment. The other stops, squats beside Kelsey and scoops her into his arms.

'Okay,' he shouts at us, 'let's go!'

I cough and wretch, staring after him as he runs towards the stairwell, Kelsey's limp arms and legs swinging.

Emily stares at me, tears streaking down her cheeks. 'You saved her life, Luke. Be happy with that. You *have* to be happy with that.' And then she finally releases her hold on me.

I roll away from her and spring to my feet. Through a burst of violent coughs, I try to yell at the fireman's retreating back, try to tell him to wait, but I can't. He disappears into the stairwell with my best friend. In that instant, I wonder if I'll ever see her again.

Overwhelmed, harsh coughs double me over. I shove my hands beneath my shirt and press them to my ribs. Within seconds, air flows into my lungs with ease, and the urge to cough vanishes. Feeling and tasting something vile in my mouth, I spit out a thick glob of black mucus.

Mum places an arm around my shoulders. 'Come on, let's get out of here.'

I let her lead me along the corridor, my mind racing with thoughts of Kelsey. As we draw closer to the stairwell, two paramedics emerge.

'You two okay?' the female paramedic asks.

'We're fine,' Mum says. 'It was the girl who—'

I suddenly double over and choke on harsh coughs, hurting my lungs and throat all over again. But I don't care. I have an idea.

Glancing up, I see the confusion in Mum's eyes, but I also see the paramedics' concerned expressions.

This has to work.

Ramping it up with more gusto, I fall to my knees and cough harder than when the smoke had actually clogged my lungs. Hurried footsteps approach as I hug my stomach with both arms and slip my hands beneath the safety of my sleeves.

'He's suffering from smoke inhalation,' the female paramedic says. 'You his mother?'

'There's nothing wrong with him!' Mum shouts, the anger in her voice coming through loud and clear.

I continue to cough, tears streaming down my face as both paramedics stare at Mum in disbelief.

The male paramedic wraps an arm around me. 'Come on, big man. You think you can walk down the stairs with me?'

I nod and cough.

'Here we go,' the paramedic says and grips me under the arm, helping me stand.

As we pass Mum, she shakes her head, barely able to contain her fury.

- 22 -

LUCAS

DURING THE RIDE IN the ambulance, I put on quite a show as I continue to cough and splutter. Mum glares at me, but can't say anything for fear the paramedics will think she's the worst mother ever. I keep my sleeves firmly fisted in my hands, Mum watching the paramedics' every move, ready to no doubt attack them should they try to free my hands. But all they do is slip an oxygen mask over my mouth and nose, and check my chest through my shirt with a stethoscope.

I do feel sorry for Mum. I don't miss the shake in her hands, her eyes darting everywhere. After all, we're heading to the most dangerous place in the world for me. She's scared. I'm not. All I care about is getting to Kelsey.

Once at the hospital, in a curtained-off cubicle, I sit on the bed, impatiently waiting for a chance to slip away from my mother. Nearly three hours have passed and I still haven't been seen by a doctor. And Mum hasn't left my side for one second.

She sits rigid on an orange plastic chair, flipping through a magazine, giving the shiny paper sharp snaps with every turn of the page. She isn't really looking at it. She's trying to calm her anger at me. And no doubt, her fear of what might happen next.

While I'd waited, I'd held a bare hand to the front of my neck and felt the sore scratchiness I'd inflicted upon myself ease away to nothing. To test it again, or maybe to get a reaction out of Mum, I let out a small cough.

Her head snaps up, her glare shooting daggers at me. 'For heaven's sake. That's enough,' she seethes. 'Once the doctor sees you and finds nothing wrong, once I get you home, you're going to be in serious trouble, young man.'

'What home?' I ask. From what I'd seen in my bedroom, I don't think there'll be a home waiting for us.

'Shit,' she says, tossing the magazine on the bed beside me.

She never swears, so I figure she hasn't even thought about the fact that we can't go home.

Pressing her fingertips to her forehead, she releases a frustrated grumble before she looks at me. 'Come on. I think we should get out of here. Now.'

I shake my head. I have to find Kelsey. She's here somewhere, and she's badly hurt. From watching TV, I know that people who are seriously hurt go to emergency first, then a place called ICU. All I need to do is get away from Mum and find the signs.

'The nurse said we had to stay here,' I argue.

'I don't care. This place is a deathtrap. You're surrounded by people we absolutely know could kill you.' She stands, splits open the curtain and peers through.

'But if they catch you trying to get me out of here, won't you be in trouble?' I ask, knowing she will be. My TV education is worth far more to me than any school lessons. Taking a kid out of the hospital when he needs help isn't something the doctors will like. They might think she's a bad mother. I'd already seen the way the paramedics had looked at her when she tried to tell them there was nothing wrong with me.

She closes the gap in the curtains and stares at me. I can see it, that doubt in her eyes, the worry. I have her.

'I'm thirsty,' I say, and slide off the bed.

'Get back on the bed this instant,' she snaps.

I scramble up. 'But I'm thirsty,' I whine. 'Aren't you?'

She swallows, pointing a finger at me. 'You stay right there.'

I study her as she opens the curtain a few inches. Her head turns left, then right. She glances over her shoulder at me.

'Do. Not. Move,' she says, her tone serious, even a little threatening.

I nod and wait as she pushes through the small gap in the curtain and hurries away. Knowing this is my only chance, I slip off the bed and duck beneath the curtain to my left, heading the opposite way to my mother.

Shoving my sleeves over my hands, I ball the material into my fists and high-tailed it past nurses and doctors who take no notice of me.

As soon as I spot the signs for the elevators, I can barely stop myself from breaking into a run. Facing two silver doors, I jab at both buttons with my sleeve-covered fist, desperate to get to another floor before searching for the ICU.

When the elevator to my right dings, I wait impatiently for the doors to open. A few people get out. As soon as the elevator's empty, I step inside and press the button for level three. Just as the doors slide towards each other, a hand reaches in and stops them.

My heart leaps to my throat, thinking Mum's found me, already. But when the doors open wide, two nurses push an elderly man on a gurney inside.

I squeeze into the corner, shoving my hands behind my back. The nurses ignore me, too engrossed in their conversation, but when I look at the old man, our eyes lock.

I can tell from the weakness in his gaze, from the strange grey colour of his skin that he's dying. I wait for my body to react, for my hands to tingle. But nothing happens. Everything about him tells me he's dying, that he probably won't make it through the night without my help, but my body, my hands, do nothing.

Something new again. Why aren't I feeling all those things I felt when I saw the injured bird, the kitten, Kelsey? What's different?

I can't see what's wrong with the old man. Is that it? Whatever needs fixing inside him is invisible to me, therefore invisible to my body.

Tears spring to my eyes. Right now, I know beyond any doubt that my mother is right about staying away from public places, that the risk to my life is real. Every instinct tells me that if I touch the old man, I'll be welded to him even though my body isn't reacting right now.

I can't explain where that knowledge comes from, except that it's from somewhere deep inside me that's never needed to show itself. Before now.

But there's something else here Mum hasn't mentioned. It's not just about the physical risk. It's the choice. The emotional damage that comes with that choice. Not only can't I help the old man because I know without a doubt it'll kill me, I also can't help him because someone else needs my help instead.

Someone more important than a stranger.

But who am I to decide who's more important? Just because one's a stranger and one isn't. Is that a good enough reason?

Trembling all over, I press myself harder into the corner of the lift, hoping the nurses won't notice the state I'm in. The old man's eyes remain riveted to me.

I hate how I feel. Overwhelmed and helpless. If I live in the real world, will that be what it's like every day? This sickening feeling in my heart, having to look people in the eye, knowing I can save them but choosing not to? Who can live with that?

The elevator lurches and a moment later the doors slide open, releasing the old man and the nurses onto the third floor. I take a deep, shaking breath, wait a moment, only moving when the doors begin to slide shut. I quickly use my arm to stop them and slip through.

Directly in front of me, over the doorway the nurses are pushing the old man through, I see the sign for the ICU. Following at a distance, I pass under the sign and enter a corridor. After a few metres, the corridor opens up to a large area with a nurses' station in front of me.

As I stop and glance around, a nurse looks at me from behind the desk. I want to ask where Kelsey is, but know no one will tell me. More lessons from the TV. I can see the nurse about to say something when a doctor in a white coat steps between us, blocking her view of me.

I hurry past the desk and along the corridor to the right. Taking in my surroundings, I glance behind me, see no one watching, and move over to the first door on my left. On my tiptoes, I peer through the window. An obese woman with her eyes closed, hooked up to machines, lies on a bed.

I move on, hoping to find Kelsey in one of the rooms. Zigzagging from left to right, I check window after window. When I look into the room on the corner of the corridor, a doctor hovers over the bed, obscuring my view of the patient. I almost move on, but the sheet-covered body is smaller than the others I've seen. Impatient, I wait until the doctor finally moves as he makes notes on a clipboard.

That's when I see the gauze covering the left side of the patient's face, her scalp mottled with patches of singed hair, a tube down her throat, machines all around her.

Kelsey.

The urge to burst in overtakes me. I place my sleeve-covered hand on the doorknob.

'I want to see her right now!' a deep male voice shouts from the nurses' station.

I stare, recognising Kelsey's father, his hands fisted at his sides. The nurse is telling him something. Then he suddenly looks directly at me. As he moves towards me, I back up a step, heart thundering, knowing I'll never be able to get near Kelsey with her father here.

Just as he takes another step in my direction, a doctor walks up behind him and says something. When he turns towards the doctor, I slip around the corner and press up against the wall.

It's not long before I hear their footsteps approach on the polished floor.

'Her doctor's just checking on her. He shouldn't be—ah, here he is.'

I hear the swish of a door opening.

'Dr Kellett, this is Shane Wells, your patient's father. I'll leave you in his capable hands, Mr Wells.'

I peek quickly around the corner to see Shane shake hands with the doctor.

'Will she …?' Shane begins, his voice strained. 'Is she—'

'She's in an induced coma,' the doctor says. 'But I won't lie to you, Mr Wells, she's in trouble. Her trachea's badly burned and she's suffering from severe smoke inhalation. That's where the danger lies, especially in someone so young.'

'Oh, Jesus …' Shane says in utter despair. 'She might not make it?'

Tears slide down my face.

She might die!

This fact hits me like a sledgehammer. All along, I'd thought it was her face I'd need to heal. But the burns aren't going to kill her.

I peer around the corner again as the doctor places a gentle hand on Shane's shoulder.

'Before you see her, why don't you come to my office so we can discuss her condition and treatment in more detail?'

Shane takes another look through the glass panel in the door and nods, tears tracking down his face.

I wait as they head along the corridor towards the nurses' station.

Positive no one's watching, I hurry from behind the corner, grip the doorhandle and enter Kelsey's room.

Closing the door behind me, I listen to the ventilator suck in air and expel it while a monitor beeps a steady rhythm.

I move closer, my fingertips already beginning to tingle. Helpless, she lies beneath the thin white sheet, the left side of her face covered in gauze. Right beside her now, my hands throb with the need to lay them on her and take away everything bad. My body's reacting because I know what's wrong with her.

I have to hurry, have to do it before her father returns or a nurse comes to check on her. I shove my sleeves up to my elbows, pinch the sheet just below her chin and pull it down.

Her naked, pale chest rises and falls along with the wires attached to her skin. My hands burn with that familiar pull. I know from TV what a trachea is, where it is, but when I think about her lungs, I hesitate.

If the doctor's right, the smoke in her lungs might very well kill her. Touching her means death. It's everything my mother warned me about my whole life, everything she said I needed protecting from, everything I feared.

Yet now that I'm face to face with it, I feel calm. My whole body thrums with the urge to absorb what's hurting her. Every fibre of my being tells me that this is what I'm meant to do. Besides, what do I have to look forward to? A life spent hiding, a life faced with impossible choices? If I have to make a choice, then why not now? Why not the one time I'm certain it's the right choice?

Bracing myself, my hands feeling like they're about to burst, I place both palms on Kelsey's ribs, her skin cool beneath my heated hands. The rush flows through me immediately, from the bottom of my feet, up through my legs and groin, through my stomach and chest. It travels down my arms, through my hands and into Kelsey, welding me to her. There's no going back. And I don't want to. The feeling flooding through me, both physically and mentally, is what I can only imagine the feeling of heaven might be like. It's glorious. And I'm not afraid.

The monitor's steady rhythm accelerates as Kelsey's heart rate picks up. With a mind of its own, my right hand slides from her ribs, over her chest and up higher until it covers her throat and welds itself there.

Much sooner than I expected, a wave of dizziness hits me, and I know I don't have much longer. The moment I feel my hand release, I reach for the gauze covering the left side of her face and peel it away.

'Hey! Stop that!' a male voice yells behind me.

Startled, I jerk around to see the doctor striding towards me, Kelsey's father close behind.

'What do you think you're doing?' the doctor demands.

I sway, grabbing the bar on the side of the bed. With my time nearly up, I turn to Kelsey and reach towards her burnt face.

The doctor grabs my arm, hauling me roughly away from the bed, from Kelsey.

'No!' I struggle weakly, any strength I have left fading fast. 'No! Her face … her face … her face …'

My knees buckle. I look up at Kelsey's father, his expression contorted in horror as he sees his daughter's exposed burns.

As gravity pulls at me, I slump to the floor, the cool lino against my cheek strangely comforting.

Then rough hands turn me onto my back and the doctor's surprised face stares at me as he pats my cheek.

'Hey, kid. Hey—'

The doctor vanishes as my eyelids close, then open with a flutter and close again. I'm not finished. I have to fix her face.

Fingertips push firmly into the side of my neck and hold steady for a moment.

'Hit that button on the wall!' the doctor yells.

I pry my eyelids open again and see Shane shuffle around me and slam a hand against a large button on the wall. Then he freezes.

Dimly, I can hear an announcement reverberate in the distance, but I'm not interested in that. I'm interested in Kelsey's father. Although I can feel myself fading, I can't go yet. I need to know she's okay.

I hear fast footsteps approaching, feel the rumble of wheels through the floor.

'She's awake!' Shane suddenly shouts. 'She's awake!'

I let my eyes close, let a wonderful drifting sensation take hold.

I've done it. I saved her.

If only I could finish what I started.

'She's choking on the tube,' Shane says, his voice far away.

I'm not worried. The doctors will help her. She'll be okay.

As I drift further away, the doctor shouts, 'He's asystole! Epinephrine!' Then the faint pinch of a needle slides into my arm, my shirt's lifted, cool hands touch my chest, then immense pressure.

Air rushes past my lips, but as the pressure vanishes, no air rushes back in.

And I don't care. I'm floating now.

'Paddles!' someone yells from much further away.

Something wet and cold spreads over my chest, but I'm barely aware of it.

'Charged!' comes a faint cry.

As every noise fades, as the darkness embraces me into weightlessness, something sharp and painful shoots through my body, sending millions of bright sparks dancing into the darkness.

NOW

- 23 -

LUCAS

COMPLETE DARKNESS.

I haven't made it.

Strange. I know I'm blinking. Though I can't feel anything else.

A cow moos in the distance.

Cows? Surely, there aren't …

Pin-pricks of light appear in the sky, dim at first, then brightening to their full, glorious beauty.

I breathe in, long and steady, filling my lungs to capacity before letting them deflate again.

Startling, icy, fresh air.

I can breathe.

When it comes to healing myself, I've never passed out before. Must have been a close call.

Searching the sky, I find only stars. No moon

tonight. As I sit up, my cold, stiff body protests. Pressing a bare hand to my chest, I find the reason I can't feel anything. I'm numb to the core. I have no idea how long I've been lying here in the sub-zero night.

Well, time to find out. I pull my shirt together over my chest, fumble with the zipper on my parka and yank it up. Taking things slow and easy, I rise.

I can't see a thing. One of the few drawbacks of rural living. No moon, no light. Simple as that.

Okay, so where the hell am I?

I'd moved through the cows, heading for the car. I turn slowly until I see it. About ten metres away, a few stars dance at eye level, reflecting on what can only be the Landcruiser's windows.

Ten metres. If I'd walked a little faster after leaving the Hargraves' homestead, I might have made it into the car without copping a bullet to the chest.

Not the case, though.

I move my stiff legs, arms out in front of me, knowing I'm close to the post-and-rail fence. When my hands bump up against it, I feel my way through the railing and stop on the other side, on my land.

Even though I'm rattled, I haven't forgotten why I'm in this mess in the first place. I remove my boots, careful not to let my socked feet step where the boots have touched the ground.

Freezing, I cross to the car and open the tailgate. Sam whines at me from the passenger seat, but she stays where she is as I search for and find an old shopping bag. I shove the boots inside, then remove my parka and shove that in too. Taking off my glove, I realise I've left the other one on Bryce's side of the fence, but I'll never find it in the dark. My jeans come off next, the frigid air sending goosepimples over my bare flesh as I shiver.

With everything that touched the ground on Bryce's property removed, I flop into the driver's seat and am instantly greeted with a barrage of licks to my face and snuffles in my ear.

Poor girl had probably seen the whole thing and thought I was dead. I give her a quick pat and gently push her far enough away so my trembling hand can turn the key in the ignition. I crank the heater, and in the glow from the dashboard lights, I notice what looks like black ink on my hand.

My blood.

I grip the steering wheel anyway and stare into the blackness all around me.

'Should've let myself go,' I whisper to the dark void. 'Let it all be over.'

Sam rests her chin on my arm and gives me a sorrowful look.

How can I even think such a thing when I have her to look after? And the horses. And my mother.

The clock in the dash reads ten past six. I'd been out for just over half an hour.

I flick on the parkers instead of the headlights. They give me enough illumination to navigate the well-known stretch of driveway without, I hope, giving off enough light for Bryce to spot me from his homestead.

Using the accelerator proves more difficult. The car surges forward, my numb foot unable to gauge the force I'm using. A few moments later, I get the hang of it and manage to drive home.

Inside, I get the reverse cycle air conditioner going, then head straight to the sink. After scrubbing my shaking hands, I scour the fridge and grab a packet of ham. Ravenous, I shove slice after slice into my mouth, barely chewing, just needing to get the fuel into my system. After giving a slice to Sam, I reach for the milk and guzzle it straight from the carton.

Sam sits to my side, her black-and-white tail sweeping the floor as she watches me with interest. Dogs know our routines better than we do and she knows something strange is going on.

Shutting the fridge door, I lean against it as the clock ticks on the mantle over the unlit fireplace. I hear my breathing, the swish of Sam's tail, the hum of the refrigerator at my back. Too much silence.

I charge across the room, turn on the TV and raise the volume, but it's not enough. I snap on the stereo and crank it up so loud the vibrations buzz through my feet. As the noise washes over me, I drop to my knees on the hardwood floor, the cacophony masking my first sob.

Sam leans against me, nuzzling me with her cold, wet nose, and that's the last straw. I wrap my arms around her, bury my face in her soft fur and let go, let it all wash over me. The trauma of being shot, of someone wanting me dead. The trauma of being treated like the freak that I am, worth nothing, meaning nothing. I cry for almost losing my life and I cry for not losing it.

I'm an utter mess and I know it. The only things I'm grateful for in this moment are my dog, and that I can't hear my pathetic self-pity. It's been quite a while since I've cried like this. I'll never forget the last time. It'd been over *her*. Because I'd failed her. Nothing since, until now.

Once I gain control of myself, I turn off the stereo but leave the TV on; a habit from childhood I've never broken, the background noise giving me a sense of company.

After lighting the fire, I search the side of the fridge for the number I need, grateful I don't rely solely on the mobile phone I no longer possess. Luckily, I've also kept my landline, although that decision had been more about dodgy mobile reception out here in the sticks.

Grabbing the cordless phone from its cradle, my fingers tremble so violently, it takes me three tries to get the number right. Although it's not late, it's well past office hours and I hear the change in the ringtone as it diverts to another number.

A male voice answers with a crisp, 'Rainey.'

'This is Daniel Clark. I'm the vet down in Cascade. Hate to say it, but I'm pretty sure we've got a case of foot-and-mouth disease down here.'

Rainey listens as I explain the symptoms I'd discovered, along with Bryce's refusal to cooperate.

'And he wouldn't listen to you?' Rainey asks.

'No, instead he threatened me, forced me to leave.' Bit of a tattler, I know. But under the circumstances, Bryce deserves it. After all, it's not like I can go to the police and have him charged with attempted murder. I've destroyed the evidence. Well, almost.

Rainey assures me he'll send a response team out first thing in the morning, and that I'm to decontaminate and quarantine myself for three days before I can resume normal duties.

I hang up, my fingers and toes tingling as they begin to thaw.

In the bathroom, I turn on the overhead heat lamps and stare into the mirror. My flannel shirt's stiff with semi-dried blood. A hell of a lot of it. When I pull the edges of the shirt together., a small bullet hole in the material rests directly over the right side of my chest. One thing about Bryce Hargraves, he had good aim. Just not good enough. Which, I guess, is another reason I'm still here. If he'd hit my heart or head, I'd be lying in his paddock, waiting to be buried.

Trying to distract myself from the morbid thoughts, I shrug out of the shirt and make a mental note to burn it later with the other items that touched the infected land. This particular piece of clothing may not have touched the ground, but it is, after all, evidence of a crime that never happened.

In the mirror, the sticky blood looks like a topography of rivers where it ran over my torso. One streak runs across to my sternum, another into my navel, the others across my ribs and down my sides.

Unsettled by the sight of what looks very much like a cross, I lean into the shower stall and turn on the water. While I wait for it to heat, I catch my reflection again and curiosity gets the better of me. I dampen a washcloth and smear the blood away from where I believe the bullet entered my body.

Not even a red mark or the beginnings of a bruise.

I stare. A bullet to my chest is the worst injury I've ever experienced. Even after living with this thing my whole life, I'm still in awe that there's not even the slightest of marks. Nothing.

Like it never happened.

Which is exactly what I'll say should anyone ask. And I'm one hundred per cent sure Bryce Hargraves won't contradict that statement.

As I step beneath the hot spray, I mull over how to deal with the whole Bryce situation. He'd told me he'd be back to bury me, so it won't be long before he discovers I'm gone. Just because I'm not where he left me, doesn't mean I haven't died elsewhere. Either way, he'll be in quite a panic.

When he realises I'm neither dead nor have I gone to the police, I have no idea how he'll react. But for now, I just want to enjoy the sensation of warming my numb body. I'll worry about Bryce later. And if the question inevitably comes up, I'll do the only thing I can do.

Deny. Deny. Deny.

- 24 -

BRYCE

AFTER GIVING THE RIFLE a thorough clean in the barn, Bryce wraps it in an old towel and hides it within the engine compartment of his tractor, where Georgia will never look.

Limping home, he grimaces with each step, the pain in his knee excruciating.

Entering the house as quietly as he can, he slips into the bathroom and washes his hands, then his face. As he pats them dry with a handtowel, he catches his reflection in the mirror. Unable to meet his own eyes, he neatly folds the towel and places it on its hook.

Heading towards the kitchen, he clenches his teeth against the pain and tries his best to hide the limp when he enters.

He needn't have bothered. Georgia stands at the

humming microwave, her back to him while he quickly makes his way to his seat. As he lowers himself into the chair, he releases a long, silent breath of relief.

'Dinner was ready ages ago,' Georgia says, her words clipped with anger. The microwave door slams as she removes a casserole dish and places it a little too hard on the table.

'You sound like your mother,' he shoots back, instantly wishing he'd kept his mouth shut.

'Good!' Plates clatter, her posture rigid as she serves their food. 'I know how she felt,' she mumbles, before letting out a long sigh.

Bryce watches her search for cutlery.

'You haven't seen those walking boots I wore in Japan, have you?' she asks, her voice almost normal. 'I know I wore them the first day after I got home, but they've vanished.'

As she speaks, the full weight of what he's done washes over him. He killed a man. A man he hated, yes, but a man all the same. He killed a man to protect everything he'd worked for, to protect his daughter, to protect the future he'd built for her. Could that be classed as self-defence?

'Dad?' Georgia asks, as she takes her seat at the table. 'Jesus. You look—'

He waves a hand at her, not sure what she sees on his face, just hoping it's not guilt.

'Get us a glass of water,' he says a little too gruffly.

She stares at him for a moment, then gets up and quickly grabs a jug from the fridge. When she passes a glass to him, he can't hide the shake in his hand. He downs the water in one go, feeling its icy tentacles spread through his stomach, wondering what it must feel like to have a bullet rip through a body, tearing apart everything in its path.

'I heard you fire a shot,' Georgia says, stabbing a piece of steak with her fork.

'Had to put down one of the herd. Twisted gut.'

Georgia frowns. He stares at his plate, noticing for the first time that she's served his favourite meal. He should have noticed the moment he walked into the house, but he hadn't. And she'd noticed he hadn't.

'This is delicious, Georgie,' he says.

'You haven't even tried it.'

'I know what it tastes like, don't I?' he snaps. Jesus, he needs to get control of himself. He's not acting normal. He knows it, and she knows it.

'Dad, it's not like you haven't put down cattle before. So, what's wrong? What was with the stupid vet?'

If only he could tell her what he'd done for her, she wouldn't be harassing him like this. But he can't tell her. Not ever. She loves him, he knows that, but he also knows she'll never forgive him if she discovers the truth.

'Dad? What's going on?'

'Why the hell'd you move the cows into that paddock so they could gorge themselves?'

She flinches at the sudden rage in his voice, rage he hasn't meant to reveal. But who can blame him? It was, after all, all her fault. He'd thrown away those damn boots she'd brought back from Japan the moment he'd seen them, but obviously too late. The stupid girl had traipsed all over the property in them without a care in the world, her head in the clouds like it seemed to be more and more these days. Then she'd gone and moved the cattle as close as possible to Clark's property.

'I was trying to do you a favour,' she says.

'Next time,' he shouts, 'don't bother!'

He regrets the words as soon as they leave his mouth.

Tears pool in her dark eyes as she bolts to her feet, the chair scraping the slate tiles like fingernails down a chalkboard. Without a word, she storms out.

A moment later her bedroom door slams, reverberating through his body like a gunshot.

- 25 -

LUCAS

AFTER MY SHOWER, the trembling gone, I dress in clean clothes. I find an old parka and a pair of boots, then grab a packet of matches from the mantlepiece and head outside. Picking up the torch beside the front door, I head down the steps to the Landcruiser.

Sam follows my every move, and I welcome the company, even though I'd rather she stay inside where it's warm.

Opening the tailgate, I remove the shopping bag with the contaminated items and hurry towards the barn. Beau rattles the gate at the back of the stables when he sees me, clearly not impressed by my tardiness. Still, he forgives me with a nuzzle to my arm before he trots into the barn, then his stall. As I make up two buckets of feed, my thoughts go to what would have happened to my animals if I'd never returned. I suppose my mother would be the first to raise the alarm when I didn't show up at work.

After feeding Beau and the pregnant mare, I find the container of petrol I use for the ride-on mower and take it out to the rear of the barn. Against the wall of the stables stands a forty-four-gallon drum I'd planned to use as a makeshift tabletop when I wash the horses. Removing the lid, I put the shopping bag in, slosh some petrol on top, light a match and drop it in with a quick step back.

The fire blooms bright, then shrinks down to a small burn. And suddenly, I'm hit with the memories of the fire, the screams, of pulling Kelsey from the inferno. The hospital. How I failed her.

I shake my head as if I can dislodge it all. I should be thinking about Bryce. And more importantly, if he's done everything possible to stop the spread of the disease he's clearly been trying to hide. I saw him in town this morning, so he hasn't quarantined himself. Does that mean he doesn't care, or does that mean he's been decontaminating whenever he leaves the farm?

Not like I can ask him.

I can only hope that after all the wrong he's done, he's done something right, something to protect everyone else.

Knowing that foot-and-mouth only affects cloven-hooved animals, my horses are safe. Which hopefully means my land has been working as a buffer between the surrounding cattle and sheep farms.

As I watch the evidence of my non-murder turn to ash, I hope that I've discovered Bryce's cover-up early enough to prevent a national disaster.

- 26 -

BRYCE

SOMETHING BUZZES BENEATH BRYCE'S pillow. He stirs in his sleep, only semi-aware of the vibration beneath his head. As the buzzing grows stronger, more insistent, it pulls him fully out of sleep.

Reaching beneath his pillow, he finds the cheap phone, brings the glow of the screen up to his face and turns off the alarm.

Two am.

Body aching with every movement, he sits up and swings his legs over the side of the bed. Waiting there for a moment, letting every muscle and joint settle, he steels himself for the pain about to shoot through his knee. When he stands, the agony is almost more than he can bear. But he has to. He has important work to do and it's going to be anything but easy. And it all needs to be done before Georgia wakes up.

Once dressed, he grabs the blanket covering his quilt and shoves it in a sports bag beside the door, picks up his boots and moves silently through the house.

In the kitchen, he collects a torch and eases onto the verandah, where he puts on his boots, flicks on the torch and heads to the barn.

There, he gathers gardening gloves and reaches for the shovel. But as he grips the handle, he stills. It's winter. The earth cold and hard. He's not worried about Georgia discovering the grave. She'll simply think that's where he buried the cow. The problem lay in the limited time and his physical ability to dig a hole large enough to bury Clark in. What he needs is machinery. Unfortunately, the tractor will wake Georgia, so it's out of the question. He has no good reason to be using machinery in the middle of the night.

Maybe he can weigh Clark down and sink him in the dam. It could work, but he's not sure if the decomposing body will harm the cattle drinking from the water, and there's no guarantee the dam level won't drop low enough to reveal the body later.

God-fucking-dammit!

He can't stand here all night and do nothing. All he can do is try digging the earth, see how difficult it is, then decide from there.

As the torch beam weaves and bounces along the grass in front of him, he makes the mistake of lifting it higher. The light hits cow after cow, their heads low, mouths drooling.

He points the beam downwards again. He can't deal with that right now. First things first.

Knowing he must be close to the fence line, he

raises the torch again and spots it. Almost there. He stops, shines the torch beam back and forth, waiting for it to hit Clark's body.

But there is no body.

He turns from side to side, trying to figure out if he's walked off course in the dark. Then he sees it. A flattened section of grass.

Training his torchlight on that area, he moves closer. He kneels with a groan of pain on the raised grass around it, arcing the torch beam slowly over the flattened area, where it illuminates a much darker patch of grass.

He leans forward and touches it, leaving dark brown stains on his fingertips. Even though it's oxidised, he knows blood when he sees it.

The torchlight catches something in the longer grass. It's too far away to reach from where he is. Groaning again, he uses the shovel like a walking stick to skirt around the blood-soaked grass to the object.

A glove. And something small and solid slightly to the right of it.

Bending from the waist, he fumbles in the grass. His fingertips pluck up something grimy but solid. Straightening, he holds it under the light.

And his heart stops mid-beat.

There on his palm, rests a spent slug coated in dried blood.

His heart kicks into gear again, adrenaline coursing through his body as he stares at the bullet. The bullet that should be inside Clark's cold, dead body.

Fear pulls at his gut, contorting his face.

It isn't possible, is it?

Unless the slug went right through Clark and exited his back. Though that isn't what these particular bullets are designed to do. And if it had exited Clark, he'd have bled out even faster.

So, where the fuck is he?

Had someone found him and driven him to the hospital themselves? But who would be strong enough to pick him up? Clark's no lightweight. And there are no marks in the grass indicating someone dragged him over to the fence.

Bryce sweeps the torchlight towards Clark's driveway. The freak's vehicle isn't there, so he hadn't made it back to the four-wheel drive and collapsed inside.

Limping over to the fence, he clicks off the torch and squints. No lights shine from Clark's house, but then again, it's two in the morning. All he knows is that Clark getting up and walking home is impossible. When Bryce left him, he was dying. There was no doubt about it. He saw the freak struggle to breathe, saw him cough up blood.

There was only one way to know.

Wait.

Bryce shoves the spent slug in his pocket, and with a head full of fear and confusion, begins the slow limp home, praying the police aren't already there waiting for him.

- 27 -

LUCAS

WHEN I WAKE IN the morning, I ring Emily before she leaves for work and, apart from the shooting, tell her what's happened. She agrees to travel into Riverview to pick up a new phone for me while I'm quarantined, though I have to talk her out of calling Bryce and giving him a piece of her mind, convincing her to wait until the disease is confirmed, just in case I'm wrong.

'You've got doubts?' she asks.

'Absolutely not,' I assure her, 'but I'd appreciate it if you kept out of it, if not forever, then at least for now.'

She grumbles something I can't quite understand and don't want to, but somewhere in there I hear her agree. That agreement, of course, will mean she'll keep her distance from Bryce, but it's in no way an agreement that will stop her from gossiping with everyone else. Nothing I can do about that, unfortunately.

After I attend to the horses, I make myself a cup of coffee and wait for the inevitable visitors to arrive. This morning, the overcast sky smothers any chance of fog. But today, I don't mind. Through the window beside my small dining table, I can see all the way to the road.

Sam curls up at my feet—or more accurately, *on* them—as I sip my coffee and wake up my laptop.

Only an hour goes by before a police car leads a procession of two white SUVs past my property's entrance, where they turn into Bryce's driveway. The response team has arrived.

How I wish I could see Bryce's face when the police pull up. No doubt he'll think they want to question him about his dead neighbour. To see the confusion on his face when he discovers it's about his neighbour's report of an outbreak of FMD, well, that would be gold.

- 28 -

BRYCE

AFTER DRAGGING HIMSELF OUT of bed, sleep having evaded him after what he'd discovered—or hadn't discovered—in the paddock, Bryce stares at his drawn, pale face in the bathroom mirror for far too long.

As the early morning had drawn on and on, he'd concluded that there was only one explanation. He'd just been too rattled to see it last night. Somone with an injured animal had come to see Clark after hours. Someone who wasn't alone. And when they'd travelled along his driveway and seen his vehicle parked there, they'd investigated. It just had to be a fact that there was more than one of them. That way, they'd have no problem carrying Clark to their car.

They, of course, would have been dealing with a

corpse. But a dead body with a bullet hole tended to attract the attention of hospital staff and police. Sooner or later, the police would arrive on his doorstep with questions. Still, what he'd figured out was the best possible scenario. He knows there's no bullet for forensic matching. He'd flushed that down the toilet before he climbed into bed.

Of course, he'd be a suspect, and possibly Georgia, too. After all, Clark was on his land.

So, he's still in the goddamn shit.

As far as he can see, there's only has one option. To fess up. But not to murder. It was an accident. He'd been putting down a cow with a twisted gut and somehow the bullet had ricocheted and hit Clark. But he hadn't realised, hadn't even known Clark was on his property.

To do that, he needs to get out there and shoot a cow. And hope that the town's limited police resources were incapable of determining the cow's time of death. He knows the fools on their tiny police force. They probably won't even think of something like that.

Bryce grips the edge of the basin hard. With Clark gone, even with an investigation, the chances of getting away with it, all of it, are looking good.

And Georgia will never have to know.

Rushing to the toilet, he leans over and vomits. As his guts clench and force nothing but water from his mouth, he embraces the purge, wishing he could purge the guilt from his mind as easily.

After cleaning up the toilet, he lowers the lid and sits, taking in gulps of air as he tries to calm himself.

What's done is done, he tells himself. Feeling guilty over killing that freak won't help anyone. In fact, when he really thinks about it, he might have done Clark a favour.

'Dad!' Georgia yells from the kitchen.

His heart jolts. Were they here, already?

'Brekky!' she finishes.

He sighs and stands, his knee sending shockwaves up his thigh and into his groin.

In the kitchen, he takes a seat and stares at the bacon, scrambled eggs and fried tomato his daughter has prepared for him. When she'd been in Japan, breakfast had been the time he missed her most.

Georgia takes her seat across from him, and even though he doesn't look at her, he feels her gaze.

'Definitely something up if you've lost your appetite,' she observes.

If only he could tell her.

'Dad?' She pauses a moment, then, 'Dad? What is it? You're freaking me out.'

As he looks up, ready to meet her eyes, they both hear it. Tyres crunching on the gravel driveway. With the kitchen at the rear of the house, he has to endure the knee pain again as he rises and tries not to limp towards the living room.

He sees a police car—no sirens, no lights flashing, he notes—pull up in front of the house. Behind it, two white SUVs do the same.

His heart thunders in his chest and bile rises in his throat.

'Oh my God,' Georgia says from behind him, a hint of excitement in her voice. 'I wonder what's going on?'

He turns to her, tries his best at a confused expression and shrugs.

The doorbell rings.

He freezes, wondering if he can really pull off the lies he's about to tell.

'Dad? What is it? What's happening?' Georgia asks.

'I guess we're about to find out,' he says. Unable to meet her eyes, he shuffles into the foyer. With a trembling hand, he opens the door and steps onto the verandah.

Officer Harry Andrews and his son, Officer Dave, stare at him. He's had many a beer with Harry on a Saturday night at the local pub over the last thirty-odd years. Harry knows him as an honest, stand-up citizen who helps the local community whenever he can. Harry would never believe he had anything to do with deliberately killing Clark. Of that, he's certain. The son might have some doubts, but his father will set him straight.

'Bryce,' Harry says. 'Got some people here who need a word with you.'

Bryce frowns as a man in his fifties with salt-and-pepper hair, looking professional even in gumboots and khakis, steps forward.

'Mr Hargraves. Jim Rainey, Department of Agriculture.'

Confusion courses through him.

'Dad?' Georgia says from behind him.

His head snaps around. 'Inside. Now,' he orders, but she remains in the doorway, her eyes wide.

'Mr Hargraves,' Rainey says, 'there's been a report of a suspected outbreak of FMD on your property.'

How?

Bryce squints at Rainey, trying to buy time to think. 'FMD?'

Rainey's mild expression hardens. 'You're no novice at raising cattle, are you, Mr Hargraves?'

'Been doing it my whole life,' Bryce admits.

'Then I'm sure you're fully aware of the signs

associated with foot-and-mouth disease.'

Bryce crosses his arms over his chest, sighing in defeat. They had him. Killing Clark had been in vain. No point lying to them.

'Yeah,' he says, aware of Georgia listening to every word. 'I guess I am.'

- 29 -

LUCAS

HALF AN HOUR LATER, as I knew one eventually would, a single white SUV makes the turn into my driveway. All my life I've avoided trouble, but when someone tries to kill you, well, I guess all bets are off.

I walk onto the verandah and wait for the vehicle to pull up. A man in his early fifties opens the door and places blue shoe covers over his boots before he climbs out. Fortunately, I have no problem talking to strangers who I'll likely never see again.

'Daniel Clark?' he asks when he reaches the top step.

'Yeah.' I offer my gloved hand, noticing the slightest frown pass across the man's face before he shakes.

'I'm Jim Rainey. We spoke on the phone last night.

Just to reassure you, my vehicle and I have been through the whole decontamination procedure before coming onto your property.'

'Right. I figured. You want to come in?'

Rainey nods, removes his covered boots and follows me inside. He takes a seat at the table where I watched the procession enter Bryce's property. While I set about making us both a coffee, I catch Rainey staring at my gloves, which of course, I haven't removed. When he looks at me, his eyes are curious but kind.

'Yeah, I know,' I say with half a grin. 'Germaphobia.' Like that explains everything. Usually, it's enough to put a stop to any questions. None come as I round the counter, slide a mug of coffee towards him and take a seat opposite.

'So, what's the verdict?'

'Seems you were right about it being FMD. Of course, we can't officially confirm anything until the samples prove positive, but that's what we're expecting and that's how we're treating it.'

I nod as Rainey takes a sip of coffee, then reaches into his briefcase, pulling out a phone and a notepad.

'Any problem if I take a statement?' he asks.

'Of course not.'

Rainey finds an app on his phone, presses a button and clicks the top of his pen.

'Right. Your name's Daniel Clark?'

I nod. Rainey raises his eyebrows and points to his phone.

'Oh, right. Yeah. I'm Daniel Clark.'

'And you're the local veterinarian here in Cascade?'

'That's correct.'

'Could you explain how you came to suspect that

your neighbour's cattle were infected with FMD?'

I give him all the details, including the symptoms I found as I made my way to the Hargraves' homestead.

'So, you informed Hargraves of your concern?'

'Of course,' I say.

'And his response?'

'He demanded I leave his property, immediately. Said I was trespassing.'

'And did you?'

'No. I thought it best if I called you right away. I have the number for the Department of Agriculture stored in my phone. When I took it out, Bryce snatched it from my hand and crushed it.'

'And then?'

'I left.'

Rainey nods as he jots down notes.

'Hargraves claims you arrived at his doorstep around five. Would you agree with that?'

'Probably closer to five-thirty. The sun had just gone down, but it was still light.'

'How long do you think you talked to Hargraves?'

'It wouldn't have been more than five minutes.'

'Then you returned home?'

'That's right,' I confirm.

'So, why did it take you almost an hour to call it in?'

I'd fallen right into that one. But I don't react.

'Mr Clark?'

'I admit, I held onto the hope that Bryce would come to his senses and call you. I wanted to give him a little time to think about the ramifications of not coming forward himself.' The lie comes from my mouth without any effort. After all, I've lied about the reason I wear gloves my whole life, so it's not like I haven't had any practice.

Rainey nods, waiting for me to continue. My lie hasn't answered his question.

'So, I took the necessary precautions with my contaminated shoes and clothing before driving home. Once here, I showered, then destroyed the contaminated clothing.' For effect, I use my gloved hands to give a little shrug. 'I'm pretty meticulous when it comes to germs and diseases. And then I had to attend to my horses. I called as soon as I came inside.'

Rainey studies me for a long moment. 'And that's the only reason for the delay?'

'That's it.'

'Hargraves didn't make you an offer?'

'What?' I don't have to fake my response to that one.

'An offer to keep quiet?'

'Absolutely not,' I say.

'So, why do you think Hargraves was trying to hide the disease?'

I shrug. 'I know he used that prized bull of his to breed a lot of his cattle. Had a bloodline that dates back to when his great-grandfather ran the farm. Could be sentimental reasons.'

Rainey nods. 'Could be. But it's a hell of a price to pay. If it is indeed FMD, he's facing quite a hefty fine for trying to conceal the outbreak.'

'What about the compensation?' I know the government has a scheme to help farmers when something like this happens.

'There won't be any.'

'Jesus,' I say. Bryce has really fucked himself over. But why? Why risk it all? Clearly, whatever the reason, in Bryce's mind, it was worth killing for.

'Lucky for the whole country he has a vet living next

187

door to him,' Rainey says.

'Just doing my job.' I try to ignore the blush creeping up my face. I don't want gratitude, I just want to get this over with so I'm left alone again. 'So, what happens now?'

'Once we get a positive on the samples, we'll destroy the cattle and bury them on site.'

That'll devastate Bryce, but what else could I do? He's not the only farmer in this area. I couldn't let it spread and destroy everyone else's livelihood, as well.

'Think you caught it early enough?' I ask.

'You know how contagious this thing is. But thanks to you, we have a very good chance of containing it.' Rainey takes another sip of coffee before he stops the recording app.

'I have to say, Hargraves was definitely covering up, no doubt hoping to wait it out until the signs disappeared,' he says. 'Let's hope his stupidity doesn't bring down the entire industry. The man's certainly no pillar of morality.'

'Don't I know it,' I mumble.

Rainey places the empty coffee mug on the table. As he stands, I rise too and follow him to the front door.

On the verandah, Rainey slips on his covered boots, then pauses and takes in the view. 'Some place you've got here. You're a lucky guy.'

I follow Rainey's gaze, taking in my property through his eyes. Seeing it every day, it's easy to forget how beautiful it is. I'm glad he's reminded me.

'You don't live on property yourself?' I ask.

Rainey shakes his head and saunters down the steps to his SUV. I follow. 'No, I'm one of those unlucky suburban guys,' he says with regret.

At the car, Rainey opens the door, throws his briefcase on the passenger seat and turns to me. 'So, you seem to know the procedure regarding yourself.'

'Sure. Stay put for three days, then life goes back to normal.' I glance towards Bryce's property. 'For me, anyway.'

'We'll have a roadblock set up about a kilometre down the road, so no visitors in that time, either.' Rainey climbs into his vehicle, shuts the door and lowers the window.

'Well,' he says, 'time to find out just how FMD ended up in this country after more than a hundred years.'

'I'd be pretty damn interested to know myself.'

'I'll fill you in. And thanks again.'

With that, Rainey drives away, leaving me wondering about the origin of the disease. It also leaves me wondering if Bryce might pay me a visit sometime soon.

- 30 -

KELSEY

I WRAP A MUG in newspaper and place it in the box at my side. Straightening, I look around at the apartment I've lived in for the last ten years. Apart from all the small items that I've already packed, it hasn't changed since the day I moved in. The furniture had come with me that day, and it'll go with me again. Sure, I've thought about buying a new couch or refrigerator over the years, but I'm the type to just keep things if they still do their job. Besides that, I don't have to worry about anyone criticising my choice of décor because there's simply nobody I need to impress.

What matters is the promise I made to myself the day I moved in. To save every cent possible until I could move to the place of my dreams. And to my amazement, that time is finally here.

When a knock comes from the front door, I look up, a memory from my childhood flashing through my mind. A memory of standing in my mother's apartment, almost in this exact position, staring at the door, willing my father to come and take me away.

I quickly brush at my clothes while my mind fights to brush the memory aside. Twenty years since the fire, and that part of my life is sometimes an elusive, disjointed dream, and sometimes as stark and clear as the scars on my face.

I remind myself that this is the reality of my life now. Nothing before the fire matters. Shaking it off, I do what I always do when the memories rise: I box them up and place them in a part of my mind I rarely accesses. And most of the time, it works.

The knock comes again, giving me a much-needed jolt from my thoughts. I hurry over and look through the peephole. Smiling, I swing the door wide. Dad only manages one step inside before I give him a tight hug. With a bag of takeaway in one hand, he returns my embrace.

'Hey, pumpkin.'

I pull away and take the food from him.

'Isn't it about time you stopped calling me that?' I ask as I lead the way to the kitchen.

'You'll always be my pumpkin, even when you're as ancient as I am,' he says, glancing around the apartment at all the empty shelves and boxes.

Sadness deepens the lines on his face. As he joins me at the kitchen bench, he puts on what I know is a bullshit smile.

'I got your favourite.' He points to the takeaway bag. 'May as well enjoy it one last time.'

I open it up and inhale the smell of Thai green curry.

'You make it sound like it's my last meal.'

'Well, it is. Your last Thai meal, anyway. It's not like you can get this in that godforsaken place you're moving to.'

Here we go. Why does it have to come down to this? Why does following a dream have to involve hurting someone in the process?

I pull the containers of heaven from the bag and push a plastic fork across to him. 'It's hardly godforsaken, Dad.' I grab a couple of bowls I left unpacked for this very reason and remove the lids from the containers.

'May as well be,' he says as he serves food into both bowls.

I know he's trying not to let his emotions show, but he's absolutely useless at it.

'It's not that far away,' I remind him.

'Five hours and twenty minutes, to be exact. Far enough so I can't just swing by and see you whenever I want.'

'I'll miss you, too.'

He sighs, puts down his fork and looks me in the eye. 'I know it's been your dream to live there for such a long time … but it's so damn isolated, Kel. It feels to me like you're moving out there to hide yourself away, and I don't like the idea of that at all.'

My shoulders drop. Sometimes he just doesn't get it. But then again, I suspect he doesn't want to understand, because understanding means accepting that no matter how small my life is, it's mine to live.

'It's here, in the city, that I'm isolated.'

He gives me a dubious look. 'Come on. That's impossible. There're people everywhere.'

I can't continue to pretend everything's okay just so

he feels better. I've been doing it for so long, it's become a habit. Even when I went back to school after the fire and was teased mercilessly over the scars, I hid my pain from him. Dealing with my own feelings had been overwhelming enough. I couldn't imagine burdening Dad with them. Not on top of everything he'd had to cope with.

But now, it needs to stop. If he doesn't understand what moving away from the city means to me, then he'll take it personally. And that's the last thing I want.

'Dad. Every day I dread walking out that door, so half the time I don't. I stay locked up in here and focus on my work because some days I just don't want to face anyone.' Uncomfortable, he moves the food around in his bowl.

'We all feel like that sometimes.'

'Yeah? How about *all* the time? I've spent twenty years with this face, and it's not getting any easier.'

His eyes flicker to my scars. He's always been the only one who never does that to me.

'You think they won't stare at you in the country?'

'I'm not stupid. Of course they will. At first. But it's not like it is here. When you walk down the street here, everyone's a stranger every day, and they can't help but gawk. I get that, and I hate that. But in Cascade, it'll be the same people all the time. They'll get used to the scars, and after a while, they'll just see me.'

'Kel—'

'No. Don't you see? I'll be able to walk out the door without feeling my insides shrivel. I'll be able to get in my car and go into town just like any other person without having a war going on inside me. That's what I want, and that's what I deserve. So please, don't try to make me feel any worse about leaving you here.'

He looks at his food for a long moment. 'I'm sorry.'

'It's okay.'

'No,' he says, meeting my eyes. 'It's not. I'm being selfish instead of happy for you. You've worked so hard to accomplish what you have, and here I am shooting you down because all I can think about is how it's going to affect me.'

I round the bench and give him a hug. 'That's all anyone thinks about, isn't it?' I feel him shake his head.

'Not a parent. I once made the mistake of not putting you first. I should know better than to do it again.'

I step away and frown at him with disapproval. 'Don't start that. It wasn't your fault.'

'I shouldn't have waited for a judge, some stranger, to tell me if I was good enough to look after my own daughter. I should've just taken you.'

'And what?' I ask. 'You're the most honest person I know. Even if you'd taken me and we'd disappeared, the lies would've killed you.' I reach out, take his hand and squeeze. 'You did the best you could, and I know that. Okay?'

He squeezes back. 'Okay.'

I return to my food, relieved we've cleared the air.

'So, when're the removalists coming?'

'First thing tomorrow morning,' I say. Turning to the fridge, I take out the solitary jug of cold water. 'They have to load me up first because there's another stop to make on the way to Cascade. So, they won't get to my place until the day after tomorrow.'

'Then you can stay with me tomorrow night,' he says, his mood brighter.

I bite my lip. 'Actually, I've already booked a motel room about halfway down there. I'll get to Cascade bright and early so I can start unpacking right away.'

That's mostly the truth. I'm also excited, wanting to get out of here as soon as possible. A night in a strange motel appeals to me far more than spending one more night in the city.

'Makes sense,' he agrees. 'Not everyone has their dream come true, pumpkin. You deserve it … and I'm proud of you.'

I smile at him. He's right. I am lucky. I now own a slice of heaven, a slice I've worked hard for. But living in Cascade's only part of the dream. My real dream, the one that never stops haunting my soul, was taken from me forever by the fire.

The memories of that summer, of the boy next door, spike into my brain. It's been a while since I've thought about him. Despite Dad telling me that Lucas didn't care, that he never even came to visit me in hospital, that whatever I thought was special about him just wasn't true, I know better. I might keep him locked deep inside me most of the time, but occasionally I bring him out.

The good and the bad.

He'd been my best friend back then, and he'd abandoned me when I needed him most. In that first year after the fire, I couldn't decide if I loved him or hated him. Probably both. I remember how close we'd been, how he thought *I* was the amazing one, when really it was him. And then the feelings of anger and betrayal after the fire, when he could have healed my face but hadn't bothered. If only he'd done that one thing for me, he could have changed my life.

Then came my utter obsession with him, demanding Dad find him so he could heal my scars. Dad trying to tell me I was being irrational, that my memories were playing tricks on me. But I'd been so worked up, so overcome with grief, I just never let up.

Close to a year later, Dad came home one day to tell me he'd finally found Lucas. And he was dead.

I didn't want to believe it. Believing Luke was dead meant my dreams were dead, too. My face would never be normal, so I'd never be the singer I wanted to be. The scars took all my confidence. And as much as I'd thought I hated Luke, knowing he was dead finally forced me to admit how I really felt about him. The fact that it hurt to the core, and that I'd cried for nearly a week after the news, told me all I needed to know. He'd been so special and magical, I'd realised my other dream had been to see him again. That my desperation to find him hadn't just been about healing my scars, but also about having my friend back again. His mother had been right. Luke had told me everyone before him with the same magic had died young.

So now, as difficult as it is sometimes, my only defence is to *not* think about him. Because as magical as our time together was, there hasn't been one bit of magic in my life since. And there never will be.

- 31 -

GEORGIA

GEORGIA PRESSES HER EAR to her father's bedroom door. She can't hear him snoring in there, but half an hour ago he said he was going to have a snooze, something he did often.

He's been moping about the place for days, barely saying a word, even though she keeps asking him questions about the disease the cattle are suffering from.

But her father refuses to tell her anything about it and keeps demanding she stay away from any of the response team who are staying on their property. Worse still, she can't even look it up on the internet since she's not allowed to leave the property and go to the local library, the only internet access she has available at the moment.

When she came home from Japan, her dad said the modem had shit itself and he was waiting for a replacement to come in the mail. Which is one of the things she hates about living here. She should be able to just go and buy one. Not in this hick town. And Bryce is so much older than all her friends' dads, which means he's old school. Apparently, old school doesn't like the modern world, especially the internet and mobile phones.

Though she has to give him some credit. He did buy them both mobiles just before she went to Japan so they could keep in touch. Unfortunately, the reception here was pitiful, especially when it came to googling anything. All she ever got was a circle going around and around. She was stuck in an information blackout.

Yesterday, when her father went for a nap, she'd almost managed to get up the guts to find one of the response team guys, but was too afraid Bryce would catch her. Right now, she's worried the stress of everything might give him a heart attack or stroke. She's never seen him so worked up, so exhausted, so cranky and short with her all the time. It's almost as if he blames her.

Besides all that, she's still waiting for the right time to tell him she wants to leave once she finishes her Higher School Certificate at the end of the year. That's definitely out of the question at the moment. Which totally sucks.

A snore comes from the other side of the door. Relief floods through her. For a little while, she's free.

Sick of being cooped up inside for the last couple of days, she shrugs on her jacket and slips from the house. As she quietly closes the door, one of the response team hurries up the driveway towards her.

Over the past few days, she's watched them from the living-room window, so she knows their routine. Sure enough, it's change-of-shift time.

Fed up with not knowing anything about what's happening on her own property, she follows him as he heads to the barn. When she steps inside, she blinks, waiting for her eyes to adjust to the darkness after the bright winter sunlight outside.

'Hello?' she calls.

'Yeah, over here,' a male voice replies.

Blinking, she walks down the centre of the barn, passing the stall her once-loved bull used to call home.

'What can I do you for, Miss?'

She stops, her vision adjusting enough to see a fold-up table and chairs at the other end of the barn. Three men play cards at the table. Halfway between the card players and herself, the younger guy she followed faces her.

'I want to know what's happening,' she says.

He gives her a strange look, almost like she might not be the full dollar. 'You really don't know?'

'I know the cattle have some sort of disease, but my dad won't tell me anything else.'

He glances over his shoulder at his team, but they're too absorbed in their card game to pay any attention. The guy moves closer until he's just a metre away.

She studies his face and discovers he's quite handsome, in a rough sort of way. Better than any of the boys around here. He takes a packet of cigarettes from his shirt pocket, pops one in his mouth and offers her the open pack.

She shakes her head and waits while he lights up, knowing her father wouldn't approve. She doesn't care either way. Plenty of kids at school smoke. It's just not something she's interested in doing.

'You're the one who went to Japan, right?' he asks.

She crosses her arms and grabs her waist with her hands. 'So?'

'So, only thing that makes any sense is that all of this is because of you.'

She stands stock-still, utterly floored.

'You really didn't know?' he says, surprise registering in his eyes.

'I … how? That can't be true.'

'How's this for true,' he says, then takes a long drag on his cigarette. 'We haven't had an outbreak in Australia for over a hundred years. Safe to say FMD doesn't exist here … *didn't* exist here, until some twit brought it here. And that twit happens to be—'

'Kyle!' one of the older guys calls from the card game. 'You're not supposed to be talking to her. Get over here.'

She remains rooted to the spot, his words like ice in her veins, freezing her. Before he turns away, the ground vibrates beneath her feet, and for a moment, she wonders if the earth's about to crack open and swallow her. Right now, she really hopes so.

Then the intense rumble grows louder and louder. A rumble she knows will definitely wake her father, if not the entire planet.

'What's that?' she asks, almost afraid of the answer.

'The excavator. It's here for the burial.'

'Burial?' The word makes her stomach roll with nausea.

'Kyle! I'm not kidding!' the older man yells.

Kyle gives her a quick, malicious wink before he hurries over to his team.

All four men stare at her. As the rumble grows ever

louder, she turns and runs, fleeing from their hateful eyes and the truth she wishes she never discovered.

After hiding in her room for over an hour, bawling her eyes out, her face buried in her pillow so her father wouldn't hear her, she finally pulls herself together. Needing something to distract her from the shame and guilt, from the gnawing dread in her stomach, she finds dirty dishes stacked high on the kitchen bench. She fills the sink with hot water and squirts in detergent before slipping on rubber gloves.

As the bubbles form, she wonders why her father hasn't told her the truth yet. Is it because he's so furious he might explode? All those strange outbursts he'd had lately … they all made sense now. They'd come from a place inside him he was trying to keep locked up.

But how long can someone keep that kind of rage deep down? And how would she ever be able to face anyone in town once the truth came out?

Sniffing loudly, trying to keep the threatening tears from escaping all over again, she grabs a stack of plates, places them in the hot, soapy water and scrubs.

Outside, a rumble catches her attention. She doesn't want to look through the window in front of her, but can't help herself. In the distance, a few paddocks away, the excavator takes a bite from the earth. She bows her head, her hands motionless in the water, as tears flow from her eyes, once again.

One thing she knows for sure, she has to get out of here.

- 32 -

LUCAS

ON MY FIRST MORNING of freedom, I'm up early and have all the horses fed and rotated to a new paddock. When I return from the stables, the thick blanket of fog glares bright with the rising sun.

On the verandah, I give Sam a quick rub with a towel to remove the slight dampness from her coat. Inside, I strip off my gloves and coat, hang them next to the door and head into the kitchen.

Eager to get to work and catch up on the backlog, I feed Sam and decide on a quick bowl of muesli. Bryce still hasn't confronted me, which I'm grateful for. Of course, he's be too busy with the response team to dare leave his property and get himself into more trouble.

Yesterday, I heard, then saw the arrival of the excavator. A devastating sight. Once the pit is large enough, the euthanised cattle will be buried. I don't wish that on anyone, not even Bryce, but it has to be done to protect the rest of the community.

Carrying the bowl of muesli to the couch, I take a mouthful as I turn on the TV. I've timed it almost perfectly for the seven am news.

As I shovel another spoonful into my greedy mouth, I freeze. On the screen, a female reporter I've seen many times before looks into the camera, her face serious. But it's not her that has me frozen. It's the man beside her, and what I see behind them.

'*I have Jim Rainey from the Department of Agriculture with an update on the foot-and-mouth outbreak here in Cascade,*' the reporter announces.

I grab the remote and turn the volume up too loud as Rainey nods and looks straight at me.

'*At this stage, the infected animals have been destroyed, and there's been no further evidence of infection in the area.*'

'*And when did the farmer in question notify you of the outbreak?*' the reporter asks.

Rainey hesitates. My heart thunders.

Don't do it!

But of course, he does.

'*Ah, fortunately, the local vet discovered the signs in the cattle. He's more than likely saved this country's meat and dairy industry from a catastrophe.*'

Shit!

The reporter's brow furrows in confusion. '*Are you saying the farmer had no intention of reporting the disease?*'

'*No comment,*' Rainey says.

I take in a sharp breath, forgetting the muesli still in my mouth, and choke. As I get up and thump my chest, I wonder why the hell Rainey didn't say those last two words at the beginning of the interview.

Too damn late now.

I wolf down the rest of my breakfast and get ready for work. This isn't going be the pleasant first day back I expected.

With Sam in the passenger seat beside me, I flick on my headlights and drive along the foggy gravel, unable to stop myself from searching out the place on the other side of the fence where I almost died. Then I hit the accelerator and rocket along the rest of the driveway.

As I round the first bend in the road, I see the signs, then the faint shape of the roadblock barriers and, blocking one lane, a trailer loaded with a large water container. Two guys wander in aimless circles in front of the barrier, their hands deep in their high-viz jackets in an effort to keep warm.

I ease off the accelerator, pull up and slide down the window, letting in a stream of frigid air. The younger of the pair makes his way to the front of my vehicle. Sam's ears prick up with interest.

'Morning, mate,' he says, sniffling from the cold.

'Morning,' I say, never eager for small talk. 'I'm Daniel Clark, the local vet. Should be right for me to go into town today.'

'No worries,' he says. 'Pete's just gotta confirm that.'

Pete wanders towards us, checking something off a clipboard. I'm guessing he's got a list of licence plates and mine's one of them.

'Morning, Dr Clark,' he says. 'You followed the procedure before leaving your property?'

'Sure did,' I confirm.

'Okay. We'll just need to decontaminate your tyres and undercarriage, then you'll be right to go.'

'No problem.'

When they both move towards the large water container on the back of the trailer, I slide my window up and blast the heater.

Sam whines. I give her head a gentle pat. 'Won't be long, girl.'

The younger guy starts up a generator, then Pete powers on a high-pressure hose. I watch in my side mirrors as Pete sprays my rear tyres, suds forming when the water hits the rubber.

As he's finishing, the younger guy taps on my window.

'Just a heads-up,' he says, 'there're some reporters further along the road. We told 'em they had to stay well clear of the decontamination area, but how well clear they've stayed, I can't tell you.'

Just what I bloody well need.

'Thanks for the warning,' I say with a fake smile.

'No worries, mate. Well, Pete's finished, so you're right to go.' He gives my windowsill two slaps and waves me on.

Pete finishes moving the portable barrier from my path, and I drive through, giving him a wave as I pass.

What I really want to do is hang a U-turn and head straight home. Only embarrassment and the knowledge that I'll have to do it all over again stops me. I need to go into work. I can't put it off any longer.

Emily's kept me up to date, letting me know everyone understood and rescheduled their appointments for my return today. The animals that couldn't wait for treatment were seen by the vet in Riverview. So, I just have to push on and face what the world throws at me.

I drive forward with caution, and sure enough, only

a few hundred metres from the decontamination station, I see the faint outline of two white vans with satellite dishes on top and a group of rugged-up people milling about.

With the temperature around zero, I'm astounded these people bother putting themselves through the discomfort and boredom of waiting for someone to drive along this deserted road. But I guess, like the decontamination guys, they have a job to do. I also guess they know this is my first day back at work.

When they see me coming, they swarm over the road, forcing me to slow to a crawl as I grow closer, then to a stop. Either that or run a couple of them over. Probably not a good look, especially since a middle-aged man with a camera is pointing the damn thing straight at me. And he's planted himself firmly in front of my vehicle. I want to blast the horn, but it's just not in me to attract more attention. I lower the sun visor and pull my parka hood over my head, hoping he can't get a good shot of me, hoping he hasn't already.

In my peripheral, I see a man with a microphone standing beside my window. I refuse to look at him. It doesn't take long before he taps on the glass.

'Dr Clark!' he shouts. 'Dr Clark? The Department of Agriculture has stated you may have saved the meat and dairy industry from catastrophe. Care to comment?'

My heart beats hard. I need to get out of here, away from the media, away from the cameras.

'Dr Clark?' the reporter yells, his knuckles tapping frantically on the window as I inch the Landcruiser forward. After I apply a steady force to my forward movement, the cameraman shuffles out of my path, and I hit the accelerator.

When my mother hears about this, she'll just about have kittens, not to mention some strong words reminding me how important it is to stay out of the spotlight.

Like I don't already know.

- 33 -

KELSEY

AFTER LUXURIATING IN A deep claw-foot bath at the quaint little bed and breakfast I'd stayed at last night, I feel renewed and full of excitement as I drive past the sign welcoming me to Cascade.

Tapping my fingers on the steering wheel in time to the beat coming from the radio, I can barely believe I'm here.

By the time I drive along the main street, the fog has burned away, revealing a gorgeous winter day to welcome me to my new home and my new life.

While I look for a parking space, I notice far more activity going on than when I'd been here to inspect the property I purchased. As I search the street, I see two news vans further along and wonder what's happening in this small town to attract the media.

Before I can think too much about it, I find a parking space in front of the café I remember fondly from the days Dad used to bring me here. Sweeping my hair over the left side of my face, knowing it only partially covers the scars, I haul myself out of the car and pull on a jacket.

When I shut the door, I notice an elderly woman staring at me from the window of the car next to mine. I quickly turn away and hurry along the street. Determined not to let anything spoil my first day in my new home town, I take a deep breath and walk into the real estate office.

Jackie Baker, who sold me the property, and who's the only agent in town, spots me immediately. She beams, rises from behind her desk and rushes forward, flinging her arms around me in an unexpected hug. Taken by surprise, I return the hug, noticing I actually like the warmth of her welcome. Just one more thing I never experienced in the city.

'Kelsey. Welcome! Are you excited?' She asks as she pulls away and pats my shoulder.

I nod, taking in her upbeat energy, how contagious it is. We're about the same age, and that energy reminds me of who I'd once been. Before the fire.

I already like Jackie, but even though we've met a few times, she still glances at my scars. I don't hold it against her, though. She's been nothing but supportive and friendly throughout the whole purchase process. I know that's her job, but can see a genuineness in her that makes me think we might soon be friends. I just need to give people time to adjust to my appearance. I have to hold strong to the belief that the more they see the scars, the less they'll notice them.

'Any idea what time the removalists are arriving?'

Jackie asks.

'I spoke to them this morning. They said around two.'

'Great. Okay, well, I'll just get your keys …'

As Jackie turns away, I glance at the young receptionist. She gives me a quick smile before putting her head down and attacking the keyboard. I have the distinct impression she isn't typing anything but scrambled letters. That's okay, too, I remind myself. How many times did that happen when I walked into any sort of office in the city? The stares, then the avoidance. It's nothing new.

Jackie returns with a bunch of jangling keys and hands them over.

'Well, that's it as far as the house goes. Now, don't be a stranger.' She takes my arm and lowers her voice. 'It'd be nice to have another friend around my own age. Sometimes I don't even know what the hell that girl is talking about.' She rolls her eyes towards the receptionist and smiles. 'I think she gets off on making me feel old.'

I grin. 'Okay, that'd be nice.'

Jackie releases me. 'Great. Oh, and I don't know if you saw the banner up over the pub? But there's a town talent show in about six weeks. To celebrate spring. We try to get everyone to participate in some way or another. It's a great way to keep the community close. And you'll be sure to meet almost everyone.' She pats my arm. 'Now there's no getting out of it, you hear me? Have a think and let me know what you might be able to help with behind the scenes. Promise?'

I try hard to hide the hurt that shoots right to my heart. Already I'm being allocated to the background, too ugly to be seen, to perform myself.

Pushing down on the lump forming in my throat, telling myself Jackie didn't mean anything by it, I plaster on a smile. 'Okay, I promise to think about it.'

'Great. Now you go and enjoy your new home. Give me a call or pop in when you're all settled, and we'll have lunch.'

'Sure,' I say, not sure of anything anymore. 'Thanks again for all your help.'

She gives my shoulder a warm squeeze before I turn and push through the door. One thing I'm not used to is someone touching me, gushing all over me and wanting to be my friend. Well, except in high school, when it was all about how cruel the girls could be by sucking me in, making me feel like I belonged, only to push me away because they just hadn't realised they couldn't possibly look at my face every day without it making them sick.

Stop it!

That's over. This is my reality now and high school was a lifetime ago. I have to stop letting it scar me on the inside, too.

Aware of the news vans further along the street, I pick up my pace, keep my head down and pretend to study the keys in my hand. As I draw closer to my car, I don't see the guy step from the café until I bump into him with a hard jolt.

Mortified, feeling everything spiralling out of control, I don't bother offering an apology, nor do I hear one from him. I keep my head down and barrel on towards my car.

'Kelsey!' Jackie calls from behind me. All I want is to get to my new home and embrace the isolation. I can do without another bonding session right now. Maybe if I pretend I haven't heard her ...

'Kelsey! Kelsey! Wait up!'

No such luck. I turn to see Jackie power-walking towards me in heels, a small set of keys dangling from an outstretched finger. As she passes the guy I'd bumped into, I make the terrible mistake of meeting his gaze.

His eyes are riveted to my scars, his mouth slightly open, a look of utter shock on his face. And then the cardboard tray containing two takeaway coffees slips from his gloved hand. They splatter on the pavement, splashing his jeans and boots. Yet he doesn't even notice. He still can't stop staring at me.

Jackie hasn't escaped the coffee splash, either. She turns on the guy, putting her hands on her hips. 'What the hell's wrong with you?'

He seems to jerk out of a trance. His eyes shoot down to the spilt coffees before he turns away and high-tails it in the opposite direction.

I stand motionless, unable to believe what just happened. Sure, people in the city always stared at me, but I'd never had a reaction like that. He'd been completely horrified by my appearance. So much so he'd apparently lost the use of his hands.

My throat closes and water springs to my eyes. From excitement to crestfallen in an instant. And I hate myself for it. I want to blame that arsehole for the way I feel, but I learned long ago that no one's responsible for my emotions but me. Still, his reaction to my face had been way over the top.

As Jackie turns towards me, I fight hard to stay in control. Unfortunately, she hasn't missed the look on my face.

'Oh, sweetie, please don't take any notice of him,' she says gently.

'Pretty hard not to.'

She seems stumped for something to say to that, so she holds up the keys. 'I almost forgot. The keys to the barn. We found them. Well, Stacy did. By accident, of course. It's not like she'd go to any extra effort to help.'

To my surprise, I find Jackie's babble calming. As my throat loosens, I hold out a hand and she places the keys in my palm.

'Thanks,' I say, giving her a weak smile. I turn towards my car, and when I open the door, I realise she's following me.

'I mean it, Kelsey. Don't pay any attention to him. He's the town freak.'

Her comment bites into me the same way the cold bites into my flesh. Before I can control myself, the words rush from my mouth. 'If he's a freak, then what does that make me?'

I see the shame on Jackie's face and instantly regret my words. Though, right now, I'm in no mood to comfort someone else. Instead, I climb into my car, start it up and reverse out too quickly.

Tyres screech and a horn blares. Slamming on the brakes, I look in the rear-view mirror to see I've narrowly missed another news van. Shaken, I put the car in gear and drive away.

Some start to the first day of your new life.

Dad isn't right, I tell myself. Even the arsehole who dropped his coffees will eventually get used to me.

Refusing to wallow in my own pity party, I look ahead in my mind and focus on arriving at my new home. Once I've dealt with the removalists, I'll be alone. Alone and free to walk out my front door anytime I choose without having to think about my face.

Something that, two decades ago, I'd taken for granted.

- 34 -

LUCAS

A COWARD. SCUM. ARSEHOLE. Jerk.

I'm all of those things and more.

In a small side alley off the main street, I lean against the wall of the local hair salon and hang my head in shame.

The shock of seeing her had utterly blindsided me. The scars were unmistakable. I'd only ever seen them once, but that's all it took to have them etched in my memory forever. They hadn't been the cause of my heart leaping from my chest, though. That happened the moment I heard her name.

Twenty years since I've heard it said aloud. The billion times I've heard it in my head don't count. Of course, there's more than one person in the world with that name. For all I'd known, it could've been a man.

Which was why I'd had to look. And there she was.

Even though she had her hair styled to cover her scars, there was only so much she could hide. Besides, that ten-year-old girl was still there in her face. A face I've never forgotten. And the vivid memory has nothing to do with her scars.

Since I'm not normal, I hadn't acted like a normal person. I hadn't walked up to her and said, 'Hi, remember me?' Nope. Instead, I'd let a flood of memories take over not only my mind, but my body, and I'd dropped the bloody coffees.

Could I have been any more of a dick? I doubt it. And when I saw the look on her face, I'd run away and hidden like the coward I am. The perfect reaction of any average, socially inept freak.

My mind replays the look on her face over and over as I try to remember if I saw any recognition in her eyes. Horror and hurt are all I can conjure up. Is that how she'd feel if she recognised me?

Jesus. Had she?

Although her appearance hasn't changed much, mine certainly has. At sixteen, I'd decided not to hide behind that long hair anymore. Emily hadn't liked the idea. She wanted my face hidden so it wouldn't be recognised should anything problematic happen. When I told her I'd do it myself, she'd given in and used the number-four clippers. I remember her surprise when she finished. She looked at me like she'd lost something. When I'd walked into the bathroom and stared into the mirror, I knew what she'd lost. The boy who'd hidden behind long hair all his life had vanished. Replaced by the man I'd started to become. After that, I'd kept it short and neat, and over time it grew thicker and darker, erasing that kid forever.

So for now, I'll go on the assumption that Kelsey has no idea who I am. Though I suppose I'm counting my chickens. She could just be visiting or passing through, but the fact that Jackie Baker handed her a set of keys seems to indicate otherwise.

And hadn't Mrs Winston mentioned something about a woman moving into the old Edwards' farm?

Oh, shit.

Fuck.

Wow!

When I peer around the corner of the building, there's no sign of Kelsey or Jackie, so I hurry towards the real estate agency.

Jackie Baker glares at me the moment I set foot inside. 'Come to apologise?'

I haven't, but I say, 'Yeah.'

'Well, you've got the wrong person,' she points out.

'Where do I find the right one?'

Her eyes widen a little. 'Ha! Nice try. As if I'd tell you anything about that poor woman.'

That poor woman.

I don't like the sound of that at all. But I know better than to stand here and argue with Jackie.

I turn away, open the door and step out. 'I'll be sending you my dry-cleaning bill!' Jackie yells after me.

Why I thought Jackie would reveal if Kelsey purchased the old Edwards' property, I have no idea. I've barely acknowledged her since I moved here. Back then, her father had been the one to sell me my property.

Hurrying towards my clinic, I'm intercepted by the same woman I saw on TV this morning. She's confident, hair and makeup perfect, clothes the expensive type no one around here bothers with. It's quite surreal seeing her standing in my path instead of inside an electronic rectangle.

'Excuse me,' she says politely. 'Are you Daniel Clark?'

I try to step around her, but she's ready for that and mirrors my move.

'Daniel Clark? The local vet. Is that you?'

'Why?' Jesus, that sounds like a yes, even to me.

'I'm from Channel Eight News. We're here to do a story on the outbreak of the foot-and-mouth disease.'

We? I glance to the left and see a guy pulling a camera from a news van. Shit.

'Sorry, don't know where he is,' I say and successfully skirt around her.

I know she's watching as I take the few steps to the clinic door, slip inside and shut it behind me. As I twist the lock, she grabs the handle, rattles the door and glares at me through the glass. I pull the blind down and let out a breath. I can't deal with reporters now. There are more important things to think about.

'What the hell's going on?'

I whirl around. Emily stands behind the reception desk.

'What?' I pretty much gulp. How did she know about Kelsey already?

'With that woman at the door?'

'Oh.' I shrug with relief. 'Who knows?'

'From the look on your face, I'd say you.'

I move away from the door. 'Some reporter about the FMD.'

'That's the last thing you need.'

'You think I don't know that?' Reporters have been one of my mother's worst fears. Which directly translates to one of mine.

'So, what now?' she asks.

'Avoid them, I guess.'

'It's going to be a little difficult running the clinic with the door locked, isn't it? You're totally booked.'

'Jesus.' Why the hell did this have to happen now? 'They can't come onto private property, right?'

Emily thinks about that for a moment. 'Well, since we're open to the public, I think they can. But if I ask them to leave, I think they have to.'

'Good. Do that. Leave the open sign on the door but keep it locked. You'll just have to let everyone in as they arrive.'

'Fine.'

I head along the short corridor.

'Hey? Where's my coffee?' she calls.

I think it's best to ignore that question, so I continue into the exam room and close the door.

All day I keep busy with patient after patient. Amazing how a few days off can spark a rush. I soon realise that most are using their pets' non-existent problems as a cover to ask for juicy details about the events at the Hargraves' farm. I suppose I knew this would happen. They're locals, after all, but I strongly suspect some of their questions are coming directly from the reporters in town.

Nothing I can do about that, though. So, I respond by telling them I know as much as they do. Most grow quiet after that. A few push, but I just shrug and focus on their pets. They can't force me to talk and they're more than familiar with my poor communication skills.

But I'm grateful for the unusually high workload. It takes my mind off Kelsey. At least for a few seconds.

- 35 -

KELSEY

AFTER SEEING OFF THE removalists, I head inside, grab a throw rug from the couch and wrap myself in the soft fabric. Stepping outside onto my new verandah, I pull on my boots and give a slight shiver against the rapidly dropping temperature.

Finally, utterly, blissfully alone.

I sigh as I walk along the wraparound verandah, which was what sold me on this place. I hadn't had a porch or balcony in the apartments I'd rented in the city. When I'd seen this verandah, I'd imagined sitting here in the sun on a cool day, soaking up the warm rays, and in the next instant I'd imagined sitting beneath the shade of the roof on a hot summer's afternoon, a cool drink in one hand, a good book in the other, my guitar at my side.

And the best thing of all? The nearest neighbours are ten acres away in every direction.

Clomping along the wooden boards, I round the corner of the house so I'm facing west. Leaning against the railing, which will need some maintenance in the near future, I gaze across the rolling hills and let the silence wash over me as I watch the last of the sun dip below the horizon.

The underbelly of the few clouds blaze in a dazzling display of oranges and pinks. I can't help but take my phone from my pocket and snap a few photos. Maybe, if any of them are any good, I can get one printed and framed to hang on the living-room wall. A first step in making my new house an actual home.

The perfect end to a not-so-perfect day.

As the light fades fast, I put the throw rug away, then almost skip down the verandah steps to my car. Retrieving a jacket and slipping it on, I hurry along the dirt driveway towards the large barn.

Halfway there, I stop and turn in a circle. The freedom of being outside without a single thought that someone's staring, is overwhelmingly liberating. I knew it would be, but to actually experience it, to know I'm totally alone, that no one will judge me, brings sudden tears to my eyes.

For a long moment, I stand in the middle of the driveway and let the water flow over my cheeks, let the slight breeze cool them against my skin until they're so icy cold I can't help but wipe them away.

Sniffling, I smile. Right out in the open, I can cry all I want, can laugh and talk to myself, and no one will ever know.

Turning in a slow circle again, taking everything in, everything that's now mine, I feel something deep down welling inside me. I stop turning to stare at the land before me; at the gentle hills that dip and rise until they meet the horizon, not another living thing in sight. And that feeling in my gut rises higher until it reaches my lungs. Suddenly, I know what it is. I let it come, *want* it to come, and soon it's in my throat.

Then I let go.

And scream and scream.

Loud and hard and with everything I've got, I let out all the torment of every rotten thing anyone's ever said about my scars, let out the fact I'll never be who I was supposed to be. I release the pain and loneliness until there's nothing left, until it leaves me so weak, it brings me to my knees.

After one final scream, I gasp for air, and it feels so damn good, like I've been freed from the prison of my past.

As my breath comes back to me, I notice the sharp stones digging into the denim of my jeans. Rising, exhaustion and elation battle inside my body. I'll sleep well tonight, and already I can't wait to wake up and live the rest of my new life in this sanctuary.

But first, I want to inspect the large barn. Even in the twilight, I can see faint traces of red paint clinging to the ageing planks of wood. More work I look forward to. I hadn't wanted a place that required zero upkeep. With an abundance of time on my hands, I need something to keep myself busy during the stretches when I'm not writing, but waiting for inspiration.

As the light dwindles, I regret not bringing a torch with me. Inserting a key into the padlock on the barn door, I twist until the rusty lock releases. Swinging the door open, darkness greets me. As I reach around the doorframe and feel for a light switch, I hear a rip and jerk my hand away.

White stuffing protrudes through a tear in the arm of my brand-new jacket.

'Damn it,' I mutter and step into the barn, letting my eyes adjust to the darkness. When I make out the white rectangle of a light switch, I turn it on. Fluorescent lights flicker until they catch and hold steady.

I finger the rip in my jacket again with annoyance. Now I can see exactly what caused the tear. A sharp but rusty nail protrudes from the doorframe. Touching it, I frown, glad I hadn't cut myself.

Suddenly, I'm ten again and back on the roof of that apartment building I've tried to erase from my memory. I see myself lifting a plank of wood and inspecting the rusty nail, can almost recall the pain of it going straight through my foot.

And then Lucas.

'Stop it,' I scold myself, shutting down the memory. No good can come of thinking about *him*. Only pain from the loss of someone so special.

Scanning the barn, I take in the four stables, two on each side, distracting myself with the thought of them housing a few horses soon. I walk along the wide corridor, and after the last stable on the left, I discover a workbench covered in dust. An old hammer rests amongst the clutter left behind by the previous owners. Jackie explained they'd moved closer to the city months ago to be near their grandchildren, the acreage too much for them to maintain any longer. Since they moved into an apartment, I'd agreed to sign the contract for sale to take possession of the property as is.

As I reach for the hammer, my phone vibrates in my pocket. I pluck it out to see Dad's face on the screen.

'Hey.'

'Hey, pump—how's—day going?'

'Hang on,' I say, hoping he can hear me better than I can hear him. 'The reception's crap. Wait a sec.'

As I hurry back the way I came, I turn off the lights and close the door, not bothering to lock up. Walking towards the house in the darkness, I notice white plumes of breath rush out before me. 'Hey, Dad. Is that any better?'

'Sounds good to me,' he answers.

'Great. What were you saying?'

'Just asking how your first day's going.'

'I'm loving it,' I tell him truthfully. Then remember. 'Except for one arsehole in town who freaked when he saw my face. Other than that, it's everything I want.'

'I'm sort of sad to hear that.'

'Dad …'

'I'm just kidding, pumpkin. I'm happy that you're happy. Can't wait to get there and check it all out. Maybe give you a hand with anything you need done around the place?'

I smile, head up the steps to my new home and let myself into the warmth.

'I'd like that,' I say. 'But I want some time to settle in first, okay?'

'Whatever you need, I'm here for you.'

After I hang up, I rummage through a few kitchen boxes until I find a packet of instant noodles. Flicking on the kettle, I start a shopping list. I'll have to brave the town again tomorrow and get some actual food.

- 36 -

LUCAS

I SEE MY LAST patient out the door just after seven-thirty. It's been a long day and Emily left hours ago, but I was determined to catch up on all the appointments I'd missed.

It's not like I needed a distraction or anything.

All day, the reporters hung around outside the clinic. Emily told me that each time a client arrived, they were accosted and questioned. She also informed me that nearly everyone was happy to answer questions and sing my praises. Seems this is the most exciting thing to happen here in a long time.

Now that I'm turning off all the lights for the night, now that there are no more distractions, she's right in my head, where I don't want her to be.

Kelsey Wells.

'C'mon, girl,' I call to Sam. She rises from her bed behind reception and follows me outside.

As I lock up, I check the street. Two blocks away, one lone news van sits outside the only pub in town. Probably having dinner, staying there the night before giving up and heading out tomorrow.

I can only hope.

Opening the Landcruiser's door, Sam jumps in and hops over to the passenger seat before I climb in after her, start the car and crank the heater.

Gripping the wheel with my gloved hands, I stare through the windscreen, completely lost in thoughts I don't want.

During my first year at university, and after almost giving up on my endless search for Kelsey, I finally tracked down her father. His name had popped up in a Google alert after he started a new job, the company congratulating their newest employee in a public blog. So, I'd hung around outside his workplace like a stalker, waiting for him to leave for the day. It was easy to spot him; he'd barely changed. But he'd had no idea who I was when I approached him. After explaining myself, the conflict on his face was unmistakable. I offered him my gloved hand to shake, and he took it, but I hadn't missed his reluctance.

We walked across the street to the park and took a seat. He thanked me for saving his daughter's life, said he was glad to see I'd survived as well. And it seemed like he meant it.

'I want to see her,' I told him.

His whole face changed, and he shook his head. 'After the fire … she insisted I find you. I tried, but I couldn't. No trace of you. Not anywhere. Your mother was obviously protecting you. Can't say I blame her.'

'I'm here now. I want to see her.'

'Can you fix her face?' he asked, looking me dead in the eyes.

I wanted to lie to him, but the fact he'd even asked that question meant something. 'I don't think so,' I admitted.

He'd thought about that for a long moment. 'Then I can't ... I won't allow it,' he said.

'I think she's old enough to make her own decision.'

'That's got nothing to do with anything. She's finally got her life on track, has a purpose, has finally accepted who she is now. She can't go through everything you'll bring up again. You have no idea the struggle I've been through with her. Unless you can do something about her scars, stay the fuck away from her. Or you'll only cause her more damage.'

And with that, he got up and walked away.

So I left it at that. Her father knew her better than anyone. He loved her and only wanted what was best for her. The last thing I wanted to do was hurt her. But I made no promises to Shane Wells. While I never tried to find her again, I did move to the one place I thought she might eventually come to. Of course, the chances were slim. It'd only been a little girl's dream, after all.

Sam whines, no doubt wondering why we're not moving. I tear my attention away from the images in my mind and look into her dark eyes.

'If she recognises me, you know what she'll want me to do, right?'

She'll want me to fix her face. She'll want me to do what I desperately wanted to do twenty years ago, but failed to.

Sam's ears twitch back and forth as she sticks out her snout and sniffs.

'That's right,' I tell her. 'And I can't crush her like that. Just have to avoid her like I avoid everyone else.'

Sam licks her lips and sits up straighter, her eyes never leaving mine.

'Jesus,' I sigh, 'I never thought she'd actually turn up.'

Sam tilts her head, one ear standing at attention.

'Don't give me that look. I didn't!'

Even Sam doesn't believe my lies. I'm sure if she could speak, she'd ask me why the hell I moved here, then. The answer to that question is so complex even I find it difficult to get it straight in my mind. I know we had a connection when we were kids. But I don't know if that's just a normal part of childhood. I know when I think of her, I feel warmth and hope. But I don't know if that's simply because she knew my secret.

Driving away from the clinic, I wonder what sort of life she's had. Unlike me, I know she hasn't followed her dream. I listen to the radio. I'm aware of the popular artists, and she's not one of them. I occasionally searched the internet and still can't find her name. If I hadn't failed her, I'm sure she'd be famous, loved by everyone.

But my mother's words come back to me. Kelsey might have had a different life, but I wouldn't have had a life at all. Saving her by healing her lungs and trachea had killed me. The only thing that saved me that day was the instant action of the doctors, and even then I spent a few days in a coma before my body recovered enough to heal itself. If I'd placed my hand on Kelsey's face, too, there would have been no bringing me back from the dead. I have no doubt about that.

Yet I still I wish I'd done it.

<><><>

The next morning, with my wipers swishing across the windscreen, I park in front of the clinic. Raising my jacket's hood, Sam and I make a dash for it and collide with the locked door. I hurriedly find the key and let us inside.

No sign of Emily. I turn on the lights and heating, then give Sam a towel dry. As she's making herself comfortable in her bed, the bell above the door jingles. Emily stands there, hair wet from the rain, eyes wide as they focus on me.

'What?' I ask, afraid she's discovered that Kelsey's here.

'You haven't seen it?'

Not Kelsey, then. 'Seen what?'

She reaches into her large handbag, withdraws a thin newspaper and holds it up. *Cascade Gazette* is blazoned in red across the top and just below that, the headline 'LOCAL HERO'.

Beneath those words is a photo. Of me.

'When did they—'

'I can't believe this!' She rushes forward and slaps the paper down on the reception counter between us.

Ignoring her hysterics, I study the photo, realising they must have taken it yesterday just before Kelsey bumped into me. They certainly couldn't have taken it afterwards. I look far too relaxed.

'Lucas!' Emily shouts, jerking me from my thoughts.

'What happened to Dan?' I ask.

'This is the last thing you need,' she snaps, jabbing at my face on the paper.

I sigh. 'Mum, no one cares. It's not like it's a story about what I can *do*. It's a story about cattle being destroyed to save the community, about a devastating disease being stopped in its tracks.'

She looks at me with scepticism. 'You haven't even read it. It's about you! About you being a hero. How you've possibly saved the whole of Australia from catastrophe.'

I shrug. 'So? They said that on the news yesterday morning.'

'Not everyone around here watches morning television. Even with those damn reporters hanging around yesterday, it still wasn't too bad. But, Lucas, *everyone* reads the *Gazette*! Don't you see? This'll make people pay attention to you.'

She's called me Lucas twice in the space of a minute. She's freaking out, but I really don't care. The only reason I've ever tried to keep people at a distance is so they won't get to know me and learn what I can do. They all know I'm a vet and they'll all know I was just doing my job.

'Nothing'll change. Sure, people might pay a little more attention to me … for all of one day, then I'll be yesterday's news. Big whoop.'

'Don't you big whoop me! You don't seem to—'

'Mum! I'm thirty years old. You have to stop this mollycoddling. This is my life, not yours. Go get your own!'

From the look on her face, I may as well have slapped her, and she may as well have slapped me back, because the words that just spewed from my mouth cut me as much as they obviously cut her.

'I'm sorry … I just … I …' Like a fool, I'm not sure how to defend myself. Probably because there is no defence.

She holds up a hand and shakes her head. 'You're right.'

I stare at her, stunned. 'No, I'm not. I shouldn't have said—'

'Maybe not, but you did.' The utter sadness on her face, in her eyes, leaves me at a complete loss as to what I should do.

'You'd better go dry that hair,' I say after a moment, seeing she needs a little time to compose herself.

'What about this?' she asks, pointing to the newspaper.

'Like I said, it's nothing. It'll blow over.'

She gives me a dubious look, then heads towards the hallway.

<><><>

Later that afternoon, I receive a call-out to a small hobby farm with a goat having a hard time giving birth. After successfully delivering two healthy kids and getting the proud mother back on her feet, I head towards town.

Driving through the rain with Sam curled up on the passenger seat, I spot a car parked on the other side of the road, hazards flashing. I slow down and lean forward in my seat. A woman squats before the front driver's side tyre. Closer now, I see her struggling with a tyre iron, clearly not having much luck.

I release a sigh as I slow even more, ready to pull over and help. Even though I don't want to, I will. I might be a freak, but I'm not a total pig.

Hearing my vehicle approach, she stands, faces me and raises a hand over her head to flag me down.

That's when I see who she is.

Kelsey Wells.

With her wet hair plastered around her face, her scars are on full display.

Unless you can do something about her scars, stay the fuck away from her. Or you'll only cause her more damage.

'Shit,' I mumble under my breath. Giving her a wide berth, I put my foot down. 'Shit, shit, shit.'

Sam looks at me with questioning eyes.

After I shoot past Kelsey, I stare into the rear-view mirror. She flips me the finger and keeps it there until I take a bend and she disappears from sight.

I can't stop the grin that stretches my lips as I glance at Sam and say, 'You see that? Pretty rude, right?'

As the bend straightens, my smile fades. Sam gazes at me with interest. I shake my head.

'No way. Too risky.'

- 37 -

KELSEY

I STARE AFTER THE absolute arsehole who just blew past me. I know whoever the creep is, he'd been about to stop and help. Before he spotted my face. Then he couldn't get away fast enough. Not that I'm surprised.

I trudge to the front of the car. Country roads and compact cars obviously don't agree with each other. The damn pothole had been filled with water, which was why I hadn't seen it. But I'd certainly felt it.

Too bad, too sad. Just get on with it.

If only I could.

Reattaching the tyre iron to the one nut that refuses to budge, I spread my hands on the bonnet for support, stand on the implement and bounce my weight on it, hoping to loosen the nut this time.

No such luck.

I growl with frustration, no longer sure if the water on my face is rain alone. Since I know how to change a damn tyre, I hate that I'm failing just because one stupid nut is stuck fast.

Then I hear the faint rumble of an engine. I look up to see the same four-wheel-drive from moments ago driving past again. Only this time, it pulls up in front of my car.

Not wanting to acknowledge my relief, I step off the tyre iron and cross my arms as the battered vehicle's door opens. And out steps the guy who dropped his coffees at the sight of my face.

'Just fucking great,' I mumble, digging my short nails into my palms as he hurries over.

He stops a few metres from me, a sheepish expression on his stupid face. 'Need help?'

'Not from you,' I snap.

His eyes widen a little, but I could give a crap about offending him.

Then he smiles. A full-on, perfect, teeth-revealing smile, his eyes coming alive as he looks into mine, blinking to keep out the rain.

My stomach lurches. No one ever looks me in the eye, not for long, anyway. But this guy's gaze is unwavering. That's when I notice something I don't want to notice at all. Even with the rain flattening his hair, he's damn good-looking. Movie-star good-looking.

Shit.

Nobody knows better than I do that appearances are meaningless, and he's already proven that beneath his surface is nothing but a total arsehole.

Spinning on my heel, I march to the boot, lift the

lid and stare inside. I have zero idea what the hell I'm looking for, only that I can't stand around staring at him. It's then I realise he never once flicked his gaze to my scars. The complete opposite of what he did on the main street when he first laid eyes on me. And worse still, the rain has drenched my hair, leaving the scars more exposed than ever. But he hadn't looked.

Unable to help myself, I peer past the boot lid and watch him squat beside the flat tyre, grasp the tyre iron and strain.

Wrenching my gaze away, I spot a hammer in the toolkit Dad insists I keep in the boot. Maybe I can bash the tyre iron hard enough to jolt the nut loose. Grasping the handle, I approach him and open my mouth to tell him to get lost.

The nut gives way and the tyre iron spins in his gloved hands.

'I said, I don't want your help,' I say, grinding my teeth.

He glances up, his eyes locking onto the hammer clutched in my hand. 'Plan on bludgeoning me to death for changing a tyre against your will?'

'Sounds like a great idea.'

Just before he turns back to the wheel, he grins. My fingers tighten around the hammer.

He's enjoying this.

'And why do I deserve that?' he asks, a teasing lilt to his voice as he unscrews the remaining nuts I'd managed to loosen.

'You think I've forgotten?'

His gloved fingers freeze on the last nut, and even though I can't see his face, I know that stupid grin has vanished. So, he did have a conscience, after all.

'Forgotten what?' he asks, his fingers motionless.

I gape at him. 'Jesus. Your horrified reaction to the sight of my face.'

Slowly, he stands and turns towards me, his expression tense. 'You think that's why?'

He's standing closer now, and even though I don't want to, I take in every inch of his face while glaring at him. 'Could there possibly be another reason?'

We stare at each other, and he seems to be waiting for me to say something, even though I'm the one who asked a question. Still, his eyes never leave mine.

After a moment, he gives a small shrug and says, 'I guess not.' Striding past me, he heads to the rear of the car.

'You should've kept on driving,' I shout after him. 'It's pretty obvious that's what you wanted to do.'

'Yeah,' he says, as he lifts the jack from the boot and carries it to the front of the car. 'Maybe I should have.'

Oh, he's got some nerve. Shouldn't he be apologising for driving past, for his disgusting behaviour in town?

He ignores me, leaving me staring at his back as he positions the jack and raises the car. Well, I refuse to be ignored. He should be embarrassed by his disgraceful behaviour.

'In fact,' I say, stepping closer, 'I'm amazed you didn't swerve right off the road and crash this time.'

He removes the loosened nuts and rocks the wheel until it falls free, and I'm sure he's going to continue to ignore me. Then he stands and looks at me with a frown.

'So,' he says, 'since you seem to want to talk about it so much, what happened to you?'

'Are you kidding me?'

'No. But if you don't want to say, that's fine.'

'As if I'd tell *you*.'

He gives me that I-could-give-a-damn shrug again and rolls the flat tyre towards me, glancing at me as he passes, once again showing no sign of revulsion in those incredible green eyes.

He hauls the spare tyre from the boot, gets it in position and tightens the nuts. That's when I notice his leather gloves are not only filthy now, but soaking wet. Completely ruined.

Good.

Not wanting to spend another minute more than necessary with him, I toss the hammer in the boot and try to lift the flat tyre. It slips from my freezing fingers and splats on the wet gravel.

'Shit!'

Before I can try again, he's there beside me, lifting it into the boot like it weighs nothing. Retrieving the jack and tyre iron, he places them in as well.

'All done,' he says, meeting my eyes again before striding away.

'Don't think I'm accepting this as some sort of apology!' I shout.

'Nobody asked you to,' he shoots over his shoulder.

I stare after him, unable to believe he didn't even attempt to apologise, let alone talk to me in such a way. What an arse.

As he climbs into his shitty car, I slam the boot lid. Marching to the driver's door, I watch as he does a U-turn and accelerates past without even a glance.

The way he's acting, anyone would think I'd been the rude one.

- 38 -

GEORGIA

RAIN THRUMS ON THE hood of Georgia's parka, her jeans growing wetter and colder against her thighs as she stands in the empty paddock. Lips trembling, her tears create warm rivers amongst the icy drizzle.

Staring down the hill, she watches a front-end loader drop soil into a massive hole filled with dead cattle. A sob escapes her throat, and she turns away in horror, only to find her father standing there.

He wraps her in his arms and rubs her back as she cries into his chest.

'You shouldn't be out here, Georgie.'

She shakes her head, trying to control herself. 'It's all my fault.'

'Don't be stupid,' he tells her.

She extracts herself from his comforting embrace

and looks him in the eye. She doesn't deserve his love, his forgiveness.

'Dad, you knew. Those boots ... I wore them on a farm tour in Japan. They're all dead because of me. Why'd you try to hide it?'

He gently squeezes her shoulders. 'Didn't want you feeling responsible or hating this place because you made a mistake.'

Georgia frowns. He'd never been like this before, had always made her take responsibility for her mistakes. It doesn't make sense.

'But, Dad ... It could've spread. It might—'

'Rubbish. I knew what I was doing.' He wraps an arm around her shoulders and steers her towards the house. 'No use fretting about it. What's done is done.'

She glances up at him, blinking away the rain. 'Is this the end of the farm?'

'Hell no,' he says, pulling her closer. 'I'll get compensation from the government. We'll buy new stock and start over. As long as we stick together, Georgie, we'll be fine.'

But they won't be, will they? Because she won't be here to start over. She just can't.

Sniffing, she lets him walk her back to the house. A house that won't be her home for much longer. She has to tell him. She knows she does. She just can't break his heart this close to the devastation she's already caused.

Not yet.

- 39 -

KELSEY

AFTER A LUXURIOUS HOT bath with a glass of wine and a good book, I place my dinner for one on the breakfast bar and take a seat. Sawing off a piece of juicy steak and chewing, I appreciate Dad for teaching me how to cook. As I prepare another perfect bite, I wonder how things might have been different had I lived with him instead of my mother before the fire.

For one, I wouldn't be a deformed freak.

But would I be here in this beautiful place if I hadn't suffered? Would the lyrics to my songs be as deep, as affecting? Would I have ever sold a single one? Made enough money to buy this property?

Maybe. Maybe not.

Without my hideous appearance, I might be the famous singer I'd dreamed of becoming. Or I could

240

very well be working in an office staring at a computer screen all day, making someone else's dreams come true.

There's always that. And I have to keep a hold of that. A very tight hold.

Okay, enough.

Reaching for my tablet, I find the email confirming my subscription to the Cascade Gazette. After entering my login details, I cut another piece of steak as the page loads. With the delicious meat halfway to my mouth, I freeze.

Staring at me from the Gazette's front page, below the headline 'LOCAL HERO', is the arsehole.

The arsehole who dropped his coffees at the sight of my face.

The arsehole who drove past when I was trying to change a flat tyre.

The arsehole who came back and helped me.

The arsehole I really should have thanked.

Forgetting the steak, I stare at the photo, studying him the way I couldn't when we were face to face.

Even though I can't stand him, I can't deny how attractive he is. My heart speeds up as I stare at the strong jaw, the sweep of his nose, his entire bone structure. But that's not why my heart's pounding. More than anything else, it's those eyes. There's something about him I can't put my finger on, something that draws me in even though that's the last thing I want when it comes to this guy.

And it feels all too familiar.

In a flash, I'm back there, inside the memories of that summer.

Watching Luke before I knew him, feeling something drawing me to him. Then the kitten. Luke healing it. Then Luke healing me. The amazing feeling of warmth and love when he did so. The magic of him, the wonder and joy he filled me with. The way he looked at me when I sang for him. The way he *always* looked at me.

And then the fire. Dad telling me Lucas never came to see me, telling me I was confused about what he could do, telling me to stop making up stories. Then learning Luke was dead.

Coming back to myself, heart thundering in my chest, I breathe fast and shallow.

Where the hell had that come from?

A tear splashes the glass screen on my tablet. Surprised, I swipe at my wet cheeks. I'm not crying, my throat isn't tight, but my eyes leak anyway.

Looking up, I stare through the kitchen window, but only see the images from that summer in my mind. I wish they'd stay buried deep down inside. At least now that I've released them, they should stay away for a while.

Maybe, I try to rationalise, it's this place. Just like when I arrived, all the hurt is coming to the surface. I suppose it's a good thing to exorcise it from my subconscious.

Even though I wish I could deny what I saw that summer, what Luke did and didn't do, I can't. It's insane, impossible, all the things Dad told me, but that doesn't change the fact that I know it's true. Every cell in my body tells me the memories are real. I'd seen it with my own eyes. He could do the impossible.

He'd just chosen not to do it for me.

I wish I knew why, but I'll never know because he's gone.

Wiping the tears from my face again, the window

swims into focus. Sighing, I have to admit Dad was right to tell me to stop talking about him.

Looking at the photo of the guy I want nothing to do with, I can't help but read the article below, desperate to know his name.

When I discover he's the local vet, the hairs at the nape of my neck stand on end.

What the fuck?

And I'm back there again, in the park, telling Luke I'm going to be a famous singer and he should be a vet. That it would be perfect because animals love him, and they can keep his secret.

Heart hammering, I read on, discovering his name is Daniel Clark. Completely unaware I've been holding my breath, I let it rush out in a hiss.

It's not him. Of course it's not him. He's dead.

Idiot.

As my heart begins to settle, I read on, an unwanted respect creeping into my gut. My fingers tremble slightly as I touch the tablet's screen.

'You're still a jerk,' I tell Daniel Clark's frozen face as I scroll, forcing his picture and the article out of sight. I keep on scrolling until I arrive at the classifieds section. Scouring the page, I finally find the heading I'd initially been looking for in the first place.

'HORSES FOR SALE'.

- 40 -

LUCAS

NOW THAT THE DANGER of the foot-and-mouth disease has passed, I find myself sitting on a hard bench at the auctions I'd planned to attend last weekend. For a few months, I've been searching for a new mare to introduce to Beau. So far, no luck.

Even though the auctions are undercover in a large arena that operates as a riding school during the week, the chill in the air keeps my gloved hands in my jacket pockets, my bidding paddle on the bench beside me.

Usually, when I attend these auctions, I sit as close to the arena as possible, but today I sit high in the stands, a baseball cap resting low on my brow, hopefully hiding my features. So far, it's working. No one's recognised me.

As a robust teenager leads a palomino mare into the

arena, I glance around the stadium. There are only around thirty or so people here, so I'm not too worried about competition should the right mare enter the ring. Unfortunately, this mare isn't the one.

While the auctioneer begins his fast-paced spiel, I tune out, my mind already eager to get onto the next exhibit so I can leave.

When the next mare appears, my interest picks up. The handler trots her out and I can see her spirit in the way she bounces, almost floats over the dirt floor. She's a bay, and although her deep brown coat's thick with winter fur, I see past that to the potential beneath.

I bid and am not surprised I'm not the only one. It gets tight—I have a budget—but as I raise my paddle for the last time, the auctioneer shouts, 'Going once, going twice …' and swings his gavel down. 'Sold to bidder two-four-eight.'

I lower my paddle, having just scraped in right on budget. I stand, eager to get the paperwork filled out so I can head home. But instead of walking down the stairs, I freeze.

Below me, hurrying in from the right, is none other than Kelsey Wells. Head lowered, concentration on the stairs, she quickly takes a seat a few levels below me.

I sink down, my need to go forgotten. She's a little late, but she probably got lost on the way. The place can be tricky to find the first time.

I stare at her back, taking in the fact that I'm in her presence again when my plan is to keep right away from her.

Trying not to think of stupid things like destiny and fate, I tell myself it really isn't that astounding to find her here. After all, wasn't it a dream of hers to own a horse? So, she came to an auction to buy one. No real mystery.

I want to get closer to her, but stay where I am. It's not like she'll be happy to see me. She made that pretty damn obvious yesterday. And I don't blame her. How can I?

So, I sit here and watch the parade of horses come and go. She bids on a few that seem like good choices, but loses. Clearly, like me, she has a set budget. Then a young gelding enters. He's full of beans and a little too alert. A guy in a cowboy hat on the other side of the arena raises his paddle.

'Four-fifty,' the auctioneer calls. 'Do I hear—'

Kelsey raises her paddle.

Damn it. I know who owns this horse, and he's got a reputation for being a little dodgy.

'Five hundred,' the auctioneer calls, pointing to Kelsey. 'Do I hear five-fifty?'

Shaking my head in frustration, I get off my arse and climb over the few bench seats in front of me until I'm sitting behind her.

The cowboy raises his paddle again.

'Five-fifty! Do I hear six hundred?' The auctioneer looks at Kelsey.

Before I can speak, she raises her paddle.

As the auctioneer bellows, I lean towards her.

'Not this one,' I say.

She jumps a little, swivels around and stares at me.

'Do I hear six-fifty?' the auctioneer calls.

'Excuse me?' she says, just as pleased to see me as I expected.

'Six-fifty!' the auctioneer yells. 'Do I hear seven hundred?'

'There're better horses,' I tell her. 'Just wait. This one's no good.'

'Who asked you?' she bites, defiance flaring in her eyes. She turns her back on me, her long hair swinging against the smooth material of her parka, and raises her paddle.

'Seven hundred!'

Unable to watch her make a mistake, feeling like I might have actually spurred her on instead of discouraging her, I get up and head towards the paperwork that awaits.

- 41 -

GEORGIA

GEORGIA STEPS ON THE brakes, the rust-bucket ute responding with a high-pitched squeal. After parking, she turns it off, and waits as the engine splutters, gives a shudder, then finally stops.

As she opens the door to yet another squeal, she winces, wondering if there will ever be a day when she might own a vehicle that doesn't constantly voice its complaints in such a loud, obnoxious way. Before pushing the thought aside, she acknowledges she might be the obnoxious one by wishing for such a trivial thing.

Glancing around, hoping the ute hasn't attracted any unnecessary interest, she reaches back inside and plucks her handmade tote bag from the passenger seat. With nobody paying any attention—because why would a bomb of a vehicle like hers draw attention in this hick town—she slips the strap onto her shoulder and puts her hand into the bag, feeling the smooth envelope.

Comfort and guilt assault her, but she hurries along the footpath towards the red mailbox, anyway.

This is your life, and nobody can live it but you. This is what you want. This is what you're good at. This is your future. This is who you're meant to be.

She grips the envelope tight and stops in front of the mailbox. With a deep breath, she removes it from her bag, brings it to her lips and plants a kiss on the address.

'Please,' she whispers. 'Please, please, please.'

Poking it through the slot, she pauses for just a moment before letting it slip from her fingers.

<><><>

Bored, Georgia pushes the wonky shopping trolley down the aisle, checking the list her dad gave her.

And there's Jo, staring at the label of a pasta sauce jar as if she's never seen the brand before. With a smile she can feel from the tips of her toes, Georgia pushes the trolley forward. Jo looks up, her neutral expression tightening as she places the jar into her trolley and takes a right at the end of the aisle.

Heart dropping, Georgia leaves her trolley behind and hurries after Jo. 'Hey,' she says to Jo's back. 'What's the deal?'

Jo freezes for a moment, then whirls around, utter contempt on her usually friendly face. 'Your dad's pathetic, that's what.'

Really, what could Georgia say? She agreed. What

he'd done was pathetic, but what she herself had done was disgraceful.

'You don't understand,' she pleads, hating herself but unable to stop. 'If you'd just listen. It's all—'

'Don't even.' Jo takes a step forward, her expression twisting into an ugly snarl Georgia has never seen on her best friend's face. 'Neither of you care about anyone else, so why should we care about you? Everyone thinks you two should just pack up and leave.'

Jo spins around and shoves the trolley until she disappears around a corner.

Tears balance on Georgia's lower lids, her vision shimmering, before she finally blinks and allows the water to flow in a warm trickle down her cheeks.

She gives herself a moment of pity, then swipes at the cooling liquid. When the time came, she'd really wanted to say a proper goodbye to Jo, but that wasn't ever going to happen.

Unless it just had.

- *42* -

LUCAS

I PARK IN FRONT of my practice and shut off the engine. From the passenger seat, Sam pants at me and lets out a small whine.

'Better stay here, girl,' I tell her.

She glances through the windscreen, and I follow her gaze into the dark night. The street's mostly empty apart from a few people waiting outside the fish-and-chip shop. The flashing string of coloured lights bordering the window illuminates their faces and the plumes of breath streaming from their mouths.

Just like I have a hundred times on the drive into town, I wonder again if Kelsey eats takeaway regularly. I doubt it. She's trim, her skin perfect.

Well, almost.

Even though I can eat whatever I want, I try not to

indulge too often, but tonight I felt restless at home, not in the mood to cook.

Hoping she's not in there, I sigh and open the door. Crisp air hits me as I tell Sam to stay, and shove my gloved hands in my parka pockets.

Apart from the pub at the other end of the street, the takeaway shop is the only other business open at this time of night.

More worried about running into Kelsey than anything else, I duck my head and push open the door. Halfway in, it comes to an abrupt stop. The noise hits me first. I look up to see the place packed with people, understanding now why some are braving the cold on the street while they wait for their orders.

'Sorry,' I mumble to the familiar middle-aged man the door bumped against.

His annoyed expression quickly turns into a grin when he sees me. Having called my order in, I ease through the largest gap I can find, squeezing past the other customers with as little contact as possible.

Suddenly, a hand grips my arm. I stop dead in my tracks.

'Hey!' a woman's voice rings out above the loud chatter. 'The doc's here!'

The whole shop falls into silence as I glance at the hand holding my arm, then at the woman grinning at me. Sharna Robinson, a middle-aged woman and owner of a healthy flock of sheep. She squeezes my arm, releases it and winks.

And then the silence erupts in a babble of voices, and people I barely recognise are patting me on the back, grabbing my gloved hand and shaking it. Eagerly.

That's certainly a first.

Jimmy Smith, one of the older farmers in the area,

leans in close as he pumps my hand and places his other on my shoulder.

'Owe you a hell of a lot, Doc. That bastard Hargraves could've ruined us all.'

I nod politely, my brain screaming to get out of here, that this is exactly what my mother wants me to avoid. Attention.

Praise and words of thanks come at me in a blur. More hands grab mine, pat my back, my shoulder, my arms.

Panic rises in my gut, my mind filling with images my mother planted there so long ago. How many nightmares have I had where everyone knows what I can do? Everyone chasing me, reaching for me, grabbing my arms, tearing off my gloves, forcing my bare hands to heal them. Everyone draining me, using me, until I'm nothing but a dead shell.

Taking a deep breath, I tell myself that's not what's happening, that it just feels that way because I'm not used to being touched at all, let alone pawed at by a multitude of people.

I push more forcefully up to the counter, where Jason Gosby, the burly store owner, slides a paper-wrapped bundle towards me. I fumble with my wallet, and as I open it, Jason says, 'On the house tonight, Doc. One-off special.'

A loud cheer erupts from the other customers.

'Not for you lot!' Jason shouts.

The crowd grumbles with good humour. Embarrassed by the generosity but eager to leave, I mumble a thanks, grab my dinner and mentally prepare for the journey towards the exit.

Smiling faces watch me, but only a few reach out and pat my shoulder this time. Just before I reach the door, a young man in his twenties, his name escaping me, blocks my exit.

'Come down to the pub, Doc. We'll buy ya a couple of beers. Least we can do.'

I plaster on a smile, the thought churning my stomach. 'Sorry, mate. Can't tonight.'

Before he can respond, I'm high-tailing it towards Sam, her front paws up on the dash, her face grinning at the sight of me.

Climbing in, I slam the door. Releasing the air I've been holding, I take in long, deep breaths until my pulse settles.

Sam sniffs at my lap. Opening the centre console, I place the food inside. With a trembling hand, I give Sam a rub behind the ears, start the car and drive.

From the corner of my eye, I see Sam lick her lips in anticipation. She knows there's an extra hamburger patty or two in the parcel for her when we get home.

Usually, I'm just as eager to get to the food, too, but for the moment, my appetite has vanished. Will tomorrow be the same? The day after and the day after that? How long until I fade back into the invisible where I belong?

I grip the wheel tighter, then relax. There's nothing I can do about it. There's no controlling what others think or do. But it *will* fade, I tell myself. Something new will come along and they'll forget all about me.

Until one of their animals needs me. Then what? Instead of a conversation about the animal's problem, will it be a conversation about what I did? Will I be forever looked at differently from this point forward?

I sigh.

Although I don't like the thought, I know it's my mother who'll worry.

- 43 -

KELSEY

I SQUINT AGAINST THE brilliant sunlight as my breath plumes in the frigid air. Directing the Ram truck and horse float, I wave my hands, indicating to the driver to continue backing towards the gate to my new horse's paddock.

When the float moves into position, I hold up my hand. The brake lights flare as it jolts to a stop, my new horse's bottom wobbling, hooves clamouring as he balances himself.

I swing the paddock gate open, and smile widely at the young man wearing a cowboy hat as he climbs from the truck and saunters towards the back of the float. Watching as he undoes the tailgate, my heart races. Having dreamed of this moment for so long, it's difficult to believe it's happening.

The young cowboy strides up the ramp, past the horse and undoes a knot in the rope attached to the halter. He makes a clicking sound with his tongue as he gently touches the horse's chest, easing it backwards from the float until they're standing before me.

I give the horse a soft rub on his white blaze, wondering what I'll end up calling him.

'In here?' the cowboy asks, nodding his hat towards the paddock.

'Yes, thanks.' Only now do I realise he's looking at my face with curiosity. I duck my head so my hair falls forward and covers the scars. As he leads the horse into the paddock, I let a smile flick at the corner of my mouth. I'd been so excited by the arrival of her horse, I hadn't even thought about how he might react. How long has it been since I've done that? I honestly can't remember.

Holding the gate, I watch the cowboy unclip the lead from the horse's halter and release him.

On high alert, ears twitching, nostrils flaring, the horse glances around his new surroundings. Suddenly, he takes off at a gallop, tail high, neck arched in excitement.

The cowboy stands beside me for a moment, both of us watching the utter freedom of the gelding as he gallops around, chuffing from his nostrils.

Eager to get going, the cowboy touches the brim of his hat. 'Good luck,' he says and saunters towards his vehicle. As he does so, the gelding slows to a trot.

That's when I notice it.

A limp.

Right front leg.

'Why's he limping?' I call to the cowboy's back.

He stops and half turns towards me with a shrug.

'Might've bumped himself on the trip here. He'll be fine. Anyways, gotta get goin'.'

Without a backward glance, he climbs into his Ram and drives away.

Turning to the gelding, I bite my lip as, clearly lame, the horse trots around the paddock. Damn it. I know owning a horse is an expensive business, but I didn't think I'd need to call a vet so soon.

Glad I took the time last night to put the local vet clinic's number in my phone, I pull it from my pocket and scroll through the contacts. As my thumb hovers over the number, I hope there's more than one vet servicing the area.

- 44 -

LUCAS

HAVING JUST FINISHED NEUTERING a much-loved kitten, I flick a pair of latex gloves into the trash and wash my hands in soapy water.

Drying them slowly on paper towels, I'm glad today's shaping up to a busy one. I came in a little later, knowing Emily wouldn't be able to question me about the gossip she's no doubt heard. By the time I stepped through the door, three patients were waiting, giving me the excuse to go straight out the back and get ready.

Now there's only one more waiting. Then I'll be in for the Spanish inquisition.

Drawing a deep breath, I ball up the paper towel and toss it in the bin. Slipping on new latex gloves, I know there's no putting it off. And really, I only have myself to blame. How many grown men have their mother working for them? I don't even bother giving myself an answer to that question.

'Snowy?' I call when I step into the waiting room. Cindy Myer lifts her white rabbit from her lap and clutches it to her chest as she stands and walks towards me. She must be all of ten, yet there's no one else in the waiting room with her.

She beams at me as she approaches. 'Mum's just gone to the butcher's. She won't be long.'

'That's fine.' I nod. 'Go on through.'

Cindy walks past, but I don't follow her. I'll need Emily to come into the exam room with me. Kids are great, but the world's crazy, so I want another adult present.

'You mind coming in?' I ask my mother without looking at her.

'Sure,' she says, rising. 'I've just taken a booking for a call-out this afternoon.'

'Right.'

'Out at the old Edwards' property. Lame horse,' she tells me.

I frown, my thoughts about last night forgotten. Playing dumb, I ask. 'What happened to the Edwards?'

'Don't you ever listen to me?' she asks, throwing her hands onto her hips. 'They moved a few months ago. A woman's living there now. Sounded pleasant enough, but another call was coming in, so I got her number and told her you'd take her details when you get there.'

I clench my hands. No need to guess who she's talking about.

'I, ah … can't make it today.'

'Of course you can. You drive right past on your way home. I've already told her you'll be there later.'

'Why the hell'd you do that?'

'Well, I don't know. Maybe because it's my job?'

I glance at her. Big mistake. She glares at me for a moment before her eyes narrow.

'Tell me, Mr Social Butterfly, what amazingly important plans do you have that prevent you from doing yours?'

She has me there. Always does.

'Nothing. Jesus. I'll do it. Get off my back.'

In that moment, Cindy's mother enters.

I plaster on a smile. 'Just in time. Come on through.'

As I wait for Cindy's mother to walk past, I can feel Emily's eyes drilling into my back. The rest of the day, I know, will be spent avoiding her.

<><><>

With four pm rolling around, I shrug into my parka and call Sam to my side. Reluctantly, I stop at reception.

'You got that phone number? I'm heading out to the Edwards' property now.'

Emily gives me a quizzical look.

'Just in case something happens on the way there and I have to cancel,' I explain.

With a dubious expression, she searches the desk, then hands me a post-it note.

'I heard about last night, at the takeaway,' she says.

'Of course you did.'

'You need to be careful.'

'So, I have to lock myself away and never come out? That's your solution to the way other people behave?'

Her mouth tightens. 'You know that's not what I mean. Maybe … maybe if you just make yourself a little scarcer around here until people start to forget …'

'Great suggestion,' I say, my tone thick with sarcasm. 'Guess I should cancel beers with the guys at the pub tonight. Oh, and that fishing trip a bunch of us have planned. What else?'

'There's no need to be a jerk.'

She's right, but sometimes, hearing her tell me what I already know gets under my skin.

'Well, since you booked that appointment,' I say, changing the subject, 'I'd better get out there before it's dark.'

I turn and stride out to the Landcruiser, Sam close to my side. I let her jump in before me and wait for her to move over.

'Heya, Doc,' a man's voice calls from the street.

I glance up to see Jason from the takeaway give me a quick wave as he walks past. I raise my gloved hand in return.

He nods and keeps on walking. I feel my heart rate drop a little. He didn't want anything from me except to say hello. I like that. And why shouldn't I? Better than being stared at or avoided altogether.

Climbing into the Landcruiser, I drive along the familiar street, though it looks a little different now. Even though it's damn cold, the town doesn't feel cold. It feels welcoming, warm, like a home away from home.

I glance at Sam and grin. She pants at me, her tongue lolling from the side of her mouth. Of course, she's always known this place as home, but it's never felt that way for me. Until now.

As we get closer to the Edwards' place, I pull over to the side of the road. Gripping the wheel, I lean forward and look at the magnificent view across the valley.

The few clouds in the sky are tinged with warm colours as the sun dips closer to the rolling hills. White sheep litter the land, their heads down as they eat from scattered biscuits of hay, their shadows growing long.

I'd been right to move here, right to make this my home. I really can't imagine a more beautiful place to be. Maybe the ocean would be magnificent, too, but I can't have everything. Though, right now, I feel like I'm pretty damn close.

Sighing heavily, I stroke Sam's fur, wondering what Kelsey will make of me when I turn up on her doorstep. She won't be happy. I already know that.

I lean my head against Sam's. 'She has no idea who I am,' I tell her. 'It'll be fine. You just wait and see.'

- 45 -

KELSEY

I PUT ASIDE MY guitar and glance at my watch. For the hundredth time. Where is this so-called vet that he keeps me waiting so damn long?

I stand and stare through the living-room window. The sun creeps closer to the horizon. It'll be dark soon enough. At least I'd taken the time earlier to catch my new horse and place him in a stable with some feed.

Frustrated, I march to the front door and fling it open, as if that might somehow make the vet miraculously appear. The chilly air sweeps over my face and into the house. I shiver, and as I half close the door to reach for my jacket, I hear the telltale crunch of gravel.

Finally!

Shrugging on the warm parka, I hurry onto the

verandah and shove my feet into the fleece-lined gumboots I found in a local store yesterday.

As I march towards the steps, I stop short when I see the vehicle approaching. The all-too-familiar beaten-up four-wheel drive.

I knew it might be him, but had hoped more than one vet worked at the only clinic in town. No such luck.

Last night, I'd been there. In the takeaway, huddled into a corner at the back of the crowd. The atmosphere had been warm and full of friendly chatter. And then *he'd* walked in. And everything changed. Apparently, the town saviour had entered. I suppose that's an accurate description. Everyone seemed to think so.

Everyone except him.

I'd watched with interest as they'd all pawed at him and clapped him warmly on the back. Nobody seemed to notice how uncomfortable their attention and praise made him. But I did. I saw how eager he'd been to leave. At one point, I even saw panic in his eyes. I'd presumed he'd want to lap it all up, not run away from it. There was something fascinating about that.

Only realising my hands are fisted at my sides when I uncurl them, I watch him park, lower his window a little and get out. Without acknowledging me, he opens the rear door and leans in.

Stomping down the verandah steps, I stop a few metres away from him and place my hands on my hips.

'What're *you* doing here?' I ask, playing dumb while trying to be as rude as possible.

He slams the door and turns to face me, a medical bag in one hand and a grin on that stupid face. 'You called for a vet, right?'

Compared to the photo I'd studied in the Gazette,

that grin changes his whole face. It's not the first time I've seen him smile, but the warmth, the friendliness coming from those green eyes draws me in again.

Jesus. Stop being an idiot.

Forcing my attention to the medical bag, I shrug.

He sighs heavily and offers his gloved hand. I note these gloves look almost the same as the ones he ruined changing my tyre, except for the fact that they're brand new.

'Hi,' he says, 'I'm Daniel Clark, the local vet.'

He stares intently at me. Usually, I'd think it was because of the scars, but his eyes only search mine, not the rest of my face. After a moment, I realise he seems to expect something from me.

Leaving his outstretched hand hovering in the air, I stalk off towards the stables. It doesn't take long before I hear his heavy footfalls on the gravel behind me.

I stop just inside the barn, the darkness almost complete. Remembering I've forgotten to hammer down the rusty nail, I carefully find the light switch and flick it on. The old fluorescents overhead flicker for far too long before remaining steady. I'll have to get an electrician in to change them over to LEDs before they give up entirely.

As he walks inside, I hurry through to the stable where the gelding waits.

'So, what's the problem?' the vet asks.

'He's limping. Front right leg.'

From the corner of my eye, I see him put down the medical bag and replace his leather gloves with the latex variety. Then, with ease and familiarity, he unbolts the stable door, forcing me to step aside to let him through. Once in the stable, he bolts the door closed. I lean against it, watching his every move.

'What's his name?' he asks.

'I haven't decided yet.'

The gelding sniffs at the offered latex glove, then his arm. When the horse takes a step closer to the vet, I stare in fascination as he actually nuzzles the guy's chest, as if he's a long-lost friend or relative.

I shake my head. I'm being ridiculous. But as he crouches in front of the gelding and runs his gloved hands over the right front leg, the horse rests its mouth on top of the guy's head and gently nibbles at his hair with its rubbery lips. I want to believe I've never seen anything like it.

Yet I have.

'Shin splint,' he says from some distant place I no longer inhabit.

Because I'm looking at Luke, at the kitten he tried to share with me, but only wanted him. At all the kittens bouncing around on him in the alley. At the healed, blood-soaked kitten curled up on his chest when I found him unconscious.

'Hello?'

I blink, bringing myself back to meet his questioning look. 'What?'

'I said, he's got a shin splint.' He rises, careful not to bump his head against the gelding's mouth. 'I did warn you about this horse,' he reminds me as he unbolts the stable door and comes out.

I take a few steps away and cross my arms over my chest. 'He wasn't limping then.'

'Guy you bought him off has a reputation for pumping his horses full of painkillers before an auction.'

'And I'm supposed to know that from you saying "not this one"?'

He shrugs as my traitorous horse puts his head over the stable door and nuzzles his arm.

'Well, that's just great,' I say.

He smiles. I wish he wouldn't.

'How long have you been riding?'

I hesitate, glancing at his scuffed, well-worn boots. 'Not since I was a kid,' I mumble.

'Right.' He strokes the horse's chin. 'So, you decide to buy a horse, hop on and hope for the best?'

'Of course not,' I bristle. 'I'll get lessons.'

'Where?'

'I'm sure I'll find someone around here.'

'Nearest instructor's in the next town over, but you'd have to get your horse over there. You have a float?'

I shake my head and watch the gelding nibble at his latex-covered hand.

'Well, you could use their horses, but they're old, barely want to move.'

Is he trying to bring me down? Isn't it bad enough I'd bought a lame horse? Now he has to belittle and discourage me?

'Thanks for that inspiring information,' I snap. 'Got any more great news? About my horse, maybe?'

I can see him trying to suppress another of those grins as he looks at my horse and runs a hand over its blaze.

'It's fixable,' he tells me simply.

'Then how about you get on with it?'

Not even my utter rudeness seems to faze him. He just shrugs, picks up his bag, lets himself into the stable and squats in front of my horse, who instantly goes back to practically kissing the top of the guy's head.

Rolling my eyes in disgust, I turn away from them,

cross my arms and lean against the stable door, stewing over his comments. Stewing because, as much as I don't want to admit it, he's right.

I haven't really planned anything. Just get a horse and go from there. I haven't even performed an internet search on the availability of riding instructors and feed suppliers. I presumed all would be available close by.

Well, I've been firmly put in my place.

And I don't like it one damn bit.

- 46 -

LUCAS

DOUBLE-CHECKING SHE'S STILL got her back to me, I remove a latex glove and quickly place my bare hand over the gelding's shin splint, making sure my body blocks Kelsey's view should she turn around.

I know I shouldn't.

I know it's wrong.

I know I'm only doing it for her.

I also know healing a shin splint won't take much out of me. What I don't know is if there's anything else wrong with the horse. That could be a problem.

My bare hand tingles and the energy flows, the sensation one of pleasure and fear. Then it's gone, the job done quickly, telling me there's nothing additional to heal.

I glance over my shoulder at Kelsey. She's still

stubbornly facing away from me, no doubt simmering over my observations about her unpreparedness for horse ownership.

For the sake of appearances, I bandage the gelding's shin then pick up my bag, give the horse's nose a rub and open the stable door.

Kelsey turns to me in surprise as I bolt it closed.

'That's it?' she asks.

'Yeah.' I put down my bag and find my leather gloves in my parka pocket. 'Keep him in here for a few days so he can't cause more damage, then he should be fine. No need to change the bandage, unless it gets loose, so just keep an eye on it.'

By way of acknowledgement, she gives me a small grunt from deep in her throat.

With my gloves securely in place, I pick up my bag and head towards the large barn door, noting the darkening the sky outside.

That's when it hits me.

The ground rises up and I stagger, feeling the bag brush against my calf and thump beside me before I realise I've let it go. I place my hands on my knees as the world heaves up and down. Somewhere in the distance, Kelsey's asking if I'm okay.

Determined to stay on my feet, I nod, my breaths rushing in and out of my mouth.

'Like hell,' she says, louder now.

I glance slightly to the side, careful not to throw myself off balance, but thankfully, I can feel the effects subsiding. She's standing beside me, and even in the poor fluorescent light, the concern on her face is as clear as day.

'It's nothing,' I tell her, purposely slowing the flow of air from my mouth. 'Just forgot to eat lunch …

maybe breakfast, too.' It isn't a lie. It isn't the truth, either.

Slowly, I pick up my bag, give her what I hope is a convincing smile and walk towards the barn door, the ground now solid and unmoving.

'I'll send you out an account.' As soon as the words leave my mouth, I remember I'm supposed to get her details so Emily can set her up in the system. I'm not sure how my mother's going to react when she's presented with the name *Kelsey*. I know she hasn't forgotten. I'm also positive she never knew what Kelsey's last name was. For now, I might be safe from her scrutiny, but as soon as she spots Kelsey in the street, sees her scars, she'll know. Nothing I can do about that. I've always known that if Kelsey ended up here, there'd be no hiding it from my mother.

For now, I'll just tell her I forgot to get the latest resident's details.

I hurry into the last visages of twilight. As I approach my Landcruiser, Sam whines, her paws on the dash, body wiggling from her wagging tail.

Pulling my keys from a pocket, I hear Kelsey's fast footfalls behind me, but it's still a shock when she snatches the keys from my hand.

'Hey!' I gulp in surprise, turning to see her shove them into the front pocket of her jeans, obviously aware I won't be game enough to retrieve them.

She crosses her arms over her chest, and I'm not sure if it's because of the cold or defiance.

'Believe me,' she says, annoyed, 'I can't wait to get rid of you, but I'm not letting you drive until you eat something.'

I stare after her as she marches up the verandah steps and disappears inside, the screen door banging shut in her wake.

I can't deny that I'm pleased, and nervous as hell about this development.

Opening the rear door, I place my bag inside, then open the driver's door and call Sam, unwilling to leave her out here in the cold.

She jumps down, stares up at me and waits for instructions.

'Come on,' I say. 'You'd better do a wee before we go in.'

<><><>

After removing my boots and placing them neatly by the front door, Sam and I cautiously enter Kelsey's home.

The smell of something delicious instantly curls into my nostrils. My stomach growls. Sam looks up at me, head tilting, one ear at attention.

I give her a rub behind her ears and notice my shaking hand. I really need to eat.

As I walk into the open-plan living area with Sam, Kelsey removes a steaming bowl from the microwave. Now I can smell what it is. Spaghetti bolognaise.

'I hope it's okay if Sam's here. It's too cold for her in the car.'

Kelsey glances at us as she reaches into a cupboard and pulls down two bowls. She smiles, the first genuine smile I've seen on her face since we were kids. Unfortunately, it's not directed at me.

'Hello, sweetie,' she says to Sam in a slightly higher pitch.

Sam's tail swishes over the polished floorboards.

Kelsey glances at me. 'Is she toilet trained?'

I quickly reach down and cup my hands over Sam's ears. 'Boy, I hope she didn't hear that. She's pretty sensitive when it comes to people questioning her intelligence and toileting skills. You might owe her an apology.'

This time she directs her smile at me. 'Do you think she'll accept a bowl of spaghetti, instead?'

'Possibly.' I grin at her, wondering if she's realised it's me who wants the apology, and it's me who'll accept that apology as an offering of food.

'Take a seat,' she says, turning to the cupboard and withdrawing another bowl.

'You don't have to—'

'No way am I feeling responsible for you killing someone on the road because you're too stupid to remember to eat. Sit.'

She certainly has a way with words.

As she takes a bowl from the fridge, I remove my jacket, place it over the back of her couch and sit at the breakfast bar. She serves plain spaghetti into the third bowl and puts it on the floor.

Sam stares at it, licks her lips but doesn't move. Instead, she looks at me.

'She doesn't want it?' Kelsey asks.

'You're kidding, right?' I glance at Sam. 'Okay, girl. You can eat.'

Sam rushes to the bowl and wolfs the spaghetti down in a few bites.

Kelsey gives me an impressed nod as she places a bowl of hot spaghetti topped with bolognaise sauce on the placemat in front of me, then the other bowl on the placemat to my left.

'Don't think this is any effort, either,' she says as she rounds the breakfast bar and takes the seat beside me.

'It's just leftovers.'

Unable to control myself a moment longer, the ferocious hunger overwhelming, I pick up the fork and shovel a mouthful of steaming pasta into my gob. Barely chewing, I repeat the action. This time, I chew a couple of times before I swallow and shovel in another mouthful.

When I glance at her, she's frowning at me. It's then I realise I can't see her scars. From this side-on perspective, I'd never know there was anything wrong with her.

I chew for a little longer, allowing the flavour of the sauce to register on my tongue. Delicious is barely a suitable word for what I'm tasting. After swallowing, I stand, pick up my stool, take it around to the other side of the breakfast bar and set it down.

'What're you doing?' she asks, her frown deepening.

I slide my placemat over the stone benchtop and resist the urge to take another mouthful of pasta. 'People usually sit across from each other when they eat,' I explain.

I pick up my fork and aim it at the bowl, which suddenly disappears. My fork clangs on the benchtop as Kelsey drags my placemat and bowl back to their original position.

'What're you doing?' I repeat the question she asked me moments ago.

'People usually take their gloves off before they eat, too.'

She has me there. And so the lies must begin.

'I'm germaphobic,' I tell her matter-of-factly, as if I've explained it a thousand times to people I've never dined with. 'So …'

She stares at my gloves, her narrow eyes full of

suspicion.

Shit. Has she figured me out?

'So, you became a vet?' she asks in disbelief.

Well, it's certainly becoming more and more obvious that she doesn't take bullshit from anyone. How I'm going to earn her trust while blatantly lying to her is beyond me. I meet her eyes for a moment. Is that what I'm trying to do? Why? I can't do anything for her. Except hurt her yet again if she ever discovers the truth.

But I can't help myself. Her approval, her acceptance, seems to matter more than anything has for ... well, decades.

'That's what latex gloves are for,' I explain, my eyes sliding away from her piercing gaze. I shrug as I stare at the spaghetti I desperately still need. 'Haven't had any complaints from my patients yet.'

When I glance at her, she's on edge, her eyes flicking all over my face, searching for something I hope she can't find.

Not out of the woods, then.

'What did you say your name was?' she asks.

'Daniel Clark.' The lie slides off my tongue like butter. Easier than the last lie. I've had plenty of practice with this one.

Her forehead creases with a faint frown. 'Did you grow up in the city?'

Shit. She's definitely fishing.

I stare at the bowl of food and swallow. 'No. No, I lived in Riverview. My sisters,' I lie, hoping to throw her completely off any thought of the boy she once knew, 'moved to the city first chance they got, but I like the peace and quiet.'

She slumps in her seat a little.

'Did I say something wrong?' I ask, even though I shouldn't push my luck.

She shrugs. 'You remind me of someone I knew once. But you can't be him.'

I look into her eyes and all I see is disappointment. My heart thunders at the idea that she *wants* me to be Lucas.

'Maybe I am,' I say, the words out of my mouth and in the air between us before my brain even understands what I've just done. Just like when we were kids.

'Why the fuck would you say that?' She glares at me. 'He's dead.'

She thinks I'm dead?

'I'm so sorry,' I say. 'I didn't mean … I don't know why—'

'Just … forget it. It's my fault. I shouldn't have said anything.' She takes a deep breath, twirls her spaghetti around her fork, then untwirls it again.

'He was someone special?' I ask gently.

'Don't.' She won't look at me now, her concentration firmly glued to her bowl.

Why does she think I'm dead?

Unless you can do something about her scars, stay the fuck away from her. Or you'll only cause her more damage.

Only her father could have put that idea in her head.

As the awkward silence stretches out, I ask, 'You want me to go?'

As if returning from some distant place, she blinks, her gaze latching onto my gloves. 'No, you need to eat,' she says. 'But you've got nothing to worry about. I haven't been sick since I was a kid. Not even a cold.'

My eyes shoot to hers in surprise. The only other person I've ever touched is my mother, who's also never been sick. Nor, on the rare occasions I've taken the risk, have any of the animals I've touched. If they come into my practice again, it's always for either yearly vaccinations or because of an injury, not an illness.

Just when I think I know everything there is to know about this thing, I learn something new. Something I suspected, sure, but something I've never been able to confirm with another person.

'What?' she asks.

Realising I'm staring at her, I lift one shoulder and grin. 'I've never been sick, either. Proves the gloves work.'

Her lips twitch and I think she's about to smile, but she clamps them together.

'I don't care,' she says. 'It's rude. If you're going to sit over there and make me uncomfortable by looking at this …' she waves her hand towards her scars, 'then you can damn well be uncomfortable, too. So, either take them off, or sit back over here.'

I hold her gaze for a long moment. She's serious. I now know I'm in no danger should she touch my bare hands. She'll never be a threat to me. Just like Sam and Beau, I can touch her without fear.

The thought floors me. I'm glad I'm already sitting down, because if I'd been standing, I think that revelation might have brought me to my knees.

Stupid, though. I kind of get the impression I'm the last person on this planet she wants touching her.

Slowly, I remove my gloves and place them in my lap. My hand trembles slightly as I reach across the benchtop and slide the placemat and bowl back. Ravenous, I shovel up mouthful after mouthful.

'Maybe you should take it easy,' she says.

'Sorry, just—'

'Starving. I get it.'

I take a deep breath, shovel in another mouthful, but this time I chew slowly while I glance around the kitchen and living area behind Kelsey. Apart from a moving box here and there, it's tidy and welcoming.

'You live here alone?' I ask as I wrap more spaghetti around my fork, finally feeling the insatiable hunger fade.

She shrugs in response, and I can't tell if she's reluctant to tell a man she lives alone, or just reluctant to tell me.

When I realise she's not going to be forthcoming with any information, I conveniently remember I need to get her details for the clinic. Putting down my fork, I take out my phone and unlock it.

'What? Now you're going to look at your phone while we're eating? Do you have any idea how rude—'

'My receptionist explained she didn't get your details when you called in. So, unless you want me to be in trouble—which maybe you do—I sort of need to do it. To get you in the system,' I babble. 'You know, so we can send you an invoice. That okay?'

She looks at her food and nods. I think she's feeling bad for calling me rude yet again, but even though I give her a bit of time by taking another mouthful of spaghetti, she offers no apology.

Opening a notetaking app, I slide the stylus from the phone and hover it over the keyboard. 'I guess the first thing I need is your name.'

'Kelsey Wells,' she says, her concentration still on the contents of her bowl.

'Okay,' I say as I type it in. 'Already know your address and your number. Email?'

She rattles it off and I type it in. There's really nothing more I need to know. But I keep going.

'Marital status?'

'No.'

I don't miss the stiffness in her posture.

'I don't think "no" is the right answer. You need to choose from—'

'No,' she says again. 'There is no marital status.'

'Single, then.'

At least that gets her to look at me. She's not impressed.

'Children?' I continue.

She gasps, eyes wide. 'Oh my God, I completely forgot!' She turns on her stool and cups a hand around her mouth. 'Hey, kids? You can come out now!' She spins back to her bowl, takes a mouthful of spaghetti and chews as she stares at me.

I huff out a laugh. 'Smartarse.'

'Stupid question.' She glances at my phone, noticing I'm not typing anything. 'What's that got to do with a client intake form for veterinary services, anyway?'

I lock my phone and put it in my pocket. 'It doesn't. Just curious.'

She points her fork at me. 'Now that *is* rude.'

'I'll have to disagree with you there. Far as I can tell, I'm just getting to know the newest member of our little community. You didn't think it was rude when you were asking me questions. Feel free to ask anything else.'

I know she won't.

She stares at me a moment longer, then goes back to her food.

'Okay, I'll go again. Did you manage to land a job in town?'

'I work from home.' She takes a bite from her fork and chews, offering nothing further.

'Doing?' I ask, not discouraged in the slightest.

I'm surprised when she finally looks at me. 'I write music. Songs, lyrics.'

My face lights up, and when she sees it, she quickly concentrates on twirling her pasta.

'You must be pretty good if you can afford all this on your own.'

Another shrug. 'A lot of well-known artists buy my work. If they do well … I do well.'

A lightness fills my chest as I study her while she stares at her food. I'm so pleased she's found a place in this world, that she hasn't let what happened to her completely destroy her dream. But there's something not quite right.

'Why not sing your own songs?' I ask.

She continues to play with her food, avoiding my gaze. 'I have a terrible voice,' she finally answers.

And now she's the one lying to me.

<><><>

After finishing the delicious meal far sooner than I wanted to, I hold the screen door open for Sam and follow her onto the verandah. Shrugging into my jacket, I turn and smile as Kelsey leans against the doorframe, holding the screen door open.

'Well, ah, thanks. That was pretty great spaghetti.'

'Whatever.'

I shake my head slightly and head towards the verandah steps. When I hear the creak of the screen door closing, I turn around, not a clue what I'm about to say, just wanting to say something.

'Hey, I …'

She swings the door open a few inches, even though

she can easily let it close and still hear and see me through the thin mesh. She stares at me, waiting.

I blurt, 'Do you have a saddle? Bridle?'

'Not yet. Why?'

I shift uncomfortably from foot to foot, nerves ripping through me, scared she'll say no. And of course, she has every right to. I reach down and pat Sam's head, the feel of her fur surprising me. I've forgotten to put on my gloves.

'I just thought of someone close by where you can get those riding lessons.'

'Oh?' she says, opening the door a little wider.

'Yeah, though you won't like who's giving them.'

She crosses her arms and frowns. 'I guess that narrows it down to you.'

Words tumble from my lips before I lose my nerve. 'I've got some great horses, plenty of tack. I'll be home all day Sunday if you're interested. I'm about five k's down the road here. Name's on the letterbox.'

Before she can reject my offer, I take off down the steps towards my car and open the door for Sam.

As I turn out of Kelsey's driveway, I glance at Sam. She stares back, her dark eyes sparkling from the dashboard lights.

'I know. I know,' I say. 'Playing with fire. But she won't turn up. You know that, right?'

Sam watches me a moment longer, gives a huge yawn, then curls up on the seat and sighs.

- 47 -

BRYCE

BRYCE LETS HIS HEAD fall into his calloused hands, wishing he could make Jim Rainey, sitting opposite him at the kitchen table, disappear.

'Mr Hargraves?' Rainey says with the slightest inflection of impatience in his voice.

'Can't I change your mind?' Bryce asks without looking up. 'Maybe I could offer you—'

'I wouldn't say any more, Mr Hargraves.'

Bryce knew the words were ridiculous the moment they left his mouth. Hopefully, Rainey won't repeat them to anyone.

'The facts are clear,' Rainey says. 'You knew your cattle were infected, and you tried to hide it. The government does not compensate under those circumstances, they issue a fine.'

Bryce finally raises his head and meets Rainey's eyes. 'How much?' he asks, his temples throbbing.

'Somewhere in the vicinity of a hundred thousand.'

Rainey stands. Bryce sees the smallest slither of sympathy in the other man's eyes. It does nothing to make him feel any better, any less guilty, any less devastated.

'This is between us,' he tells Rainey. 'My daughter doesn't need to know.'

Rainey reaches the kitchen door, then pauses. To Bryce's utter relief, Rainey gives a nod before he opens the door and leaves.

Alone now, with nothing but his thoughts tumbling over each other in a jumble he can't seem to untangle, Bryce swallows over the lump in his throat.

- 48 -

KELSEY

FIVE HUNDRED METRES BEFORE reaching my destination, I pull over to the shoulder of the road and grip the wheel, trying to calm the butterflies in my stomach. If only I can decide whether or not I actually wants to spend time with Daniel Clark.

Without a doubt, I wholeheartedly want to learn how to ride. That's a no-brainer. I just can't decide how I feel about Daniel.

Daniel Clark.

Even his name doesn't sit right with me.

'Daniel,' I say aloud. Nope, that doesn't work. It just sounds wrong.

'Clark,' I try. A little better, but not much. Do I need to call him anything at all?

Maybe it's better to just turn around and go home,

where I feel comfortable, where my stomach isn't fluttering and doing flip-flops every time I think about seeing him again.

That'd be easy. That's exactly what'll make me feel better, safe, protected, in my element.

But is that living? Haven't I been doing that most of my life? Where has comfortable, safe and protected got me so far?

A career writing music. Nothing wrong with that. But I should be writing music for myself, not selling it to other artists.

A nice house in the country, exactly where I dreamed of living. But as lovely as it is, I'm still as alone as ever.

And what had I promised myself when I made the move? That I'd get out in public, socialise, make connections.

I just hadn't planned on it being with *him*.

Does it matter? Who cares who I socialise with? It's about making the effort. That's what matters. Besides, I'm not really socialising with Clark. He's giving me riding lessons, that's all. If anything, it's good practice, right?

My hands grip the wheel tighter, then relax. I'll do it. I'll learn to ride, and in the process, I'll spend time with another human being. How hard can it be?

In fact, after our dinner together the other night, I already know it won't be hard. He lets me get away with my sarcasm and rudeness, all traits I know I use to keep people at arm's length. But he doesn't seem to care. And I like that. I also can't deny I like the way he looks into my eyes.

Why that scares me as well, I don't know. But I do know I want more of it. And the wanting more wins over the fear.

Taking my foot off the brake, I check my mirror and pull onto the road.

After I park in front of his house, I expect him to come and greet me. When there's no movement at the front door, I steel myself and get out.

Still no sign of him.

Sighing, my heart rate increasing, I climb the steps to the front door and raise my fist to knock, but hesitate.

In the city, I would never, ever have gone to a guy's house on my own. Let alone the home of a guy I really don't like. But here I am, in the middle of nowhere, just about to do that very thing. And out here, nobody'll hear me scream.

I know I'm being ridiculous, know my brain is making up excuses to avoid anything new. Still, I can't seem to stop my feet from backing away.

No!

The scream comes loud and strong in my head.

Get over yourself and face up to your idiotic fears. No one cares about your stupid face, no one cares what you've been through. They've all got their own problems to deal with. Get out of your head and get on with it, for fuck's sake, woman.

Fists clenching at my sides, I take a deep breath, quickly brush my hair over my scars and turn towards the door.

- 49 -

LUCAS

TENSE, I SIT ON the couch, Sam at my feet, giving me that look of hers that always shoots guilt into my heart. I wait, realising I'm actually holding my breath. Nothing happens, so I release a silent exhale.

'See,' I whisper to Sam, 'she's changed her mind.'

I heard her arrive. Then nothing.

Sam cocks her head, her look quizzical, but I can't tell if it's directed at me or if she's listening.

After dinner with Kelsey the other night, I'm still deciding on what her revelation means here and now. Does believing I'm dead work in my favour? I'm leaning that way. She clearly thinks there's something about me that reminds her of the boy she knew, but the fact she thinks that boy is dead means that's all I am; a reminder. So, if I just continue to be Daniel Clark the local vet, then I can't disappoint her, can I?

And there's something else I've thought about, too. Now that I know she thinks I'm dead, I want to get to know her as Daniel. I want to see if she'll like me without the knowledge of what I can do influencing her. I've never forgotten her admission that she'd only made the effort to get to know me because of what she saw me do. I'm sure, if she'd never discovered my secret, we never would have become friends.

There's only one way to find out.

At this point, though, I'm not too sure she'll ever like me. But I have to try. It'd be damn nice to have a close friend again. And I think my best shot is to let her continue to believe I'm dead.

Which, of course, means lying to her. Something I really don't want to do.

What a liar.

I can still hear her little-girl voice accusing me that day she saw me heal the kitten. Guess I haven't changed all that much.

A soft knock comes from the door. I snap to my feet at almost the same speed as Sam, wipe my clammy hands on my jeans and grab my gloves from the arm of the couch.

Don't need them.

Except I've backed myself into a corner that's a little hard to worm my way out of.

My heart races as Sam trots towards the front door, a spring in her step, tail wagging blissfully. If I had a tail, I'm sure it'd be tucked between my butt cheeks right now.

Maybe she'll leave, think I've forgotten, think no one's home.

Sam barks.

Well, there goes that hope.

I hurry over, pull on my gloves and open the door before I have one more thought about anything.

She snaps her hand back to her side as if she'd been about to knock again.

'Hey,' she says.

'Hey.'

'I, ah, I thought maybe you'd forgotten.'

'Sorry, caught me while I was in the bathroom,' I lie. 'You want to come in?'

She peers around me, frowning. 'You have horses to ride in there?'

I grin, the tension leaving my body. How can I not like her? Especially when I see sparks of that little girl still existing within her.

'Actually,' I say, 'I moved them outside a while ago. They needed a toilet break.'

The corner of her mouth twitches as she suppresses a smile.

'Lame,' she says.

'No, that's your horse. Mine are fine.'

'Oh, so funny. Give me a millisecond to compose myself.' She gives me an exaggerated eye roll and steps aside so I can come out.

I lead her through the barn, where I already have the tack organised and waiting.

'Wow,' she says, taking it all in. 'I suppose it's a little nicer than mine.'

'It wasn't always. I've spent a lot of time swapping out rotten wood and restoring stable doors. Loved every minute, though.'

'How long did that take you?' she asks, genuinely interested.

'Probably got it to where I wanted it over two or

three years, but then, of course, there's the ongoing maintenance, too.'

'Great,' she says, sounding a little deflated.

'I'd be happy to help you,' I blurt, once again not thinking before I open my mouth.

'I wasn't asking,' she shoots back.

'Just offering.'

I keep moving and she follows me out through the other end of the barn, across the small yard and over to the paddock gate where I keep Beau and Perry separated from the mares. I give a loud whistle, watching as Beau spots me and breaks into a gallop. I should have known. He reaches me in record time, giving a loud snort when he shoves his head over the gate and nudges me.

'Not you,' I tell him, stepping to the side so I can see around him. I give another whistle and see reliable old Perry in the distance, slowly trotting towards us.

As I turn, Kelsey tentatively holds out her hand to Beau and lets him sniff her. Transfixed by him, she reaches up and traces her fingers over the scars across his face. Sometimes I forget about his injuries. I just don't see them anymore.

'Who's this?' she asks, without taking her gaze from his scars.

I sidle closer and Beau instantly comes to me, nuzzles my glove, then presses his face into my side. I rub his whiskered chin.

'This is Beau. He's standing at stud. Has all the fun around here, don't you, fella?'

Heat floods my face. What the hell did I just say? I give Kelsey a quick glance, but her expression hasn't changed. Maybe she didn't hear me. Or maybe she doesn't care for my stupid comments.

'What happened to him?' she asks, her gaze firmly fixed on Beau.

'Got himself caught in a barbed-wire fence when he was a foal. I bought him for next to nothing at the auctions when I first moved here. He was only a yearling then, but I knew he was perfect.'

'Perfect?'

'Well, I wanted a stallion with not only a great temperament, but the looks to match.' I scratch his forehead. 'I got lucky, didn't I, fella?'

Her brow crinkles. 'But he's ... scarred.'

'You can't see past that?' I ask gently.

Our eyes lock. I keep completely still. It's not long before she glances away, but it's the longest she's looked at me. I'm aware that the sight of Beau's scars should confirm that I'm most certainly not the boy I remind her of. As I study her face, her tough, guarded expression melts into vulnerability.

I take a tentative step towards her, not sure what I'm planning to do, only that I need to be closer to her. Lucky for me, the sound of trotting hooves turns our attention to Perry, a placid gelding perfect for a new rider.

After tethering Perry to a ring attached to a column far older than me, I take a few steps away and lean against a stable door, where I've already placed the tack.

Kelsey runs her hand over Perry's neck before turning to me with a questioning look.

'Okay,' I say, 'saddle blanket first.'

'Me?' She blanches, eyes widening a little. 'I'm just here for riding lessons.'

'They'll be difficult without a saddle.' I manage to tamp down on the stupid grin that wants to spread across my face.

She lets out a huff, strides over to where I'm leaning and tugs at the blanket beneath the saddle. Holding it in her hands, she looks at me.

'Just place it gently on his back,' I tell her.

She does so, talking so softly to Perry I can't understand her words, but know they're to help keep him calm. Not that he needs it. A bomb could go off and he wouldn't even flinch. Only thing he's scared of is water. But I let her handle things the way she wants.

Without me telling her, she retrieves the saddle and hauls it onto Perry's back, still chatting to him.

'How's that?' she asks.

'Pretty good for a newbie,' I say. 'But the saddle could do with being just a little closer to his withers.'

She adjusts it accordingly and glances at me for approval.

'Now the girth,' I say.

As she reaches under Perry's belly, I'm impressed by what she remembers from her trips here with her father.

'Make sure you get it tight,' I tell her. 'Don't want you and the saddle sliding off.'

Turning her back to Perry's head, she leans against him for leverage and cinches up the girth. As she strains, Perry whips his head around and nips her backside.

'Ow!' she yelps, more in surprise than pain, I'm guessing. Which is why I feel no shame chuckling.

Face reddening, she glares at me as she rubs her butt cheek. 'It's not funny!'

'You want me to take a look, make sure he didn't break the skin?' I offer. Then realise I'm not joking, because my hands are tingling and the pull is there, urging me to go to her. But instead of thinking about taking away her pain, my imagination goes into overdrive. I see myself walking over to her, removing my gloves, letting them fall to the ground as I pull her in close, slide a hand down her back, dip into her jeans and cup her injured cheek.

'Hey, smartarse,' she says, jolting me out of my head. 'Can you tighten it up for me?'

For a moment, I have no idea what she's talking about. I'm only aware of the blood rushing to my groin and how grateful I am that I'm wearing clothing that hides what I most certainly don't want her to see.

'Well?' she asks, squinting at me in confusion, still rubbing at her backside.

'I could,' I say, 'but that'd mean I'd have to be around every time you want to go for a ride.'

'Can't have that.' She marches up to Perry's head, shortens the lead and gives the girth another try.

And now I can't stop myself from looking at her backside, imagining what it'd be like to touch her. Not because of the pull, not because I want to heal her. But because I want to feel her skin against my hands, feel her react with pleasure.

Jesus.

As my heart gallops in my chest, I tell myself the only thing I want from her is friendship, that same connection we had as kids. Thinking of anything more is crazy.

She's closed off, damaged, angry, sad and lonely.

Just like me.

I release a long, silent breath. I suppose I should stop lying to myself. I can't deny the thought hadn't crossed my mind when I moved here. But to be fair, it'd been a fleeting idea. I had no way of knowing what sort of person she'd become. Ten-year-old kids aren't thirty-year-old adults. It was stupid to even consider it.

Now, here she is in front of me, and I know all her insults, anger and sarcasm are a way to keep people from getting close to her, from hurting her. I know she's living by the 'get them before they get you' motto.

Not much different from me, really.

'Okay,' she says, staring at me, her head slightly cocked. 'What now?'

<><><>

Over the next few weeks, I introduced her to everything she needs to know about riding safely, starting with her walking Perry in the round yard, teaching her how to rise and fall in rhythm with Perry's trot, then onto cantering.

Breaking my usual routine, I even rescheduled appointments myself so I could teach her after work and keep my mother out of the loop.

It didn't take long for her to relax around me, and after such a short time, we've developed an easy rhythm between us.

Now that I feel she's in total control, I saddled Beau up for our first ride outside the round yard.

Beside me, Kelsey saddles up Perry, her movements fluid from practice. I notice today that she's bought herself a proper pair of riding pants. Pants that hug every curve of her thighs and backside.

She catches me staring and I quickly say, 'You all set?'

'The question is, are you?'

'You think the pupil has overtaken the teacher?'

'I guess we're about to find out,' she says, the spark

in her eyes lifting my heart. She's having fun. Although I know it's because she loves to ride, I also want to believe it has something to do with me. With us. How we are with each other.

As she slides into Perry's saddle, I lead Beau from the barn and open the gate to the largest of my paddocks. Once she's through, I lock the gate and swing myself onto Beau's back.

I start off at a trot, taking it easy, letting Kelsey get a feel for the wide-open space, where she has the freedom to make Perry go anywhere she likes.

Before I know it, she canters past me, urging Perry on. I smile and give chase, happy she's confident enough to do her own thing, happy she's now a competent rider. And unhappy she may decide she has no need for me and my lessons anymore.

After exploring the land for over an hour, I lead her to the crest of the highest hill on my property. We stop beside a single ghost gum and take in the view. White puffy clouds dot the blue sky, the breeze gentle, the sun bright.

'Oh, wow,' she says in awe.

'I've been looking forward to bringing you up here.'

'It's incredible,' she says, a huge smile on her face.

'It's not just the view.'

She looks at me. 'No?'

'Just listen.'

She closes her eyes. 'Tell me …'

'Up here, it can seem like you're the only living thing on the planet, but there's so much going on. Listen to the leaves in the gum tree, the birds, the horses breathing.'

Her face relaxes as she takes it all in.

'Feel the breeze on your face, in your hair, the feel

of the horse beneath you, the sun on your skin.'

As she tilts her face up to the sun, she releases Perry's reins and slowly holds her arms out to her sides. Stretching her hands, she moves her fingers as the breeze flows through them.

And I know I'm in love with her.

When she opens her eyes, she lets her hands drop to her thighs.

'How do you feel?' I ask.

She looks into my eyes. 'Like I'm not alone.'

I nod, unable to find any words.

'Thank you,' she says softly.

'You're welcome,' I say, my voice thick with emotion.

She hears it, sees it in my eyes. I know she does, because she digs her heels into Perry's sides and walks him towards the downward slope.

As she disappears, I follow her. I can't help the way I feel any more than she can. And I don't think she feels the same way. At least, not yet.

By the time I see her again, she's cantering down the hill. Beau wants to catch up, but I rein him in a little.

Her hair bounces as the wind blows it back, her seat in the saddle solid as she rocks with Perry's canter. I grin, feeling a tug of pride at what I've given her; a freedom and joy she'd never experience in the city or the suburbs; a freedom and joy that until now, she only knew as a memory from her childhood, from a time before I failed her.

With my concentration on her, I completely forget about the creek at the bottom of the hill. A narrow channel of shallow water that Beau and I have leaped over countless times.

As Perry approaches, I see his tail give a sudden flick

as he spots the glint of sunlight on the liquid surface. I know it's going to happen before it does. I open my mouth to shout a warning, but Perry skids to a stop so fast I only get out, 'Kel!'

She flies over his head, her feet thankfully coming free of the stirrups before she lands flat on her back in the water with a splash.

'Go, go, go!' I urge Beau on, streaking down the hill towards her.

I'm out of the saddle and running before he stops.

She lays there, unmoving, the water pooling against her side. My heart bounces around in my chest so hard I think it might bruise my insides, but I don't care. I don't care about anything but Kelsey.

Splashing into the shallow water, I drop to my knees beside her, suddenly struck by déjà vu.

'Kelsey? Kel?'

No movement, no acknowledgement.

Fuck!

I take her face in my gloved hands, barely feeling the icy water seep into my jeans.

'Kelsey? Kelsey?' Nothing. 'Shit.'

But something's not right. I don't feel the pull, the tingling in my hands I always feel when there's an injury before me. Then again, I can't see any injury. But my concern for her is so intense, I release her face with one hand and bite the tip of my glove.

And freeze.

She's grinning.

Grinning!

And now she's squinting up at me.

'You're way too easy,' she says, a chuckle escaping her throat.

Relief floods through me. Staring into her eyes as

they dance with mischief, I gently stroke her cheek with my gloved thumb. And something between us shifts. I'm touching her, caressing her, but I'm not. There's still that barrier between us, but whatever's happening has nothing to do with a physical touch. Her smile fades. She's feeling it, too. While I don't feel the pull of my hands, there's a pull within me all the same. Without realising I've shifted my gaze, I find myself looking at her lips, wanting them against mine.

Suddenly aware I'm giving her a strong message, one she might not want, I try to meet her eyes again, but I can't. Because now *she's* staring at *my* lips.

My heart pounds so hard it throbs in my temples. The urge to kiss her is almost impossible to resist, because as far as I can tell, she wants me to.

Then she meets my eyes. As colour rises in her cheeks, she blinks fast, frowning a little.

'Aren't you going to help me up?' she asks.

Releasing her face, I stand and offer her my hand. As she grips onto the leather, I once again hate the damn things. I want the sensation of her fingers wrapping around mine, her palm against my own.

When I pull her up, I use a little too much force. She bumps into me and grabs my upper arm to steady herself. We're so close, our hands still clasped together against my chest, neither of us making any effort to move away.

Now that she's upright, a drop of water drips from her wet hair and slides down the side of her face. With my free hand, I gently wipe it away as another follows its path.

'Are you sure you're not hurt?' I ask, trying to distract her from my gloved fingers as they continue to wipe away the drips.

Her grip on my arm tightens. I meet her eyes again, and as she watches me, I squeeze her hand between us. When she squeezes back, I know she wants me to kiss her.

Then Beau's there, his nose nudging my arm, forcing my fingers from her face as he lets out a snort.

Kelsey laughs, releases me and steps away, the moment broken.

Damn horse.

Trying to act like I'm not disappointed at all, I give Beau a quick rub on his nose, before turning to find Perry right beside him. I grab Perry's reins and glance at Kelsey.

'Sure you're not hurt?' I ask again, knowing damn well she isn't.

'I'm fine. Just sopping wet.'

'Tends to happen when you decide to go for a swim.'

'Wasn't exactly my decision,' she says.

'What matters is, are you okay to get back on?'

She nods, moves over to Perry, and hauls herself onto his back.

I move up beside her and adjust her wet boot in the stirrup, giving myself an excuse to grip her calf. When I look up at her, she's watching me.

'Don't do that again,' I say gently.

'Do what?' she asks, confused.

'Trick me into thinking you're hurt. It didn't feel great.'

She catches her bottom lip with her teeth and nods. 'I'm sorry. It was pretty stupid.'

I squeeze her calf. 'Just scared the hell out of me, that's all.'

I release her and climb onto Beau.

'Better get you back before you freeze to death.'

'Race you?' she asks, that spark in her eyes appearing once more.

Before I can respond, she digs her heels into Perry's flanks and takes off up the hill, leaving me staring at the gelding's flexing rump as they grow further away.

She scared me. Scared me because I care. Way too much. I care in the way my mother warned me about. And it seems her warnings are right on the money. Because if Kelsey had been hurt, I know I would have done whatever it took to remove that hurt.

Even if it meant showing her who I am.

I love her, and after what just happened, I think she's catching up to me. Fast.

As I give chase, a memory hits me like a sledgehammer. The park, the swings, Kelsey flying through the air and crashing to earth. Lying there, eyes closed, not moving. Tricking me, saying the same words.

You're way too easy.

My heart stops for a moment. If I remember, does she?

I shake my head. She probably does, but in her head, that memory involves a boy who's dead. A boy who isn't me.

When I draw level with her, I slow Beau to a canter that matches Perry's.

I glance over, and see a woman enjoying the freedom of riding a horse like she's dreamed of doing. When she smiles at me, her eyes crinkle with genuine happiness.

She's changing. Has already changed. She's not the defensive, angry, insecure woman who arrived in town. That little stunt she pulled at the creek, that was the

Kelsey I knew from our childhood. The Kelsey who was full of life and spark and cheek. And she'd been brave enough to let that girl come out and play.

She trusts me enough to do that.

The thought warms my body and my mind. There's so much hope in my life now, I'm not sure what to do with it.

Leaning forward in the saddle, she urges Perry on faster. I give Beau the reins and chase after that hope.

- 50 -

KELSEY

AFTER CLARK GIVES ME a towel from the tack room, I dry my hair as much as I can, then unsaddle Perry, place a halter around his neck and tie the lead to a ring on the stable. Undoing the correct buckles on the bridle, I slide it carefully over Perry's face, releasing the bit from his mouth.

The horse gives his head a good shake before I secure the halter over his nose and buckle it up.

'Good job,' Clark says. 'Are you sure you're not too cold? I can finish up here if you want to go.'

'I'm fine,' I tell him, though he's right. The chill's seeping into my skin, my wet clothes clinging to me in a way that makes me desperate to strip them off. I should hurry home and do just that. Slip into a hot bath and warm my bones.

'Can't neglect my duties just because I fell off, right?' Even though I'm cold and uncomfortable, I don't want to go home.

He smiles, shrugs off his jacket and holds it up. Grateful, I slip it on, the warmth left within from his body embracing me.

He picks up the saddle and bridle. 'I'll put these away while you brush him down.'

I grab the brush and sweep it over Perry's coat just once before I give into temptation and look over my shoulder. Although I don't want to, I can't possibly miss the tight, long-sleeved T-shirt he wears, the way his muscles move beneath the stretchy material as he carries the saddle.

Pathetic.

Here I am, ogling someone because of their appearance. Again.

Turning to Perry, I concentrate on brushing him properly, and smile to myself as I think of what almost happened.

When I fell off Perry, the shock of the fall itself, the freezing water, the blue sky staring down at me, had left me frozen. Amazed I hadn't winded myself, I'd thought about getting up. Until I heard the thunder of Beau's hooves, then Clark's shouts and his feet pounding towards me. I'd snapped my eyes closed and lay motionless.

With no clue as to why I was pulling such a stunt.

What had I expected him to do?

Was it attention I wanted? More than he'd already given me?

Deep down I knew. I'd wanted to see how he'd react, what he'd do if he thought I was really hurt. But it'd turned into something else, entirely.

When he'd cupped my face in his hands, I hadn't felt the slightest urge to jerk away, even though one hand was over my scars. Maybe it'd been because of his gloves, the barrier they created between us, but I think it had more to do with the fact that he didn't care about the scars. Then I'd opened my eyes and made a joke of it, and his relief had been palpable. I'd really scared him, and I'd felt like a total idiot.

Until he'd stroked my cheek tenderly with his thumb, the leather soft against my skin, but frustrating all the same. With him leaning over me like that, with him looking into my eyes then at my lips, I'd thought it might happen, had wanted it to.

But when he'd caught me looking at his mouth, fear and embarrassment had taken over. I'd hoped by asking him to help me up, the moment between us would be broken. I'd been wrong. It seemed my body had its own ideas and I'd held onto his hand instead of releasing him. Squeezed his hand when he'd squeezed mine, letting him know I wanted what he wanted.

And if it hadn't been for Beau's interruption, I know it would have happened. I also know my disappointment at that interruption means I want him as far more than just a friend.

Shaking my head, I let out a breath.

It's hard to admit, but that thought feels wonderful. And for just a moment, I bask in the warmth of the feeling that someone else besides Dad actually cares about me. But what I can't wrap my head around, is why he wants me. He could have anyone. Why me?

'Alright,' he says from behind me. 'Let's get him back into his paddock.'

Jerked out of my thoughts, I quickly release Perry and lead him from the barn, following Clark towards the paddock gate.

'I think I'm ready to give my own horse a try,' I tell him as he swings the gate wide.

Brushing my hand with his glove, he takes Perry's lead from me, unclips it and gives the horse's rump a firm pat. Perry trots into the paddock and gets busy eating.

'Yeah,' he says as he closes the gate. 'I'd say you are.'

He doesn't seem too happy about that fact. Neither am I. It'll mean he no longer needs to be around when I ride. He'll no longer have any reason to see me at all.

'I, ah, I was wondering, though … if maybe you could come around and ride my horse first? You know, just to make sure he's okay?'

'Sure,' he says, as if it means nothing.

I silently release a breath, heart beating a tiny bit faster. Like it does every time I'm around him.

Not sure what else to say, the slow clomp of hooves draws my attention. I turn to find a very pregnant mare approaching from the other paddock. Reaching over the railing, I give her head a pat.

'Wow, she's huge.'

Clark joins me at the fence, his arm brushing lightly against mine as he strokes the mare's neck. Fully aware that he's right in my personal space once again, I briefly consider moving away, but even though he's barely touching me, the warmth radiating from him feels too good to give up. So, I hold my ground. I might even lean a little closer to him. Only because I'm patting the mare, of course.

Besides, he seems oblivious.

'So,' he says, glancing at me, 'how come you ended up moving out this way?'

I want to clam up just as much as I want to open

up. When he holds my gaze and cocks his head, the words tumble from my mouth.

'I thought … maybe I could be part of a community. When they get used to me, that is.'

He nods thoughtfully. 'They're going to love you.'

Surprised by his comment, I'm even more surprised when his face reddens, when his eyes quickly leave mine and return to the mare.

My stomach flips the way it had when I was a kid, when I'd close my eyes on the swing and let myself fly.

'She's due anytime now,' he blurts.

My heart drums in my chest, and for some stupid reason, I want to smile, but I don't want him to know his reaction has evoked my own. 'I've never seen a foal being born.'

'You want to?' he asks, his eyes meeting mine again, the colour in his face fading back to normal.

This time, I let the smile take over. 'Yeah. I'd really like that.'

<><><>

After a hot shower, I blow-dry my hair, dress in warm pyjamas and slip on a fluffy robe just as a knock comes from the door.

I freeze, instantly wondering if it's Clark. Not liking that my mind goes straight to him, I reason that it really couldn't be anyone else.

With a little more enthusiasm than I like, I hurry to the front door and swing it open.

'Surprise!' Jackie sings, holding up two bottles of champagne.

'Jackie,' I say, hoping there's not a trace of

disappointment on my face. 'Come in.' I swing the door open and Jackie breezes inside, looking quite different in jeans, runners and a knitted jumper.

'Oh, wow,' she says, taking in the open-plan living area. 'This is so cute. I love it!'

I'm not sure if 'cute' is a nice way of saying my furniture's old, but I don't mind.

'Thanks.'

Striding over to the breakfast bar, she places one bottle of champagne on the bench and the other in the fridge. 'So, where're the glasses? Let's celebrate your new home.'

I blink at her.

'I'm sorry I haven't made it out earlier. Kids, you know. This's the first night my husband's been home early enough. His brother's staying a couple of nights, so it was the perfect opportunity for me to get out of there. And don't worry, he's coming to pick me up about tenish. Hope that's okay with you.'

'Of course,' I say, hurrying into the kitchen and foraging around until I find a couple of old wineglasses I've never used.

After pouring the champagne and giving a toast to my new home, we sit on the couch. Getting comfortable, Jackie slips off her shoes and curls her legs up like she's been here before.

We chat about all sorts of things, from the most mundane tips in the kitchen to Jackie complaining about her husband not being around enough. To my surprise, I'm enjoying the other woman's company, and even though she occasionally glances at my scars, those glances seem to be getting further apart, just as I'd hoped. She's so easy to talk to and so warm, that I can't help but open up to her, too.

It's finally happening. I'm making friends, fitting in.

When she gets up to retrieve the second bottle of champagne from the fridge, she asks, 'So, why're you in your PJs so early?'

'Oh, I, ah, I fell off a horse.'

Jackie's eyes widen as she plonks on the couch and opens the champagne. 'Are you okay?'

'Yeah. I landed in a creek. Got pretty wet and cold, but that's all.'

Jackie squints at me, then fills our glasses again. 'If I remember rightly, there's no creek running through this property.'

'No, I ... ah, was at Clark's.'

She pauses, her glass halfway to her lips. 'Clark's?'

'The vet,' I answer, a little confused.

'Oh! Right, of course. I've just never heard anyone call him *Clark*. It's usually just Doc.' She gives me a curious, sideways glance. 'You were at his house? Daniel Clark's house?'

I hesitate, wondering why she sounds as if she doesn't believe it. 'Yeah ... is that not okay?'

'Of course it's okay, it's just ... I don't think I even know anyone who's been over there.' She cups her glass in her hands and lock eyes with me. 'But why? We *are* talking about the same guy, right? The one who dropped his coffees when—'

'Horse-riding lessons,' I blurt before she can say anything she might regret.

She gives a thoughtful nod. 'Hmm. Never heard of him giving riding lessons before. Ned Jamison's the one to go to for those.'

'The one in Riverview?' I ask, remembering what Clark had told me.

'No.' Jackie shakes her head. 'That's Bernie Wriggly.

Ned's only a ten-minute drive from here. He's been doing it his whole life.'

'Oh.' This isn't making any sense. 'But I don't have a float, so I can't get my horse there.'

'No need to. He's got heaps of horses to ride.'

She must see the confusion on my face, because she leans forward a little, clearly intrigued.

'What exactly did the doc ... Clark tell you?'

'Pretty much that he was the only one I could go to.'

'So, let me get this straight,' she says, a spark in her eyes. 'He told you he's the only one who gives lessons, and that you'd have to go over to his place to get them?'

I nod and take a sip of champagne.

'Well, that's definitely something.'

'He lied to me?' I ask.

'Well ... I suppose, but ... how much is he charging you?'

For the first time, I realise he's never asked me for any money. Then again, I haven't even asked him what he charges, nor offered him anything for his time. I'm a total idiot.

'Nothing,' I answer.

'Then I guess he didn't really lie, since technically he'd be the only person around here who doesn't charge for lessons ... if you want to look at it that way.'

'Right,' I say. He'd purposely eliminated all my options so he was the only choice I had. Why?

'So,' she says, 'what's he like?'

'You'd know him better than I do.'

Jackie shakes her head. 'Nope.'

'But ... hasn't he lived here for years?'

'About five or six. I can't remember exactly. But

nobody really knows him. I mean, up until the whole foot-and-mouth thing, he's been background furniture.'

'But you told me he was the town freak. What did that mean?'

'I shouldn't have said that,' she admits, her gaze sliding to her drink, shame written all over her face.

'But it meant something,' I push.

'It's just the whole gloves thing. Even in the middle of summer. It's a little weird.'

My mind races back to my childhood, to Luke and his sleeves. The middle of summer and he always wore a long-sleeved shirt. Using it to cover his hands.

My heart drums in my chest, but before I can think too long about it, Jackie continues.

'And then there's the way he barely interacts with anyone.' She gives a little shrug. 'I mean, he's great with animals, a great vet, but try to get a word out of him ... well, he's pretty much the most unsociable person around here.'

I let out a scoff.

'What?' she asks with a raised eyebrow.

'He doesn't seem to have any trouble talking to me. Sometimes it's hard to get him to shut up.'

'That doesn't sound like him at all.' She takes a long sip of her drink. 'Now that I think about it, after the coffee-dropping incident, he did come into the office wanting to know where he could find you so he could apologise. *That* definitely wasn't like him, either.' She stares into her glass for a moment, then looks up. 'You don't think ...'

'What?'

'That maybe he likes you.'

Instant heat hits my face, and it has nothing to do

with the champagne. I can't deny I think Jackie's right. Not after today, on the hill, at the creek. Not after wishing he'd kiss me.

Jackie clears her throat, bringing me back. 'Wherever you went just now, you looked pretty damn happy.'

It's only then I realise I'm smiling, that she's right. The very thought of him fills me with something I've never had before.

Jackie grins. 'I'd say it looks like you might like him, too.' Apparently pleased with herself, she gives my knee a little pat. 'Well, this isn't the conversation I thought I'd be having tonight.'

'I didn't say—'

'I know,' she says, and gives me a wink. 'You don't have to say anything.'

After Jackie's husband picks her up, I climb into bed, lie in the dark, and thinking about Clark. Although Jackie hadn't told me much of anything about him, she had given me one thing I'd been unaware of.

He lied about the riding lessons. At the time he'd offered them, I'd done nothing but treat him terribly, and while yes, I'd fed him, I hadn't exactly been warm about it. And he'd been fully aware I could get lessons somewhere else. So why lie?

Only one answer made sense. He wanted to spend more time with me. What didn't make sense was why he'd want to spend more time with someone who gave every indication she wanted the opposite.

If he'd offered now, after getting to know each other, that might make sense. But it hadn't made sense when he asked me. All he knew of me then was that I was angry and upset with him. Surely, any normal guy would've run for the hills.

But not Clark. He'd wanted to get closer to me.

Apparently, he hardly interacted with anyone, but he wanted to interact with me. Was it just some sort of weird attraction on his part? Did he think that because I'm also damaged goods, we might get along, understand each other? That, at least, made some sort of sense.

I just can't get over how much he reminds me of Lucas, how comfortable I am with him, like we've always known each other. And those eyes. Sure, other people have green eyes like his, but it isn't just that, is it? It's the *way* he looks at me. I can fantasise all I like about Lucas being alive, but I know two things. One: Dad would never lie to me. And two: Lucas would have healed his stallion's scars.

I groan in frustration. If I keep running it over and over in my head, I'll end up with no sleep and a headache. And it'll all be for nothing.

Maybe Jackie's right. Maybe Clark just likes me and it's as simple as that. He'd certainly given me a very strong message today. I might not have any experience with guys being attracted to me, but I'm not stupid, either. I don't need experience to understand how it felt when he looked at me the way he did today. Words had been completely unnecessary. That moment between us had been as natural and solid as gravity holding us to the surface of the earth.

That's what I need to hold onto, not some ridiculous fantasy about a magical boy from the past. The boy who'll only ever exist in my mind.

As I roll onto my side and close my eyes, I decide it's time to lock him away in that deep part of me again.

Maybe it's time to make room for someone real, someone alive. I just wish I could figure out why that someone is interested in me.

- 51 -

GEORGIA

GEORGIA TAKES HER FOOT off the sewing-machine pedal and bites her lip. Her gut tells her something isn't right. She pulls at the fabric and examines the stitching.

As a tightness forms across her forehead, she rolls her chair over to where her notepad rests on the desk and stares at the evening gown she sketched a few hours ago. The waist, she thinks. It looks right in the drawing, but it's not coming out that way on the machine.

A quick rap of knuckles on her door makes her jolt. In a panic, she shoves the sketch in a drawer full of fashion magazines and slams it shut.

'Yeah?' she says a little too loudly.

Swivelling in her chair, she meets her father's eyes

as he pokes his head around the door he's partially opened.

'Auctions are on today at Riverview. Can't buy anything yet, but it'll give us an idea of what's out there for when we can. You coming?'

Georgia can't think of anything more boring. 'Nah. Gotta repair these old clothes.' When his face drops, she adds, 'Maybe next time?'

'Right,' he says. 'See you later, then.'

Feeling like the worst daughter in the world for lying to him yet again, she waits until he closes her door before releasing a long breath. She hates this feeling. Deceiving him, knowing she doesn't want to be part of this life anymore, is killing her. It isn't him she doesn't want to be a part of, just the farm, the rural life, the boredom of doing the same thing over and over, every day blurring into the next with nothing new to look forward to.

Tears prick at her eyes. What she should do, what a good daughter would do, is stay here and work her butt off to make it up to him. She should be thinking of ways to make the farm bigger and better than ever. What she shouldn't be doing is running away and leaving him to deal with this mess on his own. Not when it's all her fault.

But it's her life, she reminds herself. And what happened was a mistake. She would never in a million years deliberately destroy her father's life. He's given her everything, especially after her mother died. He could have withdrawn into himself, closed himself off to her in his grief, but he hadn't. He'd put her first, her grief first, and he'd helped her through it all as best as he could.

Even that isn't enough. Not when she has this

yearning that lives in her very soul. Clothes call to her wherever she looks. Just walking along the street in town, she can't help but evaluate everyone she passes, mentally re-dressing them in either entirely new styles, or making modifications to the clothes they wear. She simply can't stop the thought process.

It's in her blood. Although Japan had brought it out stronger than ever, it's been that way for her from the moment her mother first twirled in front of her and asked if she liked the dress she'd been wearing for a rare night out. That moment, at the age of four, had been what started it all, and it's never let go.

Passion swirling inside her gut again, Georgia opens the drawer and removes the notepad. Running her fingers over the sketch, her mind whirs as it tries to figure out what's wrong.

Outside, her father's ute starts up and the familiar sound of crunching gravel fades as he drives away.

She rips the baseball cap off her head and shakes her long hair free, giving her scalp a good scratch. Staring at the dress on the sewing-machine, she frowns again, then stands. Maybe, if she tries on some of her other dresses, something will come to her.

She flings open the wardrobe doors and grins. With a loving touch, she runs her fingertips over her unique jackets, skirts, tops and dresses. When she reaches the dress she designed from memory—the dress her mother first asked her opinion on—her fingers pause, then pluck it from the wardrobe and hold it up in the sunlight streaming through her window.

Yes, she thinks. *This is going to be my life.* It's what her mother would have wanted for her. She knows it with all her heart.

- 52 -

LUCAS

I SPRAY DISINFECTANT ON the examination table and give it a good wipe before removing the latex gloves I'd just used to examine Rufus the tabby, the pride and joy of seven-year-old Ella.

Pulling on fresh gloves, I wander along the hallway to see who's next.

To my surprise, an anxious Mrs Winston and a trembling Poppet both sit in the otherwise empty waiting room.

I move forward, giving Emily a quick glance before setting my sights on Mrs Winston.

'Something wrong with Poppet?' I ask.

'Oh dear, yes,' she rushes. 'Her little foot's all red. I think she has something stuck in there, but I can't get a good look.'

I nod with concern. 'Bring her through,' I say, indicating for her to go ahead. As she rises with Poppet in her arms, I add, 'How's Mayor Winston today?'

This is so unlike me, it stops Mrs Winston in her tracks. She glances at Emily and raises her eyebrows in what I can only interpret as approval.

'Why thank you for asking,' she says with a smile. 'He's in quite good spirits, actually.'

As she walks towards the examination room, I catch Emily's baffled expression. Before she can say anything, I hurry after Mrs Winston and follow her into the room.

I wait for her to place Poppet on the examination table. The moment the little dog's right front paw touches the cool stainless steel, she lifts it, holding it beneath her small body.

I let Poppet sniff my glove, and in a few seconds her trembling stops, allowing me to gently examine her tiny paw. Sure enough, something's imbedded itself between her first and second toe.

'Looks like she might have a grass seed in there. You mind if she comes with me for a moment?' I ask Mrs Winston.

'Of course,' the elderly woman says with a nod.

I scoop up the three-kilo dog and carry her through to the operating room, gently kicking the door closed behind me, already knowing what I'm going to do. And why not? It'll basically cost me nothing.

With Poppet in the crook of my arm, I remove a glove and place her on the operating table. She stares up at me, watching my every move as I take her paw and spread her toes apart, all the while gently murmuring nonsense words. There's a little pus and a lot of angry inflammation around the seed.

Then I do what I'm made to do and hold her infected paw in my hand. That energy flows through me, feeling like it's coming from my heart and radiating down my arm until the heat hits my hand. Then it leaves me and pours into Poppet.

As I stand there, my hand welded to the little dog's paw, my mind once again drifts to Kelsey, how I'd been so damn close to kissing her, and later at the fence, how she'd leaned into me instead of away from me.

She likes me. I'm not so socially inept that I can't pick up on that.

I only realise I'm grinning like a fool when I notice Poppet licking my hand with uninhibited enthusiasm.

The familiar rush of euphoria spikes within me as I release her paw and stare at the grass seed in my palm.

As I follow Mrs Winston to the waiting room, she tries to get a good look at Poppet's paw.

'But I don't understand,' Mrs Winston repeats. 'I thought it was infected. It was all red and angry, and—'

'Once the grass seed came out, she was fine,' I reassure her. 'And no charge for today,' I say, hoping that puts a stop to her questions.

Mrs Winston beams at Emily, who tries to hide the disapproval that flashes in her eyes.

'Well, that's so very generous of you,' she says as I open the door and give Poppet's head a quick pat.

Smiling widely, I say, 'Hopefully, we won't see you too soon.'

She chuckles and wanders out, raising Poppet's perfectly healed paw and waving before she leaves.

'What's going on?' Emily snaps as I close the door.

I shrug. 'It won't hurt to give her one freebie.' I'm playing dumb, and by the look on her face, she knows it.

Ignoring her, I walk behind the reception desk, open a drawer and find one of the chocolate bars she keeps for upset kids. Tearing off the wrapper a little too enthusiastically, I take a huge bite.

'I don't mean just her,' she says, staring at me with piercing eyes. The eyes I haven't seen since I was a kid. The eyes that I've given no reason to look at me that way for … well, about twenty years, I guess.

My mouthful of chocolate awards me some precious time to try to come up with a bullshit story she might buy.

'Well?' she demands.

I lick my teeth and gums in an effort to clear the chocolate coating every surface of my mouth.

'I think it's the foot-and-mouth thing. Guess I'm not the town freak anymore.'

Emily sighs heavily, shaking her head.

Well, it sounded good to me.

'No,' she says. 'It's you, not them. I can hardly ever get you on your phone anymore because you're too busy doing God knows what. You're smiling more, and …'

Her eyes widen, and my stomach drops. Mothers. Apparently, they know their kids too well.

'You've met someone.'

It's not a question, so I don't answer. Instead, I swallow and look at the floor. Really, there's no need for words when it comes to my mother.

You've met someone.

I roll the words over in my mind. I can't deny they're true. At least, for me. But they only really mean anything if they're true for Kelsey, as well.

In my peripheral vision, I see Emily stand.

'Who?' she asks. 'Who in this town is interested …

it's the woman who moved into the old Edwards' farm, isn't it? The woman you've conveniently forgotten to give me the details for so I can put her in the system.'

I shrug, a little surprised the gossip hounds around here haven't mentioned her to my mother. Even if they don't know her name yet, they'd be sure to bring up the scars on her face. That'd be more than enough to tip her off.

'Oh, Luke ...' she says. 'You can't—'

'Don't tell me what I can't do,' I bite, anger suddenly bubbling up inside me. Always denying me, always trying to stop me from finding any happiness in my life. 'And it's Daniel, remember?'

I see the hurt in her eyes, but I'm not giving in.

'I know exactly who you are,' she says as she steps forward and grips my arms.

I make a half-arsed attempt at pulling away, but she holds on tighter.

'Don't you think I want you to fall in love and enjoy all the wonderful things that come with it? But it's too dangerous. You damn well know that, Lucas. Getting close to someone means certain death. Just like the others, you won't be able to help yourself. None of you have lived long for that very reason. Love is a death sentence.'

My heart pounds as I give her a long, steady look. The words I'm about to say will hurt her, but they'll also be the most truthful thing I'll ever tell her.

'I don't care. She's worth it.'

<><><>

As I stride along the street, I feel like a heel, but also lighter, even ... yes, even happy. When was the last time I'd had that thought? I know the answer, of course. Everything positive always came back to Kelsey.

None of which means she'll let me into her life. For the moment, as I enter the café, I push that thought aside and just enjoy the notion that there's hope.

From behind the counter, Jo gives me a huge grin, which I can't help but return. I don't miss the surprised expression she unsuccessfully tries to hide.

'Hey, Doc. The usual?' she asks, already turning towards the coffee machine before I answer.

'Thanks.'

As the machine hisses and spits, Jo gives me a sideways glance. 'How's everything?' she asks.

'Actually, pretty good,' I reply, again seeing surprise spring into her eyes.

On the street, a hot coffee in my gloved hand, the sun warm on my face, I take in the trees lining the street, the tiny buds dotting the branches, and for once in my life I feel in sync with nature, the prospect of a new life before me, ready to bloom.

Until she finds out who you are.

I push the thought aside as a local man I can't recall the name of approaches.

'Hey, Doc. How's it going?' he says as he walks within earshot.

I raise my coffee and nod my head as he passes by.

On the road, a car horn gives a couple of sharp toots. I look over and see Rob Cunningham giving me a thumbs up through his open window. I raise my hand in acknowledgement.

When I turn my attention back to the street, my smile falters and I stop.

A few metres away, Bryce stands motionless, staring

at me. It's hard to tell whether it's utter hatred or fear on his face. With all my spare time spent with Kelsey, I've forgotten about him. It's actually quite a feat that I haven't run into him until now, but I guess he's been a little busy.

I stare at him as I take a sip of coffee. 'Bryce,' I say by way of greeting.

'Keep away from me, you ...' Bryce clenches his fists at his sides. 'Whatever the hell you are.'

We stare at each other. Me staring at a man who tried to kill me and destroy the whole town's farming community. Bryce staring at a man who defied death and exposed his negligence. Well, we can't stand here like this all day.

I take two steps closer, and in a low voice say, 'Not dead, is what I am.'

Unnerved, Bryce takes off across the street, an angry horn blaring as an SUV slams on the brakes, barely missing the old man.

'Well, that wasn't very smart.'

I turn to find Jackie emerging from her real estate office. She sidles up to me, her eyes still on Bryce as he hurries along the opposite side of the street.

Turning her attention my way, she says, 'I hear you've been giving our newest resident riding lessons.'

I suppress a smile. So, Kelsey's been talking about me. That feels pretty damn good.

Playing it down, I shrug. 'No one else around here to do it.'

'I thought Ned Jamison gave lessons?' Jackie says, the corner of her mouth twitching.

I shrug again and take a sip of my cooling coffee.

'Well, either way,' she says, giving me a knowing look, 'it's very nice of you.'

I gulp at the coffee to take the pressure off trying to have a conversation with her. There's really only one thing I want to ask her. *What else has Kelsey said about me?* But I'm sure if I do, it'll get back to Kelsey in no time, and I'm looking forward to seeing her this afternoon. I can do without other people offering her an opinion on me. Though lately, everyone seems to see me rather differently than they did before she arrived. I guess I really should thank Bryce for that. But I won't.

'Also,' she continues, 'I was wondering if you'll be attending the spring talent show this year? We'd love to have our local hero there.'

I shift uncomfortably. 'I really wish you wouldn't call me that.'

A little further along the street, I notice an elderly couple I've never seen before approach the pedestrian crossing.

'I'll make you a deal. If you promise to attend, I'll call you Dan. Or is it Clark? That's what Kelsey calls you.'

Oh, she does, does she? This is news to me. My mind searches through our time together and I can't for the life of me remember her calling me anything at all. Interesting.

As I think about what that might mean, the elderly woman comes to an abrupt stop halfway over the crossing.

'I, ah … I'm not sure,' I say, unconsciously taking a step towards the crossing.

'Well, have a think—what's …'

The elderly woman's legs buckle. As her equally elderly companion tries desperately to stop her from falling, a single thought races through my brain.

Not now!

'Oh no!' Jackie yells beside me. High heels clicking on the pavement, she dashes precariously towards the couple.

Unable to help myself, I race after her, but as she reaches the crossing and other bystanders begin to gather, I feel that incredible pull. Instead of embracing it, I try to push it down.

'It's her heart!' the elderly man, presumably her husband, yells at no one in particular. 'Somebody help! Please!'

His wife lies flat on the crossing, her husband on his knees beside her as she gasps for breath, her eyes wide, helpless.

Help her!

One bystander says he'll get Doc Evans, the local GP, and takes off towards the doctor's surgery.

My hands tingle with anticipation, but I don't move. Even from where I stand, I can see the life draining from the elderly woman.

'Please ...' the elderly man begs, his voice quieter. 'Somebody ... please ...' He looks up at the gathered crowd, tears slipping over his wrinkled cheeks.

I resist every urge in my body to go to her. I resist because I know what will happen if I touch her. Not too long ago, I might have seriously considered it. The way I felt then, I might have been willing to give my life for hers. Better than dying from Bryce's bullet. But I'm not the man I was that short time ago. Everything's different now.

Now I have a reason to stay alive.

Now I have a reason to be selfish.

I fist my throbbing hands at my sides and swallow over the lump in my throat.

Across the street, Doc Evans pushes through the

gathering crowd. I make my move while no one's watching and step back. As more locals hurry from stores along both sides of the street, I walk away.

Heart pounding, knowing the elderly lady's heart has probably already stopped, I walk faster and faster until I break into a run. Even though running might attract attention, I can't stop myself. I have to get as far away as I can.

The pressure of it all, the impossible choice, is something I can't seem to outrun. Who am I to decide whether she lives and I die? Who am I to decide whose life is more important? As I try my hardest to outrun the impossible, nausea sweeps over me.

Bolting past my clinic door, I take the corner. Bracing myself against the old brick wall, I break into a sweat as saliva rushes into my mouth.

I lean over and vomit. Warm coffee projects from my mouth and hits the cracked pavement, splashing the wall and no doubt my shoes and jeans.

As I tremble all over, I realise something else.

I'm alive because I *did* make a choice. And I made that choice for a reason. It's time to stop fucking around and make the most of that reason.

- 53 -

GEORGIA

GEORGIA TWIRLS IN FRONT of her bedroom mirror, inspecting the perfectly fitted formal gown she's just finished. Eyeing it from every angle she possibly can, she clasps her hands in front of her and beams at herself.

Releasing a tiny squeal of delight, she performs a little happy dance before carefully removing the dress and laying it on her bed.

After pulling on her robe, she glides her fingers over the silky, cranberry-coloured material. When she reaches the neck, she touches the hand-stitched label. The raised letters read GEORGIA.

Spinning on her heel, she opens her closet doors, grabs a pretty summer dress and turns it inside out. Then she plonks down in front of her sewing machine, grabs a GEORGIA label and pins it to the dress.

As she positions the garment and label beneath the needle, the doorbell rings. Hesitating, she cocks her head and listens to her father's heavy footfalls. Curious, she leaves her dress and parts her curtains just enough to see a black SUV parked in the driveway.

She'd been so engrossed in her work, she hadn't even heard it arrive.

As the doorbell rings again, she crosses the room and quietly opens her bedroom door.

- 54 -

BRYCE

'ALRIGHT, ALRIGHT,' BRYCE GRUMBLES as he reaches the front door and wrenches it open.

Two men in suits stare at him. Bryce squints at them with suspicion.

The older of the two speaks first. 'Mr Hargraves?'

'Who's asking?' he snaps, wanting nothing more than to slam the door in their faces. When has anything good come of two suits turning up on a man's doorstep?

The older suit glances at the younger one, which seems to be some sort of permission for the young man to speak.

'Mr Hargraves, we're from the Quarantine and Inspection Service. The Department of Agriculture has lodged a full report regarding the foot-and-mouth outbreak on your premises. I'm here to confirm their conclusion that the outbreak resulted from your daughter's recent trip to Japan.'

Just as he thought, nothing good. Bryce glances into the house, and satisfied, lowers his voice.

'Yeah, that's right,' he says. 'So it's confirmed. Now piss off.' He takes a couple of steps back and swings the door closed.

'I'm sorry, sir,' the older suit says, placing a firm hand on the door before it closes. 'It's not that simple. There are substantial financial penalties for such an offence.'

Barely able to contain his rage, Bryce swings the door wide and moves into the suits' personal space, forcing them to retreat a few steps. Closing the door behind him, he scowls at the two men.

'She's seventeen, for fuck's sake. What the hell do you want from her?'

'That's quite irrelevant,' the older suit says. 'Someone must be held accountable. We're here to discuss what that's going to look like.'

- 55 -

KELSEY

MUSIC BLASTS FROM THE stereo in my living room as I sit on the couch and scrawl furiously on a thick notepad. After a moment, the pen pauses. I bite my lower lip, think, then write and write.

Tossing the pen on the coffee table, I place the notepad beside me, pick up my guitar and position it on my lap.

As I study the words on the notepad, I blindly reach for a remote control, press a button and plunge the room into silence.

Plucking at the strings on the guitar, I fumble and start again. This time, the melody runs through my finger like I've played it a thousand times. Studying the notepad, I begin to sing the lyrics.

I start soft and tentative, slowly increasing the

passion, building upon the build. Unlike when I lived in an apartment and had to worry about how much noise I made, I let loose, let my voice soar with all the emotion the lyrics convey.

The power of the music runs through my entire body, buoying me up, higher and higher until the final few notes bring my voice back down to a soft, emotional tone.

As I strum the last note, I break into a grin, heart ticking fast in my chest. This one … this song, comes from somewhere new inside me, somewhere I like. A lot.

For the first time, I'm not going to sell the lyrics to another artist. This song is mine, and only mine.

Still grinning like a fool, I put the guitar aside and rise. When I glance through the front window, I notice Clark's vehicle in the driveway. I check my watch. He's early, but instead of being annoyed, I'm glad.

Cheeks aching, my smile widens as I hurry into the hallway. Before I reach the front door, I stop at the hall mirror, give my hair a primp, then roll my eyes at myself.

'Yeah, that'll help,' I mutter.

Taking a moment to wonder why I care about my appearance anyway, I reach for the door before any more stupid thoughts can cross my mind.

When I open it, the verandah appears empty. Wondering if he went straight to the stables, I push through the screen door and heads towards the steps.

'Hey.'

I whirl around to find him leaning against the house beside the living-room window. Placing a hand over my heart, I gape at him.

'Jesus. How long have you been here?'

'Long enough to know you lied.'

'What?' I have no idea what the hell he's talking about, but I know one thing. 'I don't lie.'

He pushes away from the wall and takes a few slow strides towards me.

'Funny,' he says, placing his hands on his hips. 'I specifically remember you telling me you don't perform your own songs because you can't sing. That's gotta be the biggest lie I've ever heard.'

Heat races through my body, burning my face. Not only is he calling me a liar, he'd been listening to me when I truly believed I was alone.

'I don't appreciate being spied on,' I snap, hoping he can hear the anger in my voice and shut the hell up about my singing.

'I wasn't spying. I believe you invited me here. And when I arrived and walked up to your door … well, there was no way I was going to interrupt the most amazing voice I've ever heard.'

Frozen, I look into his eyes and all I see there is honesty. He's not fucking with me. He means it. And that moves something deep inside me, something I can't quite grasp, but know is important, good. Maybe even more than just good.

'Did you bring the saddle?' I ask quickly, trying to distract him by getting back to why he's here in the first place.

The cheeky bastard knows it, too, because he gives me that lopsided grin of his. 'It's in the car.'

I stomp down the verandah steps and head towards his four-wheel drive. As I reach the tailgate, he catches up, his grin fading a little.

'So, why lie?' he presses.

'Is it open?' I ask, astounded he's still pushing. I

reach for the tailgate handle, but before I can wrap my hand around it, the car lets out a chirp, followed by a distinctive clunk. I turn, spotting a key fob in his hand.

Folding my arms over my chest, I stare daggers at him as he moves up beside me and leans on the dusty vehicle.

'Well?' he persists.

Why does he care what I do or don't do? Breaking eye contact, I look at the gravel between us. 'It's a stupid question.'

'I think it's perfectly logical. You write music, you must want to—'

'No one wants to look at this.' I point at the scars on my face and glare at him. 'No one gives a shit how well anyone sings anymore. It's all about looks and sex appeal and bullshit.'

Embarrassed, wondering where that rant came from, I take a breath and release it, willing my heart to stop racing. I shouldn't give a rat's arse what he thinks, but I do.

'Now,' I say, 'can I get the saddle?'

He unlocks the car, opens the tailgate and removes the saddle. When he straightens up, he says, 'But how can you deny—'

'Oh my God!' He just won't let up. 'I don't need the third degree about my career. All I want is for you make sure my horse is safe to ride. Speaking of which, how much do I owe you for the lessons?'

The faint smile remaining on his lips completely vanishes. 'I don't want your money. What I want ... well ... I'd hoped I was more to you than just some riding instructor.'

I can see it in his eyes. I've hurt him. And I don't like that feeling one bit.

Turning away, I walk towards the stables so he can't see how much I regret causing him pain. Behind me, his footfalls crunch on the gravel.

'Come on, Kelsey,' he says, 'I'm interested. I want to know … how can you deny your dream—who you are—just because of what others might think?'

He's not blind. He knows why.

'You were never supposed to hear me,' I say, walking a little faster.

But he's right there beside me, glancing at me, having no trouble keeping up.

'Have you even tried performing in front of anyone?' he asks.

'When I was a kid. Before …'

'And that's it?'

I nod, wishing he'd stop.

'Then you don't know, do you? If you haven't tried … you're actually the one judging people before they ever have a chance to judge you.'

'Easy for you to say,' I bite back.

'You seem to forget, I'm the town freak. I know what it's like.'

I scoff, pull up and face him. 'Bullshit. You're the town hero. Besides that, you can take off those gloves anytime you like and no one'd know you're any different. But I can't take off my face.'

'You'd certainly get some stares if you did.'

Despite myself, I smile, and before I even know what I'm doing, I backhand his arm. 'You're an idiot.'

'And that's news to you?' He winks at me, then glances towards the stables. 'I'm not sure why you're standing around insulting me. I thought you wanted to ride?'

'Maybe insulting you is more fun,' I admit.

He chuckles. 'Oh, now you have no problem telling the truth.' As we both walk towards the stables, he gives me a playful bump.

Relaxing now that he's not interrogating me, I ask, 'So … you like listening to music, songs?'

'Yeah,' he says. 'Does something for the soul. At least, that's how it makes me feel when I listen to something amazing. Something like what I just heard—'

'What's your favourite song?' I blurt before he can start in on that again.

He rubs his chin. 'That's a hard one.'

I watch him from the corner of my eye as he thinks.

'Well, it's an old one. I doubt many people know it.'

I grin, gently elbowing him. 'The suspense is killing me. Spit it out. It's no big deal.'

He laughs. 'I'm not so sure about that.'

'I'll tell you what mine is if you tell me yours.' I want to stop walking and face him, want to know what moves Clark to his very soul. Something I completely understand. But if I stop and look at him, he might realise that I *do* think it's a big deal.

He gives me a quick glance, then looks towards the stables as we approach. 'It's called "Don't Let it Show" by Alan Parsons. Heard of it?'

I shake my head. 'I don't think so.'

'Well, like I said, I don't think it's all that well known. So, let's hear yours.'

'Oh, if I told you that, I'd have to kill you.'

He stops. 'Hey! Wait a minute.' I keep moving but turn and walk backwards as I grin at him.

'You said—'

'You said I was a liar.' I shrug. 'Guess you're right.'

<><><>

The light outside fades as I slip a halter onto my horse, who I've finally decided to call Frankie. Taking a sugar cube from my jacket pocket, I feed it to him, enjoying the tickle of his whiskers on my palm.

Everything had gone perfectly with Clark riding the gelding, then handing the reins over to me once he believed Frankie was safe. A little nervous at first, I'd quickly realised my own horse was just as easy to ride as Perry.

On the one hand, I'd been elated that I hadn't made such a bad purchase, after all. On the other hand, I felt a dull disappointment in the pit of my stomach.

Glancing up, I watch Clark brush Frankie with firm, long strokes. He catches my gaze.

'Well, you're all set to ride on your own now,' he says.

As his gloved hand glides over the gelding, I'm fully aware of why I'm feeling that dull disappointment. I no longer have a reason to see him anymore. My riding has come along in leaps and bounds because he's a fantastic teacher, has generously given me more of his time than expected, and now my horse is safe to ride.

Trying to think of a reason to see him again, I realise there doesn't need to be one. Isn't it enough that we enjoy each other's company?

'Would you like to stay for dinner?' I ask before I chicken out.

His hand stills on Frankie as our eyes lock. Suddenly shy, I glance away and give the gelding's head a scratch.

'Well,' he says slowly, 'I guess, since you didn't kill me last time, that'd be okay.'

'I feel so privileged.' I press my lips together to keep from grinning like an idiot. 'How about you go turn on the lights?'

He gives me an amused smile and saunters towards the door. As I walk Frankie to his stall, I find myself staring at Clark's backside. Again. A little ashamed, I unclip Frankie's lead from his halter and close the stable door.

When I look in Clark's direction, he's standing in the open doorway, staring at the red-streaked clouds.

Seeing him lost in the sky's beauty makes me smile. He really appreciates all the world has to offer, taking nothing for granted. I admire that about him.

Watching, I wonder if I should join him. Then I take that thought further. Imagine standing beside him, watching the colours of the sky change as everything descends into night. Imagine looking at him and him looking at me. Imagine him leaning in and kissing me.

I shake my head. Sure, I'd often wondered what it would feel like to be kissed, but I'd never had a particular person in mind. A person I *wanted* to kiss. I'd certainly never encountered a man who actually wanted to kiss *me*. Is that what my dinner invitation is all about?

Releasing a long breath, I wrench my eyes from his silhouette and glance at my watch.

Barely able to see the time, I call out, 'Lights?'

Clark jumps a little, glances over his shoulder at me and quickly stretches towards the light switch.

Suddenly, he jerks back. 'Ah, shit.'

That doesn't sound good. As I hurry towards him, his silhouette clamps a hand over his ribs.

'What is it?' I ask, flicking on the lights.

He hesitates a moment, his expression trying to hide what I can only guess is pain.

'It's nothing,' he lies.

I frown at the hand covering his ribs, which doesn't quite cover the tear in his shirt.

'Oh my God,' I gasp. 'What—'

I glance at the rusty nail I'd forgotten about.

'I'm so sorry,' I say, facing him again. 'I meant to hammer the bloody thing down. Let me see.' As I reach towards him, he takes a step away.

'It's nothing,' he repeats. 'Just a scratch.'

Not believing a word of it, I move closer. Again, he retreats. That's when I notice blood seeping into his shirt below his gloved hand.

'You're bleeding.'

He shrugs. 'Scratches tend to do that.'

'Not that much.' When I step closer, he moves away.

'You know,' he says, giving me a lame smile, 'I think I should get go—'

'Oh, for God's sake,' I grab his arm and pull him through the doorway towards the house. As I drag him along, I wonder why he's acting so weird.

- 56 -

LUCAS

MY MIND RACES AS Kelsey leads me through her living room and down a hallway. I really need to leave so I can fix what I know is a large gash over my ribs. Even with the pressure I'm applying with my hand, I can feel the blood oozing from the wound, can definitely feel the pain.

So stupid. I should have paid more attention to what I was doing instead of being off in dreamland, running over the time I'd spent with Kelsey, over the fact that she doesn't need me anymore, doesn't have any reason to see me on a regular basis. And running over how I can get around that problem.

Because it's now the biggest problem I have.

As she leads me into her small bathroom, my heart hammers in my chest, and it has nothing to do with my injury.

'Sit,' she tells me as she releases my arm and places a hand on my shoulder, applying pressure until my arse rests on the side of the tub.

When her hand disappears, I miss it instantly. Even with the searing pain over my ribs, having her touch me again sends all sorts of wonderful reactions through my body.

As she opens the medicine cabinet above the sink, a growing sense of trepidation overwhelms me, and I stand. But she's blocking my path to the door, and without pressing right up against her, there's no way out.

'I really have to go.'

She gives a little snort and frowns at me. Placing some cotton swabs on the vanity, she grips my shoulders and forces me back down.

'Don't be such a baby,' she admonishes. 'Take off your shirt.'

I suppose, in her eyes, I'm acting like a total wuss. Well, even in my eyes.

'I don't think that's—'

She puts her hands on her hips and glares at me. 'Do it.'

Bossy, but I know she's only trying to help. With a half-hearted effort, my gloved fingers fumble with my shirt buttons.

'Oh, for heaven's sake,' she says, and brushes my hands away in frustration. She works the buttons, starting at the top and moving down quickly. Fascinated, I watch as my shirt opens, as her bare knuckles accidentally brush against my skin. Reaching the last few buttons, her fingers—so swift before— now tremble and fumble.

'You know,' she says, avoiding my gaze, 'you could do this yourself if you'd take off those gloves.'

'Why would I want to do that?' And I mean it. For once, they're working in my favour.

Our eyes lock for a moment before she glances away and finishes undoing the last button. Hands shaking, she brings them up to my chest and slips them beneath each side of my shirt. As she eases it from my shoulders, her fingertips brush against my skin. Her touch, so light and sensual, takes me completely by surprise. My breath catches as I look up into her face, aware of just how intimate the moment is … and aware that she could have moved my shirt aside without touching my skin.

As the shirt pools at my bent elbows, she gasps, her eyes snapping to mine. 'That's no scratch.'

I gaze at the angry tear a few inches below my right pec. Blood oozes from the open wound, and it hurts like hell. I'm not used to enduring the pain of an injury for more than a few seconds, but right now, I simply don't care.

'You'll need stitches,' she says.

I stand, forcing her back a step.

'Not this instant. Let me patch you up or you'll bleed all the way to the doctors.'

Tense, I wait in the cramped space as she runs a washcloth under the tap. Of course, it isn't all bad. Being so close to her feels nerve-racking and like coming home all at once.

She turns to me and presses the warm washcloth to my skin just below the wound. My heartbeat accelerates. I want to feel the touch of her fingers again. Very slowly, she gently wipes away the blood, taking great care not to get too close to the wound and cause me more pain. I can barely stand it.

'You are, you know,' she murmurs.

I have no idea what she's talking about, so I wait. But as she works the washcloth on my skin, I get the feeling she's changed her mind about whatever she was trying to tell me.

'I am what?' I ask.

Whether to steady herself, or get better leverage, she brings up her free hand and places it on my side. Against my skin. The deliberate touch is electric, and I hitch in a sharp breath, letting her know the effect she's having on me.

She meets my eyes, the washcloth motionless between us. I see it then. She's dropped her guard, and I'm looking into eyes that want the same thing I do.

'You are ... more to me than just a riding instructor,' she breathes.

My heart stops in my chest for a moment, before thundering with hope. Even though she'd ignored me when I said those words, she'd heard me. Of course, she might mean she sees me as a friend. But there's no denying the charged atmosphere around us, the way she's deliberately touched me. Twice. This time, I have to know. I need to start living. And that means taking risks.

With our eyes locked, I lower my head. Slowly. Waiting for any indication she doesn't want this. Her eyes flick from side to side as we stare at each other, and her fingers tighten on my side.

I close the gap, making my intentions completely clear, and when she still doesn't move away, I press my mouth to hers. So soft, so warm. Easing the pressure a little, I brush my lips over hers in a whisper of a kiss. And to my surprise and delight, I feel the slightest movement beneath my mouth, just enough to understand she's tentatively kissing me back.

But more than wanting my lips on hers, I want to know what she's thinking.

When I lift my head, she stares at me. And I see desire reflecting back. *Thank God.* I kiss her again, this time opening my mouth enough to gently draw on her lower lip. She matches me, pulling on my top lip, and a low rumble vibrates through my body as I reach for her with my clean glove, place my hand on her hip and inch her closer.

Still pressed against me, the washcloth slips. She gasps and pulls away.

I've blown it.

Unnerved, swallowing hard, she retreats a step. 'I think you ...' her voice trembles as she trails off.

'Should go?' I finish for her, even though it's the last thing I want to do.

She hesitates for a second. When her gaze slides from mine, she nods and retreats another step.

Suddenly, the pain from the gash comes rushing back. I hadn't even realised it'd vanished until this very moment.

'I ...' But I don't even know what I'm going to say. Not the truth. Not that I don't want to go anywhere. That'll only scare her. And I don't want to freak her out any more than I already have. 'Mind if I clean up first?'

She gives me a slight nod, turns and closes the bathroom door behind her.

I draw in a deep, shaky breath, place my hands on the side of the basin to steady myself, and meet my eyes in the mirror.

What the hell have I done? Have I ruined

everything? Or started something new and wonderful? How can I know? What experience do I have with anything like this?

Emotions whirl and ebb through my entire body, drawing my attention right back to the painful gash.

I straighten up, remove my left glove and place my hand over the wound. Feeling the heat radiate into my palm, I can't help but remember the warmth of Kelsey's hand on my skin. The only person to ever touch me, the only person I ever *want* to touch me.

Jesus. How am I supposed to forget her touch, forget the feel of her lips against mine?

Remembering I'm supposed to be leaving, I turn to the basin and see the blood I've left smeared on the porcelain.

Taking the wet washcloth, I clean up and quickly button my shirt. When I look at myself in the mirror, I can see straight through the tear in the material, straight through to my completely healed skin. I should have waited until I was in the car before healing myself, but I'm not thinking clearly.

I shove my glove on, open the door and place my hand over the revealing tear in my shirt. From the hallway, I hear fast footsteps coming from the polished floorboards in the living room. They stop, start again. Stop, start again. She's pacing.

When I walk down the hallway and look in at her, she stands stock-still apart from her hands clasping and unclasping in front of her.

'Should I drive you?' she asks, the worry on her face, in her voice, more than evident. 'I should—'

'No,' I blurt. As much as I'd love to have her in the car with me, I'm not going anywhere but home. That'd be a little hard to explain. 'I'm fine,' I reassure her. 'I'd better get going.'

Careful to keep one hand over my torn shirt, I open the front door.

'Hey?' she says from close behind me. Still not using my name, I notice. Even though her voice is cautious, it's also curious and soft. A spark of hope leaps inside me as I turn towards her.

'I'm sorry,' she says, her eyes finding mine, then skittering away. 'I just …'

I wait a moment, but can see she's stuck, so I let her off the hook. 'It's not your fault. I should've been more careful.'

I give her a smile, walk out the door and gently shut it behind me, knowing full well she wasn't apologising to me for getting injured. She was apologising for not being ready for what I want between us.

- 57 -

GEORGIA

IN A PARKA, JEANS and gumboots, her hair tied back and a beanie on her head, Georgia stands in the paddock, staring into the distance towards the end of the driveway.

She wonders if today will be the day that either begins her life or ends it. Those are the only two possibilities. There's no in between.

'Georgie,' her father says in frustration.

Snapping out of her thoughts, she tries to focus on the task at hand. She feeds the wire she's been clutching through a star post, grabs the end and walks it to the next post, watching the coil of wire spool off its spindle without tangling.

She repeats the process five times before she reaches her father and hands him the end of the wire.

He uses pliers to wrap it around the post and secure it in place so the sharp end safely tucks in on itself.

'Dad?' she asks, hesitant.

He grunts in acknowledgement as he places the pliers in his toolbox and removes the tensioner.

Georgia's heart beats a little faster. 'Haven't you ever wanted to do something else?'

Bryce secures the tensioner and gives her a perplexed look before tightening the wire. 'Hell no. This is who I am. It's my life, our life. Who'd wanna leave all this?'

Not the answer she wants at all. Watching as he picks up the star-post banger, she notices how much he strains when he straightens. She stoops down, grabs a couple of star posts and follows him at a ninety-degree angle to the fence they'd just completed. She hands him one of the star posts.

'I just thought … maybe, since you're getting older, it might be harder to do all this physical stuff.'

He lines up the star post with the end of the other fence, gives it a good whack into the ground with a hammer, then strains again as he lifts the banger up high and lowers it over the post.

Georgia presses her fingers to her ears, waiting for him to start the noisy process of driving the post into the ground. Instead, he's looking at her. She takes her fingers away from her ears.

'That's a strange thing to ask. Why do you think I've been teaching you your whole life? Just like my father taught me and his father before him. All this is yours, Georgie. I'm not about to let anything ruin that. Not even that prick next door.'

'He was only doing his—'

Bryce holds up a finger. 'Don't you dare say that.

Don't you dare.'

He turns away from her and slams the banger down on the post before she can cover her ears. The sharp clang of metal on metal makes her wince.

Pressing her fingers to her ears, she jumps with each clang as her father drives the star post further into the ground.

She wants to run away, but stays put and blinks back the tears that threaten to slip from her eyes. All she can do is hope against hope that soon she'll be gone.

- 58 -

KELSEY

WITH MY GUITAR RESTING on the couch beside me and a notebook on my lap, I press the tip of the pen to the empty page, but it refuses to move.

Clark's favourite song comes into my head again. Of course, I'd played it as soon as he'd left and I'd calmed down. Putting on headphones to block everything out, I'd lain in bed with the lights off and let the words wash over me. After just a few lines, tears had spilled from my eyes. By the time I'd listened to all the lyrics I'd been a blubbering mess. The words could be interpreted in so many ways, but I understood how Clark connected with them, why they moved him and why he'd been that little bit reluctant to let me into his world in that way. What I hadn't been prepared for was how I'd connected with the words, as well. Had he known I would? Had he deliberately chosen that song for that very reason?

Or am I reading too much into it?

I sigh in frustration and slam the notebook down on the coffee table.

I haven't written anything in what, three days?

Has it been that long since he'd kissed—

My phone rings. Clark's name appears on the display. I blink at it, wondering for a second if just the thought of him somehow made him think of me.

Again.

Like every other time he's called me in the last few days, my heart gallops, and I bite my lip, hard. I want to answer, want to hear his voice, want to see him. Want all those things more than anything. Even more than my need to sing.

But I can't. I can't put myself through what I know will eventually lead to my heart breaking. He's too good for me, too handsome, too kind, too caring, too everything. He deserves someone beautiful in his life, not a hideous creature.

When the ringing stops, I wait for what feels like an eternity. Maybe this time, he'll give up and not bother leaving a message. But when I hear the familiar chime telling me he's done just that, relief washes over me.

I grab the phone and dial message bank as fast as my fingers possibly can.

Putting the phone on speaker, I wait as the automated voice tells me I have one new message and five saved messages.

'Hi, Kelsey. It's been a few days and ... well, you haven't called back. I don't like being a pest, so I won't bother you anymore. I just thought ... I thought maybe we could have that dinner we missed out on? Will you give me a call? Even if it's

just to say no.'

When the automated voice asks me what I want to do, I replay the message. Twice.

I can hear it in his voice; the sadness mixed with hope. He tried to bury it, but I know him too well now.

My fingers itch to call him. It's mean of me to ghost him like this. I know it and hate myself for it.

'Fuck,' I say under my breath. 'Fuck, fuck, fuck!'

Standing, I stalk into the hallway, take a deep breath and stare into the mirror.

As I study the scars on my face, I glare at myself. Even contemplating letting him get closer is so ridiculous I can't fathom how such a stupid, self-centred thought ever entered my head.

But it had, and it's still there. Tormenting me.

If only he hadn't kissed me. I can't wrap my head around what he'd been thinking. Nor can I do the same about my own actions. It wasn't as if I'd pushed him away, told him to get lost, that I'd never think of him like that.

I should have. Instead, I'd kissed him back. Not once, but twice. Sure, I'd come to my senses, but how had that kiss even happened in the first place?

Because I'd wanted it to.

I need to stop lying to myself. I'm clearly falling for Clark, whether I think I deserve him or not.

The worst thing is, I don't just hope to kiss him again. No, that's too simple. I want everything, all of him. To hold him and have him hold me. To have him inside me, in my life. Permanently. To combine our lives and be a couple.

I want all of it. And even though I know it's crazy when I've known him for such a short time, it feels right.

Except for one minor detail.

My face.

No one wants to look at my scars for the rest of their lives.

Glaring at myself in the mirror, I try to summon all the anger I can usually conjure up when I think about the injustice of this world, of what happened to me. Of how it all could have been different if Luke had done that amazing, magical thing for me.

But as I pull my hair away from my face, the anger doesn't come to save me like it usually does. This time, I let the sadness slip in.

- 59 -

LUCAS

I WIPE DOWN THE operating table, and the second I finish, I grab my phone and check it.

There's been no beep or vibration to tell me I've missed a call or received a message, so when I find no sign of either, I shouldn't be disappointed.

But I am.

She kissed me back, I remind myself. And now she doesn't want anything to do with me.

Reaching into my pocket, I find my leather gloves and wrench them on, hating them all over again.

God, I wanted to touch her with my bare hands. The way she touched me. And I knew I could, that I'd be in no danger. She wasn't sick, and she never will be. If nothing else, at least I've given her that.

The thought doesn't help much. I fist my hands,

loathing the feel of the leather tightening over my knuckles.

Stalking out, I head through the waiting room, thankful it's empty. From the corner of my eye, I notice Emily's head snap up, but I avoid her gaze and hurry towards the door.

'Where're you going?' she asks.

'Lunch.'

'You could offer to get me something.'

I don't even try to hide my annoyance. Spinning on my heel, I face her. 'What do you want?'

Her eyes widen a little, then settle on mine, studying me.

'Well?' I ask impatiently.

'It's that … Kelsey girl, isn't it?'

So, she does know.

'Don't say it like that,' I snap.

'How do you expect me to say it?' She stands and leans against the reception counter. 'You think I've forgotten what happened last time you were involved with her? I almost lost you that day.' She takes a breath, her eyes boring into mine. 'Why didn't you tell me who she was?'

'Because it's none of your business.'

'Did you really think you could hide her from me? In this town? I've been waiting for you to tell me for weeks.'

I almost laugh. She's acting like I'm a kid again, like she has control over the situation.

'Stay out of it,' I warn her.

'I will not. You're all I have. And look at you. One minute the happiest I've ever seen you, the next all riled up. What's happened?'

I soften a little. She's right. I shouldn't be taking out

my frustration on her. 'Listen, she doesn't even know who I am. To her, I'm Daniel Clark, the local vet. That's all.'

As that sinks in, her brow furrows. 'Then … I don't understand, Lucas. If she doesn't know who you are, why is she here? Of all the places on this planet, she just happens to show up in Cascade? That makes no sense.'

I suppose I should come clean about that, even though it won't help, but I've had enough of lying. I shove my hands in my pockets.

'When we were kids … she told me this was her favourite place, that one day she'd move here, so I thought … I don't know what I thought, just that I've never been able to get her out of my head. She was the only light in my childhood. And I fucking failed her.'

Emily moves around the reception desk and places her hands on my upper arms. 'You know that's not true. How many times did we go over that? You saved her life, Lucas. And it killed you. You literally couldn't have done anything about her burns.'

I shake my head. 'But it's how I feel, how I've always felt. Reason doesn't make it go away.'

She squeezes my arms, and I know she's going to say something I don't want to hear, so I head for the door.

'Lucas? That's exactly why she's dangerous for you.'

I freeze, my heartrate cranking up. How many times has she used my real name this time? I know that's how she expresses the importance of her words. Well, I've got some important words for her.

I face her again, every nerve in my body raw. 'So what?' I ask, just short of yelling. 'Who cares about danger? For the first time, I feel like I'm actually alive, not just killing time in some void. A void you seem happy to keep me in. But not anymore. I'm never going back to that existence.'

I wrench open the door and burst outside, pissed off that I can't slam it behind me.

On the street, I pass the crossing where my choice saw a helpless old lady die. I let out a huff of air, wondering what my mother would think of that. Would she be happier if I'd killed myself by saving an old lady who didn't have much time left, anyway?

I crush the thought, hating myself for even thinking that way. Everyone's life has value, no matter what their age.

Wondering if I'm once again lying to myself, I pause just outside the café's doorway and take a few deep breaths. I need to calm down. Taking my anger out on other people isn't going to help. It won't make Kelsey love me.

As frustration whirs through my bloodstream, I tune into the conversation inside the café.

'How's Freddy Krueger Hands going?' a male voice asks.

'Stop calling him that,' Jo says.

'It was your idea,' the male protests.

I know I should stop eavesdropping, but I can't help myself.

'Yeah, well, it's stupid, so stop it.'

'Oooooh,' the male says in a sing-song voice. 'You got a thing for him? Bit late. He's already found his perfect match.'

'What perfect match?' Jo asks.

'One guess.'

Enough, I think, and step inside.

From behind the register, Jo spots me and

straightens up. Standing in front of her, his back to me, Mike leans over the counter.

'Forget it, alright,' Jo says, grabbing a cloth and wiping the counter, forcing Mike to straighten up.

'Come on,' he coaxes, 'it's obvious.'

Jo widens her eyes at him, giving a small shake of her head.

'Freddy Krueger Hands has found a Freddy Krueger Face,' the idiot says. 'You know, that new chick—'

I don't even remember crossing the space between us. My hand clamps down on his shoulder, then I spin him around and slam him up against the counter.

'I don't give a shit what you call me,' I almost spit in his face, rage surging through me, 'but don't you ever talk about her like that again. You got that, you little fuck?'

The wide-eyed idiot nods vigorously. I twist a gloved hand in his shirt and pat his cheek with my other hand, getting him right up close to my Freddy Krueger hands. Then I release him and watch him bolt for the door.

'And don't come back!' Jo shouts after him.

Suddenly ashamed of my behaviour, I scratch the back of my head and glance at Jo. 'Sorry about that.'

'No way.' She beams at me. 'I've been trying to get rid of that creep for years.'

Unable to help myself, I grin at her, and let the anger fade away.

- 60 -

GEORGIA

AS GEORGIA SITS AT her sewing machine, the faint rumble of an engine in the distance catches her attention. Glancing through the window, her heart jolts in her chest as the postie stops at the letterbox down the end of the long driveway. After a moment, the car drives off.

She bolts from her room and races to the front door. Unsure of where her father is, she calls to him, waits, but hears no response.

Confident he's outside somewhere, desperate to get to the letterbox before he does, she slips out the front door and shoves her runners on. She wants to sprint all the way there, but if her father sees her running, he's going to wonder why.

Heart thundering, she calmly walks down the steps,

listening intently to any sounds that will give away her father's location. There's nothing but the crunch of gravel beneath her shoes.

Trying to keep calm, she tells herself that just because the postie stopped, doesn't mean there's any actual mail. Even out here, they sometimes get junk mail. It might be nothing at all.

But the timing is right and something in her gut tells her today's the day. The day her life will either end or start.

Finally, after the longest-ever walk down the driveway, she reaches the letterbox and removes a bunch of letters. She flicks through them, taking in bill after bill. Until her hands freeze.

There it is. The insignia of the Academy of Fashion and Design.

She gulps in air, her hands shaking violently. Shoving the others in the waistband of her jeans, she tears this envelope open and pulls out the letter, knowing the first words she reads will be the most important.

Dear Ms Hargraves,

We are pleased to inform you of your acceptance into—

Unable to contain herself, she squeals in delight. With the letter clutched firmly in her hand, she turns in a circle and performs a victory dance.

Sucking in air and letting it out, she rests her hands on her knees, the smile on her face starting to hurt. Recovering, worried her dad heard her squeal, she straightens up and looks at the homestead. There's no sign of him, but the smile slips from her face as all the implications of the letter come crashing down.

Even now, she can't enjoy the utter exhilaration she wants to feel. Because she has to face up to the hard part. She has to figure out how to tell her father she's leaving not just the farm, but him. Probably forever. She can't imagine coming back here, not now, not when she's destroyed everything.

Placing the letter in the envelope, she swaps it for the bills in her waistband, and with dread in one side of her heart and joy in the other, she heads to the house she no longer sees as her home.

- 61 -

KELSEY

I TEAR A PAGE from my notebook, screw it up and toss it on the floor with all the other failed attempts at a decent chorus. At this rate, I'll have to scrap the whole piece.

Not one to give up easily on a song I damn well know has promise, I poise my pen over the empty page.

My phone vibrates on the coffee table.

I try not to look at it. Before I started on the song, I placed it on silent and turned it facedown for a reason. Staring at the empty page, my grip tightens on the pen as the phone continues to vibrate. But when it stops, I know it's useless. I grab it and light up the screen.

A missed call from Clark.

Surprise, surprise. Didn't he say he wasn't going to bother me anymore?

The worst thing is, I'm most definitely not annoyed he's broken his word.

Releasing a groan of frustration, I wait for the phone to tell me if there's a message. In a few seconds, I have my answer. Dialling message bank, I put the phone on speaker.

'*You have one new message and—*'

'I know!' I yell at the voice.

When prompted, I hit number one.

'*Hey, Kelsey,*' Clark says, followed by a pause so long I wonder if he's going to say anything else. '*I know you're probably not interested ... but I said I'd let you know if my mare was about to foal. Looks like it'll be sometime tonight.*' Another long pause. '*I hope ...*' The message ends.

I hang up, stare at the phone, then down at my notepad.

Don't think about it.

'Fuck it.'

Tossing the notepad aside, I hurry into my bedroom, dress in my most flattering jeans, a long-sleeved shirt and a figure-hugging parka. Checking my reflection in the mirror, I wonder if I should put on a little makeup.

Stop thinking.

Pulling on a pair of boots, I grab my phone and keys from the table in the hallway and rush to the car. Of course, once I climb into the driver's seat, I can't stop my mind from racing, analysing.

Technically, he hadn't broken his word. He'd actually kept it. I can't be angry about that. But I need to be angry about something. He'll ask where I've been, why I haven't taken his calls. What am I supposed to say? That I believe he deserves someone better? That his kiss terrified me as much as it thrilled me? That I can't decide which reaction is more important?

Well, that's a lie. I know exactly which reaction I favour. Which is why I've avoided him. And why I'm in my car right now, rocketing towards him.

I grip the wheel tighter and give it a shake.

If I really believe there's no future with him, why am I going over there? And what did he hope? Why didn't he finish that sentence?

Shut up!

By the time I pull into his driveway, I'm almost on the verge of turning around. But I don't. Instead, I park next to his four-wheel drive and look towards the barn where dim light seeps around the edges of the door.

I take a deep breath and get out, surprised my legs don't buckle beneath me, surprised they carry me easily. When I reach the large metal door, I hesitate and close my eyes.

What's the worst that can happen? He rejects me? Since when have I ever been accepted?

But he won't reject you, will he? He invited you here. Even though you've ignored him, he hasn't given up. Because he wants you.

I push at the door, and as it slides, it releases a loud rumble. I slip through the opening and close it. Sam bounds towards me. Happy for the distraction, I squat down and greet the excited dog.

'Hello, girl,' I coo, running my fingers into her thick fur. 'How've you been?' Sam tilts her head in response, then takes off. A few metres away, she stops and looks at me, then bounds around in a circle before taking off again.

I get the message and follow the black-and-white

fluff ball until I can no longer avoid Clark's gaze. I catch his smile before quickly looking away, studying the scene before me, instead.

The rear barn door stands wide open, a gentle light illuminating the yard beyond where the pregnant mare paces over thick straw. A metre or so from the open doorway, Clark's placed four hay bales together and covered them with a thick blanket.

I put my hands in my parka pockets and move closer, my legs steady, somehow hiding how fast my heart beats.

Sam jumps up beside Clark, sniffing at what looks like a picnic basket behind him.

'No, you don't,' he tells her. Sam jumps off and watches me as I round the hay bales and take a seat next to him.

I force my gaze towards the mare, but from the corner of my eye, I know he's staring at me.

'How is she?' I ask, nodding towards the horse.

'Fine. I missed you.'

My eyes snap to his. He's not smiling anymore. He's serious.

I want to tell him I missed him, too, but the words stick in my throat. The intimacy of saying I missed him … won't that mean I've been thinking about him? Because clearly, he's been thinking about me.

I focus on the mare and see him do the same in my peripheral vision. The horse twitches, whips her head around to look at her stomach and flicks her tail.

'You see that?' he asks.

I nod.

'That's a contraction.'

'She seems to be handling it better than just about every woman on the planet.'

He gives a snort of laughter. 'Kelsey …'

'I've been busy working on a song,' I blurt.

'Sure you have.'

I look at him, trying to put on my best offended expression. Because I am offended, right? I *have* been working on a song. Well, trying to, at least.

'I have,' I protest.

Raising his eyebrows, he grins. 'Uh-huh.'

I backhand his arm. 'Shut up.'

Our eyes lock for a moment too long. I let my gaze skitter down to his torso, suddenly remembering what caused all this. I haven't even asked if he's okay.

I meet his eyes again. 'How many stitches did you get?'

He stares at me, utterly confused. I frown at his torso.

'Oh, ah … seven,' he says abruptly.

I nod. 'Impressive.' Whatever the hell that means.

'No,' he says, 'this is impressive.' He sweeps an arm behind him towards the picnic basket. 'Take a look.'

I swivel, grip the lid and lift. Inside I find two thermoses, a plethora of sandwiches, biscuits, cake, soda and a bottle of scotch.

'There's enough for an army.'

'These things have a way of dragging on all night,' he explains, and waits until I look at him. 'I'm glad you're here.'

I want to tell him I am, too. Instead, I focus on the mare. Who decides at that moment to lie down in the thick straw.

'Think I spoke too soon,' he says.

Removing his leather gloves, he tosses them on the hay bale beside me and fishes a latex pair from his medical bag. Then he offers me a pair.

'We probably won't need to do anything, but just in case, would you like to help?'

I nod, take the gloves from him and slip them on.

As Clark predicted, the birth goes smoothly, steam rising from the wet amniotic sack as the foal comes into the world without any help from anyone but its mother.

As the mare licks her new baby, I take a seat beside Clark on the hay bales. When he removes his latex gloves, I do the same. Trying not to look like I'm watching, like I'm only interested in the foal, I notice him pick up his leather gloves, but instead of slipping them on, he places them on his thigh.

My heart thrums. This might be my only chance to put an end to all this turmoil. He could put them on at any moment. What I need is something that'll distract him, that'll make him forget all about them.

It'll cost me, but I can't go on wondering.

'How come … why haven't you asked what happened to me?' My body tenses as I wait. It's strange he hasn't asked.

'I did ask,' he says gently.

I meet his eyes. 'No, you haven't.'

'When I changed your tyre, I asked.'

'I don't remember that.'

The corner of his mouth twitches. 'I think you said something along the lines of *fuck off.*' His eyes crinkle as he grins.

'I did not!'

'Maybe you didn't use those exact words, but that was certainly the message.'

I bite my lip. 'I'm sorry. I was awful to you.'

'You had good reason to be. I was a jerk, but …' He looks into my eyes. 'I'm so glad you forgave me.'

He reaches into the picnic basket and removes the expensive bottle of scotch. His bare hand reaches in again and fishes out two small glasses.

'So, I figured you'd tell me when you're ready. Are you?' he asks.

As my gaze latches onto the scotch with trepidation, I give a single nod. To my surprise, the words tumble from my lips. I've never told anyone my story, always convinced myself it was nobody's business but mine. But the truth is, it simply hurts too much.

Now, with him, it flows from me like air on a sigh. As I describe what happened, I see the flames. I can taste the toxic smoke in my throat, can even remember the world going black as I looked out the window to see my mother dead in the alley.

'I can't remember anything after that,' I say, seeing nothing but compassion in his eyes. 'Until I woke up in the hospital … with this face.'

- 62 -

LUCAS

IT'S AS BAD AS I suspected. She had no idea I'd been there, that I'd dragged her out of the fire. And why would she? She'd been unconscious, right up until I'd healed her lungs in the hospital. Of course, she hadn't seen me then, either. Because I'd been on the floor, dying.

I study her profile as she stares at the mare and foal, watch the tears shimmer in her eyes. Glancing at her hand resting on the blanket between us, I simply can't help myself.

Gently, I place my bare hand over hers.

Her eyes instantly snap to my touch, then flick to the gloves resting on my thigh. A little sneaky of me, I know, but it seems natural to have forgotten to put them on after watching the mare give birth, after listening to Kelsey's story.

Then her eyes meet mine and that thrill of love and desire rushes through me. But whatever she sees unnerves her, because she glances away. I do too, and together we watch the newborn foal struggling in the straw as it tries to get those long legs to cooperate.

It's then I realise her hand hasn't moved from beneath mine. I take that as a good sign, and with a tenderness that comes from the depth of my soul, I stroke my thumb against her little finger.

As if drinking in my touch, her eyes drift closed. To my utter surprise, she turns her hand until our palms touch and our fingers entwine.

The feel of her actually holding onto me spikes right through my heart. Her touch tells me she hasn't regretted kissing me. She's just been scared, just needed time to think this whole thing through.

And now she's here, holding my hand.

The foal wobbles to its feet, and as it does, I move a little closer to Kelsey. She tenses, but before I can say anything, the foal loses its balance and drops back into the straw.

Concerned, Kelsey rises. I don't let go of her hand.

'She's fine,' I reassure her. 'Just finding her legs.'

I can see she's not going to sit back down, that she's avoiding me, even though she's made no attempt to extract her hand from mine.

I stand and move in front of her, blocking her view of the mare and foal. Completely frozen, she stares at my chest. Releasing her hand, I gently touch my fingers to the underside of her chin.

After a moment, she raises her face and looks right into my eyes.

And I kiss her. My head spins when she leans into

me without the hesitancy of our first time. I feel her hands fist into my parka, and I deepen the kiss, not really knowing what the hell I'm doing, just going with my instincts.

And it's working. Her lips explore mine just as much as mine explore hers. As the intensity between us grows, I'm only half aware of her hand sliding down my right arm, her fingers encircling my wrist. I'm only half aware as she guides my hand higher, sliding it over her jacket, over the swell of her breast beneath all that padding. Tentatively, she touches her tongue to my lower lip and I'm barely aware at all as she guides my hand over the side of her face. Then my fingers are in her hair, my palm covering her scars.

It's only when she presses her hand over mine, holding it in place, that I come back to myself. I lift my mouth from hers, our breaths colliding. Even though I've pulled away, her eyes remain closed, my hand firmly trapped over her scars.

Fear pulses through me.

She knows.

She's trying to get me to heal her.

Not wanting to startle her, I slip my hand from beneath hers and place it on her shoulder. Her eyes snap open and stare into mine.

I wait, reminding myself that I know nothing. I have no idea what's going on inside her head. Then I see the tears well in her eyes. Hiding her face, she drops her forehead to my chest and shakes her head as she draws in trembling breaths.

'Hey,' I whisper, trying to get my own breath under control. Playing dumb seems like the best option. Gently, I say, 'Don't do that, Kel. Don't you want this?'

'I don't think *you* do,' she says, refusing to look at

371

me. It hits me then. She was testing me, trying to see if touching her scars disgusted me. And what had I done? Pulled away as if they did.

'I have no doubts about what I want,' I reassure her.

Slowly, she looks up at me, her expression filled with conflict and doubt. 'You say that now, but you don't want to be stuck looking at this every day. Fuck. I can't even stand to look at myself.'

I'm not letting her get away with that rubbish. 'If you saw someone on the street like you, would you judge them the way you judge yourself?'

She thinks about it for only a moment before she bites her lip and shakes her head.

'So, forget the pitiful excuses. What I care about is what you want.'

'I ... a long time ago,' she says, staring at my chest, 'I resigned myself to never ... being with someone.'

'Me too.'

She looks up at me again, searching my eyes. 'Then you know it's not a belief you can change in a split second.'

I nod in understanding. Of course I know. I've been living it my whole life. The only hope I ever had was when I met her. Back then, ten-year-old me saw hope because of her friendship, her spirit, her nature.

'Yeah,' I say, cupping her face in my hands. 'But you know what? I started rethinking the whole thing ... about the same time you moved here, I think it was.'

She tries to resist, but it's futile. A huge grin breaks across her face. I can't be sure if that smile is because of my words, or because I'm showing her I'm not afraid to touch her scars. But I still see that doubt lingering. She needs to get her head around the fact that someone loves her for who she is, not what she looks like. I get it.

'So,' I say softly, 'we just give you a chance to get used to the idea. I'm not going anywhere.'

The uncertainty remains in her eyes, but there's relief there, too.

I gently brush my thumbs over her cheeks. 'It's in your hands, Kel. You decide when you're ready. And when you are, you make the first move. And I'll wait.'

She hugs me then, forcing my hands from her face as she wraps her arms around my waist and rests her ear against my chest. I fold her into me, a little overwhelmed by the feel of her pressing against me, holding me.

'Thank you,' she whispers.

- 63 -

KELSEY

I TRY TO STIFLE a huge yawn as Clark walks me to my car. Shivering against the chill in the air, I'm a little disappointed he's not holding my hand, though he's walking so close, our arms keep grazing.

'Tired?' he enquires.

'Exhausted.'

After everything that's happened tonight, my head's spinning. Trying not to think about it yet, I fish my keys from my jacket pocket. Before I know what's happening, he swipes them out of my hand and steps back.

'Hey!'

'You know,' he says with a cheeky grin, 'driving exhausted is far more dangerous than driving on an empty stomach.'

'Very funny. Not. I live five k's away. Hand them over.' I extend my hand, noticing he still hasn't put on his gloves.

'Most accidents happen close to home,' he states.

'You're a statistical encyclopaedia now?' I stare at my keys, then meet his eyes. 'If this is some sort of ploy—'

'Oh, it is,' he admits, jerking me wide awake. 'A ploy to keep you safe. If something happened to you … well, I just found you.'

Touched, I search his eyes. 'Don't say stuff like that.'

He lets out a little scoff. 'Better get used to it. It'd be pointless to pretend we don't know how I feel. As pointless as you pretending you don't like it.' He winks at me, turns and walks off towards the house.

I like that he's so right about me. I also can't deny I like how open he is with his feelings. No embarrassment, no beating around the bush, just stating a fact that he's completely unashamed of.

I more than just like it.

After a moment, I hurry after him, meeting him as he steps inside.

'No funny business,' I say, knowing full well he won't do anything I don't want him to.

He holds the front door open for me. 'In fact,' he says as I brush past him, 'I insist you take the couch.'

<><><>

After Clark stoked the fire embers back to life and helped me make a comfortable bed on the couch, I listen to the shower running in the bathroom. Quickly changing into his long-sleeved T-shirt, I wrap myself in his white bathrobe and pull on the thick socks he's given me.

Comfortable and warm, with the scent of him all around me, I plonk on the couch. I wasn't lying when I said I was exhausted. It's well after midnight, and although I won't admit it to Clark, I'm grateful I didn't have to drive home. The darkness out here is thick.

Desperate to crash, I run my tongue over my slightly fuzzy teeth. No way can I go to sleep without cleaning them, no matter how tired I am.

I plump the pillow, glance at the bathroom door and as I wonder how much longer he'll be, the shower stops. After waiting a moment, I walk across the floorboards to the bathroom where a thin strip of steam seeps from beneath the door.

Tentative, I rap lightly and wait. 'Hey? Just wondering if you have a spare toothbrush?'

'Just a sec,' he calls out.

A few moments later, the door opens. I expect him to hand me a toothbrush. Instead, he swings the door wide, letting a cloud of steam escape.

Taken off guard, I can't help but openly stare at the sight before me, like some sort of dream emerging from the swirling mist. As casual as can be, he dries the back of his head with a towel draped over his right shoulder, the muscles in his arm flexing. As the wet hair around his face drips onto his chest, I watch the drops race over his flawless skin, down into the sprinkle of hair that disappears beneath the towel around his waist.

'Kel?' he says, his voice like gravel.

My eyes snap to his. Instant heat hits my face.

'Sorry, I …' I can't even remember why I'm

standing here. Until one corner of his mouth turns up. Jesus, I'm giving him the wrong impression. 'I can't sleep unless I've cleaned my teeth.'

He nods, and to his credit, I don't even see the slightest sign of disappointment in his steady gaze. Then he opens a drawer and rummages through it.

'I think I've got a spare here somewhere.'

With a mind of their own, my feet carry me a few steps into the bathroom as I watch the muscles in his back move beneath his flawless skin. Why I find it so fascinating, I'm not sure. Well, maybe it has something to do with the fact I've never been this close to a man who's clearly naked under a towel.

It takes me a moment to realise he's stopped rummaging. I shift my gaze to the mirror. He's watching me watch him. It sends a jolt right through me, and my gaze skitters to the floor. Fortunately, I don't think I can blush any deeper than I already am.

He turns towards me and holds out a toothbrush still in its packet.

'I mean it, Kel. Unless you make the first move, nothing'll happen here. So relax.'

As I take the toothbrush, our eyes lock. A powerful moment passes between us, and I want him right then so badly it hurts in places that have been asleep my whole life. Every cell in my body responds to the perfect specimen of the man before me.

Shy, wanting him but not knowing what on earth to do, I drop my gaze again, scanning the well-defined muscles, wishing he'd get rid of the towel over his shoulder that's hiding half his body.

Then he reaches towards me and touches the lapel of the bathrobe I'm wearing.

'I'm really liking this look on you,' he says, a cheeky

spark in his eyes. 'Kind of looks like you live here … It's sexy as hell.'

I burst into laughter, releasing all the tension. 'You're so full of it.'

He chuckles as he turns away, returning with a tube of toothpaste. 'Here. You can use the kitchen sink. Glasses are in the cupboard above the microwave.'

'Thanks,' I say, heading to the kitchen.

'Kel?'

I stop and look over my shoulder at him.

'I'm not full of it,' he says, before he closes the door.

It's like he can reach into my mind and pluck out exactly what I want to hear.

Grinning like a fool, I clean my teeth and rinse. Back at the couch, I take off the robe and socks and snuggle under the blankets.

A moment later, he emerges from the bathroom. I close my eyes, pretending to be asleep. Hearing his footsteps draw closer, I know he's looking at me over the back of the couch.

''Night, Kel,' he whispers.

''Night,' I mumble, relief sweeping through me when I hear him move away. I wait for the sound of his bedroom door closing, but it doesn't come. Curious, I sit up. His door stands open, but I can only see partially inside. A moment later, a lamp clicks off, plunging his room into darkness.

I flop back on the pillow, my mind racing when it should be shutting down. I think about how disappointed I'd been after he gently removed his hand when I'd made him touch my scars, how I thought I'd been right all along. As wonderful as he is, even he can't stand to touch them. But then he'd gone and proven me wrong by cupping my face in his hands and looking at me like he wanted nothing more than for me to love him back.

So, here I am. I've found a man, a real man—not some fantasy—who can see past the scars and wants me for who I am on the inside.

I need to move on with my life, have to start living.

And it's obvious that Clark is the person to move on with. While I don't need him in my life, I want him in it. I can't continue to live in a fantasy world, dreaming of a dead man, when the reality in front of me is pretty damn wonderful. And is it really a bad thing that Clark reminds me of Luke? Will it matter if sometimes I let myself imagine he is Lucas? As long as he never knows, who will I be hurting?

If he had a billboard with flashing lights, he couldn't make it any clearer how he feels about me. And even though I believe he deserves better, it's not my decision, is it?

Heart thundering, I stare at the soft firelight flickering across the ceiling.

What are you waiting for?

I grab the robe from the back of the couch, get up and shrug it on. As I pad across the floorboards towards his bedroom, I wonder if he left the door open as an invitation, if he knew I'd change my mind.

When I get to his doorway, I hesitate on the threshold.

His lamp snaps on. As if he's been waiting for me. He sits up in bed and swings his feet to the floor. The comforter slides from his bare chest and pools around his waist. That's where he stops and waits.

I take a step into his room, noticing Sam in a bed in the far corner. I'm an idiot. That's why he left the door open. So Sam can get outside if she needs to.

'Kel?' he whispers.

My gaze snaps to his. I study his face, see the hope and love in those incredible eyes.

'Are you sure?' I ask.

'I'm sure. You know I'm sure.'

Now that I'm in here with him, all my doubts vanish. I love him and he loves me. It's so simple.

As I shrug out of the robe and let it drop to the floor, he rises from the bed, waiting for me to go to him. I move slowly, feeling the long-sleeved shirt he gave me brush against my thighs as I take in his body again, take in that he's only wearing tight boxers.

Finally, I reach him, and step right into his personal space. My skin prickles with excitement as he waits, letting me take the lead.

I find his bare hands with mine and entwine our fingers, pressing our palms together. Our eyes lock and he squeezes my hands. I squeeze back, the simple touch so intimate. It gives me a thrill that he's not afraid to touch me. He trusts me, and that makes me feel so special because he doesn't even seem to remember he never touches anyone.

Rising on my toes, I kiss him, and when he kisses me back, I know this is right, that this is where I'm meant to be. Releasing his hands, I slide my fingers over his forearms, then higher, delighting in the tight muscles beneath my touch.

His chest rumbles as his hands slip around me, skim down my spine then over my backside, bringing me in flush against his body, letting me know how hard he is for me.

He's so tender and gentle, and that reminds me that I need to be careful with him, too. Slipping my hands from his arms, I run my fingers gently over his ribs, searching for the gauze covering his stitches so I can navigate around it.

As he kisses me, as his hands caress and melt me, I try to picture him standing beside the bed, try to remember seeing the white dressing on his otherwise perfect body.

But I can't.

My brain fires with a million thoughts all at once.

Until it settles on just one.

I let my heels drop to the floor, ease my mouth from his and take a small step back, his hands coming to rest on my hips as I watch his chest rise and fall.

I don't want to look, but my gaze drifts lower, anyway. For a moment, I can't comprehend which is his right side, which is his left. But it doesn't matter. Because there's no dressing, no gauze, no injury.

My fingers tremble as I brush them over his ribs, over his flawless skin.

When I look up at him, his eyes are almost closed, as if he's lost in my touch.

'There's nothing …' I whisper, though I want to scream. 'No stitches …'

His eyes snap wide open and I see the naked fear there.

I step away, feeling his hands slide from my hips, feeling the cold closing in.

'It *is* you.'

He reaches for me, but I take another step away.

'Kelsey. I wanted to tell you. I—'

I spin around and run. I don't want to hear it, don't want to hear another lie from his mouth ever again.

- 64 -

LUCAS

IN A STATE OF shock, I stand there like the fool that I am, staring at the empty doorway.

Fucking idiot! So stupid!

I hear her feet pound the floorboards, the rattle of keys, the front door slam.

Move!

I sprint after her.

How could I have forgotten? Because my head was in the clouds, too distracted by her finally wanting me, distracted by her touch and all the physical reactions she aroused. Why, in that moment, would I be thinking about an injury that doesn't exist?

But I wonder if, somewhere in the back of my mind, I'd deliberately revealed who I am. I wanted her to fall in love with Daniel Clark, the average rural vet. I wanted to know that she loved him, that her love wasn't coming from any place that believed I could heal her. But there's also that part of me that wants her to love the real me and everything that comes with being Lucas Daniel.

I wrench open the front door just as she reaches the bottom verandah step. Dressed only in my shirt, she hops on one leg as she tries to shove a foot into her boot. She almost falls, but somehow, in her desperation to get away from me, she rights herself.

Racing after her, not giving a damn about the sharp gravel cutting into my bare soles, I know I won't reach her in time.

She climbs into her car and slams the door. With too much momentum behind me, I smash into the driver's side and fumble for the doorhandle. The lock makes a dull *thunk* just as my fingers clasp the handle and pull.

I know I'm probably scaring the hell out of her, but I'm more than scared. I'm terrified. I can't lose her.

'Kel,' I plead. 'Come on. Don't run away.'

Her face whips towards me, and for the first time, I see tears streaking down her cheeks. As much as I want to draw hope from those tears, I also see fire in her eyes.

'What?' she yells. 'Like you did?'

What is she talking about? 'I never ran away from you.'

She glares at me through the window. 'How can you look at this face and say that?'

I place my hands on the glass. 'I wanted to, but—'

'I was your best friend, and you couldn't even be bothered to do the one thing you were capable of. I really thought you cared about me. But you were more worried about yourself, about people finding out.'

Is that really what she believes?

'Kel, that's not what happened. You don't underst—'

'Yes, I do! I was supposed to have another life. I was supposed to be someone else. You could've given me that … so easily.'

Sobs burst from her throat as her words wash over me. She starts the car, her hand reaching for the gearstick.

'No! Kelsey, wait!' I beg, banging on the window.

She floors it, forcing me back, the tyres spraying up gravel. The car fishtails slightly before she regains control and rockets along the driveway.

Devastated, I stare after her. My knees want to buckle, but I'm so frozen, I stand there like a statue.

This is so much worse than I ever imagined. All this time I thought she'd want me to heal her face, thought I'd break her heart when I revealed it's not something I can do. It never crossed my mind that she thought I'd deliberately chosen *not* to heal her.

Fuck.

Gradually, I become aware of the icy air. But it doesn't feel like it's seeping into my bones from the outside. It feels like it's coming from the inside.

I crunch towards the house, still not caring about my sliced feet.

There's only one thing I care about, and she hasn't just walked away from me. She's bolted.

- 65 -

KELSEY

HE'S ALIVE.

I pull into Dad's apartment complex parking lot, punch in the code, and wait for the security gate to rumble open.

The sound reminds me of Clark's ... no, Lucas's barn door.

Clark. Lucas. Lucas. Clark.

The tears start again.

I swipe them away with one hand, steer with the other, and pull into the guest spot beside Dad's car. As it's only seven am, he hasn't left for work yet.

After speeding home from Clark's—Lucas's—I'd packed a small bag, made a coffee in a travel mug and left. I remind myself again that I need to call Jackie and see if she can organise someone to feed Frankie.

The thought of the horse makes my face crumple and once again I let the tears flow, let my body hitch and shudder with the pain, the lies, the deception. All of it.

What the hell had he been thinking? That I'd never find out? Or that he'd get to screw me before that happened?

None of it makes any sense.

Well, some of it does.

Now I know why he reacted the way he did the first time he saw me in town. Obviously, he knew who I was. It was all over my face. And then when he changed my tyre, how he'd stared at me when I'd pointed out that reaction, how he seemed to be waiting for me to what? Recognise him?

Of course, I'd been too caught up in the humiliation of having to accept help from the first person to freak out at the sight of me. Besides, he looked nothing like the boy I'd known.

Except the eyes, I remind myself. Those eyes.

The day I saw the photo of him in the local paper, that'd been the moment. The photo he obviously hadn't realised was being taken. The photo where those green eyes were completely unguarded, completely real. I knew those eyes.

Then, when I'd questioned him, he'd lied about growing up in the country, about having sisters. Why? To throw me off? If that's what he wanted, then why not just stay away from me? Why inject himself into my life? Why live in Cascade?

The puzzle went round and round in my head, again and again.

As I suck in air on hitching, gulping sobs, I think about the sight of him in my rear-view mirror as I drove away. In the red glow of the taillights, he'd looked so crushed, so broken, as he stood there watching me leave.

And so he should be.

But it doesn't help. Because I also remember his eyes staring at me through the car window, his confusion just as prominent as his fear and pain.

What he was confused about, I don't know. But I do know one thing. He could have healed my face. And he hadn't.

End of story.

But evidently, it hasn't been the end of the story.

As much as I'd hated him for what he'd refused to do for me, I'd always held something deep in my heart for him. How could I not? He'd trusted me with his secret, made me feel like I was someone special, someone worthy of knowing that magical boy.

And how many times had I wondered what he might have looked like as a man, even though I'd been told he was dead?

Which is why I'm here. To confront the person who made me believe that lie.

I grip the steering wheel hard. Clearly, walking away from me after the fire hadn't been the end of the story for Luke, either. He'd moved to Cascade because of me, because I'd told him that's where I wanted to live. And sure, it'd been a stupid little girl's dream. Yet, there he was.

And he'd become a vet. That had been my idea. When he'd had no clue what he could do with his life, I'd told him to be a vet because the animals wouldn't be able the tell anyone his secret.

Jesus.

He'd listened to everything I'd said. And he'd

followed through. Why? Why would he do such a thing if he hadn't cared? It's crazy.

If he cared that much about me when we were kids, he would have healed my face, saved me from a life of misery and isolation, something he knew all about, even at the age of ten. My burns weren't life threatening. Sure, he might have passed out for a while after healing them, but it wouldn't have killed him.

So, why the fuck hadn't he done it?

I want to scream out my frustration, but I'm in the city, and even here in the parking garage, I can't do it. All I can do is confront Dad and hopefully stop the incessant merry-go-round in my head. And I desperately need sleep.

Grabbing a wad of tissues, I blow my nose and calm down.

By the time I ring Dad's buzzer, I finally feel in control.

Until he opens the door, his surprised expression quickly changing into a warmth I know all too well. When he holds out his arms, I fall into them and fall apart all over again.

'Kel,' he says in that same soothing tone he'd use when I woke from nightmares of the fire. 'What is it, pumpkin?'

- 66 -

BRYCE

BRYCE SITS IN HIS office chair, his back to his desk as he stares through the window at the bright, sunny day.

He should be out there. Doing what exactly, he can't quite fathom. He's never been at such a loss. After repairing the fence with Georgia, and with no cattle on the property, there really wasn't anything else to do.

Thinking of Georgia, he frowns, remembering her question the other day. She'd never questioned him before about his love of working on the land. Was it really all about him getting older? He suspects that's not why she asked at all.

Feeling a stone take form in his stomach, he jolts out of his thoughts when the phone rings. It's a number he doesn't know. Probably another scammer, but his curiosity gets the better of him and he answers.

'Yeah?'

'Bryce Hargraves?' a male voice asks. There's no telltale delay, and the guy has a perfect Aussie accent.

'Who wants to know?'

'Mr Hargraves, this is Dean Wilson from the bank. We need to have a conversation about your mortgage.'

Bryce grips the mobile so hard he's surprised the screen doesn't crack. 'I talked to someone else there not long ago. I've got an extension. Why is it you lot can't talk to each other? Surely, it's on my file.'

Wilson remains silent for a moment. Bryce presumes he's actually reading the file like he bloody well should've done in the first place.

'I can see here, Mr Hargraves, that the extension you requested has already expired. You're now in arrears to the tune of—'

'Listen here, you little punk,' Bryce spits into the phone. 'I've been a customer at your bank for—'

'I understand, Mr Hargraves, but you made an agreement and you've broken—'

'Just give me another extension. I'll make it up. I always have. Check your records.'

'As you're aware, the last extension was your final one. If you're telling me you don't have the money to pay your arrears today, then we'll have to start the process of—'

'Go to fucking hell!' Bryce roars down the phone. Heart hammering, he wants to throw it at the wall, but thinks better of it. One more thing he can't afford to replace.

Instead, he settles for swiping everything off his desk. Sucking in air, he watches overdue bill after overdue bill flutter to the floor.

Clark, he thinks. *This is all Daniel Clark's fault.*

- 67 -

LUCAS

I DRIVE HOME FROM Kelsey's house in utter despair. Of course, she wasn't there. I thought if I gave her at least the morning to think about the relationship we've developed, she might calm down enough to let me explain. But her car was nowhere to be found. I tried her phone twice, but her refusal to take my calls sent a clear message.

Feeling like a stalker, I drive into town, knowing I'll pass her if she's on her way home. I don't. I can't find her car in town, either. I have no idea where she might have gone, but I won't harass her, which in itself is infuriating. From what she said to me last night, she doesn't know the truth. How can I tell her what really happened if I can't see her, speak to her?

By the time I get home, my heart's like a lead weight

in my chest.

Unable to sit still, I go out to the barn, Sam at my side, her usually pricked ears flat against her head. She knows my moods too well.

Inside the barn, I snatch a lead off a hook, intending to catch Beau and go for a long ride. Halfway there, my breath catches in my throat. As much as I try not to think about what's happened, it's there, snapping at my soul in an unrelenting attack I can't outrun.

I lean against a stable door, allowing my legs to buckle beneath me. Releasing the rope, I drop my head in my hands and finally let go.

When I feel pressure on the back of my hand, I look up to find Sam touching her nose to my glove. My breath hitches in and out, my throat sore and tight. Poor dog must be sick of seeing me like this.

I wonder now if I'm better off alone. I'd thought the pain of loneliness was bad enough, but this crushing agony that consumes everything is a million times worse.

Sam touches her nose to my glove again and gives a little whine. I take it off, slide my bare hand beneath my shirt and rest it over my heart. Waiting a moment, I stare at Sam, glad she's here with me.

'It's not working,' I tell her. 'It still hurts. I can't fix that, either.'

She tilts her head and whines again.

'I know, girl. I know.'

Then something catches her attention, and she takes off towards the house. That's when I hear it. The sound of an engine, tyres crunching on the gravel.

Kelsey.

I bolt after Sam.

Until I see an old ute skid to a stop at the bottom

of the verandah steps.

Fuck!

Bryce flings open the door and barrels out, heading towards the house.

Just what I need.

I take a step backwards, hoping to disappear into the shadows inside the barn before he sees me.

Sam barks. Bryce stops, changes direction and heads straight towards us.

'Home. Now,' I tell Sam.

Tail between her legs, she hurries towards the house, giving Bryce a wide berth. Poor girl thinks she's in trouble, but she's not. I can tell from Bryce's stiffness, the rage on his face, that he's not here for a social visit. I don't want Sam getting hurt.

I can't say the same for myself.

Bryce charges towards me, his face almost purple. I stand my ground. I'm not afraid of him.

As he draws closer, he raises an arm, pointing an accusing finger at me.

'I shot you!' he yells.

I shrug. 'You just grazed me.'

'Bullshit!'

He stops close enough for me to hear his ragged breaths.

'Maybe,' I say, knowing full well I'm antagonising him, 'you're not the great shot you think you are.'

With a speed and agility I hadn't expected from the old farmer, he swings, his fist connecting hard with my temple.

I stagger, stunned by the sudden violence, and to my horror, I trip and crash to the ground. In shock, my head throbbing, a warm trickle slides from my eyebrow into the corner of my eye.

Bryce advances and stands over me. I make no move to get up or protect myself.

'You should be dead, you dog!' he roars, spittle flying from his lips. 'Now I'm losing everything!'

The warm trickle finds its way into my eye. I blink and wipe at it, inspecting the blood on my glove.

Bryce leans in closer, his hands on his knees to keep himself steady. 'I'm gonna get you, Clark. I'm gonna expose whatever it is you are. That's a promise.'

He straightens, turns and strides away.

Why not just 'get me' now? Why walk away when he has me on the ground? Rage pulses through me. I stagger to my feet.

'Hey!' I yell at his back.

He stops, faces me, and tries to hide his surprise. I can only imagine how dark and ugly my face looks.

'You wanna know what I am?' I've lost control, and I don't give a fuck. I rip off a glove and touch the split in my skin where he punched me. When the pain vanishes, I swipe my hand over the spot, clearing away the blood, giving him a good view.

Bryce's eyes narrow, his face twisting with confusion.

'What? Not enough for you?' I thunder, tearing my throat with the effort.

My sanity on the verge of non-existence, I take a few strides to my right and slam my palm down on the hook that earlier held Beau's lead rope.

The sharp point pierces straight through my palm and out the back of my hand. The pain is excruciating, but I don't care. I glare at Bryce, who's staring at me with alarm ... and fear. I know what he's thinking. He thinks I'm insane, and an insane person can be as dangerous as a wild animal. There's no reasoning with insane.

I wrench my hand free of the hook, and this time my vision fades a little. I can't pass out now. I hold my hand towards Bryce.

'You see what I am?' I yell, my voice rough, hoarse. As I grab my injured hand, I realise how this might look to Bryce. Like some sort of religious wound.

Let him think what he wants.

When the pain vanishes, I wipe the blood on my jeans and show him my perfect palm.

'You see?' I rage at him. 'So what're you gonna do, Bryce? Tell the cops you shot me? Who's gonna believe you? Everyone'll think you're crazy, because there's no fucking evidence, is there?'

Bryce shuffles backwards, blood draining from his face.

'You think you've lost everything?' I continue, unable to stop. 'You know nothing! I've been dead inside my whole life. So you can't hurt me, you piece of shit. You got that? You. Can't. Hurt. Me!'

Bryce turns and breaks into what I guess, for him, is a sprint.

Gasping for breath, I rest my hands on my knees and suck in air.

After a moment, I hear the ute door slam, the engine start and rev hard as he takes off.

Just like Kelsey.

Everybody ends up running from me.

'Fuck!'

- 68 -

KELSEY

AFTER TALKING TO JACKIE, who reassured me Frankie would be well looked after, I convinced Dad to go to work and let me sleep. When I confront him, I want a clear head.

By the time he walks through the door after work, I've showered, found a bottle of wine in the pantry and taken delivery of my favourite Thai.

'Smells amazing, pump—Kel.'

I shrug, take a bite and find it tasteless. But I chew, knowing I should eat something.

'So,' Dad says, 'from what I witnessed this morning, you're not just here to see your favourite person.'

I take a deep breath, then a sip of wine. This isn't going to be easy to admit. Jeez, I can barely admit it to myself, but I need to say the words out loud. The truth has to start somewhere, and it may as well be with me.

Giving him a steady look, hoping my voice doesn't crack, I say, 'I think I'm in love.'

Floored, Dad gapes at me. He blinks rapidly and I can only guess that he's trying to decide if those words actually came from my mouth. Then, like flipping a switch, his whole face lights up.

'That's fantastic,' he says, studying me. When I don't return his smile, he asks, 'Isn't it?'

'Well, I don't know, Dad. Since according to you … he's dead.'

He gives me a blank stare before his gaze flickers to his wineglass.

'Dad. You know who I'm talking about. You lied to me.'

His guilty eyes meet mine as his shoulders slump in defeat. 'That night, the night of the fire … his mother told me he was dying. At the time, that's what I believed.'

I shake my head in confusion. 'You're not making any sense. Why would he have be dying?'

'Because he saved your life.'

I stare at him. 'How could he save my life when he wasn't even there?'

'He was there.' The shame on his face is unmistakable. 'He was there at the fire … and the hospital.'

'But you said—'

'I lied.'

I can't believe what I'm hearing. 'You told me he never came to see me in the hospital. You told me he didn't care!' I slam my palm on the table, almost sending the wineglass flying. 'Why?! How did he save me? Why lie about that?'

Dad holds up his hands, trying to slow the questions spilling from my mouth, questions I desperately need answered.

'I can explain,' he says, regret in his voice.

'Go!'

'I'm trying to ...' He takes a deep breath. 'He was the one who pulled you out of the fire.'

'You said it was the firefighters.'

'Kel, this is hard enough. Just let me get it out, okay?'

Hard for him! I'm the one who's been lied to all these years. But losing my shit won't help. I nod, take a trembling sip of wine and wait.

'Later, when I spoke to the firefighters, they told me it was you, the boy and his mother they found in the hallway, outside the apartment. You were unconscious, and the boy was coughing his guts up. His mother wasn't. Somehow, that little kid pulled you out of that inferno.'

I want to cry, imagining Luke, scrawny and small, running into the burning apartment, risking his life. Pulling me out of there. It seems impossible.

'Dad ...'

'I saw him in the hospital when I arrived, outside your room. He was filthy, looked so out of place. I didn't know who he was. Not then, anyway.'

His shaking hand picks up his glass, and he takes a long swallow of wine.

'He took off when he saw me looking at him, but somehow he must have heard the doctor telling me you might not make it, telling me what your injuries were, what the biggest concerns were when it came to you surviving ... or not.'

I lean forward, heart thundering.

'I know I let you believe your only injuries were the burns to your face, but they were the only injuries you had that weren't a threat to your life.' He takes a gulp of wine, and this time, when he finishes, he manages to look me in the eye. 'Your trachea was badly burned and then there was the severe smoke inhalation … all those toxic chemicals. You were intubated. It was touch and go.'

'Jesus, Dad, why—'

'Kel, please.' He sighs heavily. 'I don't know how, but the boy—Lucas—he managed to get into your room. Your doctor and I, we caught him in there … touching you.'

I draw in a harsh breath. 'Touching me?'

'He had his hands on your chest … your throat. He knew exactly where you were hurt the most. And I remember him peeling the gauze from your face, but the doctor … he grabbed the kid and pulled him away. I'll never forget him struggling, screaming …'

He trails off, apparently lost in the memories.

'Screaming what?' I ask quietly.

'*Her face, her face* over and over until he … collapsed.'

My throat tightens and for a moment I can't even draw a breath. When my body finally demands it, air wheezes into me, coming out as a sob.

How am I supposed to comprehend all this new information? Information that changes absolutely everything I've ever believed. He'd pulled me out of the fire. He'd healed my life-threatening injuries despite the danger to himself. And then he'd tried to heal my face.

He'd tried. He'd cared.

Hot tears flow from my eyes and drip off my chin, but I get out, 'He collapsed?'

Dad nods. 'His heart stopped, but they got to him so fast, got it going again.' He pauses, and I can see he doesn't want to continue.

'Then what?' I wipe the tears from my face, but they keep coming. 'Dad?'

'While he was dying, while they were fighting to bring him back … you woke up. That's when I knew. I remembered what you'd told me about your friend, about what he could do. So, once everything calmed down, I demanded they assess your injuries again.'

'And I was fine, wasn't I?'

He nods, draining the last of his wine. 'Except for your burns, you were in perfect health. The doctors couldn't explain it. But I knew. You'd never lied to me before, and you hadn't lied to me that day you told me what he could do. I'm sorry I didn't believe you.'

Seems I'm the only one who doesn't lie, but right now, that doesn't matter. 'If they saved him, why did you think he was dead?'

'I thought, if there was even the slimmest chance he could take away your burns, I had to try. So I found his room. He was in a coma … he looked exactly the way you'd looked … before he touched you. His mother was there, and I begged her, but—and rightfully so— she demanded I leave. She said he was dying. When I came back the next day, desperate to convince her, they were gone. The nurses refused to tell me anything, so I presumed he'd died.'

I cover my mouth and try to stifle the sobs that wrench from my throat. As the truth comes crashing down, anger explodes inside me. I suddenly spring to my feet so fast the chair crashes to the tiled floor.

'How could you?! All this time … I thought he didn't care about me because of your lies! Why the fuck, Dad! Why?!'

He flinches at my outburst but remains silent. As he reaches for his empty wineglass, I sweep my hand out and knocks it flying off the table. It shatters on the floor like a bomb going off.

'Why?!' I scream, slamming my hand on the table.

'You needed to forget about him,' he says softly.

'*What?* Why would I need to forget about the boy who saved my life?'

He rises and comes around the table towards me. I take a step away. Holding his hands up in surrender, he stops.

'Kel, you have to try to see this from my perspective. You almost died. Your mother *had* died … right in front of you … and then I believed your friend died … because he saved your life. On top of everything you'd been through, how could I put that burden on you, too? I couldn't, Kel. I just couldn't do it to you.'

I stare at him, at the sincerity and despair in his eyes, and this time, I know he's telling the truth.

As much as I don't want to admit it, he's right. I'd blamed myself for my mother's death, knowing if I hadn't thrown that bottle of scotch—if it hadn't fuelled the fire—things might have turned out differently. If I'd found out then that Luke had died saving my life, it would have been too much to cope with. I would have been overwhelmed by guilt.

'But it didn't work,' he continues. 'You were obsessed with him, constantly begging me to find him. I think part of it was a way to avoid your grief. I thought you'd eventually forget about him, but after a year, you were only getting worse. So, I told you I'd tracked down his mother and found out he was dead.

It was the only thing I could think of to stop your obsession, to help you get past it all. By then, I felt it'd been long enough since the fire … since your mother … and it worked. You stopped talking about him.'

Frozen, all I can do is stare at him as everything sinks into my muddled brain.

'But he's not dead, is he? And you weren't surprised by that,' I remind him.

He glances away, the look of shame on his face intense. Taking a deep breath, he releases it slowly, clearly stalling for time.

'Dad … tell me. I need the truth. All of it.'

He gives me a brief glance. 'He must have told you.'

'He hasn't told me anything. I didn't let him, because I believed your lies. Tell me!'

'I'm so sorry, Kel.'

I can see the pain in his eyes, but it's not his life these lies are affecting. It's mine.

'Dad! Just say it!'

'When you were about eighteen or so, he found me, wanted to see you. Shocked the hell out of me. Because I truly did believe he'd died after saving you.'

Unsure if I'm trying to stop a scream, or if I'm just in shock, I bring a hand to my mouth.

He'd tried to find me.

I swallow over the lump in my throat. 'But he never … What did you do?' I accuse.

'I couldn't have you go through all that trauma again … not unless he could make you whole … heal you. So I asked him if he could … and he said he didn't think so.'

My mind races. 'And then?'

He swipes a hand over his face and meets my eyes.

'I told him to stay away from you.'

My legs buckle, but before I fall, Dad's arms are around me, holding me up, pulling me into a tight hug. Pushing against him, I try to escape, but he refuses to let go.

'Kel, you have to understand. Please.'

Shaking my head against his chest, I try to comprehend it all. It's almost too much to take in. The one person I trusted most in this world had been controlling my reality, bending and distorting it.

'Kel. Everything I did, every lie I told you, it was all to protect you. You were so fragile after the fire … and when he turned up years later, you were finally getting your life together. I could see it coming apart if he came back … if he couldn't help you. How could I let him disappoint you? Kel … I just wanted you to move on. I couldn't bear to see you dragged back to that dark place again. Not when you'd dug your way out.'

I want to hate him for what he did, but can't. Even though I don't agree with any of it, I understand. He was trying to protect me. He was just being my dad.

Slowly, I hug him. 'He saved my life,' I choke.

'More than once, pumpkin. More than once.'

Later, after we'd cleaned up the shattered wineglass and eaten a little more food, I sit on the couch with him and tell him all about Luke. He listens with rapt attention, and when I finally get it all out, I ask him why he thinks Luke lied to me about who he is.

'I'm not sure, Kel. But if I had to guess, it's because he can't do what you want him to do. Maybe it's as simple as that. He doesn't want to hurt you, either.'

I think about that, about how it makes me feel. For so long I thought he was dead, that I'd never be healed. But now, it's hard to believe there isn't hope.

Then I remember Beau and the fact that Luke hasn't done anything about his scars. Maybe he hasn't healed the stallion because he won't be able to explain where the scars have gone, so he's played it safe. That made sense.

But I have another problem. I'd made him touch my scars, and nothing had happened. No wonderful feeling like the other times he'd healed me, no change to my scars. But what if, after all these years, he's figured out how to control it? What if he can turn it on and off at will? Could that be it?

If that were true, none of it explains why he's hidden who he is from me, why he hasn't helped me. There's only one way I'll find out.

'You really love him?' Dad asks.

'I don't know what else to call it.'

He nods, places an arm around me and pull me close. 'I know I'm not your favourite person right now, but you're so lucky. If you have any feelings for him at all, you should run towards them, not away from them. He clearly loves you, Kel. If I had someone in my life like that, I'd be in their arms in a heartbeat.'

I look up at him, at the sadness in his face, and realises that he's suffered through all this, too. He'd always been there as much as he could when I was a kid, but after the fire, he'd been there for me twenty-four-seven. I'm sure he must have had a few flings here and there, but never anyone important enough to bring home. And even after I'd started my own life, he'd never introduced me to anyone.

'Dad ...'

'Kel, I know you might never trust me again, but ... if you love him, then go love him. You need to trust me on that.'

Darcy Daniel

- 69 -

BRYCE

BRYCE PLONKS DOWN AT the table for dinner, his mind a whirlwind of racing thoughts he still can't get his head around. What he'd seen Clark do was impossible. Yet he'd still seen it.

Georgia places a plate of lasagne and steamed vegies in front of him and takes a seat.

What did make sense now was why Clark was still alive after he'd been shot. And just as Clark said, it also explained why he hadn't gone to the cops. Can't really tell them you've been shot when there's not a mark on you.

'Dad?' Georgia asks softly. 'Please tell me what's wrong. You look so scared.'

He glances at her and sees the worry in her eyes. But what can he tell her? The truth? Like Clark said, if he tries to tell anyone, he's going to look like he's lost his mind.

'Just feeling sorry for myself,' he says and lowers his gaze to the food she's dished up. It smells delicious, but he can't even find the motivation to lift his fork.

Georgia nods in sympathy. 'You should go see the talent show tomorrow night. It'd do you good to get out. Maybe the guys have forgiven you by now.'

'Have your friends?' he scoffs.

Her face drops. 'They're teenagers, Dad. What do you think?'

He shakes his head. 'I'm sorry.'

'Stop saying that. I'm the one who's sorry. It's my fault.'

He can see she's close to tears again, but this time, he just can't deal with it. He rises, leaving his food untouched.

'Sorry, Georgie, I'm not hungry.' He walks away, needing time to think things through.

- 70 -

LUCAS

I FOLLOW MEGAN CAMPBELL and her Great
Dane, Ralph, down the hallway into the waiting room.
Clearly excited to be going home after his yearly shots,
Ralph drags Megan towards the door. With the dog
outweighing her, she's not going to win. Embarrassed,
Megan looks over her shoulder at me, then Emily, with
helplessness.

Amused, Emily waves at her. 'I'll email your bill.'

And with that, Megan opens the door and gets
wrenched through, then dragged along the street.

Any other time I would've had a chuckle, but not
now. Nothing's funny anymore.

I head to the door and turn the sign around so the
word 'open' faces me, then pull down the blind.

'You can go,' I tell Emily as I wander towards the

hallway, intending to clean up the exam room. Anything to delay going home. Back to the emptiness, to where Kelsey discovered I'd been lying to her, to where she ran away from me.

I've lived there on my own for years, and yes, while I thought I'd been a hollow shell, lonely, wondering what the point was, I realise that I knew nothing. Having just lived through the best weeks of my life, of truly connecting with the woman I love, feeling like I belong, like she loved me, too, and feeling the hope of a future I never thought I'd have right at my fingertips … what I feel now is so, so much worse than anything that came before.

Just as I get to the hallway, Emily says, 'Luke?'

I stop, frowning. 'It's Daniel, remember?'

'I've been trying to get a chance to talk to you all day …'

She trails off, waiting for me to face her. I don't want to. I don't want to do anything, and I certainly don't want to talk to my mother about Kelsey.

'Lucas, please.' Her voice is so close, I give in and turn around. She's standing only a couple of feet away, her expression almost as miserable as my mood.

'I don't need another lecture,' I tell her, my tone too harsh.

'Good. Because I'm not going to give you one. Just … talk to me, Luke.'

She's looking at me like she really means it. My throat closes. I press my thumb and forefinger into my eyes and shake my head, desperate to stop the tears from coming.

Then her hands are on my arms, rubbing them in that way mothers do to offer comfort.

'Okay,' she says. 'Then let me talk … and it's not a

lecture.'

I take a deep breath, getting myself under control again, and look at her.

'I understand, Luke. I understand how you must be feeling.'

'Mum ... you've got no idea.' My voice is thick and clogged with emotion I really don't want her to witness.

'I've wanted to tell you for a while, and I guess now is as good a time as any. I've been seeing someone.'

The turnaround from this being all about me to all about her has my muddled head spinning. What the hell is she talking about?

'You've noticed I've been late into work a few times, lately.'

Jesus, she's serious.

'Who?' I ask.

When she hesitates, for a terrifying moment, my irrational brain thinks she's going to say Bryce Hargraves.

'A psychologist in Riverview.'

I blink at her in confusion. I don't know if we have our wires crossed or not.

'As in a ... relationship?' I ask. 'Or a patient?'

'Patient,' she says, her voice a little softer. And that's when I really look at her, really take in the sadness shadowing her face. Her eyes water a little, but she's keeping the tears in check.

'Oh.' For a moment, I'm at a loss for words. Then, 'Okay ... why?'

'I just ... well, let's just say, I understand how you feel ... about the loneliness.'

I stare at her, and for once I don't see my mother before me. I see a woman who's been deprived of a relationship for just as long as me. When I was at university, I had suspicions that she may have been involved with a man here and there, but clearly nothing serious. And since moving to Cascade, I'm certain she's been single the whole time. How have I not even thought about that until now? How selfish and self-absorbed am I?

So, we're more alike than I thought. Just like me, the pain of loneliness has caught up to her.

While she looks at me, worry and sadness mingling in her eyes, I do the only thing I can do. I hold out my arms, and as the first tear slips down her face, she moves into them and hugs me.

As I wrap her in my arms, she shudders a little and I know she's trying to hold in the sobs she needs to release. With a gloved hand, I give her back a comforting rub. The contact, although foreign, feels good, and I realise that because our lives are so closely entwined, we never do this. I'm sure if we lived apart, only saw each other occasionally, a hug might be normal.

'Hey,' I mumble. 'It's okay.' Though I'm not sure it is. If she feels the way I do, then we're both a goddamn mess.

She sniffles slightly against my chest.

'You'll find someone,' I say. 'I'm sure of it.'

A small huff of a laugh escapes her throat, and she releases me, giving her eyes a quick wipe with the back of her hand. With a sad smile, she says, 'Small towns don't really lend themselves to a lot of possibilities.'

I nod, unable to argue with that. 'You know you don't have to stay here, right?'

She waves a dismissive hand in the air. 'I'm not going anywhere. And don't you go worrying about me.

I'm just feeling a little down. I'll get over it. That's why I'm seeing someone.'

'Well, you know where to find me if you need me.'

'I just wanted you to know I really do understand. And lately, after seeing you so happy ... and now, like this ... I've been wrong, Luke. You deserve to have love in your life.'

It's hard to believe I'm hearing those words come from her mouth.

'Yeah, well. You don't need to worry about that anymore.'

Her lips form a thin line as she walks over to her desk and turns off the computer. Grabbing her handbag, she says, 'Any chance you're coming to the talent show tonight?'

'Yeah, right,' I scoff.

She gives me a concerned glance before turning towards the door. I follow so I can lock it behind her.

Her hand hesitates on the doorhandle, then she turns to me. 'I really think you should come.'

Does she even know me at all? Since when would I attend that event under normal circumstances, let alone now?

Annoyed, I sigh. 'I'm not interes—'

'Jackie came in earlier,' she interrupts. 'She told me about a last-minute entry.'

I want to say *so what?*, but something in her eyes stops me. She's scared.

'Mum, I'm not going—'

'Luke,' she says, continuing to break her own damn rules. She places her hand on my arm and looks up at me with frightened eyes as she squeezes.

'It's Kelsey,' she says so softly I only just catch it.

My whole body goes rigid.

Kelsey.

Emily gives me a worried smile, pats my arm and opens the door. 'I'll see you there, then.'

Her fear now makes perfect sense. Not only has she just told me I deserve love, she's pushing me towards it. She could have kept that information to herself, and I'm sure deep down she wanted to. But more than that, she understands what we all need.

I step outside and call out to her. She turns, giving me a sad smile.

'Thank you,' I say, meaning it from the bottom of my heart.

She gives me a hesitant nod, then walks away into the cold night.

<><><>

I race home, feed the animals, shower, shave and dress in clean jeans and a shirt. After telling Sam she can't come with me, I get in the Landcruiser and drive into town.

Of course, there's not a single car space left in the parking lot, so I find a spot way down the street and hightail it to the pub.

I don't know what the deal is with these talent shows, so I'm scared I'm going to miss her, that she'll think I don't care. Hurrying through the crammed parking lot, I pull on the pub door and enter. Cheers and applause wash over me, the atmosphere full of laughter and happiness.

On the stage, a couple of teenage girls wearing wigs and outrageous costumes bow at the applause, then run off into the wings.

I scan the audience, wondering if Kelsey's watching

the performances, but I don't see her anywhere. As I make my way to the bar, I spot Emily at a table with her friends. She catches my eye and gives me a tentative smile. It's obvious she's worried, but it's also clear she wants me to be happy.

Moving further into the pub, I'm greeted with pats on the back and a couple of handshakes, but nobody stops my progress. By some miracle, I find a seat at the bar. When I swivel around on the stool, I've got an unhindered view of the stage, smack bang in the centre. Why no one else has snavelled this prime position, I don't know. I glance around, worried I've stolen someone's seat, but nobody seems to care.

After ordering a Coke, I swivel around again to face the room. Hoping to spot her, I search the crowd. After no luck, I presume she's backstage somewhere.

Unfortunately, as I'm swivelling towards the bar, I catch Bryce glaring at me with disgust. He sits on his own, beer bottles littering his table. Looks like he's had more than one too many and I briefly wonder how he's getting home. But what do I care?

- 71 -

GEORGIA

GEORGIA STANDS IN FRONT of her open wardrobe, one lone dress swaying on a hanger. She reaches in, grabs it and turns towards an overflowing suitcase resting on her bed.

With tears streaming down her face, she places the dress on top of the others, packs them in as tight as she can, then closes the lid. She leans her full weight on top of the suitcase, squashing it enough to allow her to pull the zipper around. Done, she drags it off her bed and rolls it next to another suitcase.

Sobbing openly, she pulls an envelope from her pocket and places it on her pillow. She doesn't know what else to do. She knows she's a coward, but she just can't face telling her father she's leaving to follow her own path. He'll hate her, be so disappointed in her.

He'll be so hurt.

Which is why she can't face him. She just can't. If she did, she fears he'll talk her out of it, lay the guilt card on her. She can't risk it, because he just might be able to persuade her to stay. And if he does, she'll resent him forever. He doesn't seem to understand she has her own dreams, and that the farm isn't one of them.

Sniffing hard, she grabs a wad of tissues and wipes her nose and face.

Looking at her bedroom for the last time, she picks up an overnight bag, slings it over her shoulder, grabs the two suitcases and wheels them out.

- 72 -

LUCAS

AS MIKE HEAD-BANGS along to his electric guitar on stage, I wish I'd taken the time to grab some earplugs before arriving. Turning away from the heavy-metal racket, I use pathetic sign language to indicate to the bartender that I need a refill.

While he pours a Coke, glorious silence descends within the pub. After a few seconds, there's a spattering of polite applause.

The bartender places my drink on the counter, and I take a long swallow.

'And now for our last act of the night,' Jackie's voice announces from the stage. 'Please welcome our newest resident, Kelsey Wells.'

My heart lurches. *Finally.* I spin around on the stool as more polite applause comes from the crowd.

And there she is.

My heart comes to a complete standstill at the sight of her walking onto the stage with her guitar. Her hair flows loose around her shoulders, strategically parted so most of it covers the left side of her face. Her pretty dress sways against the middle of her thighs, her sexy boots stopping just below her knees. I realise it's the first time I've seen her in anything but jeans and jodhpurs. She's stunning. And she clearly doesn't know it.

As she takes a seat on a stool, adjusts the guitar on her lap, then the microphone height, I see the tremble in her hands. She's so nervous, so painfully self-conscious. So beautiful.

I want nothing more than to protect her from those nerves, but she has to do this on her own. My entire body tenses. Apart from the contest she won when we were kids, she's never done this in front of an audience.

As we all wait, I hear the occasional cough, clearing of a throat or two, shuffling of feet. Her frightened eyes quickly scan the crowd, then lower to the guitar, to her fingers on the neck.

She starts to play.

And fumbles, stops.

She looks so lost, so scared.

Have I done the wrong thing by encouraging her, pushing her into something she really doesn't want? Given her false hope? I want to race up there and drag her away from what I know she believes is a judgemental crowd. No one's making any noises now. They're waiting patiently to hear what this new resident has to offer.

I want them to hear her.

I want the world to hear her.

She bites her lip and repositions her fingers.

I release a long breath. She's not giving up.

But before she begins, she looks out at the crowd and searches the audience. Then she finds me.

I can't stop the huge, stupid grin from forming on my face. I give her a nod. When she doesn't look away, I think she's frozen. But I'm wrong. With our eyes locked, she begins to play.

The melody washes over the packed room, filling it with an entirely new atmosphere. It's haunting and beautiful, transporting me somewhere I didn't know existed within me.

Then she sings. And everything changes. I actually hear the woman beside me gasp.

Kelsey's voice fills the dim room with light, her eyes never leaving mine for a second. Her fingers expertly work their way over the strings now.

As her words wash over me, I suddenly realise she's not just performing a song at a talent show.

She's singing *to* me.

She's singing the story of us.

She's telling me there's hope.

I'm so moved by her bravery, by the words she's singing, the power of it wells in my eyes and flows down my cheeks.

As the song builds, as her voice reaches amazing notes filled with emotion, I notice the audience is just as captivated as I am. I know there'll be no stopping her now. She's going to have everything she ever wanted.

When she plays the last note on her guitar, the audience remains utterly silent. I know they're overwhelmed by what she's just given them, but I see the confusion on her face, the insecurity in her eyes.

I take off my gloves and start to clap. That's all it takes. Suddenly, the whole place erupts in applause so loud it gives Mike's heavy metal a run for its money.

She breaks into a wide smile, her eyes never leaving mine. I want her to take in the crowd to see how much she's affected them, how much they love her. Instead, she stands, her hands shaking as she slings her guitar onto her back.

I think, like the other contestants, that she'll walk off into the wings. But she moves forward on the stage, finds the steps and weaves through the tables.

As the applause dies down, I realise all eyes are on her.

And she's coming my way. I remain rooted to my seat, taking her in as she draws closer. Unlike on stage, she seems determined, full of purpose.

Then she's right in front of me, her eyes searching mine, suddenly not so sure of herself. I grin.

The pub and crowd disappear, and it's just us. She steps between my legs, places her hands on my chest, leans in and gives me a shy, tender kiss.

My hands find her waist and pull her closer. Wrapping my arms around her, I kiss her back, my heart and mind racing with everything this means.

It's not until we break apart and she rests her forehead on mine that I hear the hoots and whistles coming from the crowd.

'Go for it, Doc!' a woman shouts. I think it's Jo.

Kelsey laughs and I laugh with her. She eases away and takes my bare hands, pulling me off the stool. I'm vaguely aware of my gloves sliding from my thigh to the floor, but I don't bother picking them up.

As she leads me to the exit, I see Mrs Winston beaming at me. Then my mother, struggling to be happy.

And Bryce. I don't hold his stare. I don't care about the utter hatred I see on his face.

I only care about the woman leading me away from everyone, leading me into my future.

- 73 -

KELSEY

AS THE PUB DOOR closes behind us, muffling the sounds of the hoots and whistles within, Luke pulls me into his arms, crushes me to him and kisses me with a passion that takes my breath away. This kiss is nothing like his other tender, sweet kisses. This is something else entirely. My knees actually grow weak from the effect he's having on my body.

Clearly, he's forgiven me for running away, for accusing him of all the lies I'd believed.

Drawing back, I look into his eyes and see the love I feared I'd ruined.

'So, I made my move. How did you like it?' I ask, giving him a cheeky grin.

He laughs. 'It was wonderful. You were wonderful ... breathtaking ... You came back.'

'My dad,' I say, resting a hand on his chest, feeling the rapid thump of his heart. 'He told me the truth this time. You saved my life, did everything you possibly could … and nearly died because of me. Luke, if I'd known, I—'

'Hey,' Jo says from the pub's doorway. 'They're about to announce the winner.'

Luke grins. 'Wonder who it's going to be?'

I look towards the door and shake my head. 'You really want to go back in there?'

'Hell no.'

<><><>

I sit in the passenger seat as he drives out of town. When we hit the outskirts, he reaches for my hand and I take it, entwining our fingers.

Now's the time to ask him everything I need to know. Well, at least the important stuff. I won't have time for everything, not before we get to his place, where I know exactly what's going to happen.

'Luke,' I say, and let out a little huff. 'I like saying that.'

He squeezes my hand. 'You have no idea how much I like hearing it.'

I squeeze back. 'Why didn't you tell me who you were? You couldn't have known what lies I'd been told, so why not tell me?'

'I, ah … I thought there were a few times there that you suspected …'

'Of course, but I thought you were dead. And you convinced me it wasn't you. So I fell for Clark, a man I thought just reminded me of you.' I hesitate a moment, enjoying the sensation of his thumb brushing over mine. 'Dad told me you tried to see me once.'

He stares at the light illuminating the dark road. 'And he told me to stay away from you.'

I notice he hasn't mentioned the part about why Dad told him to stay away.

'But you moved to Cascade,' I point out.

'It was a long shot.'

'And how long would you have waited?'

He takes his eyes off the road for a moment and looks at me. 'Forever.'

I blink fast, trying to stop the tears welling and spilling over. Who would ever say something like that to me? Only Luke.

As we drive in silence for a while, I realise how close we're getting to his home, and I still need to ask him the hardest question of all. And I need to do it before we get there. Once I'm in his arms, I won't be able to.

A wave of nerves washes over me. He won't like the question. He'll probably think that's why I came back.

'Luke?' I say quietly, the fear inside me just as strong as the hope. 'I have to ask you something, and it seems wrong and improper,' I rush, 'but I can't help it. I have to know.'

He looks at me and I can tell he sees something in my expression he doesn't like. When he extracts his hand from mine, I think I've ruined everything. Until he turns on the indicator and steers into the driveway.

'Please don't,' he whispers.

'You don't even know what—'

'Yes, I do,' he says, his hands gripping the wheel so tightly his knuckles whiten in the dashboard light. 'Please … don't ask.'

I study his face, watch a darkness come over him.

And suddenly, it all makes sense. How could I not have seen it all along?

He didn't want me falling for him because of what he can do. Because of what he can do for *me*. He wanted me to love him without any of that. To love him for just being him. My mind flashes back to when we were kids, when he asked me if I only wanted to be his friend because of his gift. I'd admitted then that he was right. But only in the beginning. When I'd really started to know him, he'd been pretty damn amazing.

'You wanted me to fall for Clark. An ordinary man.'

He seems to think about that for a long moment, then sighs. 'That's part of it.'

Only part of it? What I don't understand is why he wouldn't *want* to help me. That, I need answered.

'I have to know,' I press. 'Don't you see? It's like you said—to pretend it's not there when it is, is futile.'

He pulls the car to a stop in front of the verandah steps, unbuckles his seatbelt and gives me a grim look. 'I don't want to break your heart all over again.'

Before I can reply, he opens his door and gets out. Disappointment floods through me. How can he say he cares about me when he won't do the most wonderful thing in the world for me? Why withhold that? It's cruel.

This time, I can't stop the tears from escaping. Just in time for him to open my door. Great. I hang my head, undo my seatbelt and climb out.

He gently touches the underside of my chin, forcing me to look at him, his expression filled with sadness as he takes in my tears.

'Kel. You're killing me here.' He closes his eyes a moment, then opens them. 'I wish I could. But I found out a long time ago, it's something I just can't—'

'But—' He places a finger to my lips.

'You've seen Beau. Don't you think if I could, I would?'

I blink up at him, taking in his words, what they mean. It can't be true, can it? I thought I'd already figured that out.

'Would it hurt to try?' I ask.

'Yes,' he says. 'It will. And I'm not talking about me.'

'I don't care.'

- 74 -

BRYCE

BRYCE SKIDS TO A stop in front of his home, gets out of the ute and slams the door so hard the vehicle rocks, imitating the way he rocks on his feet as he stumbles into the house.

That fucking prick.

Getting everything he wants.

Everything going his way.

Everyone thinking it's all so fucking wonderful.

He stalks inside and slams the door.

'Georgie?' he yells, wanting to tell her about the injustice of it all.

Getting no answer, he heads down the hallway towards the bedrooms.

'Hey, Georgie? I'm home!'

He stops at her door and pounds on it too loudly.

He knows he's had too much to drink, knows how bad it would have looked if he'd crashed on the way home. As far as he can tell, though, they can't hate him any more than they already do. Not one of the arseholes who once called themselves his friend came and said a word to him the whole night.

Fuckers.

Then that ugly bitch had walked on stage and wowed them all with that stupid voice of hers, topping it off by kissing the fucking freak in front of everyone. Like they were rubbing it in his face.

He shakes his head, instantly regretting it as everything wobbles in front of his eyes. He leans on Georgia's door until the dizziness dissipates.

'Georgie?' he calls again. Why isn't she answering? It's not possible she's slept through the commotion he's just created.

He opens her door and lets it swing inwards. As he steps into the room, he freezes. Dread grips his gut.

Her bed's empty. And there's an envelope on her pillow.

With great reluctance, he tumbles onto the bed and grabs it. Tearing it open, he unfolds the note within, squinting at it in the dim light.

I'm so sorry, Dad. I just can't live your life. I need to live mine.

I love you,
Georgie.

No. No, no, no, no, no. This isn't happening.

He struggles on the mattress. Finally managing to stand, he crashes into her wardrobe with a groan. Clutching the handles, he flings the doors open. A couple of metal hangers clink against each other in the otherwise empty space.

He crumples to the floor, and for the first time since he was a little kid, he cries.

- 75 -

LUCAS

AGAINST EVERY OUNCE OF my being, I agree to show her what I can't do. This night, having started out so promising, is quickly running off the rails. And once she sees the truth, I'm betting it'll be completely over.

But it's what she wants, so I'll do it. I can barely handle the pain I already see in her eyes. I don't know how I'm going to cope when the truth stares back at her. It comes to me then, our kiss in the barn after the foal was born. She knows that didn't work. So, why doesn't she believe me? I consider asking her, but I think, maybe she just needs to see it for herself.

I want to hold her hand as I lead her to the bathroom, but I'm not sure she'll want me touching her ever again after what I'm about to show her. I flick on the harsh light and wait as she positions herself in front of the mirror and brushes her hair away from her scars. Moving up behind her, I meet her hopeful gaze in the reflection. Before I even do a thing, I'm already grieving the loss of her.

'Please,' she whispers.

I take a deep breath and gently touch my fingertips to her scars, then flatten my hand over them completely. In the mirror, she closes her eyes, almost as if she's praying. But I know it's pointless. There's no pull, no tingling in my hand, no rush of energy leaving my body. Nothing but the feel of her scarred skin against my palm.

She opens her eyes. As I start to remove my hand, she covers it with hers and holds it there.

'I don't feel anything, Luke. Not like when we were kids. I'll never forget that feeling.'

I shake my head, and she lets her hand drop to her side. I watch as she stares at her reflection. And sees nothing has changed.

I wait for her tears to come, but they don't. In the mirror, her eyes meet mine.

'This,' she says softly, 'this is why you didn't tell me who you were.'

I nod. She's nailed it. And I have to live with the consequences. I guess if I'd told her up front, I never would've fallen for her. I'd have only wondered what might have been.

'I knew you'd get your hopes up,' I tell her. 'Knew you'd think I could ... fix you. But I can't heal something that's already healed, no matter how imperfectly.'

To my surprise, instead of moving away, she leans into me. I take my chances, wrap my arms around her and pull her closer.

'I'm so sorry, Kel.'

'It's okay. It was a little girl's fantasy.' She runs her hands over mine, then grips them in hers. 'But what isn't a fantasy anymore is you … you being alive … you wanting me. That's a million times better than anything you can do with these hands.'

My heart swells with hope and overwhelming relief. I press a gentle kiss to her scars. 'You have no idea how much that means to me.'

She looks at my reflection with what I can only describe as pure love, then she turns in my arms and kisses me until all the pent-up fear evaporates.

But I'm not sure what she wants right in this moment, how far she wants to take it. I don't want to rush her, pressure her. Breaking the kiss, I look into her eyes. All I can do is be honest.

'You know I want to make love to you, right?'

She gives me a cheeky smile. 'I was hoping …'

'Nothing has to happen now,' I say quickly. 'We can take things as slow as you like.'

I feel her fingers lock together against the back of my neck.

'Well,' she says, 'you told me nothing would happen unless I made a move. I'm pretty sure the whole town witnessed that move. I'm done waiting.'

Without another thought, I sweep her up in my arms and carry her into my bedroom.

Placing her on her feet beside the bed, I turn on the dim lamp. Sam looks up at us from her spot in the corner. I feel like a heel, but she's not watching.

I step to the door and look at Sam. 'Come on, girl, out you go.'

The good girl that she is, she gets up and walks slowly from the room.

'Awww,' Kelsey sighs.

I close the door and turn to her. 'You want an audience for this?'

She shakes her head and lets out a little chuckle. I grin stupidly at her.

'Are you as nervous as I am?' she asks, her eyes sparkling in the lamplight.

'Yeah.'

'Good.'

She unzips her boots and wrenches them off. I follow her lead. We stare at each other like a couple of fools, both waiting for the other to make a move.

'So,' she says, running a trembling hand through her hair, 'I don't think I'm quite at the point where I'm ready to do a strip tease for you. How about you?'

I laugh. 'Definitely not.'

Closing what seems like a vast distance between us, I walk over to her, wondering if my heart's going to fail after using up too many beats all in one night. Standing right in her personal space, loving that I can do so now without fear of her retreating, I take her hands in mine.

'I was so scared we'd never get here.'

'But here we are,' she says softly.

'Here we are,' I repeat, having no idea what my next move is going to be.

'So, since we're not doing a strip tease, can I undress you?'

'Oh, so bold,' I say, surprised and amazed.

She grins up at me. Releasing my hands, hers brush against my hips, then lift, bringing my shirt with them. Raising my arms, I help her slip it off.

Instead of moving closer, she takes a step back, her gaze making a leisurely journey from my shoulders all the way down to my jeans. I'm rock hard and I know she sees it when her eyes quickly snap to mine.

'Can I touch you?' she whispers.

'I don't know about that,' I tease.

'*Lucas* ...'

I chuckle, hoping I'm taking away her nerves. Though she seems to be doing a pretty good job of hiding them.

'So, you've been thinking about that, huh?' I ask.

'Have you *seen* your body?'

'Oh, I see. I'm just a body to you.'

She steps close and looks into my eyes. 'The only body I want against me ... in me.'

Jesus. She's a never-ending source of surprises. I want to pull her against me, but her hand reaches out. And I wait.

Then she touches me, her fingers tentative on my chest. Placing her other palm against me, her heat seeps into my skin as I watch her eyes follow her hands. The sensation is incredible, new and exciting and more than I ever imagined being touched this way might feel.

I close my eyes, relishing every moment. Her warm hands travel over my torso, down lower and lower, then finally stop at the top of my jeans.

Well, one hand does. The other hesitates a moment, before continuing on its journey. My eyes snap open to find her staring at me as she slides her palm over my erection. I'm thankful for the thick material between us, but I gently take her hand and guide it back up my body, then trap it over my galloping heart.

She releases a little huff of a laugh. 'Is there a problem?'

'There will be if you do that again,' I almost growl at her, straining with the effort to keep control.

Her laughter engulfs me and I'm so glad she's

happy, that we're still us even in this very different situation. Her eyes crinkle when I reach out and touch her dress.

'How do we get this off you?'

She reaches behind her, lowers a zipper and lets the dress slip to the floor. Her smile falters and suddenly she's gone from bold to insecure. I try to think of something amusing to say to put her at ease, but her beauty disables that part of my mind.

I take in her lacy white bra, the pink nipples visible through the material, her trim waist, the swell of her hips, the white lacy underwear.

Breath explodes from my throat. 'You are so goddam beautiful. I can't even—'

She presses against me, kisses me, and I know she's doing that so I'm not looking at her anymore, but I don't mind, because the feel of her skin against mine takes my breath away.

I wrap my arms around her, hold her tight against me and feel her press against my erection. As our mouths explore each other, I glide my fingers along the curve of her spine until my hands find the rough lace covering her backside. Without a thought I slide them beneath the material and cup her firm cheeks.

Soft little groans escape her throat. Then she breaks the kiss, our breaths rushing in and out in sharp, harsh gasps. Her eyes search mine.

'What do you want?' I whisper.

She breaks our eye contact, drops her forehead to my chest and slowly shakes her head. For a moment, I think she's having second thoughts. Then her fingers brush over my stomach, fumble with my belt and slide it free of its buckle. When she starts in on the button, the brush of her knuckles against me becomes too much. I take over, my own hands trembling as I decide to just get rid of everything. I drag down my underwear and jeans, forcing her to take a step back.

There's no hiding from her now. Not that I want to, but I also don't want to freak her out. I'm acutely aware that she's never done this before, either.

As she takes me in, I see the shock in the slight widening of her eyes, but it's just a flash, and then she's smiling again, meeting my eyes.

'Jesus,' she murmurs. Taking a deep breath, her hands disappear behind her. A moment later, her bra crumples, and the straps slide from her arms.

The sight of her bare breasts has me rooted to the spot, and it's my turn to feel insecure. What if I touch her the wrong way? What if she doesn't like it? I don't know what the hell I'm doing.

She must sense my hesitation because she takes my hand in hers, her eyes never leaving mine, and places it on her stomach before slowly gliding it higher. I feel the ripple of her ribs, the underside of her breast, then her hard nipple presses into my palm.

We both draw in a breath. Moving on my own, her eyes close as I explore all the shapes and textures I've never felt before.

'You're incredible,' I rasp beside her ear. She sinks her fingers into my hair and kisses me, her tongue gliding over mine.

My control is spiralling dangerously. I want to be inside her so badly it actually hurts. I've never felt so much all at once and I think I'm going into sensory overload.

I pull back, needing to breathe, needing to not have any sensations for a moment.

Staring at her beauty before me, I reach out and

draw her lacy underwear over her hips until she wriggles out of them, and they fall to the floor.

And now she stands naked before me, totally exposed and vulnerable. Yet instead of the self-conscious look I expect when I meet her gaze, she's smiling at me with so much love, tears prickle the corners of my eyes.

'You have to touch me, Luke. Right now.'

'Bossy,' I say, trying to skirt around the emotion that feels like it's about to consume me.

'Damn right,' she says, taking my hand again, angling it down, moving my fingers between her legs where it's so slippery and warm. My mind explodes, instantly imagining how it'll feel to sink into her.

And then I focus, concentrate on what she's doing, how she's guiding my fingers, sliding them over the centre of her, the heat there incredible, then gliding them higher over that nub which makes her draw in her breath.

She's trembling now, and before I lose it, or maybe she does, I sweep her up in my arms and lay her on the bed. I know I'm not going to last long. And from the way she's looking at me, she knows I'm not going to, either.

As I kneel on the bed, she boldly opens her legs to me. The sight is incredible. Her hooded eyes watch me as I position myself between her thighs.

But I don't move over her like she expects. Instead, I slip my hands beneath her gorgeous backside. She tenses, realising where I'm heading.

'Luke, I'm not sure—'

But my mouth is already on her, kissing her as I keep my own body away from hers. I don't miss her gasps, don't miss the fact that words are no longer coming from her mouth.

Then I touch her with my tongue, right where I'm supposed to. Her backside clenches in my hands and she rises off the bed a little, pressing herself against my mouth. She's so hot and wet, I know what I'm doing is working.

So I stop, lift my head and look at her. She's staring right at me, her eyes half closed.

'What're you doing?' she breathes.

'I thought you weren't sure,' I tease her.

'Luke … Jesus Christ …'

I grin. 'Close, but not quite.'

She laughs and bites her lip. 'Oh God … don't make me laugh *now*. Keep going … please. Keep going.'

I press my mouth to her again, swirling my tongue over her. Her thighs shake against my arms. In my hands, her muscles clench even tighter and suddenly her fingers are in my hair.

'God, Luke … yes … keep doing—" She strains against me, fists my hair, then releases breathy, shallow groans that grow deeper and longer until I feel all the tension in her backside melt away.

Through ragged breaths, I hear her murmur my name, feel her fingers tugging on my hair. I trail wet kisses over her stomach, between her breasts and up her throat until I reach her mouth. She's grinning at me in a way I've never seen before.

Satisfied, I think.

But before I can enjoy the satisfaction and relief that I'm not a complete failure at this, she raises her hips beneath me, and I feel myself slip against her wetness.

'Now,' she says simply.

And as easy as that, I slide into her slowly, deliberately, completely. And it's everything I never imagined. As I look into her eyes and she looks at me, I feel more than the sexual need. I feel the connection between us, so damn strong, I know it will never be broken.

'Kelsey,' I breathe, 'Kelsey …'

She cups my face in her hands, kisses me and moves her hips beneath me.

The sensation of sliding within her is too much, and I finally let go.

- 76 -

KELSEY

I LIE IN LUKE'S arms, completely and utterly and deliciously spent.

His fingers make languid trails up and down my spine, over my waist and hips, over my backside—where it tickles so much it almost borders on pain. He can't seem to get enough of touching me; my skin, my hair, my breasts ... my sex.

It's exactly the same for me. Having never touched anyone like this, neither of us wants to stop now. My own fingers track through the sprinkling of hair on his chest, over his pecs, his stomach, still amazed by his perfect physique.

'You're looking for trouble,' he says, his voice rumbling into my ear through his chest.

'Well, I wouldn't want that,' I murmur.

'You sure?'

I grin, press against his side and raise my head so I can look into those amazing eyes.

'Aren't you exhausted yet?'

He grins. 'Yeah … but if you wanted to …'

'I think I'll always want to. But … you know I should be pretty sore, right?'

He gives me a smug grin. 'You're not?'

'You know damn well I'm not. You're getting way more sex than you should be … and I think that's kind of cheating.'

He gives me a wink. 'Fantastic, isn't it?'

I laugh and punch his arm. 'Hell, yes.'

As our chuckles die down, he touches me under my chin, his face suddenly serious. 'I think I forgot to tell you something.'

'What's that?' I ask, a little concerned by his intense expression.

'I love you, Kelsey Wells. There'll only ever be you.'

My heart inflates. Even though I have no doubt how he feels about me, to hear the words out loud is something else, entirely.

'Right back at you,' I say, not understanding why I can't say the same thing to him.

His eyebrows shoot up. 'Right back at you?' He chuckles, then grabs me, tickling me until I beg him to stop.

Rolling me onto my back, he gives me a long, sweet kiss, filled with no demand other than love and affection. I press against him, kissing him, wanting to tell him I love him, too. But don't.

When he pulls away, he rests his head on his pillow and faces me, searching my eyes.

'When we're married, when we have kids … do you

think it'll still be like this?' he asks.

Warmth floods through me. 'We're getting married? Having kids?'

'Of course we are,' he says, as if it's the most normal thing in the world.

Heart kicking into high gear, I touch his face. 'This is the first I'm hearing about it.'

He takes my hand and holds it between us. 'You don't want to?'

'Of course I do,' I tell him without hesitation.

'Well, there you go. We just got engaged. How easy was that?'

I try to frown, but my smile wins. 'I think you tricked me into that.'

'You want to get out of it? I can take it back.'

'Don't you dare!'

We both laugh like fools, and I have that feeling of letting go of the swing and flying through the air, of crashing to earth beside each other in fits of giggles. We were so free in that moment, so happy.

When we calm down, I ask, 'You really want kids?'

'Yeah.'

'What about … if they're like you?'

He gives me a lopsided grin. 'If that happens, it won't be like it was for me. I'll be here for them. *We'll* be here for them. They'll have me to teach them everything there is to know about this thing … these hands. And they'll have a mum who's going to be around for them for a very long time.'

'I am?' I ask, not sure what he's talking about.

'I'd never been able to confirm it before you told me, but my mother … well, she's never been sick a day in her life since I came along. I'm guessing it's something that gets passed on when I do my thing.

You'll never have to worry about getting sick, Kel. At least that's something I've given you.'

I look at him with wide eyes. 'You're serious?'

He nods, reaches out and touches my scars with tenderness. 'I'm just so sorry I can't fix this for you.'

I take his hand from my face and kiss his fingers. 'How did you figure it out?'

'There were a few things along the way, when I was growing up. Guess it makes perfect sense, since scars are the body's way of healing itself.'

'I'm so sorry I ran away from you, blamed you. You didn't deserve that.'

'Hey,' he says, 'you only knew what you were told. Just like me, you had a parent who was trying to protect you. I'm sure we'll make mistakes, too.'

He's right, of course. I give him a gentle kiss, and when I pull back, I say, 'Speaking of parents, that'll be interesting.'

He releases a little puff of air. 'Yeah. My mother's not going to know how to handle having someone else in her life who knows the big, bad secret.'

'Don't forget about my dad, too. It's not like they'll be able to avoid each other.'

He chuckles.

'What?' I ask, loving the way his eyes crinkle.

'Wouldn't it be something if those two end up getting along? For once in her life, my mother will have someone else to complain to about me.'

I grin at him. 'What're we getting ourselves into?'

He pulls me closer. 'It all sounds so complicated, so wonderful. It'll be our adventure. And I'm going to love every minute of it.'

And then he's kissing me again. This time it's filled with passion, and I return it hungrily, forgetting about my exhaustion. I want him again and my body has no problem telling me it agrees.

He draws me into his arms and slides my thigh up to his hip, opening me just enough so he can ease inside me. With one arm wrapped around my waist and the other beneath my head, our bodies are so incredibly close, I really do feel at one with him.

Already, he knows how to angle his hips to meet me just where I need him to. As I tip over the edge oh so easily yet again, I can only wonder at how my world has changed so radically in the space of twenty-four hours.

- 77 -

LUCAS

I LAY CURLED AROUND Kelsey, her back against my chest, her bottom pressed against my groin, her hand loosely holding mine against her stomach. After drifting in and out of sleep for hours, I wonder if I keep waking because I'm afraid this is all a dream.

But I am awake, and as I listen to her soft breaths, feel the gentle rise and fall of her body against mine, I remind myself again that the woman in my arms is going to be my wife. I grin stupidly to myself, remembering how casually I'd made my weird proposal, but remembering how afraid I'd been that she'd think I was moving too fast, that I was out of my mind.

I suppose I was, still am. But if this is what being crazy feels like, I never want to be sane again.

Prying my eyes open, I study her smooth shoulder illuminated by the moonlight. I hadn't shut the blinds earlier. I'd been a little too occupied. The silver light seems to caress her skin, and I want to touch her again, but I know I should leave her alone. She needs to rest. So do I.

As I let my eyes drift closed again, appreciating the feel of her against me, a gunshot rips through the soundless night.

I bolt upright, heart pounding.

From the living room, Sam lets rip with a stream of non-stop barks.

Beside me, Kelsey stirs. 'What was that?' she asks, her voice still full of sleep.

'I don't know,' I say, even though I'm more than a little familiar with the sound of a gun being fired.

I swing my legs over the edge of the bed. Sam's barking isn't calming down. Someone's out there. Someone with a gun.

I grab my jeans off the floor, frantically pulling them on. In bed, Kelsey sits up, the moonlight revealing her bare breasts, the worry on her face.

I shove on a T-shirt, lean over and give her a quick peck on the mouth.

'Stay here,' I say, and as I turn away, I grab my shoes and jacket.

When I open the bedroom door, Sam's right there, her barks frantic, her need to tell me someone's out there intense.

Fear thrums in my chest. I can only think of one person who might be out there with a gun. The one person who hates me, fears me, blames me.

I shove my shoes on and hurry to the front door as I pull on my jacket.

If it is Bryce, I don't want Sam anywhere near him. I turn to her, tell her to sit, to be quiet. She does what she's told. Then I tell her to stay.

And I open the door and go out into the freezing night.

Right away, I see light streaming from the partially open barn door. I know I haven't left it on. I never do unless a mare's about to foal. If I owned a gun, I'd have it in my hand, but I've never had any need for one.

Pounding down the stairs, I spot a shovel leaning against the railing in the garden surrounding the house and grab it. Over the crunch beneath my feet, I strain to hear any noises coming from inside. But there's nothing.

Heart hammering, I reach the door, which is open just enough to step through. And I do. I squint against the light. Even though it's dim, it's brighter than the moonlight outside.

I see nothing out of the ordinary. The aisle between the stables is empty, all the stall doors shut. But the smell of gun smoke in the air is unmistakable. This is where the shot was fired.

And I feel a presence that isn't the horses.

The hairs on the back of my neck and arms stand to attention.

He's in here. I know it.

I also know I should turn around and leave. But I can't have him follow me to the house. I can't let him get anywhere near Kelsey. No, I need to confront him now, do whatever it takes to stop this before it gets even more out of control.

Clutching the shovel handle, I change my grip so I'm holding it like a baseball bat, ready to swing the sharp metal blade. Slowly, listening for the slightest noise, I creep along the aisle, my footfalls almost silent on the soft dirt.

To my left, I ease over to the stall housing the mare and her new foal. She stares at me, the foal in the straw beside her, its head nodding as it drifts off to sleep.

Crossing to the other side of the aisle, I glance into the stall I placed Beau in before going into town.

And I freeze.

There on the ground, blood darkening the straw, Beau lies motionless, a bullet hole in his empty eye socket. His dead eye seems to stare at me, but I know he's gone.

My stomach churns.

And then I hear movement behind me.

'How does it feel, you fucking freak?'

I whirl around, my nausea forgotten. Bryce stands at the far end of the barn, apparently having hidden in the very last stall. He takes a few steps towards me, brings up the rifle—the same one he used on me last time—and levels it at me.

'What the hell—'

'You took every single thing I loved,' he says, the pain and anger in his voice all too clear.

My grip on the shovel tightens involuntarily, even though I know it's useless. He's too far away. He'll shoot me well before I can reach him and swing it at his head.

I realise my only hope is to no longer be in his sights. If I can get to the open door, slip behind it, make him come after me, I might be able to get the better of him as he's coming through the doorway.

Releasing my batter's grip on the shovel, I keep it in one hand, hold up my other, and take a step backwards, towards the door.

'I was only doing my job,' I try to reason with him, though I know from the look in his eyes that he's about as sane as I was last time I saw him. 'You can't blame—'

'Whatever the fuck you are,' he growls, 'you're gonna die.'

'That won't work, Bryce.' That's not entirely true, and I realise that he knows it, too. He shot Beau in the head for a reason. He knows if he shoots me the same way, I won't survive either. But I have to try to convince him, anyway.

'You know you can't hurt me,' I tell him.

He lifts the rifle, digs the butt into his shoulder and glares down the sights at me. His finger tightens on the trigger.

'Oh yes, I fucking can,' he says.

I hit the dirt, knowing even as the shot rings out, that I'm not faster than a bullet. But as I wait for the pain to rip through me, I feel nothing.

I look up at him just as he shoves the rifle's barrel beneath his chin and fires. I turn my face into the dirt, not wanting to see more than I already have.

It all happened so fast, I can barely comprehend it. I don't understand how he missed me, why he didn't try again before he killed himself.

Behind me, I hear the rumble of the barn door. Turning towards the sound, I see Kelsey wearing my white bathrobe.

She's leaning against the door as it slides open, trying to hold onto it, trying to keep herself upright. And she's pressing a hand to her chest, her eyes wide with terror.

I scramble to my feet, sprint to her, blood blooming in the white material as she collapses to the dirt.

'Kelsey!'

Reaching her, I slide to my knees and pull her into my arms.

This can't be happening!

She blinks up at me, her breaths ragged. 'I'm ... sorry,' she gasps, tears spilling down the sides of her face.

I frantically part the bathrobe. Right between her breasts, blood oozes from a bullet hole. Without a single thought, I place my hand over the wound and instantly feel the pull, feel my energy flowing into her.

She's shaking her head, gripping my wrist weakly as she tries to force my hand away.

'You're safe,' I tell her. 'I promise.'

'No,' she cries. 'Please ... don't.'

I kiss the top of her head and rock her. 'It's okay,' I whisper. 'It's okay.'

The euphoria coursing through my entire being feels immeasurably more powerful than anything that's ever come before. I know what's happening and I'm so fucking happy. Happy because it's working. She's going to be okay. And this time, I'm not going to fail.

She's breathing easier now. Her hand on my wrist tightens and there's strength in it as she tries to separate my hand from the wound, but she can't. Until I'm done, it's welded to her body.

She lets go of my wrist and pummels my chest with her fists. 'Stop!' she screams. 'Stop it!'

I shake my head, everything becoming clearer even as it fades slightly. I know I don't have long, know I have to say what I can now.

'I can't, Kel. The point of this thing ... it keeps coming back to you.'

Suddenly my hand drops away from her, and I feel

the slippery bullet slide from my palm.

'No!' she cries. 'I'm nobody. Nothing. You're—'

'This is who I am, Kel. Promise me, you'll go be who you are.' With everything I have left, I lower my head, kiss her lips and try to tighten my arms around her, but I'm faltering, swaying, tilting to the side.

She lowers me to the ground and crouches over me, clings to me. The world in my peripheral vision darkens. I've been here before, but this time I know it's the last time.

'Don't go,' she cries. 'Please, Luke, please don't leave me …'

Her warm tear splashes my cheek as the world grows darker. I'm not sure if I'm smiling or not. I hope I am.

'My best friend,' I say. 'Forever.'

I blink, trying to clear my vision so I can hold her in my mind as I go.

'I love you, Luke. I love you so much those words just aren't enough … they'll never be enough. I love you … I love you. Lucas …'

And suddenly, I'm back on that swing, grinning at Kelsey as I swoop downward, then up and up … and I let go, rising into the air … weightless, waiting for the pull of gravity. But it never comes.

I just keep flying.

EPILOGUE

KELSEY

THE FUNERAL IS A blur, but I do remember some things.

I remember the sun being so warm on my face at the gravesite. It should have been comforting, but it wasn't.

I remember the whole town being there. It should have been comforting, but it wasn't.

I remember my father's arm around me, his hand squeezing my shoulder. It should have been comforting, but it wasn't.

I remember Emily reaching out and holding my hand through the entire service. Her tears racing down her face just as fast as mine. Even when his coffin was lowered into the ground, she never let go. It should have been comforting, but it wasn't.

I remember thinking that nothing would ever be comforting again.

Not without him.

But I was wrong.

<><><>

Two months later, I found comfort while hunched over the toilet bowl, throwing up the tiny bit of toast Emily insisted I eat.

The woman was relentless. After the funeral, Dad came to stay with me, but that didn't stop Emily from coming to see me every single day. I didn't want her there, thought she should hate me for what I'd done to her son, but she didn't.

Instead, she told me he knew all about the danger of falling in love, and he'd done it anyway. He'd told her I was worth it. That almost stopped my heart.

Which is what the coroner believed happened to Luke. Everyone knew that Bryce had killed himself in front of Luke. And Luke's heart had just stopped. Having no medical history, that's all the coroner could come up with. Freak things like that happened sometimes. What else could the coroner find? Nothing he could explain.

Emily continued to fuss over me. When she saw how skinny I was getting, she cooked for me and watched me eat until she was satisfied I'd had enough.

I really didn't care what she did. I didn't care about anything at all. If she'd stopped coming, I wouldn't have cared, I wouldn't have eaten, I probably wouldn't have even noticed. I think I would have just withered away. What did I have to live for?

But after a while, I resented her presence, resented the reminder every single day of what we'd both lost.

When I snapped at her and told her to get out, to go to hell, to leave me the fuck alone, she never even flinched. And when she let herself into my house and found me throwing up in the toilet, she told me off, thought I was purging.

After convincing her I wasn't, that I was sick, she gave me the strangest look.

'You can't be sick,' she said. 'You've never been sick a day since he touched you, right?'

'Well, I am now. Probably your cooking,' I mumbled.

She sat on the edge of the bathtub, ignoring my insult.

'Kelsey,' she said slowly, the wheels turning over in her head as I tried not to throw up again. 'Did you and Lucas ... did you use protection?'

What the hell sort of question was that? 'None of your business,' I snapped, too nauseous to try to understand what she was getting at.

'Well, it very well might be my business ... if it means I'm going to be a grandmother.'

That shattered my little pity party.

What?

'You won't ever be ill, Kelsey. Seems like morning sickness to me.'

I stared at her, still trying to understand what she was saying.

'When's the last time you had a period?'

I blinked fast, tried to think, tried to understand why I hadn't noticed. But grief had obliterated everything.

'I don't think I have,' I whispered.

She clasped her hands together. 'Right, let's get you to the doctor's then and find out.'

Helping me up on trembling legs, I couldn't look at her, couldn't see the hope in her eyes. What if she was wrong?

What if she was right?

She came with me, waited at my side in the doctor's surgery as he put a strip in the urine sample I provided. Unable to help myself, I clutched her hand, the suspense absolute torture.

When he delivered the news, we hugged each other and cried.

He was with me, *had* been with me the whole time.

After calming down and leaving the doctor's, Emily told me that while she had to raise Lucas alone, it wouldn't be that way for me. I had two people in my life who'd be there for us. My dad, and her.

The relief was immense. I was a mess, couldn't even look after myself, let alone a baby.

I knew Luke was gone, but I also knew a part of him lived on inside me, and I'd soon meet that little boy.

Emily and Dad both came with me to the ultrasound. I'd already told them I'd name the baby after his father. Emily was a little uncertain, but I thought she'd come around to the idea.

Imagine our shock when we discovered the baby was a girl. I hadn't even considered it. But as the months passed, as I ate properly and did everything I was supposed to do, the feel of the baby girl inside me faded the grief by giving me purpose.

We didn't think she'd be like Luke. After all, the others had been male. But if she was, I'd have two people who knew what the risks were, who could help me protect her.

Emily was with me in the delivery room, vigilant that the doctor and nurses wore gloves and long sleeves.

Then little Luka came into the world, screaming her head off and covered with gunk.

These Hands

I never thought I could love anyone as much as Luke, but I'd been wrong about that, too. The moment I heard her, she took my heart. The moment they laid her on my chest, she took my soul.

I cried with the love I felt for her, and I cried because Luke wasn't there to meet her.

But he was there *in* her. At least I'd have that.

Once we were alone with her, Emily and I debated how best to figure out if she was like Luke.

As awful as it seemed, we decided that if we gave her a tiny scratch on her arm and she was normal, then everyone would think she'd scratched herself with her fingernails. But if she *was* like him and she healed herself, at least it wouldn't take anything from her. She was so tiny, I couldn't risk hurting myself only to have her heal me and suffer for it.

Emily had to do it; I just couldn't. She'd brought a new packet of pins with her and dragged the tip of one across Luka's arm. Just enough to draw blood.

Luka screamed and squirmed, but when I took her hand and held it over the scratch, she grew quiet.

Lifting her hand away, Emily wiped at the tiny droplets of blood. Leaving clean, unmarked skin.

We both cried again as Emily expertly put on the little mittens the hospital provided to prevent babies scratching their faces.

At least Luka would know the touch of her mother and grandmother. As long as we weren't injured, we would forever be able to safely touch her.

I wished with all my heart that she wasn't like him. But I was also glad she was. As horrible as it seemed, it felt like he was truly with me when I was with her.

<><><>

Three years later, and I'm standing on the stage at the biggest venue I've performed at yet.

Every time I step on stage, I hear Luke's words, to go be who I'm supposed to be. So I have.

He gave me that, the courage to ignore all my insecurities, the courage to believe in my voice, my words. And it seems he was right. So many people apparently agree.

Of course, Luka's my motivation, too. I have to support her, give her a life where I can protect her by surrounding her with the two people who can help do that. They've given up their lives to be with us, to travel the world, to keep watch over her when I can't.

Now, as I sing the last lines of my final song in front of the enormous crowd I only ever dreamed of as a little girl, I glance into the wings and see her there. She has my nose, my mouth, my chin. But those green eyes are all her father's.

She beams at me, wearing her pretty little pink gloves, one hand in Emily's, one in Dad's. She wiggles her butt to the music, making them both laugh.

I think they're finally sleeping together; the way they look at each other, the little touches I've seen between them. They think I don't see, but I do. I'm sure they've been trying to hide it from me, thinking I'll see in them what I should have had with Luke. But I'm so happy for them. They deserve to have joy in their lives.

Maybe I'll find that again one day. I think Clark taught me that I'm capable of loving someone else. But if I am, it won't be for a long time.

Although Luke's gone, he gave me more than just our daughter. He gave me a mother again, one who loves and cares for me. He brought Dad to Cascade.

He surrounded me with family. He surrounded me with a community that cares.

And as I sing the final notes of my own words, Emily and Dad let go of my daughter.

And she runs onto the stage and into my arms.

THE END

If you enjoyed this book, the most wonderful thing you can do is leave a review letting other readers know. Even a few words are so appreciated.

ALSO BY DARCY DANIEL

Playing the Part

The Devils' Cradle

Deceivious

ABOUT THE AUTHOR

Darcy Daniel enjoyed reading from an early age and fell in love with many genres, but was drawn most of all to romance. Darcy enjoys life in a picturesque, small historic town just outside Sydney, Australia.

Printed in Dunstable, United Kingdom